I0764436

Oath of Allegiance

By

Peter Jonas

Order this book online at www.trafford.com/03-0617
or email orders@trafford.com

Most Trafford titles are also available at major online book retailers.

Note for Librarians: A cataloguing record for this book is available from Library and Archives Canada at www.collectionscanada.ca/amicus/index-e.html

ISBN: 978-1-4251-8411-7

We at Trafford believe that it is the responsibility of us all, as both individuals and corporations, to make choices that are environmentally and socially sound. You, in turn, are supporting this responsible conduct each time you purchase a Trafford book, or make use of our publishing services. To find out how you are helping, please visit www.trafford.com/responsiblepublishing.html

Our mission is to efficiently provide the world's finest, most comprehensive book publishing service, enabling every author to experience success. To find out how to publish your book, your way, and have it available worldwide, visit us online at www.trafford.com/10510

www.trafford.com

North America & international
toll-free: 1 888 232 4444 (USA & Canada)
phone: 250 383 6864 • fax: 250 383 6804 • email: info@trafford.com

The United Kingdom & Europe
phone: +44 (0)1865 487 395 • local rate: 0845 230 9601
facsimile: +44 (0)1865 481 507 • email: info.uk@trafford.com

10 9 8 7 6 5 4 3 2 1

FOREWARD

I am Peter Jonas, a native of Hungary, a small European country. Hungary is a dry, "land-locked" country; we don't have oceans or seas. We do have a history of having conquered lands that bordered three seas. However, when I was born in 1967, this was only a distant memory.

I'd like to take you on a journey back in time over 200 years, when most of the world was still unknown. I would like to have you travel with me to Australia where this story begins in the summer of 1770.

You can be a spectator to a mutiny, witness the revenge of power, and observe how life can continue when people almost give up hope. Only two survivors continue the journey into the unknown. Life bounces them left and right, through good times and bad.

The journey is long and hard, but you can learn from it. The well-planted tree produces wonderful fruit. Never give up hope.

TABLE OF CONTENTS

Oath of Allegiance

Introduction

Our story begins in the last quarter of the 18th century. Great Britain was hungry for expansion again. Exploration, colonization, and the acquisition of natural resources were their goals. The British Admiralty commissioned several voyages around the globe, one of the most significant being the exploration of the renowned South Seas. Captain James Cook had been assigned by the Admiralty to lead the expedition and gather information about the new territory. Due to the growing economic crisis in England at the time, crime was on the rise. The House of Lords gave orders to transport criminals to the remotest of the new colonies. There, they would labor for the mother country, and in this way contribute to the restoration of Great Britain's peace and prosperity.

On August 26th in the year 1768, Captain Cook weighed anchor in Plymouth and sailed south. His company included three merchants and four lady members of the House of Lords. They spent six months off the coast of New Zealand until they became convinced they had still not reached their destination. Sails spread anew; they now tacked a more westerly course. Finally, on April 19th, 1770, they caught sight of the New Holland coast. Ten days later they dropped anchor in Botany Bay. Setting sail from there, a new danger awaited the voyagers. Gigantic shoals loomed up ahead of them. Captain Cook instructed the lieutenant, with the help of eight of the rowers, to press farther north of the shoals in order to determine their span. One mile from shore, their voyage was delayed an entire week. They could do nothing but wait for the team to return.

Into the Unknown

Daybreak. The sun's crimson rays lavishly color the eastern sky. Waves storm around the fiery orb as it ascends, dazzlingly, from the foam. The ship is tossed hither and thither. The cries of hungry seagulls can be heard overhead. Under the sun's strong rays, the fog was dissolving, though the vessel itself was still engulfed by it. Its yards were aslant; as if to show that it's powerful body -- like that of a sleeping lion's -- could spring into action at any moment.

There was sudden movement on board. The first officer appeared, holding a telescope in his hand. The lookout was on the alert, alarmed by the morning's unrest. The first officer, paying no attention to him, mounted to the quarterdeck, and with the telescope now fully extended, took a lengthy survey of the coast. He saw nothing out of the ordinary. The lookout appeared then and after saluting briefly, said, "Sir, the captain is waiting for you down in the parlor. It seems the crew is beginning to get restless."

The first officer nodded, closed his telescope, and headed for the ramp. Summoning the Bo, "Son, he shouted gruffly: "Mr. Nightingdale! Whistle for the crew to fall in. Everybody on deck!"

"Yes, sir!" With that, the first officer proceeded to the quarterdeck, where the captain's cabin was located.

In the parlor, breakfast was still being served. He found the captain in the company of his guests, who were enthusiastically discussing what would happen when they finally discovered the continent. English industry would boom beyond belief, they were saying. Lord Gredford, who owned impressive steel and coal factories, painted a vivid picture of the new continent for the four ladies. Then the sound of a bugle call and the heavy stomping of feet on deck, quickly ended Lord Gredford's account, and the vibration sent the crystal glass and the porcelain table service shattering.

"Captain, sir, the crew awaits your orders!"

"Thank you, Mr. Brady." The captain turned to his guests. "Ladies and gentlemen," he said, "please follow me." He took his cane and started for the door. The uproar on deck died down with the appearance of the officers and the guests. Captain Cook studied the men assembled and said: "Our search team returned last night. It seems that the shoals, deemed to be of considerable span, have made further advance impossible. We have no other choice but to turn back and approach from the south."

"But sir...!" exclaimed one of the sailors, removing his cap. "The west coast is wild and infested with bloodthirsty Papuans. And what about food and water...?"

"There is a price for everything, Mr. Anderson. We have come all this way to explore a continent. As of this moment, our rations will be reduced to half."

The sailors' grumbling filled the ship.

"For how long, Captain, sir?" Phillip Morrel asked.

"According to my calculations it should be about 10 to 12 weeks before we've circled the continent."

Once again the sailors' grumbling filled the deck. Captain Cook's expression hardened, and he eyed them all sternly. He turned to his first officer: "Mr. Selkirk, everyone to the sails! Direction: south-southwest!"

"Yes, sir!" The first officer clicked the heels of his boots together and at his order the crew went to work immediately.

In no time the spars of the Endeavour were covered with canvas. The huge ship groaned as it circled. A fresh morning breeze fluttered the sails. Every rope was tied to the breaking point. And the great vessel was once more underway.

The officers and guests turned back with the captain, while the ladies returned to the parlor to discuss the dramatic turn of events. They discovered that with the aid of a full meal they were now perfectly able to drown out the crew's grumbling about their newly enforced diet. Their privileged status absolutely forbade that such an event should dampen the excitement of their new adventure. And so they immersed themselves in mindless chatter.

Meanwhile the prevailing mood in the sailor's quarters was growing gloomier by the minute. The men were eating their meager rations in silence. It was Phillip Morrel who put an end to the torment. He suddenly jumped from his chair and threw his gun on the table. Within seconds the angry sailors were on their feet. Seizing weapons and knives, they all rushed toward the deck.

In the parlor, at this time, the explosion of pistol shots unhappily coincided with the serving of tea. The ship's officers took their weapons and hurried to the deck ramp. Soon they found themselves face to face with bayonets. In front of the boatswain five sailors broke into the room. Captain Cook was taken aback at the sight of the weapons. Mutiny had broken out!

From above, scuffling and more pistol shots could be heard. The retired soldiers had no way of preventing the sailors from getting their hands on the weapons. Everyone was pushing and shoving their way to the deck, where the battle was at its height. To make matters worse, the most unexpected thing of all occurred at this moment. It happened that the women were discussing matters with Lord Gredford. Lord Gredford was standing directly in front of Morrel, the leader of the rebellion. "Mr. Morrel," said Lord Gredford. "We would like to inform you that we are completely on your side. If we sail north instead, despite some risk to the ship, we would at least be assured of good hunting and fresh water. Everybody knows that the west coast is utterly uncivilized. That's why I want to ask you to allow us on your side... I mean, as business partners. Just think how rich we will all become if we were to find the right ore or mineral!"

This sight dumbfounded Captain Cook. To him, Lord Gredford was as much a family friend as he was a business partner. Oh, he thought to himself, what strange cards life dealt one at times.

During the night the soldiers had succeeded in crushing the rebellion. The sailors were now waiting in chains for their fate to be determined.

The military court convened the next day at noon. As the leader of the mutiny, there was a good chance Phillip Morrel would be executed. Six of the other sailors, who were considered accomplices, were given the same verdict. But the biggest surprise during the trial came when Captain Cook pronounced the four ladies, along with Lord Gredford and the two merchants, accessories to the crime. The trial was fast and simple. Execution was frowned upon as being too severe so the guilty were forced to leave: All the mutineers and their sympathizers were expelled from the ship and placed in the dinghy, with some provisions, tools and a few rifles, then abandoned to their fate.

They sailed along the continent for 21 days until they found a place to drop anchor along a small riverbank. Exhausted, sunburned and famished, they had almost reached the end of their strength. It was in this condition that the first settlers of New Holland, later to be called Australia, arrived on the continent in June of the year 1770.

Under the circumstances, the voyagers had only one choice for a leader, Phillip Morrel, the fallen mutineer. The former boatswain led his little troop into what appeared to them to be the blackest of futures. Nevertheless, they tried to draw strength from his words.

"They exiled us to the bleakest of shores," he explained. "It looks as if we'll simply have to make the most of our situation...with whatever time remains to us. Our chances of escape are minimal. It may be years before another ship passes this way. I say first thing tomorrow we travel upstream about half a mile. At least there we'll be safe. We'll build houses in time for the rainy season. If not, we'll be wiped out by fever."

The others agreed in silence. The men supported the women, who were weeping and inconsolable and sought shelter. They distributed what crumbs of food they had for nourishment, and bedded down for the night.

In the morning they gathered their belongings and sailed upstream. When the current became too overwhelming, they went ashore. That night they sat gloomily around the fire. They ate their miserable ration of food, appointed night watches, and went to sleep. It turned out to be a long sleepless, night, as strange animal sounds made even the thought of rest impossible.

The next day the little river narrowed, which meant they had reached the end. They divided into two groups and investigated the territory. Lord Gredford's group, coming upon a picturesque valley, saw the place where they were to build their houses. They fetched the others to show them the discovery and the decision was settled when it was determined there was fresh water in this area as well. In the clearing they spied a place to set up camp.

A new chapter of their life had begun. Within a two-month period of time, three houses were built and a year later they had built six. The group soon realized their survival and future depended on their creating lives together.

Lord Gredford soon confessed his feelings to the charming Miss Elizabeth and they married. Thomas Hawkins -- who had a degree in theology and for unknown reasons had become a sailor on Captain Cook's ship -- performed the marriage ceremony. Later the other three women followed their example in finding suitable husbands.

In the course of time they began working the land and succeeded in cultivating some fruits and vegetables. They also discovered sugar cane, corn and wheat, and flavorful forest roots, which were added much variety to their diet. The men learned to hunt with arrows, to fish, and to shoot rifles. Obviously, they couldn't risk the loss of a single bullet.

From spoiled prima donnas, the women became perfect housewives. In other words, life had not ended for these people but, on the contrary, civilization was budding all over again.

Then one day an incident occurred that threatened to disturb their newfound peace. In the course of hunting, four of the men had wandered very far south. At sundown they set up camp, made a fire, and roasted the meat they'd caught. Over the course of time they had grown used to the sounds of the forest, but now they had heard something that filled their hearts with fear. It was the dull pounding of drums...

Quickly kicking dirt over their fire, the men took up their weapons. They began to creep through the thick of the forest toward the source of the noise. The moments passed in terror. They could feel their heartbeat in their throats. Emerging from the thick forest, they found themselves in a wide grassy clearing. In the middle of the clearing burned a huge bonfire, and around this bonfire grotesque figures were performing a war dance. Papuans! The pounding of the drums quickened. Then the natives, raising a loud cry, broke apart. Six Papuans forced three bound hostages into the fire. The spectators' blood froze as they watched; the victims were all white men. The Papuans cut the victims' ropes and tried to force them to stand, as the victims persisted in falling to their knees with pleas for mercy. Then the warriors' spears were raised high... and down on to the victims.

Terror struck the men as they watched this scene. It was inconceivable that these savages were less than a day's journey from their homes. Fear gave them wings and they flew for cover, looking neither left nor right, running as far as possible. They wanted to be as far as possible from this horrible spectacle. Their fellow white men had been butchered alive to provide meat for these animals! But there was nothing they could do: the Papuans were 300 in number. Silently they prayed for the salvation of the victims. For a long while they were confronted with a long swampy stretch, and decided that to continue in the darkness would be too dangerous; there were crocodiles and venomous snakes in these parts. They chose a large tree for their resting place. They climbed up the tree and hid there, trembling, waiting in silence for morning to come.

When dawn broke through the swampy forest trees, the men cautiously descended from their hiding place and continued on their way. They tried, from the position of the sun, to determine where the shore was. Soon they found themselves in a rocky area with a stream that ran through its center. Kneeling beside it, the men quenched their thirst and attempted again to orient themselves. It was then that they happened upon the cave. Curious, they lit torches and entered. Hanging above their heads, blinking sightlessly at the intruders, were hundreds of bats. One of the sailors stepped into a hole, lost his balance and fell face first into a puddle. His companions helped him to his feet. They observed that their companion's clothes were covered with glistening mud, and eagerly held up their torches for a closer look. The mud on his clothes sparkled with gold dust! Pushing each other aside, they pressed on into the cave, which was progressively narrowing. After a slight bend the light of their torches reflected off the walls of the cave with a hundred times its former strength. They couldn't believe their eyes with what they saw: The walls were covered with solid gold!

The next night they returned to their village, where their loved ones were waiting impatiently, afraid that something dreadful had happened to them. They had a hard time believing that the men had returned virtually empty-handed. Instead of fresh meat, a small sackful of items was emptied onto the table. The tiny gold nuggets sparkled in the russet glow of the campfire. They could hardly believe their eyes. Soon, dozens of questions were thrown at the men.

They recounted the story in detail. The audience trembled amid tales of life-threatening danger with the Papuans and the prospect of immense wealth with the gold they'd found As they dreamily fingered the nuggets, two thoughts occurred to them; claiming the immense treasure, and seeing their homeland, England, again!

The next morning the little village teemed with life. Seven of the men returned to the cave and within a matter of days, managed to procure two chests full of gold nuggets. The whole matter of the Papuans was quickly forgotten. From that day on, they stockpiled huge ricks of hay to be used as bonfires to signal any ships that should appear on the horizon. But the horizon remained empty.

Soon 25 years had passed and yet the village flourished in spite of the many hardships and tears. Hopes dwindled, dreams faded and a new generation was emerging in the heart of the wild.

The New Generation

April 14, 1795

It was eight o'clock in the morning. The settlers had been up since dawn, where the morning sun found them hard at work.

Sparkling sunbeams caressed their houses, and nothing had as yet disturbed the tranquil peace of their little village. The men worked the land as usual, and the women looked after their homes.

A young man emerged from the forest and walked over to the nearest house. He walked nimbly along the path, carrying a bow and arrow in a leather quiver. In his hand were tiny birds he had shot during shooting practice. His name was William Anderson. William was a handsome young man of sixteen years. At five feet, eight inches, he possessed his father's bear-like strength and his mother's quick wit, as well as the nobility that coursed through their veins. His bronzed skin, from constant exposure to the sun, deep brown eyes and strong features gave him a look of confidence and defiance. Above all, though, he exuded strength and intelligence. He was quick-handed when it came to hunting, but had a very romantic side --even though this particular illness, so feverish yet refreshing at the same time, was yet unknown to him.

He climbed the rough-hewn wooden staircase and opened the door. When he entered, his mother turned to him.

"William! I'm so glad you're finally back. Your father will be here any minute. Quick, go wash up for breakfast."

"Morning, ma... look what I have here!" William put his things on the ground, and went behind the house to a canal that had been built from the river nearby. Rolling up his sleeves, he bent over the water and washed. Then he saw her, in the field on the other side of the canal; a beautiful girl, Susannah Gredford. He ducked down beside the riverbed and observed her every move as she was gathering flowers and humming a tune.

"William, come to breakfast!" his mother called.

"I'm coming," he replied. Then after drying his face on his sleeve, he tried to catch another glimpse of the girl, but she was gone. He stood and walked back to the house. As he turned the corner he saw Susannah again who, occupied with her flowers, was taken aback at the sudden appearance of the young man. William stood face to face with the beautiful girl.

"Sorry. I didn't mean to scare you!" he said softly. Susannah fixed her gaze upon him and their eyes met.

"You didn't scare me," she replied, and closing her eyes she began to blush. She attempted to escape, but the path was so narrow, surrounded with a thick hedge, that as they passed each other their hands accidentally touched. The girl shivered and ran away.

William looked as if he'd seen a ghost. Running, Susannah cast a brief glance back to see if he was still watching her. And then -- perhaps intentionally -- she dropped her flowers and continued to run. William went to the bouquet and gathered the scattered flowers together. He took a leather string from his pocket and tied them together. At a loss as to what to do with the flowers, he threw them into a thorn bush. Hearing his mother calling him again, he went inside the house. He had no way of knowing that the girl was watching him from a nearby bush. She went to the thorn bush and carefully removed the bouquet. A smile came to her lips. She hugged her treasure and ran home, which was on the other side of the village.

William sat at the table without saying a word. His father had arrived home at the same time. Hull Anderson was middle-aged, 48 years old. His wife, Leonora, once a very beautiful lady of the court, was 44 years old. The one-time elegance of her hands had faded. But even the twenty-five harsh years surviving on the island wasn't enough to erase the beauty and nobility of her features. They never spoke to their son of their former life; he probably wouldn't have been able to even imagine what busy England was like. The twenty-five years had sunk into oblivion. The new generation had no idea what had happened a mere two and a half decades ago.

They ate without speaking, then Hull finally asked his son: "Where have you been all morning, son? You've been up since dawn."

"I was out hunting!" William jumped up from his chair, and proudly showed his father what he'd caught. Hull nodded in approval.

"We saw a spotted wolf roaming these grounds. Be sure to stay out of his way. He has a mate and pups with him. He'll attack anything that he thinks might make good eating."

"If he's smart he'll stay as far away from me as possible! One shot of my arrow and he's gone!" William exclaimed, proudly.

"Be very careful son," his father said. Hull stood and turned to his wife. "Today we're going to the south side. The kangaroos have ruined the crop again. Send William with lunch, will you?" As he said this, he left the house.

William began packing at once.

"When the sun is pointing south I want you home, you hear me, son?" said Mrs. Anderson. "It's a long way to the south side." "Yes, Ma," her son replied, and slinging the bow and arrows over his shoulder he went on his way. Leonora shook her head. Her son's boldness worried her at times. But deep down she trusted him. Leaving the house, he went straight to the bush, but to his great chagrin the bouquet was no longer there. He frowned and looked around. Aside from the nosey and rude parrots that shrieked down from the top of the tree, he was alone. He continued on his way deep into the woods, where he felt most at home. Deep in thought, he kicked a stone and pondered the day's latest events.

William had never been in love before. Perhaps he had no idea what he was feeling now. Had anyone so much as hinted that he was what they called "lovesick", he would have scoffed at the notion. As an only child, he had grown accustomed to being alone and always had his own ideas about everything. Isolation had made him reserved. He put great faith in his own strength and courage, and achieved every goal with seeming effortlessness. This was the first time his rock-hard foundation had been shaken by a pretty face, that of a 15-year-old girl. Closing his eyes, he tried to recall her, fluttering like a carefree butterfly, adding to her bouquet with one beautiful flower after another.

The light breeze tossed her thick dark curls into her coral-tinted face. Beautifully chiseled hands chased the curls away and revealed her splendid almond-shaped eyes. Her red lips, as she hummed a happy tune, broke into an everlasting smile. Her fine features, even from a distance, gave evidence of her noble blood.

As she knelt down, the daring cut of her dress subtly revealed her bosom, a reflection of the daring fashion of the times. But what truly captivated William were her beautiful blue eyes. They were as blue as the ocean. Looking into them was like seeing into his future...

No matter how hard he tried, he couldn't take his mind off Susannah. Love at first sight, we might say, but here in the heart of the wilderness everything was different. There were no benches where pupils could daydream about each other behind the teacher's back. The school here, in any case, only taught Tom Hawkins' sermons and lectures. Their schooling was, in truth, the school of survival and nothing else. The young people of the island were like fragile flowers in the midst of a horrible swamp always in constant threat of being swallowed by the wildness of the island. And yet even this couldn't stop the noble roots from taking hold under the surface of mediocrity. The immaturity of their feelings was balanced by a love of nature, which is what the nomad substitutes for civilization. In their isolation they had become precocious: their young blood, if needed, could be riled in an instant.

Hull Anderson joined the other men. Gathering their tools, they rose and set out for the fields on the south side, where they were growing corn and wheat, but their crops were at the mercy of the wild animals. Sometimes they had to chase as many as 200 kangaroos or wallabies off their land. Over 3/4 of the crop was destroyed. The increasing number of rodents also led to devastating losses. Still, they had enough to somehow put bread on the table. By now, the village had a population of 23, whereas the original village consisted of a mere 14. The second generation had nine youths in all. Lady Elizabeth Raymond had borne three children to Lord Gredford. Her son Daniel was 24; her daughter Elizabeth was 18, and the youngest, 15-year-old Susannah. The second couple consisted of Lady Betty and one of the former sailors from the Endeavour, Altamont. They, too, had three children. Stewart, 19, was the oldest, Thomas was 17, and the beautiful Mary was their younger sister. The third couple consisted of Lady Cora and the former rebel Phillip Morrel. They had two children, a 20-year-old son, Robert and a 17-year-old daughter named Sarah. We have already met our friend William. He, of course, had no brothers or sisters. The remaining six men resided in two cottages under the leadership of old Mr. Johnson. Lacking wives, they remained bachelors and spent their free time playing cards and dice. Whomever they had left behind in England when they were expelled from the boat, were now, so many years later presumed dead.

William, all this time, had been thinking how he could win Susannah's favor. He wanted to surprise her with something; and knowing she liked flowers, he set out to pick her the most beautiful flowers he could find. Once he'd gathered them, he tied them together, and returned to the place they had met the first time.

Suddenly he heard a faint rustling sound and knew immediately what it was. Quickly he reached for his bow and an arrow. His instincts had been right, as usual: a mere 30 feet away he saw the giant spotted wolf coming towards him. Stopping in its tracks, it sniffed the air with its sensitive nose, trying to determine what character had dared to block its path, but the acquaintance was soon ended. The wolf, his huge mouth hanging open, would soon rush to its demise. William aimed at the animal with fierce determination. The string of his bow grew tighter and tighter, then the arrow landed right between the wolf's eyes. Had William shot the wolf with a rifle, the beast would have died immediately, but the arrow had not caused the wolf's death, and the bleeding animal now sprung at William with every bit of its remaining strength. Quick as lightning, he ducked, and the deadly paws whirred over his head.

Having missed, the wolf landed on its back, then sprung up to leap at William again. However, William was prepared. His next arrow pierced the beast's heart. If anyone else had the presence of mind to do what our hero had done they would most likely have fainted from the trauma of the experience. But William was a 'child of nature' and didn't know fear. He walked over to the dead animal and started to lift him, wanting to carry him home. Realizing the enormous weight of the dead animal, he decided it wiser to return with his father. Before heading home, he gathered some branches and lit a fire around the body, so no scavenger would get at his trophy while he was gone. When the fire was burning well, he took up the bouquet of flowers and went on his way as if nothing unusual had happened.

The brush became sparse and the clearing came into view. But he was out of luck. Susannah hadn't returned. He suddenly had an idea:

"I'll leave the flowers on the steps, and when she comes out of the house she'll see them." So that was what he did. He stole up to the house and when he was sure nobody was looking, he hurried up the steps. He put the flowers down, ran toward the woods, and lay down to wait. Still, there was no sign of Susannah. He soon realized he had severely miscalculated. Now, instead of Susannah coming out of the house and discovering the flowers, it was the older Gredford daughter, Elizabeth, who opened the door instantly. She discovered them, and thinking they were for her, glanced around slowly, and picking up the flowers, she disappeared inside the house.

William was furious with Elizabeth; the flowers were not intended for her. But he blamed himself even more. How stupid he'd been to put them where everyone could see!

"Another time..." he grumbled to himself as he walked away. Again the green dimness of the forest greeted him as thousands of carefree birds chirped and twittered above his head. Following his instinct, he found himself following the path to the shore. Within half an hour he reached the shore and sat on a rock. In front of him stretched the monumental and seemingly endless Great Barrier Reef. His father had told him about it and he had heard that beyond the reef stretched an ocean without end. But as to the question of how his father had come into such information, there was no ready answer. It's true that at that point in his life he wasn't overly concerned with making a connection. In his young mind, there was still quite a bit he didn't consider important yet.

With hungry eyes he searched the distant horizon. His imagination called up visions from the unknown. But now as he took in the ocean, he suddenly spotted a huge sailboat. The vessel slowly navigated between the coral reefs in search of open water.

William jumped from his seat and stared dumbstruck at the sailboat, which now, like a white ghost, simply vanished from sight. He knew exactly what he had to do. He started running to where his father and the others were working. In order to save time he took a short cut through the brush.

Luckily, they were still there. They had just been about to leave when he arrived. Anderson could see immediately from the way his son was running that something serious had happened. He ran to William as the others stopped to watch them.

"There's a big white ship or boat out there heading for the shoals, going south!" hollered William, who was still far away.

"To shore!" yelled Anderson. The men all dropped their tools and started running. Hull Anderson began running home. Entering, he threw open the door with such force that he gave Leonora a start.

"Leonora, where's my telescope? Our son saw a huge ship going south. This may be just what we've been waiting for all these years!"

"It's over there in the trunk!" she replied. Anderson quickly emptied the contents of the trunk on the floor until he found what he was looking for.

"Come with us!" he told his wife. They ran out of the house.

This was some event... Imagine the settlers, in the course of 25 years, had not seen a single ship. Anderson impatiently escorted his wife, who had already grown short of breath. The moment they reached the shore, William was already screaming: "Look, there it is!" Everybody looked.

"A three-master Spanish frigate," Morrel remarked thoughtfully, taking the telescope. Suddenly he added: "Why that's the Santissima Trinidad! A three battery-decked battleship launched in 1769... I see they've rebuilt it."

The others were familiar with the sailboat, which had caused such a sensation in 1769. William glanced questioningly at Morrel.

"But Uncle Phillip, have you seen that ship somewhere before?" Morrel put down the telescope. He stared gloomily ahead. After a while he continued: "One of these days you'll understand everything, son..."

But William had clearly not understood. He knew that it was useless to try prying information out of old Morrel when he was reluctant to give it.

"One day you'll understand..." the words echoed in him. And from that moment, he decided he would do everything in his power to discover that secret, the secret they were keeping hidden from the new generation. There was no knowing why. Why, if there were people on that great ship, and the ship belonged to some great nation, and if their parents were from the same place, then what in the world were they looking for in those godforsaken parts? Many secrets had yet to be discovered, and William decided they must be revealed. Just then he heard his mother's voice.

"Couldn't we send them some kind of signal?"

"Unfortunately not. By the time we got the fires going the Trinidad would already be gone again, between the shoals. Pity, it would have been so good to return to England..." Morrel said softly.

"Mother!" cried William. "Is there such a thing as another world outside this one?"

Leonora turned her tearful gaze to him. "Yes, my son," she answered softly.

William, feeling his mother's pain, decided it was better not to bother her with any more questions. His hunting gear in hand, he returned to the forest.

The adults were still standing there in silence, watching the ship's slow departure.

William suddenly remembered the wolf.

"Father, come quick and help me with the spotted wolf I killed today. He tried to kill me but I was faster!" The words interrupted the growing silence. Leonora ran to her only child to make certain that no harm had come to him. The men, hardly able to believe their ears, followed young Anderson.

Arriving at the scene of the struggle, they discovered the dead wolf. They heaped praise on William and three of the sailors hoisted the animal on their shoulders to head back to the village. Back at home, word had already spread about William's sighting of the ship, and now they were bombarding him with questions. Then, on sighting the giant kill, our hero became even more wonderful in their eyes. William's father was the most outspoken in his praise. All this time, William was trying to catch a glimpse of Susannah. When he spotted her, she was holding her sister's arm and looking at him. He fixed his gaze on her for a long time. The girl became embarrassed, lowered her eyes and blushed.

Suddenly William realized that this event was drawing too much attention to him; and at a loss for what to do, he withdrew to the forest. He climbed to a high branch, put his face in his hands, and thought back on all the strange events of the day. Everything had happened so fast and so many things were still so unclear to him. He didn't know where to turn for answers.

When William left, Gordon took out the dagger and went to work skinning the animal. He had decided to surprise William with a leather outfit in a few days. Everybody watched in silence as Gordon worked.

"Today we saw a ship going south and were unable to send any rescue signals. It was probably an exploration ship, which means it may return this way. I recommend that we put bonfires on the shore in as many places as possible. If it's meant to be that this ship is the one to rescue us, and if it comes by again, we can signal it. At least that way we'll increase our chances of being rescued." Having finished his remarks, he turned to the villagers who had gathered there in expectation.

"We'll take your advice, Gordon. Perhaps the Trinidad will spot our signals and try to reach us," Morrel replied. The others agreed with this and headed back toward the village.

Arm in arm, Susannah and her sister returned home, talking excitedly about the events of the day.

Meanwhile new ideas had begun to form in William's mind. That night he would listen in on his parents and try to learn as much as possible about the secrets they were withholding from him.

And after dinner, as planned, he listened to his parents from the next room. First, he heard his father's voice: "It's too bad we missed that boat. Imagine what it would be like to start a whole new life in England..."

"Actually, you know, I've grown accustomed to this place," his wife replied. "I don't miss the good life. I don't miss the social life. It's no longer for us, Hull. I really don't miss it anymore."

"You know, I think you're right," said Hull. "Too bad Phillip spilled the beans when the boat was passing by. I hope you realize that William will do everything in his power to discover the truth."

"Perhaps it's for the best," said Leonora, wiping a tear from her eye.

"If the Trinidad takes us on board we'll have to tell William everything in any case," said Anderson.

"If it takes us on board! You don't think they'd mistake us for savages, do you!" his wife declared. With that they stopped talking, and only occasionally could William hear a sigh or quiet word. Soon the house was silent. William felt he had learned enough for the present. He quietly climbed back into bed.

That night in his dreams he traveled to England, and majestic mountains surrounded him. Then suddenly radiant England appeared before him with its many houses and many inhabitants. Needless to say, he could only imagine what England looked like. In reality, he had no idea how to imagine England with all its hustle and bustle. He thought everything there was the same as here, just many times bigger.

His mind, occupied with these thoughts all night, awoke the next morning from a deep sleep. He washed quickly, dressed and left his room. His mother was standing in front of him, having just brought water in from the canal. He ran over and took the bucket from her. His mother served him breakfast, which in his hunger he devoured. He then said goodbye and left the house. His path led him directly to the woods. His first task for the day was to pick flowers for Susannah. Half an hour later he emerged from the woods with a beautiful bouquet and headed for the Gredfords' house.

He held the bouquet at his side; in case anyone was coming along, he could drop it immediately without the other person noticing. He knew if he were seen with the bouquet, there would be many embarrassing questions to answer. As he entered the clearing, William crouched down on the ground and crawled to the nearest bush. He peered out towards the house but Susannah was not there. He crawled forward again, and when he was sure nobody was looking, he stood and hoping for the best, quickly ran to the house. Just as he was about to set down the bouquet, Elizabeth opened the door. With a look of wonder, her eyes were opened wide.

"Well, well, if it isn't William," she called out in a shrill voice. "So you are the secret deliverer of the flowers!" In her question there was a hint of mockery that made William's blood boil. William had been completely taken off guard as he fumbled for words. The appearance of Elizabeth had embarrassed him so much that he found he couldn't speak in his own defense. Elizabeth watched amusedly as William's face changed from ghost-white to crimson.

"But now you'll 'fess up that it was you who sent the flowers yesterday and today, won't you, William?"

A furnace would have been cooler than the way he felt now. Elizabeth took this to be a confession. But he would show her, he would get her mind off the matter, and he would soon be free from this ridiculous predicament!

"The person who sent these flowers wishes to remain anonymous for reasons I'm unable to discuss."

"And just what reason would that be?"

"That if the young lady were to find out she would feel very ashamed of herself." As he hadn't been able to come up with anything better, he walked away from the awkward scene. Elizabeth stood petrified for a while and then finally took the bouquet and hurried into the house. She hadn't understood what William had said, but she sensed that something just wasn't right. William ran away knowing the truth. Free of the girl's embarrassing questions, having reached the edge of the woods, he stopped to catch his breath. Summing up his failures, he decided to postpone any more flower gathering for the moment. He had to find something that Elizabeth wouldn't be able to poke her pretty nose into...As was his custom, he retreated deep into the forest...

Hopes and Dreams

One fine morning Gordon's daughter Mary, together with Elizabeth Gredford, was strolling along the shore. It was their custom to come here whenever they had something important to discuss. Elizabeth was leading the conversation, discussing the very important matter of the flowers. They had been trying to name the person responsible for sending the flowers with William. There was a long silence, and then Mary spoke:

"First, let's try to figure out how many eligible men live in the village."

"Well," began Elizabeth, "there's your brother Stewart..." She blushed. "Then there's Robert, the Morrels' son..."

"See how well we've managed to narrow your admirers down!" Mary laughed.

"That's right, it could only be two," she admitted. "Or else William was just doing it to poke fun at me!"

"What do you mean by that?"

"Well, when I asked him why he wouldn't tell me the name of the sender, he said that if I were to find out I'd be ashamed of myself."

"Well, isn't that strange," Mary remarked. "Then isn't it possible you were the butt of somebody's joke, Elizabeth?"

"That thought hadn't occurred to me. Ooh, if I could just get my hands on that William now! I wouldn't stop until I got the secret out of him! Now I see how stupid I was to let him get away without telling me." With this Elizabeth, finished her fretting. They continued walking slowly along the shore.

On hearing these last remarks, William withdrew his head from between the branches, where he had been eavesdropping. Not too thrilled with the idea of having his ears boxed by them, he jumped down and ran in the opposite direction of the women. It made his blood boil to recall the humiliating incident with the flowers, and Elizabeth. Now, just as he was about to turn back into the forest, he was startled by a high-pitched shriek. The sound had come from the direction of the girls. That could only mean they were in some kind of danger. William quickly turned around and followed silently in their tracks. Returning to the place where he had been eavesdropping, he saw no sign of the girls. He had a bad feeling about this. Taking giant leaps, he reached the thickets. He cut across the bend and peered between the leaves. A small boat that had been dragged halfway onto the shore caught his gaze. Around it lay people he had never seen before. Then with searching eyes, he spotted a ship out in the harbor, a two-master, its sails down, standing about a half mile from the shore. The decks were lashed relentlessly by the waves. William's sixth sense told him something was wrong.

His only thought now was to find the girls. Elizabeth and her friend were fearfully hiding in a nearby bush observing the suspicious-looking newcomers fearfully. Luckily only William's sharp ears picked up Mary's stifled cry. The strangers seemed not to know where they were, as they kept searching the beach and the surrounding area. They wanted to fill up with water so they could continue on their journey, but fearing wild animals, they dared not venture into the forest.

"Look here, Commander Donald, sir!" mocked an evil-looking man named Smith. "You can do whatever you want, I'm going back to the British colony."

"You're not going anywhere until I give the word," replied the so-called commander, and then added: "All seven of you know that if we'd don't find food and water quickly we'll all die!" He said this with meaning.

"Then what are we waiting for?" interrupted Frank, who was lying nearby.

"Who's going for water?" asked Donald.

Three of them volunteered: Hooper, Antonio and the runaway slave, Ziba. Two of them took the buckets. One was armed with a rifle. They set out to find water...

William was shocked when he saw that they were heading towards him. He didn't dare run for fear they would see him. His instincts told him he needed to steer clear of these characters. Most likely, the same thoughts had occurred to both Elizabeth and Mary.

How did the men end up on this coast? The answer is simple: They were escaped convicts. Over the past two decades large convict colonies were being established down south, under English rule. Several thousand were deported here, and they lived under miserable conditions indeed, so far from their mother country. Their provisions were so paltry that they nearly starved to death. Local authorities often embezzled the government aid they were supposed to receive. Often the only supplies they could get their hands on were from bootleg ships that appeared now and then. The coast guard often went to war with these ships, but they returned anyway, because the convicts always traded them whatever they had in exchange for a few essentials.

The eight convicts had escaped using one of these ships. Under cover of the night, they boarded the boat and killed everyone who resisted. The remaining passengers simply threw themselves overboard. The men didn't have to fear retaliation, as the ship was on the coast illegally. Three months had passed since their escape, but lacking a map, they became caught between the shoals. By trading with a nearby Papuan tribe they had managed to obtain enough food for a few days, but the ship was empty when they took it over. The Papuans could not appreciate the value of gold or paper money because they could not trade them. The tribal leader had met white men before, and knew a couple of words in English. He made the men understand that only by trading their arrowheads, knives, or gems could they get food from the tribe. The men were forced to move on, but at the next bay they dropped anchor again. They were down to practically nothing in supplies; only a few weapons remained now and very little food and water. The Papuans, however, did not attack, in spite of the fact that the tribe numbered several hundred. The convicts had to find a way to get food and water...

The three men, Silvanez in the lead, were hardly a meter away from the girls who held each other in fear. Help was nowhere in sight. Meanwhile, William kept his eyes out for the girls. "Where could they be?" he asked himself. The convicts were coming closer and closer. William's heart was beating wildly, but he knew if he kept still they would not notice him.

"How the hell did we end up in this damn forest, anyway? There's no water anywhere in sight," grumbled Silvanez and scornfully spat on the ground.

William remembered the creek scarcely 300 yards away that flowed into the bay. It occurred to him that if they found the creek they would continue ahead because there was a salt-bed at its mouth, making the water there undrinkable. They were then sure to discover the path, which if followed to the end, would lead them directly to their village in the valley.

"I've got to find a way to keep them from going there," he thought. He went to work immediately. He glanced toward the boat. The other five men were resting in the shade of a giant palm tree. They looked briefly in the direction of the men who went to fetch the water and just now disappeared into the forest. William leapt out of hiding and with silent steps, slunk into the forest. Cutting through the thicket, he was quickly ahead of the men. Ducking behind a mangrove stump, he imitated the howl of a dingo. The three men stopped dead in their tracks.

"What the hell is that?" asked Ziba, frightened.

"How should I know," grumbled Hooper.

"Put the barrel down and don't make another sound!" he ordered his partner, Silvanez.

The strange creature's howl sounded angrier by the second, but it was nowhere to be seen.

"He's nowhere in sight, even though I've looked everywhere."

"Maybe the devil has pups."

"Then I wouldn't recommend going there!" Ziba whined.

"You nearly peed your pants, didn't you, you black mule!" Hooper scoffed.

"Should we go around?" Silvanez asked indifferently.

"No!" We'll be more vulnerable in the forest...Let's go the other way, maybe we'll find water there. Hurry, Ziba's going to need a change of pants pretty soon!" jeered Hooper.

"You've got a big mouth, you white bum. Hey, go right on ahead. Ziba's only got one life to live!" Then they turned around and started back.

One can imagine how relieved William must have been to hear these words. The timing had been perfect, as his voice had begun to grow hoarse. When he was a little boy his father had brought him a dingo cub and they played together all the time. When the animal grew and began yearning for a partner on moonlit nights, William used to imitate its howl. Like all young children, he was quick to pick things up. This was not the only time the trick had come in handy. But he knew now that the most important thing was to find and save the girls. He carefully scurried back to where he had been hiding. Now and then he would give a spine-chilling howl, and watch amused as the men quickened their steps.

Elizabeth and her friend, meanwhile, were wondering how they would make their escape. They watched, surprised to see the men returning so quickly. The other five men laughed when they heard the bungled account of the men who went for water.

Mary looked around in search of an escape route, when her fine lips curved into a sudden smile. Elizabeth looked at her quizzically.

"Look!" Mary whispered, pointing toward the forest, where William's head could be seen between the branches of a mangrove tree. He waved to them, climbed down and made his way toward them through the high grass. Reaching them, he gave them no time to ask questions, but said: "Listen. When I give the signal, I want you both to run as fast as you can in the direction I just came from." Then, turning his back on them, he wriggled like a snake back into the foliage. Following his proven tactic, he howled, then waved for the girls to run. Using the decoy as their cover, the girls followed the path that would lead them into the sheltering forest.

The convicts gave a start at the renewed howling, but it only lasted a second. The convicts, rifles in hand, divided the food. They postponed the search for food and water until after the meal. William ran after the girls and, having caught up with them, said: "We have to go back to the village and warn the others!" Without waiting for a reply, he was on his way. Having reached the canal, he decided to take the path that led to the fields as he thought it unwise to spread panic among the village women. The girls followed him to the fields and from a distance started calling to their fathers. The men took up their tools and began running anxiously toward the children. Breathlessly, William ran to his father. The first words that came to his lips were: "Father. They're here!"

"Who is here, son?"

"Some evil-looking men! They came by ship. The kind of ship we saw last time, only smaller." Anderson sat his son down under a eucalyptus tree. "Start from the beginning, son. Tell me everything." William told his father everything that had happened, beginning with Mary's shriek. Then the girls came over and confirmed William's account of the story.

Hull Anderson looked over at his companions and yelled: "Hey, Bolton, Bafin, follow me! We've got to get to that storage attic and get the remaining weapons. "We've got to take every precaution until we know these strangers' motives."

"Meeting in the village square, now!" Morrel announced. Everybody followed him.

"From this moment on, nobody is to set foot near the shore, you hear. Hopefully the strangers haven't discovered any traces of our presence here," remarked Hull Anderson, looking around for his son.

All of a sudden it occurred to him how smart his son had been to divert the men from the creek path. His father looked around anxiously... but William was long gone. Hull knew his son and how he couldn't tolerate praise and questions, but that it was danger and adventure he loved. He was sure he knew where William had gone. He had more than likely gone back to where the strangers were. And that meant his son was in immediate danger. "Quick, everyone follow me!" he yelled and started running. "It's William!" But by the time his father had discovered his absence, many things had already occurred.

William was, in fact, on his way back to the shore. He wanted to know what had become of the uninvited guests.

Reaching the shore, William looked cautiously around, and then fixed his gaze on the ship. He crept over to the boat that had been pulled ashore, soon discovering that he had nothing to fear, for the men had all fallen asleep under the palm tree. He approached them fearlessly, stopping just a few feet from the man called Donald. He studied their stubbly, unwashed faces. What happened next can only be credited to William's great courage. With complete composure, he walked over to the sleeping Donald and carefully picked up the rifle that was lying beside him. He examined the novel firearm. His father's guns were blunderbusses; this was of a much more advanced caliber, a fast shooter. Slowly he raised the sight to his eyes and picked out a seagull flying above the water. He pulled the trigger! William dropped the weapon and ran for cover. The men were on their feet in no time. The appearance of the young man had so surprised them they didn't have the presence of mind to fire at him, in spite of the fact that their guns were loaded.

Anderson and the others had reached the shore by now. Thousands of frightened seagulls flew off, screeching helplessly. Hull Anderson knew there was trouble in store for them.

William, seeing his father, ran toward him. Hull Anderson hugged him and ordered him to get behind him. The convicts could scarcely believe their eyes when they saw the settlers. But they quickly realized whom they were up against. Their ridiculous choice of weapons was a good indication.

Donald Hawke, the leader of the gang, smiled his most charming smile and spoke respectfully: "Now that we're all here, I guess we should officially introduce ourselves! The name's Donald Hawke, and these here are my friends." He pointed around himself, where the other convicts, fingers on the trigger, were wondering what Donald was up to. They knew that just one round of fire would have sufficed to finish the settlers off.

"We were out here fishing along the shoals, but as we were nearly out of drinking water, we had to come ashore. And maybe a little wild meat wouldn't hurt either!"

Phillip Morrel studied the speaker carefully before saying anything.

"If you like, we wouldn't mind offering you some of our meat and water..."

"Well, speaking for my friends, we would all be much obliged at the offer!" Donald said, bowing slightly, and holding out his hand. Looking back at his companions, he motioned for them to follow his example. William didn't miss a thing.

"Follow us, Mr. Hawke," Morrel said and they started for the village. The strangers lagged behind a little, and put their heads together conspiringly. This, too, did not escape William's attention.

Back at the village, everybody was anxiously awaiting news from the shore. As the men approached, they observed the newcomers in silence. They smiled at the villagers in anticipation of the provisions they had been promised.

In spite of the shaky introductions, the villagers eventually got along fine with their new guests. Three of the convicts returned to their boat to fetch a case of rum. Night had already fallen, but the men's singing could still be heard through the forest. Around midnight the villagers escorted their guests to the shore and said goodnight. The eight convicts took in the oars all the way to the boat, and bedded down for the night.

Donald woke his men at dawn the next morning. The men didn't understand what was happening.

"Look here," he told them, taking a gold nugget from his pocket. His companions could hardly believe their eyes. "Last night the village head, Morrel, let me in on a little secret...Our poor fellow citizens aren't so poor as it seems. There are gold mines hidden in this forest! I think we should have a look before we blow their brains out."

The other convicts stared at their leader in awe.

"How are we going to find out where the stuff is hidden?" inquired Cooper.

"In their storage cellar they've hidden two whole chest loads of gold! There's also a map leading to the mine." The men listened to their leader's words with huge eyes. "We wouldn't be able to get in there without violence, but I have a plan, and we'll find it useful in more ways than one. This afternoon all eight of us are going hunting. Believe me, there'll be more food and gold than we can carry, and all this without firing a single bullet." Then he revealed to them his wicked plan . . .

Alone

Back at the village, everyone was jumping for joy at the new turn of events. They were finally returning to Europe!

Donald Hawke prepared a going-away supper for his hosts on the ship for the next evening. Prior to this, the eight men went hunting as planned, so that, as they said, they could restock their food supplies. After lunch they set out, promising to be back by noon the next day.

Meanwhile the villagers went straight to the business of packing. The excitement of the coming trip to home shone from every face. Phillip Morrel was planning to give Donald a little bag of gold by way of payment for their traveling expenses. His companions thought this was a good idea, as they didn't want to take advantage of the men's goodwill. Their plan was to return later for the gold. The two trunk loads of gold would be more than enough to assure their futures in Europe. However, they did all agree that great care had to be taken to not tell their guests about the rest of the gold...

Unfortunately, Morrel had already said too much in the course of drinking, his head woozy with rum.

William, on the other hand, could not stop thinking that something was very wrong. Right from the beginning, he had strong doubts. Donald had given him a knife with an insignia of the convict inscribed on it. He told William it was a gesture of thanks.

The next evening, as agreed, the villagers set out for the boat. They were wearing their best clothes; after all, this was indeed something to celebrate. After twenty-five long years as castaways, they were finally going home!

The Andersons were also busy preparing for the journey. As the boat had to make many trips between shore and ship, the couple wanted to be the last to go aboard as they were still waiting for William, who after all this time had still not turned up. Hull angrily searched the premises without success. Losing his temper, he threw open the front door. "We're going without him!" he informed his wife and that was that. They headed for the shore.

William didn't want any part in the supper. He had no tolerance for strangers and he knew in his gut that something was very wrong. He wandered to the back of the village and came upon the Gredford house. He heard voices coming from the house and saw two figures standing near the window. Without thinking, he peeked through the window and saw Daniel, who was whispering something to Elizabeth. The girl laughed aloud. "All right, I'll go and tell Susannah!" With that, she stood and went into Susannah's little bedroom. William snuck over to the other window and pricked up his ears. At first they talked in hushed tones, then Elizabeth's voice broke out with: "Please, Susannah, I beg you! Won't you do me this tiny little favor?"

"No, I don't want to. I hate him!" Susannah protested.

"But, Susannah, how can you say such a thing?" her sister snapped back at her. "Mr. Hawke has agreed to take us on his ship and the gold will pay our way. All you have to do is hand him the bag and give him a little peck on the cheek! You can't say I'm asking a great deal!"

Susannah was filled with teenage rebellion. "If it's such a small thing, why don't you kiss him yourself?"

"Why, Susannah, I'm a full-grown lady! And you're just a stubborn little girl!"

Susannah crouched helplessly on the edge of the bed and glared at her older sister. Then Elizabeth lost her patience altogether, threw open the door and with a look of disgust, told her: "That's it. You're not going anywhere...And you're not getting any supper either." She slammed the door and was gone.

Susannah's eyes filled with tears now. Having been witness to all of this, William retreated from the window, and straightening up, took a better look at the beautiful girl, seeing that she was now sobbing.

The family then left the house and joined the Andersons. Within a matter of minutes the little village was deserted.

Susannah was still crying softly, maybe not so much because her pride had been wounded, but because with the onset of night, fear was beginning to creep into her mind. We can imagine just how frightened she was to hear William's voice behind her. He murmured only two words, and they were intended to console rather than blame her.

"Don't cry..."

Susannah screamed and looked fearfully toward the window where she saw William standing in her room. Her frightened expression met William's inquisitive one. "What are you doing here?" she asked, more calmly now, though her heart was beating wildly.

"I was passing by when I heard you crying and I just thought..."

"I wasn't crying," she cut him off, but immediately put her hands over her face, which had reddened with embarrassment. William laughed at her feeble defense.

"Well then, you were sniveling because your parents wouldn't take you along."

"What gave you that idea?" Susannah asked, taken aback by the fact that her secret had been revealed so easily.

"I just guessed. Anyway, everyone's gone, they're all down at the boat." He said this mischievously. The girl smiled a little smile.

"Well, yes...I had to stay here because my sister's angry with me."

"I'm not surprised," he retorted. "I wouldn't like it a bit if years from now, I had to remember that my very first kiss went to Donald Hawke!"

"What did you say?" the girl sprang up, turning bright red. "How did you know? Unless...unless... Unless you were spying on me!"

"The dingo doesn't have hearing as sharp as mine!" William burst out laughing.

Their eyes met again... and this time the girl didn't close her eyes, as she had at their first meeting, but endured the fire in his eyes. Soon they realized the distance between them was shrinking and that they were moving closer and closer to each other. William reached for her hand and Susannah let him hold it, though she lowered her head shyly and blushed. He slowly pulled her to him. Outside, the sun had set and in an instant, night had descended. But for them, it seemed as though the sun was still shining brilliantly, like a rainbow appearing in the midst of storm clouds. Their hearts were racing as their gazes nearly set fire to one another. Their lips met and their eyes closed tightly. The world vanished. It was just the two of them in the midst of the immense forest, inside one small room of the house. But their souls rose higher and higher on the wings of a cloud. Although the night had blanketed them, their eyes fused together like burning stars. Their senses were woven into one, and time had stopped completely, around them. The spark of their love blazed into a thousand flames.

William was the first to speak, but he could hardly find his voice. "Susannah...I want to tell you something..."

"Not now," she cried. She freed herself from his embrace, and ran out of the house. He happily followed after her.

They ran with all their strength until they finally reached the ocean shore. Out of breath, Susannah collapsed on the sand. William caught up and sat down beside her. They sat silently for a while, listening to the waves gently lapping at their feet. The ocean breeze turned chilly and Susannah shivered. William removed his coat and placed it around her shoulders. Brushing against her skin, he could feel her whole body trembling. He also felt himself under the sway of a force that was new and strange. Tenderly he held her against him and their gaze wandered to the sky, filled with millions of stars. The bright silver moon cast its enchanting glow and the constellations, especially the Southern Cross, caught their attention. They gazed at the stars for a long time, as if the heavens were blessing their newfound love. Suddenly one of the little stars stirred and began to fall in a wide arc into the ocean. William wanted to speak, but the girl prevented him.

"Wish for something, William," she urged. But he could see only her. "Do you hear me, William, wish for something." He cast her a mischievous look. "Don't you want to?"

"Yes!"

"I wish that this girl would be mine forever and ever...!" The words drifted into the night, reaching to the highest heavens. Nevertheless the triumphant cry was extinguished immediately as Susannah slapped his face. But William just lay there happily taking the beating, laughing without pause.

Deep in his heart he could feel a vibrant tingling sensation. When the girl finally tired of the battle, she suddenly cast a fearful look at the sky. The little star had at that moment descended into the ocean to disappear without a trace. Susannah dropped her head sadly and became very quiet. William couldn't understand what had happened; the girl had been so happy only a moment before.

"What's wrong, Susannah?"

"I didn't wish for anything," came the disappointed answer.

"What would you have wished for?"

"Just that...that everything would stay just as it was before. That the strangers would go on their way again...without us!"

"Don't be angry, I just..."

"I'm not angry," she interrupted. "I just don't understand why everything has to change just when I was beginning to be so happy...with you!" She turned her beautiful head to him now. Tears were streaming down her face, shining silver in the moonlight.

"Don't cry...I'll always be right beside you. Life is beautiful, you'll see, we'll have everything we need in the new world."

"But we have everything here..."

"But the world is such a big place, and we've hardly experienced any of it yet."

"But people are evil, William. Happiness can only be found here," was the unexpected answer. William stroked her face. "Everything will be fine, you'll see..." With both his hands he pulled the slender girl to him; their lips met. Hand in hand, they returned to the Gredfords' house and Susannah's room. As they lay down in one another's embrace, all they could hear was the pleasant sound of their breathing. Their hearts were beating in sync, and they felt that their whole lives were ahead of them. It was indescribably wonderful.

As they fell asleep, their ocean of dreams carried them toward a bright future. All their worries had vanished. Neither of them had any idea what would happen if Susannah's parents were to find them here, with a coat spread over them, but they did not care. There was only one thought - that they loved each other and nothing or no one could ever come between them.

As the inquisitive moon shone down on them at that moment they somehow already had a sense that something wicked was about to happen. Some unexplainable tragedy was about to take place, the likes of which might have irreversible consequences.

Susannah was the first to awaken. She had no idea how long they'd been asleep. Astounded, she saw that a crowd bearing torches was gathered outside. She shook William to wake him up. He sat up as fast as lightning and ran to the window. What he saw outside was terrifying. Strange characters were everywhere. Torches were held high as they broke down the doors of the houses. Already several of the homes were on fire. Susannah hid behind him and observed with terrified eyes what was happening outside. The cries of the strangers were incomprehensible -- more like yelps or barks than human sounds. The youth carefully approached the door. Now there were noises from the other room as well. William's hand was on the latch when it lifted suddenly and a grotesque native figure appeared. In his hand he held a long spear. It was lucky for them that he wasn't carrying a torch, and, with the exception of the spear, he was carrying no other weapon. This way, he was unable to see the young couple. The savage was instinctively trying to find his way around the room. He began rummaging through the table in front of him. He growled like a dingo, fingering whatever objects he could find. All this was done in silence, as if not to arouse the attention of his tribesmen. William didn't remain passive. He waited for the intruder to turn his back, and then knocked the giant to the ground.

The man fell without making a sound, landing at William's feet. In spite of her fear, Susannah helped drag him away from the door, and they quickly bound him hand and foot; they gagged him and left him there on the floor. They had to hurry and reach the forest as fast as possible. They knew that if a native carrying a torch were to discover them, it would be the end. Hand in hand, William and Susannah silently crossed the threshold. Outside they ran towards the back of the house as they witnessed the horrible scenes of the night. Most of the houses were burning. The sound and smell of the burning houses was dreadful crackling into the night and painting the sky crimson. Their progress at this point was hampered, as they had to cut through the clearing. They couldn't go in the other direction;

that was where the savages were. Then William dropped to the ground suddenly and began to crawl, catching Susannah's legs until they were both crawling through the grass. To their misfortune, Susannah was unable to suppress a soft cry. Two natives had been approaching all this time, but William only noticed them at the last moment. The two natives became suspicious. One gave a strange shriek from deep in his throat, and their fellow tribesmen ran to the clearing from all sides. Urgent barking sounds filled the air, and then with torches raised and spears ready to be hurled, they began combing the area. The land was covered with thick grass, and the visibility was poor. The young heroes held each other close. They held their breath. Their eyes gleamed with fear. Their parents had told them stories about these savages, how they dragged their captives off to their villages and then tortured them. In the midst of war dances, they killed them and cut their bodies into pieces. In those days, the children had laughed with disbelief, taking the stories to be mere adventure tales. They would never in their lives have imagined that something like this could actually happen.

It seems that destiny still hadn't favored the two young people. Suddenly they found themselves illuminated by torchlight, surrounded by grim forms. Susannah held as tightly as she could to William, who could feel her entire body shaking with fear. The crowd began to back away and make room for a painted man. He pushed everyone out of his way roughly and, snatching a torch from one of the warriors, thrust it into William's face. He could feel the scorching flames of the torch. Strands of his hair were singed as the wind blew them into the flame. He tried to throw his head back, and get a better look at his captor. He wanted to read the motives that were written on his face. But the Papuan's face reflected only savagery and twisted hatred. The staring match lasted only a few seconds and then the chieftain took a closer look at Susannah. As the torch got closer to her face, the girl jumped back in fright. William reached for her and they were now on their feet. Now a cruel smile appeared on Mintnao Kombalun's face. He muttered something to his prisoners. He called one of his warriors over to him, but without taking his eyes off Susannah for even a second. The Papuan seized the girl, wanting to take her with him. The instant the rough hands touched her, she cried out. William threw himself on the man and hit him, pulling the girl towards him. He held his hands up in protest to show that Susannah belonged to him, that nobody else had a right to go near her. The circle of warriors widened again and Kombalun looked back questioningly as his allies, Donald Hawke and friends, stepped into the torchlight. The two young people's mouths dropped open with disgust. So that had been Donald's plan! But why? It soon became clear enough...

The "hunters", during the past couple of days, had gone to talk with the chieftain. They conspired with him to attack the white village. With regard to the booty, the Papuans could have the people and any of their personal belongings. In exchange, the convicts demanded help mining the gold from the caves... It may sound strange, but the Papuans had not once set foot in the territory of the white settlers in the twenty-five years they had lived there.

Their reasons were religious in nature. The territory was taboo to the Papuans. It was a holy place on which neither the chieftain nor any members of his tribe were allowed to set foot. These were ancient burial grounds. One night, during a victory celebration over their vanquished enemies, a great spirit had appeared to them and frightened them from the property. When this had happened, only some of the oldest surviving Papuans still knew. But the superstitious tribe had not dared since that time, to break the taboo. Kombalun, however, was more greedy than superstitious. Dreaming of treasure beyond compare, he had his medicine men break the taboo, and called his nation to war.

Three of the convicts had died in the battle. The five remaining were here now to discuss their plans. Donald greeted Mintnao Kombalun like an old friend. Seeing the two youths, his brow darkened for a minute, he informed the chieftain that the two must also die. This news did not please the tribal leader, who pointed agitatedly to William and Susannah, gesticulating wildly. He mixed a few English words into his lively banter. Donald appeared to understand the Double Dutch as if the chieftain had been speaking to him in his own language. At the end of the speech, he grinned and stepped in front of William. "The chieftain says that after you've been fattened a bit you'll be killed. Until that time, he and the girl can't marry..."

"What did you say? You mean that beast wants to marry Susannah?"

"Listen here," Donald yelled at him roughly. "If it was up to me you'd have been fed to the fish. Be happy you've got a few days left to live."

"You bastard," shouted William, striking the despicable face. The natives sprang into action, pinning his arms behind his back. Donald's eyes flashed wildly with anger and he began to reach for his knife, and then thought better of it. "Get ready, son," he warned, "You're going to be the main course at their wedding!" Williams eyes widened in disbelief. Suddenly, Susannah fainted without so much as a whisper.

Soon, the natives set out for booty. What they considered superfluous was tossed into the fire. The little village became desolate. Twenty-five years of bitter struggle, hard-earned progress now lay covered in dust and ashes. William looked around tearfully: there was nothing here to come back to. And their lives were hanging by a thread. Making fists and clenching his teeth, he was pushed along in the line and they penetrated into the deep of the forest. Doubt tormented him throughout the entire journey. They attached a snare to one of his legs so that he wouldn't escape. Behind them, two Papuans goaded them on with spears. They didn't tie his hands, so he was able to support "his lady". In the remaining hours of the night they had not stopped to rest. By dawn they were far from the shore and by morning they marched ceremoniously into the village of the Papuans. Susannah was unconscious from exhaustion. The trials of the past hours had consumed every last drop of her energy. William had to lead her the whole way and later carried her.

The warriors returned to the village with great enthusiasm. The villagers who'd remained at home now eagerly fondled all the stolen valuables. The two youths, even in this hard time, were not allowed to be together. Kombalun assigned Susannah to a separate tent, where she could rest from the journey. William was put in a cage where he would have as little space as possible to move around. It was so small, in fact, that at most he could only kneel. Standing was not even an option. They saw to it that the feeder was immediately filled with food, and guards prodded him from all sides with spears to see that he had his fill...

Kombalun hung around Susannah's tent heaping his presents on her, but the girl did not accept anything. When she awoke she could not find William anywhere. She tried desperately to leave her tent, but the women who had been set to guard her would not let her go. When she had tired of her attempts to escape, she began to cry softly. Later she decided that she had to stay strong and hope they might have the chance to escape. She closed her eyes to sleep, but her mind kept on whirring like mad after all the horrors she had just been through. She knew only her parents and her brother and sister, all her life up to now and they were dead. She knew nothing would ever be the same again. All the others were dead – only the two of them remained. They had to face the evil white men and the bloodthirsty Papuans alone. How could they find the way out? Was there a way out at all? She bowed her beautiful head and cried herself to sleep, swallowing her tears…

William was given so much food that he felt as if his stomach would burst. Soon afterwards he got rid of most of it when he saw the corpses of the other convicts being taken to the village. Then he caught sight of the bloody bodies of his parents and the horror of it made him want to cry out. He pressed his face tightly against the bamboo bars and could not turn his eyes from the terrible picture though he felt as if he would go mad. "None of them have survived… they are all dead..." he murmured, staring, half way to madness in his pain. The hypocritical face of Donald appeared in front of his tear-filled eyes, and he felt he now understood everything… He felt a burning pain in his fingers. He noticed that blood was flowing over his hand. It was his own blood. He had driven his nails deeply into the bamboo bars in his shock just before.

After a while he began to get over the shock induced by the first despair. His mind was filled with a single thought: escape…

He shifted around, trying to find a comfortable position. The only thing he was afraid of was what might happen to Susannah. But he was glad that she did not have to see the butchery that was soon to start. Then eventually blessed sleep overtook him as well, and he slept through the whole day.

Susannah had to put up with Kombalun's attentions nearly every hour. The Papuan chief took presents one after the other to the guests' tent; presents that naturally originated from among the things they had so recently stolen. Among them the girl recognized her mother's pearl-encrusted mirror, which she hid under her mat.

The village was preparing for a rich feast. They had lit a large fire, and after the opening war dances they began their cannibalistic gorging, which is better left untold…

As evening fell, the satiated Papuans lay down around their fire and gazed on the valuables they had stolen. Kombalun kept on moving around them, and when something caught his attention he immediately seized it, in most cases taking it off to the girl's tent soon afterwards.

Susannah's guards explained to her what an important feast they were missing. The girl understood from their sign language what was happening outside. She mourned the death of her parents with bitter tears… Later, using signs, she tried to learn from them where William was. In answer to her questions, one of the women took her by the hand and led her to a tent, opening it slightly. Susannah immediately caught sight of William inside: he was asleep, leaning against the bars of his cage. The girl asked why he was being kept there, imprisoned. She did not understand the answer, but the woman's motioning disgusted her: she was pointing at him, saying 'yum yum' and stroking her belly. The next time Kombalun appeared, she did not send him away, but asked if she could leave her tent. In the chief's eyes a flash of doubt appeared, but he was honoured that the white beauty had talked to him. Finally, he condescendingly agreed to her leaving the tent together with the three other women, but kept on hovering around until Susannah sent him away. The girl's path led first to the cage where William was being held. She watched him sleeping for a while, and then stepped in and knocked on the bamboo bars. The native girls were anxiously pointing towards Kombalun's tent, but the girl took no notice of them. William moved and opened his eyes, blinking. He was very happy when he caught sight of Susannah.

"Do you mind my waking you up, Will?"

"Oh, not at all." William smiled, and his eyes eagerly watched the features of the girl. "Tell me, have you already thought about escaping?"

"Hush, one of the bandits might hear you!"

"They can't – they left for the gold mines this morning... Listen, Suzy! I wasn't searched before I was shut in here, so I still have my dagger with me. I think I will be able to cut through the bars overnight. If I succeed, we can escape from here tomorrow night. I can see that you are guarded as well, but you might gather some food for the journey. Can you manage that?"

"Of course I can, the chief has brought me so much food that there's hardly any room left in the tent. I think I can fool them they are rather simple-minded. But I must go now. We must not attract their attention."

She rose and kissed his lips through the bamboo bars. Then, waving good-bye, she returned to her tent, accompanied by the Papuan women. William lay back on the floor, satisfied and engrossed in his thoughts.

Night fell on the jungle without any transition, darkness conquering everything. The warriors had re-kindled the fires and were eating noisily. The remains of the feast glowed a ghostly white in the moonlight. Soon after came the call of the first hyena, who scurried in to clear away all the edible remains of the feast. Then, a small rasping noise mingled with the voices of the animals – a noise caused by a hunting knife cutting bamboo bars. William had started his night work. Within three hours he had managed to cut through four bamboo bars. When he removed them he was able to climb out of his prison, which hung one and a half yards above the ground. He took a long walk around the village, stretching his stiff legs and arms. After he had exercised his limbs enough, he lay down under a eucalyptus tree, and did not climb back into his prison until just before dawn. He carefully placed the bamboo bars back into position, and waited for the morning to come as if nothing had happened.

As the sun rose in the east from beyond the depths of the jungle, the Papuans, who were used to waking early in the morning, also arose. The women began their work in the fields, and the men got ready for the hunt. Donald and his companions returned from the gold mine at the same time. They had spent the night there, having made a site check the day before. Today they planned to take some natives with them to extract the ore. Kombalun also came up when the five convicts arrived. He had chosen eight strong warriors and had put them at the disposal of his "brothers". They had taken all the tools they needed from the ship the previous day. Their plan was to make the Papuans do all the work while they looked on from under the shade of the trees. Suddenly, Santiago had an idea. He told the others, who received it with great cheers. His plan was to ask the Papuan chief for five girls to make the dull hours pass more quickly. Now they just had to get Kombalun to agree to their plan. At first he listened to their request with a long face, but when Donald gave him a knife as a present, he immediately became more understanding. It did not take long to choose the five girls, as none of the women were wearing anything but a loincloth. All of them were tall, pretty women, but still Donald took his time, choosing carefully. The other convicts soon chose their women. They decided to have the Papuans start and take the girls to bathe at the seashore before following them.

William could see everything that was happening through the bars of his cage. He saw them picking the girls, but he was concentrating on watching Susannah's tent. A Papuan woman carrying an earthen vessel left the tent. He called to her; she turned, shocked, and ran back into the tent when she saw who was calling. But she must have understood something, since Susannah's face soon appeared in the opening of the tent. She waved to William, who was glad of the greeting. They watched each other lovingly for a while, and then Susannah suddenly disappeared back into the tent. Kombalun was approaching, bringing with him a beautiful Papuan girl who could not have been more than fourteen or fifteen years old. Her face had not yet been spoiled with tattoos and sticks. They were coming straight to William's cage. Kombalun said in broken English, "you lord white woman… I lord Papuan woman. You white woman me… I Papuan woman you!"

William immediately understood the meaning of the words. He, William, could get the Papuan girl as a wife in return for giving Susannah to the chief. He shook his head violently, pointing at the girl. But Kombalun misunderstood him, and thought that William did not like the girl. So he acted on what he had experienced with the convicts, thinking that he wanted to try the girl before the exchange. He nodded to William's guard, who unlocked the cage and motioned for him to get out. William jumped down from his prison with a bad feeling about what was going to happen. Kombalun called the two other warriors, and the three of them led William to a smaller, round room no higher than a carved baobab tree. The walls were covered with animal skins, and there was a fine mat on the floor. There were two holes in the wall – one on the western and one on the eastern side. High above his head there was a third hole, which probably served as a kind of chimney. The chief left him with the girl, but William could see that there was no chance of escape, since the warriors had been left in front of the door, which was covered with a thick mat.

The girl walked up to him and brought his hands to her breasts. Strange, feelings began to come over him, feelings he had never known before. The girl's breasts felt like great oranges, which seemed to grow as he touched the soft skin. She slowly drew his body towards her. William stood, hesitating, but as the girl stripped off his clothes and removed her loincloth, he started to feel something he had never experienced in his life. He entered the school of sensual pleasures, a school that this young girl seemingly had already passed. As they lay down on the skins he simply relied on his instincts, not needing to be shown the way of physical love.

The world around them no longer existed. William's initial resistance soon became just a pretence, and then dissolved altogether; his lust spread over him, and he could no longer rule his mind...

Minutes later, or was it hours, they were lying side by side, trembling and weak, their throbbing blood still pulsing in their foreheads. Their hearts were jumping behind their ribs like unbridled steeds. The girl pushed her hot forehead to William's face and embraced him tightly.

Suddenly, movements could be heard outside. Kombalun entered, pulling aside the mat curtain. A broad grin appeared on his face. The situation was unmistakeable: the young man had accepted the bargain. William already knew he had lost: whether he wanted it or not, Zormin had become his wife. There was nothing he could do. He nearly went crazy at the thought of giving Susannah to Kombalun without her knowledge. He freed himself from Zormin's embrace, stood up and looked into Kombalun's eyes... Driven by sudden emotion he hit the face of the man who was his captor. Papuans invaded the room upon hearing Kombalun's horrified cry. William was caught and led to his prison, his captors beating him all the way there. Hearing the great uproar, Susannah looked out and was afraid when she caught sight of William lying bloody on the floor of his cage. She wanted to run to him, but remembered his advice. Whatever happened, they had to escape that night. So she remained in her tent, brooding in doubt. She did not want to attract Kombalun's anger, so she waited patiently for the night. From time to time she looked out at William's prison. The angry Papuans had beaten him unconscious. She also gathered food for she knew they would need it. If they were chased, there would be no time to search for food. So far she had not thought about what they would do if they finally got free again. Which way should they go? Where should they go?

William did not recover until after dark, so he could not see that the mortally offended chief placed a guard under his cage. His head felt as though it were splitting, so he closed his eyes again…

When night fell, fires blazed up again. The Papuans, tired from the day's work, prepared their dinner and then lay down on the warm ground…

The ore miners had not yet returned. They had set up a camp by the quarry. The happy whoops of the convicts disturbed the silence of the night. They were frolicking around in high spirits with the girls. The yellow metal extracted during the day was lying in a pile by the largest fire. Its vulgar twinkling showed its value. But the vast treasure was tainted with fresh blood.

Susannah had not dared to leave her tent that afternoon, and she became more and more anxious as night arrived. Eventually she went to bed, but the native women did not leave the tent as usual, but stayed by the girl, talking to one another quietly. The girl did not know what to make of this stricter guard. Nevertheless she recognized that it would be impossible for them to disappear unnoticeably if it continued…

William's thirst brought him to. He felt a stabbing pain in his ribs when he moved, and an acute pain in his back. He had to use his hand for support when he sat up. The floor of the cage was marbled with blood, and he was beginning to feel how much blood he had lost. His eyes slowly got used to the darkness. Then he caught the sound of a small twig cracking under him, and saw the Papuan guard sitting on the floor below his prison. He realised he had put all his eggs in one basket. He had to escape that night. It was clear what was going to happen to him if he stayed. That evening he had not even been fed, but not because he had missed the evening's feasting. This made him realise that if he did not hurry up, he would soon become a delicious lunch on the table of the chief. He did not much relish the idea of ending his short career on earth in the stomachs of the Papuans. He had to act that night…

An hour later the Papuan village became silent, and the pale moon rose over the inhabitants of the jungle. William carefully watched his guard, who had already become bored with his monotonous post. The guard took a look at his prisoner and, seeing that he still appeared to be unconscious, sat down under a neighbouring tree and started eating quietly. From time to time he looked around anxiously. Maybe he had been forbidden to eat, or perhaps he simply did not want to share his dinner with anyone. After the meal he lay down, breathing heavily, and rested his head on the tree. Any hope of escaping depended on the guard falling asleep, thus giving William a chance to act. He waited, anxiously. Finally the moment had arrived; he sat up noiselessly and approached the bars he had cut through the night before. He carefully took out the loose bars and laid them down across the grid of the floor, so that they wouldn't fall down and make a noise that betrayed him. He crawled out and landed with a quiet thud. Taking out his hunting knife, he approached the guard, ready to stab. The only way of escape and to Susannah's tent led directly past the sleeping Papuan. He carefully watched the breathing of the oblivious man. Slowly, feeling the way with his feet, he closed the distance between them, then, after what seemed like an eternity, William passed him without any problem. But just then a night bird, startled by something, began to sing piercingly. The Papuan gave a loud snore and stretched out on the ground. A few minutes later he was lying limp. A last silent rattle left his throat: a farewell to life. William pulled his knife out from the Papuan's chest. He wiped it on the grass and continued on his way. Reaching Susannah's tent, he could not see the female guards anywhere. He suspected that the girl was being guarded in the bedroom. He went around the tent and listened at the back…

There was a numb silence in the tent. Quietly he took out his knife and began to slit the thick cloth that formed the back wall of the tent. The blade slowly cut through the fibres… He heard a quiet scraping from inside, then a timid voice, "Is it you, Will?"

"Yes," he whispered back, and went on cutting the fibres with greater impetus. A tiny little hand appeared in the slit, and then Susannah's slim body was pressed through the opening and William could finally embrace her, who was trembling with fear. He led her quickly to the chief's tent. It consisted of two parts. The inner room was the bedroom, but the outer one was unguarded. The chief's personal property was kept here. Anyone daring to steal from Kombalun would have to pay with his head. William went in to retrieve his bow and arrows, which the greedy chief had confiscated as well as his leather suit and hunting bag. As soon as he held his bow and arrows, his confidence returned. He felt he could now face a whole group of natives. Susannah held the small bundle in which she had packed the food. They crept silently out of the sleeping camp and threw themselves into the underbrush…

When they were out of hearing distance, William curiously asked to where the women had disappeared. The girl explained that at first they had not wanted to leave her alone for the whole night. She had nearly come to accept that the escape would fail, when Kombalun's smirking face appeared at the door of the tent. Susannah looked at him in disgust, but then suddenly she had a good idea. She knew the chief would do anything to court her favour, so she began to point at the native women and, using simple words, she told him that she would only sleep alone. At first the face of the chief darkened at the request and he looked at the girl resentfully. Susannah, overcoming her revulsion, breathed a hot kiss toward his face. He immediately sent the women away, but then stood there in expectation of further rewards. But she sent him away, saying that the next day he could expect more from her.

William listened keenly to Susannah's story. At the end he embraced her and said, "I knew you wouldn't leave me in the lurch. You know, if we hadn't been able to escape tonight, I would have become a banquet lunch tomorrow."

"Will, if I lose you I will take my own life…"

They carried on forcing their way forward through the bush. They could not afford to decrease their speed, since they had to get a long way through the jungle before morning. Once Kombalun learned of their escape he would not easily give up the chase. The pale light of the moon found its way into the thicket here and there, and thus with difficulty they could grope their way through the vegetation. Deep in the jungle, where even the broad light of day could not penetrate, they had to rely completely on their other senses. William led Susannah with a wonderful instinct. He always found openings in the impenetrable thicket, though in many places he had to cut a way through with his sharp knife. He could smell the salty scent of the ocean clearly, even when they were still miles away from it, and they pressed on towards it. Finally, as dawn came, he sat the exhausted girl down on the seashore. There they filled their stomachs with food. They would not be able to stop again until evening fell. They had to go as far as possible from the place where they had left the jungle. They were very lucky not to have met any wild animals during the night. They would have been easy victims in the thicket. Perhaps a higher power had been helping them to get so far on their desperate way. The instinct to stay alive was also very strong in them. They had as much a right to life as anyone else…

After the meal, at William's suggestion they waded into the ocean up to their knees, and continued their journey walking along the shore through the waves, where the water generously smoothed away all traces of their passing…

In the morning, the Papuan camp awoke to a horrifying shout. The guard who had come to relieve his friend found him lying in a pool of blood underneath the hanging prison. He ran up and down the central village square, shouting and calling until all the people came out of their huts.

Kombalun also appeared, adjusting his large, ornamental feather headdress. He walked in a stately manner towards the shouting man. This was his big day. Today he would finally be able to lead the beautiful white woman to his tent. The Papuan crowd parted for their chief. The warrior pointed fiercely towards the dead man and the empty cage. Kombalun stood and stared stupidly for a while, as it was yet early morning and he was still rather heavy headed. Slowly he began to come to his senses. He roared, and then pushing aside those standing in his way, he raced to the girl's tent. He pushed aside the mat and disappeared from view. When he stepped out again, his face was distracted. His fear had become a reality; his bride had been abducted.

Within minutes an army stood ready with weapons, all set for the chase. Kombalun stood at the head of the group prepared to go after the escapees. His scouts easily found the place William had entered the thicket. The trampled vegetation showed their direction of travel. But there was one thing helping the escapees. In the dense thicket there were places where two people could easily find a way through, but where thirty men armed with long spears and large bows had to cut a real trail to be able to go on. Nevertheless, their great experience in the jungle enabled them to gain quickly. Yet the young pair had a few hours advantage. They had long been on the seashore when their followers started on their trail. Still, Kombalun would not easily renounce the white beauty. When after the early morning hours the sun began to beat down, it turned the jungle into a hot kettle. Water evaporated from the vegetation and the saturated soil, and the group had to continue through suffocating humidity.

After a further two hours of walking the growing breeze began to have a salty tang. The thicket gradually became sparser, and a cool sea wind touched the warriors' tired and wet bodies. They immediately found the footprints in the sand. They also found the traces of the dawn camp. But the tracks from here led straight into the ocean in an incomprehensible way... Kombalun was shocked. His science ended here. There were no traces on the water. They might have sailed away. But where could they have found a boat? Many questions arose in his head, but finally he had to admit that he was defeated. He looked at his people and saw the longing for the cool seawater in their eyes. In the end he could not do anything but give permission to stop and swim. The warriors, throwing away their arms, burst out in shouts of cheering and ran into the cool waves. The chief did not join them, but followed the tracks from the forest to the shore again and again. He slowly began to realise that he had lost the game; the cunning young man had outsmarted him. No matter where he looked, he could not see any boat or ship on the sea. He saw only the endless water stretching out to the horizon, and the waves frothing on the rocks of the shore.

The sun slowly reached its noon position in the sky. William and Susannah were walking in the blue seawater hand in hand. They had crossed several curves and bays since morning, and were already far away from the place of their morning camp. William looked around carefully and said, "We don't have to walk in the water any further. Kombalun will not have found our tracks anywhere. The only thing he will have seen is that we went straight into the sea. Maybe he thinks we will swim across the ocean in our fear of him." Then he winked at the girl. "But he's wrong." They both laughed. They walked up to the sandy beach. While Susannah rested under a giant fern, William broke off a leafy branch and wiped away any trace of their tracks. In the meantime the girl watched a group of koala bears joyfully hopping about in a eucalyptus grove. The amusing, loveable animals were moving from one tree to the other, carrying their cubs on their backs and peacefully nibbling the young shoots. William returned and saw the Susannah's delight in the bears. He stood by her and quietly said, "We will stay here for the night. I saw a freshwater stream near here, but we have to go a little further up it. It is flowing, but the water is salty so close to the sea, you know."

Susannah nodded her assent. She turned away from the forest and looked back along the shore. "You were clever to cover up our tracks; the sly Kombalun might divide his army and send them in two directions, but this way they cannot find us."

William received her appreciation with a smile. He picked up their small pack and started up alongside the stream. Jungle soon surrounded them again. They arrived in a landscape broken by giant rocks. Trees grew on every inch of the soil, so they had to go to one side. They had hardly advanced a few hundred meters when they heard voices from deep within the forest, and the sharp, hard clanking of tools echoed among the rocks. William immediately crouched down in the grass and pulled the girl close to him. Susannah's first thought was that their pursuers had discovered their tracks. She could almost see the evil grin on Kombalun's distorted face. But William knew whom it was the bush hid. The voices revealed the cheerful mood of Donald and his companions. Further on, the Papuans were carrying rocks mixed with gold out into sunshine.

Susannah hid in the bush while William approached the glade, creeping skilfully as a cat, hidden by the vegetation. His ears immediately caught the words of his detested enemies.

"Soon we can leave this hot kettle and sail back to Europe," came the voice of Donald Hawke.

"What wealth awaits us there!" called John Pedro.

"What luck that three of us have bitten the dust! The share per person will be higher this way," Frank Jose interrupted ironically.

"How wise you are, Frank! If you go on like this, you'll be able to count all ten of your fingers twenty years from now."

"My friend, it's enough for me to be able to count up to nine", he said, holding out his hands, which were missing one finger. "Nine hundred kilograms of gold, and I will swim in beer till the end of my life, surrounded by the nicest girls!" Frank laughed and slapped the bottom of the Papuan girl embracing him.

"You cad!" William exclaimed softly. Seeing the carefree way the scoundrels were behaving, he was suddenly seized with the thirst for revenge. He swiftly came to the decision that he would silence them one by one. He would follow them like a ghost, and kill each of them separately, just as they themselves had done with his parents and his friend. He would not let them enjoy their freedom in that far away Europe. He would also settle the account with Kombalun, and with everybody else who was responsible for their misfortunes. These thoughts filled his mind and were nearly responsible for his downfall: he had to withdraw rapidly into the bush to avoid being captured by some approaching Papuans. They passed right by him. The natives talked rapidly to the convicts, gesturing with their hands and feet. They were running out of extractable ore. The convicts could see it happening with their own eyes. They had a look at the day's results. Enormous riches awaited the five of them. They did not have to fear being unable to reach an agreement: even twenty could become rich on this amount of money. They looked knowingly at one another…

"We are rich!" they exclaimed to each other. But Donald, always the practical thinker, cooled their hot heads.

"No, we only will be. First we have to reach an inhabited area where we can make use of our spoils... And now, let's go. I want to see the shores of this continent behind me as soon as possible. I think that's how we all see it!" His companions eagerly agreed. Donald ordered the natives to gather their things and go back to the village.

William returned to Susannah. He told her about the convicts' plans in detail, and then moved on to talk about the possibility of revenge. But the girl did not want him to be exposed to danger, so she tried to persuade him to abandon the plan.

"Don't do that, Will! If I lose you, there'll be no one else left on earth for me. Let's go far away from here, please! To a place where none of our enemies can reach us."

"It's not possible, my darling." William replied. "I saw how our parents died. I have decided that I will take revenge for them as soon as I get the chance. These evil white men cannot leave, become rich and live it up in peace on the treasure our parents discovered. They have to die, as they deserve. All of them." Susannah turned away in sorrow. William sank down onto a rock weakly and buried his face in his hands...

The convicts were happily walking back towards the Papuan village. They passed along the seashore, turned onto the main trail, and arrived at the camp soon after sunset. Donald Hawke went immediately to Kombalun's tent. The chief received him coolly, and Donald soon learned the reason why. The man did not even like mentioning William. He thought that William would soon be planning something against them. Stepping out of the chief's tent, he walked straight to his companions. That night they started packing immediately.

Kombalun shut himself in his tent, and would not let anyone in. Zormin, the young Papuan girl, fled into the guests' house. She lay down on the mats and caressed the surface with her charming hands. Her thoughts brought William's face back to her. She could not imagine why he had left her for that white-painted, pale-faced girl. She thought she could really have made him happy. She could have given him half a dozen healthy boys if he wanted. Kombalun's face was dark both inside and out; William could even have taken the throne away from him. And she could have become his deserved wife. Their children could have risen to power all around the country. How beautiful it could have been. Zormin stretched her arms longingly in the dark to embrace William's strong body again, the man who had kissed her on the mouth so strangely. The young lads of her tribe could not kiss; they just bit her breasts and soon became violent. The white-faced stranger was different. First he had been shy, then burning, but it was clear he was of a higher class than her tribal mates. The Papuan girl put her hands on her belly and hoped that her son would at least resemble him. She would do her best to protect him from the others, since there was no doubt he would rule the tribe one day. Would he bear the crescent-moon shaped birthmark on his neck, which would demonstrate his special privilege from the moment of his birth? Zormin's outstretched hand caught only the empty air. The white stranger had left her, and might never return. But if he were to return, she would wait for him faithfully. She would never let anyone else touch her. She would wait to get her lord and master back…She sat up, pulled her knees up to her chest, and tilted back her head. She stared with dreamy eyes into the dark. The moon watched her through one of the windows, softly stroking her hair with its silver light. Teardrops twinkled in her eyes like falling stars, then rolled down her face and dropped silently onto her breasts.

Ship on the Shore

All this time William was swimming toward the boat in the quiet sea. The convicts had moved the small sailboat much closer to the Papuans' camp, anchoring the boat in the little bay.

Susannah sat on the shore watching the boat, clearly visible in the moonlight. Worried about their fate, she quietly murmured prayers to herself.

It had been a long time since William left. She started to worry about him. Her concern grew when a horrible explosion coming from the sea suddenly shook the air. With eyes wide with fear, she stared at the burnt wreckage of the boat that was quickly disappearing in the bubbling water. Dead silence descended on the seashore. The convicts were now captives of the shores of New Holland!

The sound of the explosion reached the village. Donald screamed, "The gunpowder!" The convicts grabbed some torches and started to run toward the sea.

William swam toward the shore with powerful strokes. He felt his strength waning.

After climbing aboard the ship, he lit a torch and ran down to the storeroom. He immediately spotted the row of barrels full of gunpowder. The idea of destroying the boat was followed by action: he cut a 20-foot rope, opened the closest barrel and dug into the gunpowder. He rubbed the gunpowder into the entire length of the rope, creating a detonating cord. He stuck one end of the rope into the barrel, dragged the other end behind him and lit it with the torch. There wasn't a moment to waste. He rushed to the deck and plunged into the sea. The flames, however, reached the end of the rope quickly and blew up the boat. William, too close to the ship at that moment, almost paid for this adventure with his life. A burning beam nearly killed him. He noticed the danger in time and ducked under the water. Even so, he almost died from the impact of the beam that hit his head.

He made it halfway to the shore; there were a few hundred yards left. He was afraid that his strength would ebb and he would go under, buried beneath the waves forever. But his luck didn't run out. He spotted part of the main mast in the water a few yards away. He used the last bit of his strength to grab it and climb on. By virtue of the rising tide he was fast approaching the shore. He felt a stabbing pain in his head and lost consciousness, collapsing onto the lifesaving beam.

The convicts ran to the sea as fast as they could. Deep down, they knew that their ship would never sail again, and without the ship all that they had fought for was lost. What so many had to die for, the reason they played this despicable role was gold!

In the recesses of their minds, where there was a shred of conscience left, they knew that this was God's punishment. Owning a fabulous amount of treasure was useless, if they could not leave this god-forsaken land. The gold was worthless here. It could not even buy food from the natives. They couldn't trust the Papuan chief either. If he thought his allies were weakened, this unpredictable man could very well attack them with his cannibalistic followers. Then the convicts' lives would really not be worth a penny.

Soon they became aware of the cool breeze coming from the sea that soothed their tired, sweaty bodies. As their path turned, the sea came into view. Their eyes automatically sought the black silhouette of the boat in the pale moonlight. But the waves of the sea had already swallowed the victim of the recent attack and the little sailboat. Only its pieces were drifting in the water, to be swept ashore by the high tide. The convicts rued the day they set foot on this continent only to become its captives.

Donald noticed a black object bobbing up and down in the water near the shore. The group rushed to the water's edge. John waded into the sea and started to swim. Getting closer, the object riding on the waves started to take shape. As he suspected, it was the remnant of the after-mast. He swam back to shore and broke the devastating news to the others. They started their dispirited trek back to the Papuan village where, once the chief learned of the new developments, might turn into a death camp. For that reason, Donald decided not to tell the truth if the chief asked why they wanted to stay longer. Soon they reached the forest and disappeared among the trees lining the path.

Susannah peeked out from behind a bush. Seeing that her enemies had left, she emerged from her hiding place and stared at the sea, tears streaming from her beautiful, sad eyes.

When she heard the explosion, she ran screaming down to the shore. She thought that the ship had exploded with William on board.

The original plan was for William to make a hole in the boat and let it sink. She was walking up and down the shore like a madwoman loudly cursing the unlucky star under which she was born. She didn't want to live without William; he was her mainstay in this world. Finally, she collapsed on the shore and stared out at the sea that consumed the only person she loved. Her heart was full of sadness and despair she had believed that Fate had sent her William to comfort her.

The "comfort" was being tossed about with the lifesaving beam. Slowly, the gentle waves deposited him on the shore, a few hundred yards away from where she was sitting. He was still unconscious, the waves washing over his head.

The blush of dawn gave way to the sunrise in the east, covering the sea in a purple hue. The quiet waves of the sea carried thousands of ever hungry, screeching seagulls that looked for a place to nest among the rocks of the shore. They angrily pecked at strangers who invaded their territory, daring to claim their well-placed nests. Perhaps they were looking for prey when they noticed the motionless body covered on and off by the ebbing waves in the dawn. Their voracious appetites were held in check, perhaps by their fear of the large body. Nothing, however, kept them from walking around the sleeping, perhaps dead man.

The sun was getting hotter and with the low tide approaching, life seemed to return slowly to the young man. He stirred slightly, but let his head drop right back on the sand. He lifted his hand to his head, the grimace on his face signalled the pain he felt. A hacking cough rose from his chest, and his body shook from the onset of a fever. As he sat up, he scared the peaceful birds on the shore that had become quite comfortable with the man lying on the ground. One of the braver ones was only a few inches away from him tending to its morning ritual in the soft sand of the seashore. At the sight of this treacherous human being that might be scheming to catch it, the bird took off with a lamenting screech. Nothing could be further from the truth. The last thing William wanted to do at that moment was capture a silly seagull. He had his own problems. He hissed as he touched the gaping wound on his head. He must have been bleeding heavily during the night, and there was still some blood seeping from the wound. He tried to get up, but in his dazed state he had trouble doing so. When he finally regained some of his equilibrium, he dragged himself to find shade because the sun was burning his wound. Overwhelming thirst depleted his energy even further. Worse than any pain was the thought that Susannah was not by his side. Squinting, he looked up and down the shore, but couldn't see a soul. Since his head wound was protesting against the sun, he staggered to the first tree. His thirst returned. He looked around for some water. His clouded vision could not find any familiar sight, so he started off in the direction of the spot where they had parted the day before, before the ship adventure. A ship adventure? Are there any ships in this world? And was it necessary to blow up the ships? In his feverish mind everything became mixed up. Last night seemed a thousand years ago.

He remembered seeing a brook that flowed into the sea. As he approached his goal in the shade of the trees, he felt very tired, close to fainting. He reached a eucalyptus tree; he collapsed and lost consciousness.

During the night Susannah patrolled the beach where she thought William might reach the shore, if he survived the blast. She cried for a long time, and even when the tears stopped, she kept remembering his attractive face. More than ever she realized how deeply she loved him. She would not survive the sorrow she felt from losing him, nor did she want to. If he was dead, there would be nothing left for her to do but end her life, as well. But deep down she felt a tiny spark of hope. She wanted proof of his death. Since night descended a while ago, she knew there was nothing she could do but wait for the morning. But she could not relax. She restlessly paced up and down at the edge of the forest, unable to settle down. She thought the morning would never come. Mysterious rustling and ominous sounds of scurrying creatures came from the deep woods. The burning eyes that watched her one moment and then disappeared filled her heart with dread. If a wild animal attacked her, she would not live to see the morning light. In her loneliness, she felt insignificant. Finally she decided to lie down near the sea; if attacked, she would escape into the water. She hoped that no wild animal could follow her there. She searched for the leather garments William removed before wading into the water. When she found them, she hugged the beloved clothing as if their owner were still wearing them.

Sleep didn't come easily. She woke up often with a start, sometimes imagining that he was whispering her name or calling her from afar. But it was the product of her tortured mind. It was near dawn when she finally fell into a deep, colorless sleep.

She slept for a long time and woke up to the blazing morning sun. She opened her eyes, blinking in the bright sunshine. She sat up, and her tired, wandering eyes halted at William's garments. She remembered her resolution of the night before, and decided to search for William's earthly remains. More than anything, her anxious heart wanted proof. She stood up and surveyed the area. The sea was lost in a blue fog, the wind driving playful waves to the shore. The birds were singing. She could see the debris that was swept ashore during the night: pieces of wood in different sizes the designation of which was unknown to her. She found the life preserver of the boat bearing the reassuring name "Nimble Fish". The heavier parts and fixtures of the ship were now among those fish after which the boat was named.

In the meantime, Susannah passed the point where she had stopped the night before. The shore turned toward the north, forming a little bay further down. Since she didn't have the sun in her eyes this enabled her to see farther. Dejected, she was about to turn back when, just a hundred yards away, she spotted footprints in the sparkling wet sand. Gathering all her strength, she started to run toward them with renewed hope. Once there, she found a piece of the sailboat, but she was not interested in it. Close to the chunk of the mast she thought she spotted the imprint of a human body. At least as far as she could judge, it must have been the imprint of a human, since this creature seemed to have stood up and walked towards the forest. She quickly followed the footprints until she reached the woods. At this point such dense vegetation blocked her that she didn't know what to do.

Again, she was overcome with doubts. It might not be William's footsteps she was following, but those of one of the convicts who had slept there. But that didn't make sense. Why would a convict sleep in this area? Was it really William who was swept ashore here? She was filled with renewed hope while trying to get her bearings. She retraced the footprints that now seemed to reflect the struggle of a wounded man. Or was her troubled mind playing tricks again? She checked the footprints again. Indeed, they seemed to originate from where she had just been, a little above the bay. She started walking quickly along the trampled grass. Soon she left the thicket behind and arrived at a eucalyptus grove. She continued with growing excitement and cried out with joy when she spotted William under a tree. She almost threw herself on him. She kissed his seemingly lifeless face. He regained consciousness for a moment but was only able to whisper: "Water!" This one word meant the world to Susannah. He wasn't dead! He was alive!

She helped him sit up, left him leaning against a tree and then ran for their belongings. She rushed back, took out one of their greatest treasures, an empty gin bottle, and ran for water to the small river. It seemed the longest few hundred yards she ever had to cover. It wasn't wise to leave him sitting against the tree. By the time she returned, William had tumbled over like a sack of potatoes. She tried to lift his head gently to help him drink some water. The first sips brought on a coughing fit, but then he settled down and started to drink in earnest. Susannah laid him down gently. Seeing the gaping wound on his head, she cleaned it, and shredded her clothes to make a bandage for it. She put a poultice on his forehead and hands. She was mothering him as the high fever caused by the wound made him faint again. She covered him and watched him anxiously. She went into the woods to gather some fruit. After all the excitement she also needed to eat. The rest of the time she stayed with him, and watched him breathing, his face red from the fever, as she anxiously awaited his awakening. Tranquillity slowly spread in her heart.

The sun was high in the sky when she heard distant thunder. She stood up and walked to the shore. Curiously surveying the sea she was surprised to see huge storm clouds gathering in the south. She knew from experience that the storm would arrive in a few hours, although storms were not common at this time of the year. She went back to the sleeping William. She knew it made no sense to wake him. In his feverish, weakened state he wouldn't be able to help her find shelter for them. She would have to piece something together herself. The realization that the cold rain would make him sicker strengthened her will. She quickly gathered some strong, dry branches, stuck them in the ground around William, and entwined them with vines to fortify them. She picked some branches with wide leaves and started the roof. She was halfway through with her masterpiece when the first gusts of wind arrived. She wondered if this wobbly structure would withstand the windstorm. Fortunately, the surrounding thick vegetation provided some protection.

By the time the first big drops of rain started to fall, landing with big thuds on the thick leaves, Susannah had finished building the shelter. She weighted the roof down with heavy branches to make sure that the powerful wind wouldn't blow it away.

The rain started to descend in buckets, and as the wind became stronger, water sometimes poured through the gaps. But this was only the prelude to the storm. Soon it became dark as night as the real sea storm broke out accompanied by thunder. The surging waves hit the rocks on the shore with an exploding sound. In such weather, those at sea can only hope for good luck and the mercy of Neptune, the god of the seas. So many were "offered work" only under the water – forever.

The storm was horrible, knocking down trees. Even the lone giant trees were bent to the ground by the wind that grabbed their thick crowns.

Susannah snuggled up to William warming him with her body. She wanted him to hug and encourage her because she admitted to herself that she was afraid. He was sleeping restlessly but was no longer burning with fever like before, when she found him. She covered him again and, also cold, she cuddled him and fell asleep, tired from the exhausting day.

William awoke around seven o'clock at night. He saw the girl sleeping next to him reached out and stroked her hair. He looked around in their little hut. He realized immediately that it was Susannah who had built it, but why? It was summer, and he would have been happy to sleep under the open sky. His question was answered as soon as he felt the wetness around them. He stirred and placed her on the leather clothes. He stepped outside into the calm, late-summer evening. His head was buzzing a little. He couldn't believe what he saw. It was obvious that a big storm had swept through. "So that is why we needed the hut!" he realized, and was very grateful for her forethought. Everywhere he saw huge trees leaning against each other, and burnt tree stumps that were chipped by lightning, although the clear, bright sky seemed to deny the devastation. The westbound sun was blazing hot, coaxing clouds of mist from the well-watered vegetation.

William didn't know how long he had slept, but it seemed to him as if his adventure had taken place weeks ago. He returned to the tent and sat down by Susannah who was still sleeping peacefully. He didn't want to wake her up. "Let her sleep," he thought, "She deserves it. Had she not searched for me, this storm would have killed me."

He caressed her lovely face and ebony hair. Then he noticed the wet rags Susannah used as a poultice that he must have shrugged off in his sleep. His head wound did not hurt quite as much as before, but the compress felt good. So he replaced the cloth the girl had torn off her dress.

He relived what had happened, but decided to concentrate only on the present and his next steps. He did not abandon his vow of vengeance against his parents' murderers, but he promised himself to be more careful in the future. He did not want to expose himself and Susannah to such a dangerous situation ever again. Susannah had proved again how loyal she was to him and how much she loved him. That was all he needed.

He bent down and kissed her red lips. She slowly opened her eyes. Seeing William safe and healthy, she hugged him. As they left the hut, Susannah was also stunned by the devastation. She found solace in the warm setting sun and in William.

They knew they didn't have much time left before the night settled, but they had to find another shelter since the ground under their makeshift hut was still wet. Against her protests, William covered Susannah with his roughly cut leather clothes still warm from his body. After a little convincing she put them on.

As soon as they found a new shelter, William realized that he was starving. They found a few fruit trees nearby and appeased their hunger. Returning to their shelter, they made their bed out of grass. They lay down; she held him close and fell asleep.

William stayed awake for a long time. Staring into the balmy night, he didn't feel cold even though he was only wearing a loincloth. He contemplated the events of the day before. He was obsessed with his vengeance. He knew that by blowing up the boat he eliminated the only chance the convicts had to escape. They had to remain at his mercy. How should he handle them? They would have to pay for every one of the crimes they had committed.

They woke up early the next morning, and wondered whether the new day would bring them good or bad tidings. They walked down to the sea to dip into the cool waves. Then they rested on the grass to dry off.

William didn't think they could survive on fruit alone, so he grabbed his bow and arrow and started off toward the forest. She followed him in silence, watching her steps.

The rain refreshed the forest; nature seemed to be reborn. The formerly withered buds were swelling, filled with vitality. The trees were blossoming, bursting with new flowers. The gentle breeze filled the air with a wonderful fragrance. The inhabitants of the forest set out with renewed energy to find nourishment.

They didn't have to go far before they spotted some tree-climbing kangaroos. William aimed at one of the younger ones and sent it sprawling with one well-aimed shot. The animal silently let go of the branch and dropped to the ground with a big swoop. The others craned their necks to see what happened when they spotted the intruders, became frightened and ran off.

Susannah pitied the kangaroo, but they had to eat to keep up their strength. William removed his arrow from the animal, threw his prey across his shoulder and they started back. While Susannah made a fire, William disembowelled the animal, skewered and roasted the meat.

They attacked their hot meat with gusto. When they had their fill, they quenched their thirst with some water from the little brook. Only then did the question emerge from Susannah: "Where are we going now?"

"I don't know, but as far away from here as possible. We are not safe here. Kombalun's hunters may come this way and discover us. We need to look for a concealed place where we can live in peace. When the time is ripe for revenge…"

"You still haven't given up on this crazy scheme?" Susannah cried in despair, "They outnumber us and will kill us. Don't you see?" She started to cry and couldn't continue. William tried to put his arms around her but she withdrew from him. "Do you want to destroy our lives?" she cried accusingly.

"Please understand," William answered with resolve. Susannah just shook her head and ran away sobbing.

William was cursing himself for raising the subject now instead of biding his time. He realized that she hadn't recovered from the shock she had suffered and needed some peace and quiet. He had to find her and promise her that they would leave this place. The revenge must wait. He hoped his enemies would not escape in the meantime. He followed her until he found her, still sobbing, lying in the grass next to a bush. He approached her. "Susannah, please listen to me. I admit that you are right. We can leave if you want to and start a new life somewhere far away." Susannah didn't answer, just kept sniveling and sulking for a while. She was still shocked by his plan that would have sent them to their graves.

Not getting any answer, William kept talking – to no avail, it seemed. He was at a loss when finally Susannah sat up and looked at him with her big eyes full of tears. He seemed sincerely remorseful. She sighed, "You see, Willy, you hurt me more than you can imagine by what you said. I don't ask for much, just not to wake up to that nightmare again as I did yesterday – without you!"

In the silence that descended between them, William reached out his hand toward her. "Shall we go?"

"Yes, let's."

They gathered up all their belongings, filled their bottle with water from the brook and then left. They continued along the seashore where the scenery remained unchanged. The sun was spreading its warmth and the sea was sparkling like molten silver. By noon it was so hot that they had to stop. It seemed as if the sun wanted to dry up the last drop of moisture. Sweat beaded their faces as they lay down under the sparse leaves of a mangrove tree. They looked around listlessly. They didn't have much water left, so they decided to sleep away the hours of the hottest part of the day.

They fell into an exhausted, deep sleep. The sound of a loud thunderclap could be heard in the distance, followed by another half a minute later, then another, waking up William. Blinking in the light, he realized that the sun was way past the noon peak around three in the afternoon. Another thunderclap shook the air. "There is a storm brewing," he thought listlessly. He got up and strolled down to the shore to survey the area. Not a cloud in the sky... Another thunderclap… "They follow in such regular intervals," he mused. His sleep-filled mind started to clear up. "Maybe it isn't thunder that's causing the rumbling." He paid closer attention to the direction the sound was coming from.

"What is this?" he heard Susannah behind him.

"I don't know, but I'm sure there isn't going to be a storm. This is a different sound."

"I think it is coming from there, behind the panhandle." She pointed in the direction from where they just came.

"Right, but I can't see anything through the trees. I may be able to see more if I swam out."

"You are still weak, William, don't go!"

"I am fine, Suzy, don't worry!"

He was already running toward the sea. He was waist deep in the water when he dove in and started to swim. Leaving the currents near the shore, he picked up speed and swam farther and farther out.

When he felt he was far enough from the shore, he let the waves pick him up and lift him. He stuck his head as high out as possible. He almost cried out, he was so surprised. A huge, three-mast sailboat was anchored a few miles away, near the shore. The boat tilted a little as if it had run aground. He didn't know how to explain the ship's arrival. Suddenly he saw white smoke emerging from the side of the ship, followed by the delayed sound of gunshots. What was this ship doing here? Perhaps the convicts had sent a signal to the crew and they came to their aid. But how was that possible? Maybe new convicts had arrived.

His head filled with the most absurd ideas as he let the strong waves carry him ashore. Suddenly, he realized that he could find more reasonable, acceptable answers to this mystery. Anybody with common sense would not come so close to a shore so riddled with rocks. Perhaps the storm swept the boat out and the captain had no choice but to move it between the sandbanks and corals. After the low tide, the ship moved closer toward dry land - another proof of the above theory. It might even capsize. Maybe the shots were calls for help.

As soon as he reached the shore, the anxious Susannah bombarded him with questions.

"What did you see? What's the matter?"

"Nothing special – I hope, it's only…"

"It's only what? Tell me already what you saw!"

William's secretiveness heightened her curiosity even more. "I saw a three-mast ship run aground a few miles down from here, close to the shore. That's the source of the shots calling for help.

Susannah's eyes opened wide. "How did it get here?"

"Most likely the storm swept it to this part of the world. I hope you know what this means." She shook her head. "The convicts may hear the shots and come to the shore. They may be able to get on the ship and sail back to Europe. In which case, blowing up their ship was in vain."

Susannah thought about this for a while and admitted that he was right. She didn't want her parents' murderers to enjoy their treasures tainted with blood. But the idea of William killing somebody was also unbearable. She wouldn't be able to be near him with the knowledge that he had extinguished the lives of human beings.

"What are you going to do?"

"I have to get to the ship. Maybe the captain will understand when I tell him about the heinous things the convicts did. It would be good if the captain and crew became their judges.

Susannah was not thrilled by the idea, but admitted that it might accomplish what he set out to do.

William's plan was to try to reach the captain unnoticed at night. He hoped this plan would work.

Donald was busy with his companions in the Papuan village. The convicts had changed their plans. Now they were making boxes that they could attach to their backs.

The leader of the convicts had decided that they would take on more porters from Kombalun, and go on foot to Sydney. There they would bribe a ship's captain to take them back to Europe. At first his companions felt the idea was madness on account of the enormous distance. But later they started to see their chief was right. There was simply no other way out of here!

Kombalun hadn't sorted any of their preparations out, though they had asked him to make arrangements for them. For days there was no word from him. He would sit under his tent and no one was allowed in to see him.

This day started like all the others. The convicts carried on building crates. There were ten natives alongside them waiting for instructions. They got no rest either: they had to go into the forest for materials for the crates, climbing the trees for wood and strong jungle creepers. With these they tied the boxes together, since they lacked nails. The sun had already disappeared behind the southern horizon when they heard the first booming noise.

“There’s going to be another storm!" fumed Jose, looking up from his work. Anxiously he scanned the sky, though there wasn't the slightest trace of a cloud anywhere. The sight surprised him, but he just shrugged his shoulders and continued his work.

Yesterday's thunderstorm had battered the camp. The people of the village were currently repairing the holes in their roofs.... A little later another roaring sound boomed over the sea. This time they paid more attention. When yet another crack sounded out, they decided this sounded like gunfire.

“Lads! I'll be blowed if that wasn't shooting!" cried Santiago. "There must be a ship nearby" added Jose. "Down to the water! Let's move!"

Robert Reid, captain of the three-master schooner the Cambridge, carried on firing the single shots. He knew there couldn't be much hope that they'd get help from the land: he’d heard enough of the cannibals who lived in this country. But he still felt that he had to try for the impossible. Maybe there might be just one civilised person hereabouts who could help them with the work in hand, getting the ship through these deadly sandbanks. He couldn't understand, though, how he had been able to get this deep-draught vessel even as close to the shore as this. It had to be down to enormous luck that they hadn’t run onto one of the sharp shoals, which would have resulted in immediate destruction of the proud vessel.

The Cambridge transported convicts to Sydney. From there they had started on the return journey, running into this powerful storm in the third week of the passage. For days they had drifted, struggling with the strong opposing winds which pushed the ship back towards the continent, until here they had run onto one of the "lucky" sandbanks which had held the craft back from hurtling on to inevitable destruction.

All hands on board had been working from early morning to clear away the sands around the ship which had been ploughed up at the moment of impact. Due to this the whole front end of the ship lay dry. They planned to dig a deep channel around the hull, which the next high tide would fill with water. They also had to repair the torn front sail, a cracked spar, and several damaged hull-rib timbers. Besides all this they had to energetically pump out the water which had come into the ship's hold. Because of these extra duties the whole crew was occupied. Only the cannon-master stood beside the captain and, using powder but no balls, fired off the signals of a ship in distress...

By now the cannon had been sounding every minute for two hours, but still no one had appeared on the shore. The only sound was the indignant screeching of gulls. Captain Robert Reid finally signalled the cannon-master to stop. Enough firing! Angrily, he went up onto the stern deck. After checking the workers and entrusting all supervision to the first officer, he went into his cabin. He stepped over to the drinks cabinet and washed down his anger with a large glass of whisky.

Captain Robert Reid was 45 years old. He had been at sea for 25 years, and had been the commander of the Cambridge for 17 of those years. Never before had he faced a catastrophe like this. But since he had been in charge of the regular shipping of convicts to New Holland, he felt his luck had left him. Even on the journey out it had been a little patchy. Then they had run into this storm and in a combination of good luck and bad luck his ship had run right up to the edge of the convict colony boundary. The only thing that would save them was news of their arrival. With the help of other ships they would be able to rescue the Cambridge. The repairs had taken weeks and now here was the latest stroke of bad luck. It still smouldered in him a little. But slowly he relaxed and calmed down. The whiskey was beginning to have a good effect on him.

On deck an unexpected shout sounded. "Men on shore! Men on shore!" A moment later the first officer knocked on the door of the captain's cabin and opened the door. "Captain! There are men standing on the shore." "Blacks?" "No sir! White men! They're waving for us to send a rowboat over to them." "How many are there?" "Five, sir!" "Organise a boat to bring the strangers aboard." "Yes sir!" His deputy clicked his heels together in a military salute and left. Outside the first officer could be heard hoarsely shouting out the commands. His sharp words flew out to the sailors. "Let down the rowboats! Four rowers start out immediately!" The creaking of the winch sounded, setting the rowboats down into the water. Within a few moments the sailors were on the shore. With the help of the incoming waves they had reached the beach quickly. Rejoicing, the five men greeted the sailors. Within a few moments, it could be seen from the ship that they had come to an agreement, and the rowboats were once again in the water with everyone in. The journey back went more slowly because the waves were against them this time. When they got closer to the three-master, the silhouette of the captain appeared at the rail. From a distance he addressed them. "Who are you?"

“Shipwrecked men, sir!" answered Donald Hawke, cupping his hand into the shape of a horn. Slowly they reached the side of the ship, and the convicts, celebrating their good luck, were standing in front of the captain before long. Robert Reid measured up the arrivals carefully. Finding nothing objectionable in them, he broke into a friendly smile and greeted his guests. Donald enthusiastically spoke to their rescuer. "Sir! God has guided you to these shores to save the lives of five unlucky men from certain destruction."

“If not God, then at least several days of stormy weather brought us here... But it is certainly a good Christian act that we can help each other. Right now my greatest worry is that we should get off these sandbanks. My men have been working without ceasing since early morning. You heard the cannon shots because I had hoped for help from the shore. I did not expect that in my position I would be able to help others. But if accident brought you here, then as far as I can I will help you, gentlemen!"

Robert Reid pronounced these last words in the captain's cabin beside a glass of whisky... An hour later the crew on the ship could see his shining face as he took leave of his guests. He commanded the sailors to transport them back to the shore and wait for their return, because they had a lot of luggage. It had been decided that the ship would continue on its way, taking the convicts with it. The convicts' calculations had paid off. They had succeeded in persuading the captain with their dirty deal. He could be bribed. And how!...

With Susannah breathing down his neck, William agitatedly ran the few miles separating them from the ship. Running in the undergrowth, he feverishly looked forward to the coming evening, when he could at last exchange words with the captain.

As the sun dipped behind the trees of the rainforest, he said farewell to Susannah. The girl tried to dissuade him from the journey, but he remained inflexible. His legs moved quickly, and soon he arrived at the part of the shore from which he only had to swim a few hundred yards to get to the boat. He wrapped his clothes in a bundle which he gripped in his teeth, and began to swim in the direction of the dark frigate at a good pace...

The ship was already at anchor in open water. With the help of high tide it had once again taken to the water. William swam right up to the ship, but saw no-one on deck. He could not find a rope ladder anywhere with which he might get up onto the ship. Beginning to despair, his repeated efforts to climb the smooth hull were met again and again with failure. Finally he discovered help in the shape of the anchor let down on the far side of the ship. By clambering up its chain he at last managed to get on board. Unseen he jumped over the rail onto the deck. It was dead quiet everywhere. He went further on and carefully looked around. Lamps burned under the deck entrance. From here the sound of human voices filtered up. He couldn't put any other reading on it but that these led down the steps to a row of cabins. He felt this had to be the captain's cabin. He glimpsed light from a newer lamp filtering out. Hurrying, he started in that direction. A blink of an eye later, someone came at him from behind. William heard the attacker and tried to turn around aggressively. The sailor had been smoking a pipe on deck when he spotted the intruder. Reasonably enough he had taken it to be a native, and so decided the man would be fairly easy to subdue. But the newcomer proved his silent strength, and the sailor had to shout to his companions for help. A whirling human ring formed briefly around the struggle. In the end William was captured and a lamp was shone on his face. Surprised shouts rang out. "It's a white boy! How did you get here? Who are you, boy?"

The disturbance alerted Captain Robert Reid. He came out and ordering silence, stepped up to the boy, who his captors released at last.

“Who are you, boy?" By way of answer, William parried "Are you the ship's captain?" "Yes!" "Captain, I would like to speak to you, but in private." Reid was momentarily taken aback, but recovered himself and said "In that case, after you, my young friend!" he invited the boy into his cabin. Smiling, he allowed the boy in front of him through the door. Unsuspecting, William stepped into the cabin. His feet became like blocks of lead when he saw who was already in there.

“Look who it is!" cried Donald Hawke. "So – the young avenger pays us a visit!" The captain, coming in behind the boy, looked at them and said "You know this boy?"

"Like a bad penny! He's the one who broke out of the Papuan camp, together with the other wildcat." William saw now that he was too late. "Where is the girl?" Reid turned towards the boy. William lowered his head and did not answer. But, the answer was soon to arrive. Another uproar broke the silence of the night outside. The sounds came ever closer. A knocking was heard, and Susannah was pushed in through the door. William's world collapsed around him.

"Susannah!", he cried, "Why did you come after me?" The girl looked up, glanced at the convicts, sobbed, and rushed to William. She clung to him as she cried. Here they were again, defenseless and at the mercy of these bandits. And the one in whom her last hopes had rested had turned against them. The corrupted captain would definitely not be helping them anymore.

The desperate situation of the two young people did not draw a single drop of sympathy from these convicts, nor from the heart of the greedy Captain Reid, filled with hopes of grand profits.

Donald hit the two with one blow and burst into sarcastic laughter "Ha Ha! These two can't keep themselves out of trouble." But he could not continue, because the boy suddenly extricated himself from the girl's embrace and whipping out a dagger, threw himself at Donald. A short struggle ensued. But, in the end other men intervened and held William down. They twisted the gasping youth's arms and held him fast. Thirsting for revenge, Donald got up and was about to attack the boy with the knife that had almost ended his own life.

The captain was not about to lose one of the souls on board and pulling out his pistol, yelled at the emboldened villain. "Leave him in peace or I'll put a musket ball in your head!"

Donald withdrew and his companions calmed him down. With a sharp movement he stuck the knife into the floor, and with his free hand he slapped the still defenseless boy. William shook his bloodied head and gave Donald a look that sent cold shivers down his spine.

"Behave yourselves!", Captain Reid ordered. "Every hand on the ship on deck – now!" Donald shook off his companions' restraining hands and turning, reached for his glass of whisky.

Captain Reid called in the first officer and had the two young ones locked into a cabin on deck. Sinking into despair, William realized he should have listened to Susannah when she tried to stop him taking this journey. Again they were captives! Perhaps their days were numbered. They may give the girl back to the barbarian chieftain. And as for him, they would simply shoot him or hang him. Susannah clung to him fiercely as her whole body shook. She lifted her tearful face to the boy.

"You see, Willy! We are in trouble again!" And whatever thoughts the boy was having before, she continued, "What if they give me back to Kombalun, and you.... they'll kill you!" In the dark of the cabin, he could sense that Susannah had turned her head towards him. From Susannah's direction a feeling of great sadness flowed towards him. But in her next words he could hear a hint of determination. "Willy! If they take you from me, I shall kill myself!" With the impact of her words, she pulled a small knife from the rags of her clothes – a knife she could use if she needed to bring on death –

and pressed it into the hand of William, shocked by her words and the knife.

"Where did you get this?" he asked. "When you attacked Donald, and distracted attention from me, I got it off the table and concealed it." "Why did you come after me?" "I just knew you'd get into trouble. And anyway, it's all the same for me. I wanted to be with you. If you have to die, we die together!"

Hearing these words, bitterness flooded through William. He stroked the girl's hair. They were both equally powerless. They would again have to wait and see what might happen. The ship rocked sluggishly with the waves. The timbers of the ship groaned, as if in pain, shifting dreams weighed down on the two young people. They slept fitfully and dreamt of sailing the seas, and for a short time they were free again.

In the captain's cabin, after the incident, there was an uneasy quiet. Donald was the first to speak freely. "I'm sorry I got so carried away Captain. The little rascal almost killed me!"

"He had good reason!" replied Captain Reid, the words sliding out of his mouth. He had heard the whole story from the convicts.

"This is none of your concern!" the convict snarled back. "What do you want to do with them?" "I still don't know. But I'm not giving them up to the savage Papuan. They're worth more than that. What if we could sell them as slaves? We can split the money. They'd both fetch a good price and repay the cost of their food with spices thrown in!"

These cruel words startled Robert Reid. "You're capable of selling them?" "With the greatest pleasure!" came back the cold, calculating answer.

The next day at dawn, the captain gave the command "Pull up the anchor! Our course is for South America!" The first officer worked out the co-ordinates. He plotted the route on the map and relayed the orders to the crew. The dull clicking of the anchor winch sounded as the sailors strained with all their might to wind up the chain. Nimble hands let down the canvas from the rigging. Within minutes a fresh ocean wind was speeding the frigate with its swelling sails away from the coast of New Holland. With the prow of the ship pointed in their chosen direction, they were on their way to South America. The convicts were able to help steer the ship through the reefs of the coral shoals, all of them being experienced mariners. Several hours later they reached open waters. Soon the prow was cutting through the water of the Coral Sea.

After a deep but uneasy sleep, our young captives woke in late morning. William opened his eyes first, and looked around in surprise. Then he realised where they were and his brow clouded over. The light trickling in allowed him to see what a cramped space they had been put in. A ramshackle desk, a chair with a broken leg, some dusty pieces of ship's gear – these were the sole furnishings of the little room. It seemed this place had not been used for some time. Perhaps the owner of the ship never thought it would be used as a slave cell again.

William's attention strayed to the face of the sleeping Susannah. She must be having a beautiful dream, because a little smile slipped across the corner of her mouth. She was a gorgeous young woman and William felt that no one more wonderful could exist on the earth. The boy didn't want to move, so as not to wake the girl who so closely embraced him. But he couldn't deny that being locked up made him agitated. He shut his eyes, but something wouldn't let him rest. He began to listen. From outside the roar of the waves sounded. He became attentive, noting how the hull stretched lengthways with the rocking of the waves. Close to the coast a boat frisked about on shore waves like a colt. Doubt suddenly filled him and he became gloomy again. The cruel truth dawned. They had already left behind the land where they were born. Anguish filled his heart. He raised his chest with difficulty and something tickled in his throat.

"What's wrong with you, Willy?" Susannah asked anxiously. She had already been watching the changes on the boy's face for some time. William turned to her with surprise and spoke softly. "Be strong, my love!" "Why?" "Because we've already left the coast behind!" "Where are we?" "On the open sea!" "But... they... they can't do this to us! Despair burst out of the girl. "They can't kidnap us and take us away from our home?" "Yes, my sweet Susannah... they can... They are stronger than we are.... We are helpless!"

Again a cry burst out of the girl, no matter how much she tried to hold it back. She sobbed so bitterly that William was deeply moved. But he was able to gain control of himself sooner than she did and he tried to comfort the girl.

"Don't cry, my love! I'm afraid it doesn't help. So far we've managed to survive every blow. Let's have faith that tomorrow will bring something better. We managed the first time! All right?" "Yes." Susannah looked at William holding her in his arms. She trusted him so much you could see it in her look and finally she was forced to smile too. "All right!" she whispered. "I'm not going to cry anymore – at least not too much!" Everything was in these few words, and William gave her a long kiss.

On deck all this time, the crew of the ship were going about their work. They rejoined chain links, they patched sails and they scrubbed the decks on the orders of the officers. It seemed as if the two captives were forgotten. If the convicts and the captain had no information about our locked-up heroes, neither did the sailors. Yet, in fact, the capture of the two young people was the topic of discussion throughout the whole ship. No one could think of why the "passengers" should have the two young people locked up. Also the sailors deeply pondered what had caused the incident between Donald Hawke and William the day before. Those who could, were constantly lurking around that part of the ship, near the captives, in the hope of some fresh piece of news.

This behaviour continued into the afternoon when William began to feel restless. Still no one opened their door, not even to give them a piece of rusk. The boy was ready for anything. He had checked how strong the door was. It was bolted from outside, but it was not a particularly well-made piece of work – a few strong slams might be enough to break it apart. But they would have to get used to confinement at least until they again came close to dry land. Right now they were sailing ever further into the open sea, and they certainly could not attempt to swim for days across the ocean.

It was Harry Jackson, a young sailor of 22 years old, who saved them from death by starvation. Harry was ordered to scrub down the companion decks. He took on the job happily, since it got him closer to the two young people. Quietly checking around he went over to the bolted door and spoke: "Hey, you in there!" Surprised, William jumped up and put his head to the door. "Who are you?" "A friend." "What do you want?" "I want to help..." The bolt creaked back and a distinctive, long-faced sailor popped into the tiny cabin. He knew he was risking a flogging if they got out. But his curiosity just wouldn't leave him in peace. He stood in front of the two, who stared at him in surprise.

"I'm Harry Jackson, a sailor on this run-down old 'dinghy'." "William Anderson", replied the boy. "And this is Susannah Gredford", he said, pulling the girl to him. "My lady!" Harry bowed in front of the girl. "My deepest respects! I'm overjoyed that we have finally had the luck to have a sunbeam move in with us. But you're so pale! If you don't get some air soon I fear you'll more resemble a weary ray of dawn light!"

Susannah reddened but managed a smile. "We can't escape and we can't decide our own fate. It seems, Harry, that you are the most kind person on this ship!"

"Thank you for rewarding me with that honour, young lady! But –" and his voice changed "– before you tell your story of how you came here, I think you must need some basic nourishment." "We haven't eaten anything since yesterday" said William. "I'll be straight back with some sustenance," said Harry confidently, peeping out of the doorway. Quickly he stepped out and bolted the door.

Just then two men, Frank Jose and John Pedro, appeared on the upper deck companionway. For a moment they watched Harry, who now appeared to be zealously scrubbing the deck, and then they moved on. Jackson watched them out of the corner of his eye, then pounced on the bucket and scrubbing brush and hurried towards the crew's quarters. Several minutes later, he was back with some food wrapped up. Again he carefully looked around and slipped into the small cabin. There he unpacked the contents, and while our two heroes keenly set to eating, he again went out and carried on working.

A few minutes later, Susannah and William, with full stomachs, saw the future before them in a totally different light. They realised that they could trust in Harry and that he would be a good ally in what was to unfold.

The next chance for the sailor to pop in on them again was only after the lunch break, when he was entrusted with a food portion for the two captives. The second officer strictly forbade him from speaking to them. Harry promised readily, but naturally didn't keep his word. As soon as they had had their food, he began pressing them with questions. William was no longer hungry, and he started relating their brief autobiography...

Jackson was ever more saddened as he heard more of the extraordinary story. After this he felt deeply for the two young people with their blighted destinies. Harry himself had grown up as an orphan, raised by foster parents. He had always dreamed that one day he would belong to somebody. But until now he had borne all this alone on the seas. He found a fixed position nowhere. And now he was hearing of the total destruction of a beautiful little town, where everybody had had a happy life...

“And this is how we stand with you "lucky" shipwrecked folk!" he muttered to himself, squeezing his hands into fists, "They bought the captain. They're taking you away from your homes, without any right, after the slaughter of your families?" he asked, still incredulous.

"That's how it was...." answered the boy, his head lowered.

"I promise I will help you. I will help you break out at the first opportunity that presents itself." The two youths looked up with shining eyes at the wonderful young man. William could not express enough gratitude. With earnest thanks he pressed the hands of the sailor. He accepted the offered hand of friendship and held it firmly. Susannah's eyes filled with tears as she said "Mr Jackson! May God help you in every way, and save you from every woe. May he give you at least once in your life a happy family circle no one can destroy!" With this she stepped up to the astonished young man and planted two wet kisses on his face. Once they had finished their thanks, Harry could stay no longer without appearing to his superiors to stay for too long. He gave them one last wink and stepped out of the door.

William turned to Susannah and embraced her. "You see! God is with us!" "As he already has been before: he's helped us enough times when everything seemed hopeless", he added thoughtfully. "Do you think he will keep his promise?" asked the girl. "I am sure of it!" "How?" "I could see it in his eyes."

Harry took back the remains of lunch to the kitchen, where he crossed paths with the first officer. "Sir!" he addressed him. "The captives could use a little air on the deck. The cabin is terribly hot and they're extremely uncomfortable. They won't be able to escape from here!" The first officer looked at the sailor with narrowed eyes. He answered in a raw voice "Jackson, don't lecture me on my responsibilities, because I locked them up! The captain left orders that they are to be kept under strict guard. Yesterday evening the boy almost stabbed one of our passengers. They are not to be let out of the cabin!" "Understood sir!" "Off you go..."

Harry slunk off, down at heart. He would have liked to lighten the long sea journey of the young pair somehow. In fact the constant rocking of the ship made them both strongly seasick, which was to be expected sooner or later. And that meant the two had to be brought out of their captivity briefly, to vomit. Mr. Dorvan did not forget that Harry had spoken up for the young couple, so he stayed on deck to keep an eye on how they were guarded. Our heroes had to bend over the rail when the motion made them ill. The sailor soothed them and the sickness passed. Three or four days of feeling bad, and after a week they were able to laugh at the whole thing. Special light food helped. After this they always got enough rusks and bitter tea from the kitchen.

The next day they again woke to strong feelings of nausea. By the third day, however, the special diet was having its effect and they didn't have to spend their whole days in the humid heat up on deck. There was now more time for chatting. Jackson told them many stories about the wider world. The couple listened to these tales gratefully and they helped them pass their time. When their sickness had passed, Harry was again ordered back to work on deck, and the couple in turn were locked up again in their cabin. But the sailors, however, were able to agree with the captain that they should come up to take some air on the deck at least once a day.

After several days the whole crew of the ship had grown fond of them. Harry asked the captain to let William work, and everyone watched out to make sure nothing bad happened to the lass. It took a lot of doing, but after a time Captain Reid yielded to the general desire and let the couple out. From this day the life of the two young people changed totally. William was able to get assigned every kind of task, and he carried them out devotedly. A week later he was among the quickest in handling the sails. Even the older sea dogs had a place in their hearts for the young apprentice sailor. Susannah, who was so beautiful that the sailors simply regarded her as a goddess, bustled around sorting out the crew's living quarters and general needs. She readily sewed up their torn shirts and jackets. She was able to help the cook in the kitchen too. She found all sorts of possibilities in the sparse rations and basic ingredients, and prepared tasty meals. Before long she was acknowledged as the real ship's cook, and could work with just the cook's boy alongside her. He was a good pupil, and bit by bit began to cook really "solid" meals, going ever further under Susannah's supervision. Altogether they made themselves indispensable to the whole ship. Later they became so trusted they were not even locked up at night. William was made to swear that he would not quarrel with the "passengers" and would keep his distance from them. The boy happily agreed, because he honestly loathed seeing them.

Often it was not possible to see the "passengers" for days on end, since they were permanently drunk. Donald sometimes came up onto the deck, and eyed up the sailors' protégés with narrow, sidelong glances. However he did not dare have them locked up any more, for he knew it would turn the entire crew against him. He sneeringly eyed them from a distance, knowing that in the end he would have the last word. His companions did nothing other than drinking and playing cards, spending their whole time in a kind of gold fever. He could not make use of them for anything.

Drunken yells often disturbed the night, but he was glad to have no worse problems with them. They continued towards their destination, keeping a good course. The Cambridge was considered an excellent sailing ship, a matter of no small pride to the captain. That satisfied his demands for the moment...

After two weeks, the three-master stopped at its first port of call on the route at New Caledonia, in a harbour called Noumea. Here they took on water and significant quantities of provisions.

On the journey there had been only one storm, which the Cambridge had handled easily. It was strongly built, and this helped the crew in their struggle with the elements.

Captain Robert Reid planned that the next stop-off would be in the Society Islands, in Papeete. This lay 2500 nautical miles from Noumea. This journey, in spite of several becalmed days with very little wind, took less than thirty days. At docking time William and Susannah were at once locked up, not to give them any chance of escape, though on these tiny islands they would not have been able to find many places to hide. After several days of rest the Cambridge again set sail. Their final destination meant their route took them past the Tuamotu islands and on to South America, where passing the legendary mariners' graveyard of Cape Horn would let them reach Rio de Janeiro. Here Donald Hawke wanted to be free of the two children. Captain Robert Reid further shrank from the slave-trade deal that the convict leader had in mind for our heroes. But if the topic came up in conversation, Donald would just flash a sarcastic grin in the captain's direction.

According to their calculations, the ship would manage the trip to Rio in less than five months. However, they had also to take into account that, although they were making good progress, it was now the middle of summer. There was a chance that they would only be able to manage the Horn next spring, since Drake's Passage became suicide with the fall of winter. Captain Reid did not want to gamble with the lives of the people on board his ship in any way. If, on the other hand, they were going to spend the winter stranded, the expenses from those three months would have to come out of tighter spending. But these were the conditions for such a major journey. So the captain changed his plans to reach the coast of Patagonia at the most dangerous time of winter, and only then to venture closer to the Horn. Captain Reid gave out the order: Set the course for Chile! Harbour of Valparaiso...

The ship set its new course and began its journey along all the nautical miles of that huge distance. They had taken on provisions at Papeete that would allow them to reach the coast of South America without having to come into port anywhere. After pulling up anchor the sailors at once set the young couple free from their tiny little prison. Soon they were in the best of health after their few days' uncomfortable confinement.

The grim-looking sailors had now completely accepted them as their own. Because of their past adversities, our heroes became fit in a short time, and looked much more developed than their age. But they still counted as young here. Next month Susannah would be 16, and William was 17 this month. Both of them looked a lot older as a result of the effects of destiny's many harsh blows, bad luck which could even have crushed an adult. The boy's strength and agility now meant something serious in the sailors' circle, one of their favourite pastimes being wrestling. On a day when there was no other work, some of their time would be taken up with wrestling. A member of the crew called Charley Dorver challenged William to a little "test session". The man was the same height as him, but his upper body was so powerfully developed that our hero was almost deterred from the outset. But then he thought to himself that to lose to this broad-shouldered, steel-muscled man would not be shameful. So he took up the challenge. The kind-hearted sailors naturally encouraged William, though they did not expect him to get far with Charley. The struggle began, and there was no doubt who was the stronger.

Both took off their shirts and Charley took up a fighting stance. The boy followed the same movement. They stood eyeball to eyeball while the others enthusiastically cheered them on. William did not know how to grab hold, and his opponent had not left him time for thought. Although the upper front part was the target, how should he start? Seeing the boy's hesitation, the other man stepped with a sudden movement to the right, and stretching out his long arms caught William around the waist. He tried to upset his balance and push him over onto the deck. The boy, however, sensed the attack, and as the two horrific arms grabbed him by the waist, he quickly slipped out of the hold. He threw his arms round the sailor's neck, and tried to pull him down. The man did not count on this, because what they later called the "embrace" was something you usually didn't get out of, but he was soon to discover himself.

Holding the boy's neck, he decided to powerfully pull him to the ground. But William didn't give up and pulled Charley with him. The watchers greeted this newest turn of events with thunderous applause and cheers. The two wrestlers rolled around on the floor, whereupon William found a good hold and gripped the sailor's neck, which was hard for the sailor to get out of if he didn't want to suffocate. Our hero took advantage of this. Slipping out of the hold he fell on him and tried to twist his arm. This was a vain fantasy, because his opponent could easily stay with one arm pressed under him.

William was in a situation where the man could at the same time press one arm to his body and easily force the other behind him. His shoulders were just a handspan away from the deck, which would mean the end of the bout. He despaired of this and made a move to the side, kicking the sailor away from him. Charley flew off him. Shrill cheering broke out from the spectators. They could see the boy's great strength, agility, and not least courage. William didn't leave him time to think and fell on him as he lay on the deck. With the greatest force he could muster he pressed himself onto the 30-year-old man. But he got stuck at a certain point. The sailor tensed his stomach muscles so that our hero was unable to press his shoulders right down. Charley stayed in this position for a while, and then repeated the boy's previous move. He sprang away from him, then threw himself after him again. William sprang up nimbly and waited for this fresh attack. The sailor approached him slowly. With a new idea William jumped towards him in a crouch. He caught his waist and knocked out a leg, and down crashed the whole height of the enormous body, with the boy clinging onto it. Again he tried to push the two shoulders down, and once more the sailor tensed his stomach muscles, against which it was futile to push. Panting with exhaustion, they looked at each other.

“I do believe you’ve won, boy!" said Charley, grinning. "Shall we take a break?" asked William. "No, I said you've won!" "But I couldn't get both your shoulders onto the deck." "Oh, but what you’ve done with me so far wasn't bad!" The sailor burst out laughing at himself, and they both stood up.

“By the time we get to South America this boy will have beaten everyone on the whole crew!" he roared mirthfully. All the sailors on deck and the boy laughed with him. The mariners proclaimed the boy the winner with a huge cheer. They caught hold of him, threw him up several times into the air, and then carried him the length of the ship. The ship took no notice of the uproar on deck and proceeded calmly on its way, carried by fair winds...

From that day on the boy had no other name than 'The Champion'. If anyone was against the fine new name, no one said anything. In the rough and simple life they had grown accustomed to, if someone achieved something outstanding, they deserved to be celebrated. Only Susannah thought differently, when she wrang the blood out of his wet clothes. Our hero also now bore a few small scars to remind him of the momentous day.

“Promise me, Willy, that you won't bloody yourself again scrapping with these rough seamen!" "I promise!" he answered, smiling, although he was not against the afternoon sport. But he still hoped he could be left in peace for a few days from renewed challenges.

Days became weeks, and weeks became months, and then the rainy season greeted them. One overcast, chilly morning the long-awaited cry sounded out on deck: "Land-ho ! Land!"

As soon as the words rang out, the deck came alive. All the folk on board had long waited for this moment, when they would again feel solid ground under their feet. The lookout sitting in the crow's nest pointed the telescope out again across the misty sea to where, in the broken morning spray, among clouds filled with rain, he had glimpsed the coast. He narrowed his eyes so that he could again make out the thin sliver which would mean that by nightfall they would reach South America. But mist again shrouded the boat. The sailors now became restless. Perhaps the whole thing was a false alarm. Sarcastic remarks about the lookout's eyesight began, but then, just as the mood might have begun to sour, a ray of sunshine penetrated the mist. At one stroke in front of the ship was revealed part of a coastline several miles off. Now the original words were on everyone's lips.

"Land!... We've arrived!... Hurray! South America!"

The captain hurried to check the ship's current co-ordinates. Not long after, he announced on deck, "We have arrived at the latest stop on our journey. By evening we will be in the harbour of Valparaiso." Then a little later came the cry "Quartermaster!" "Yes sir!" "Give every member of the crew a double portion of rum at once!" Whoops of joy broke out among the sailors. "Hurrah for the captain! ... Strike the rum barrel!" Almost at once two of them rolled out a ten-gallon barrel and stood it against the main mast. Susannah and William were present at the great celebration which marked the end of each large section of the sea journey. Harry – who had from the first day become a firm friend of William's – stepped over to him and pressed a mug of rum into his hand. Without any doubts, the boy took the measure and drank deeply. Taking his draught like a hearty seaman!.... until the pain. Suddenly he felt as if the whole of his insides would swell up. He broke out in a hacking coughing fit, to the amusement of the sailors. When at last he could come up for air and clear his windpipe his first words were: "I've never had a drink like that down my throat in my life!" With these words such enormous hilarity roared out that the very joints of the Cambridge creaked as if in a storm. The boy was embarrassed as he began to understand, and the blood came to his face.

"Don't be upset William! I didn't know that you'd never drunk rum!" said Harry, grinning. "Because we – " he indicated his mates standing round " – drink nothing but this when we get the chance." "If we've got the money!" cut in Butterson, one of the sail-riggers. "If we're forced to, we have to drink 'filler' instead." The boy realised there was no need to be angry, and laughed freely along with them. Susannah became curious about what had had such an effect on our hero. She stepped over to a sailor and took a mug from his hand. The boy shouted, "Don't drink it Susannah!" He was alarmed without cause, because the girl only sniffed it, and, her nose wrinkling, gave it back to its owner. "This is what you drink on celebration days?!" she said in the direction of the boy in a sad voice. William at once understood. He nodded. He remembered those celebration days like this. And at the last such gathering, everyone but themselves had lost their lives!

But Susannah didn't want to stir up those powerful, bitter memories, so she at once changed the subject. She asked Harry if he had ever been to South America before. Jackson started to tell stories. The topic moved on to his childhood and all the adventures that befell him then. The other sailors flocked round the group of speakers and listened. When he finished another sailor immediately started to tell a new story. This way they filled an hour until the lookout's voice again sounded from the masthead. A small boat was approaching the ship, and soon the harbour pilot stepped onto the deck. According to the usual protocol, the captain explained to the newcomer their intended destination, and made him acquainted with the cargo manifests and other paperwork. Once the pilot had discovered that everything was in order, he personally steered the Cambridge into harbour.

By late afternoon, the sailing crew of the ship were gone, sent on shore leave for a two-month break. They had pay for two months with them too, so most of the crew had gone to carouse in the port. Many of the old sea dogs among them had been in Valparaiso before and so knew the ropes there. Which is to say they knew where to find the main taverns. Nonetheless, there were a good few of these in the harbour and the town.

Susannah and William were enraged when on Donald Hawke's orders they were locked back in their cabin on arrival in the harbour. For the course of the trip so far it had only been possible to see the "passengers" together when – as now, permanently – they got hold of enough alcohol and their whole bodies were saturated with drink. They had only just now come alive so they could "have one for the road" in some small dive on shore. They took with them the captain's payment for the trip, which was readily at their disposal against the gold nuggets. The captain knew what he was doing. Whenever a convict produced a gold nugget and asked how much he would give for it, Captain Reid quickly answered and paid. He knew very well that the gold nugget was worth treble the money he was paying for it. So the convicts got a substantial sum of cash, disembarked and soon disappeared into the whirling twilight crowd. Only a few people stayed on board. The officer on duty, the captain, several guards, and William and Susannah. Captain Reid was really softhearted this evening, letting the young couple out of their cell and entrusting their guarding and supervision to Harry. The young man was happy to stay with them, since he had grown truly fond of the pair these last few months.

“Why don't you go into town?" asked Susannah. "Because when we drew lots, it was decided that I had to do the 12 o'clock watch." "Do you always draw lots to decide who is on watch?" "Yes. And it's possible that the dice want it to be me again soon. We've done it like that here for a long time. That way there's no argument." "What do the others do in the town?" "Well.... they usually go to drink in some bar." "There's no other pastime apart from drinking?" "Well, of course. There's other things to do as well." "What?" "Well they usually...." and with that he went quiet. Something wouldn't come out of his mouth. What he could have said to the young lady was that once they had sufficient "spirits" in them, the crew would be seeking the company of ladies of the night. Now he began to feel bad that he had helped the conversation get on to this topic. "What do they usually do then?" persisted Susannah, and in her heart she was secretly enjoying how embarrassed the sailor was getting. Harry uncomfortably fidgeted for a moment, then said, "In a word, what they get up to are.... things not for the ears of a young lady... and how does the young lady like the harbour?"

The girl saw that the young man was now totally embarrassed. Although she would have liked to press on further with this topic, she didn't. She would have gone completely over the boundaries, and she didn't want to hurt the sailor. "The harbour is very beautiful. Now I'm seeing it for the first time in my life... It would be so good to walk in the streets. Mingle with the throng. To see all those things which you told me about, Harry."

"But we are captives!" William came over and brought the daydreaming girl back to the sad present. Up until now he had been leaning on the ship's rail and gazing at the blue distance from which the Cambridge had come... Over there was hidden another world, with the name of New Holland. The place where he had been born. Where perhaps he had left behind every happiness. But here was someone he still had to look after. Someone to protect from danger, to encourage if they lost heart, to comfort if they were sad, and that was Susannah... This dreamy girl who – though he didn't realise – he had rudely deprived of her illusions and dreams with his interruption. Susannah heard, and hung her head. William slowly began to understand the feeling she had just been experiencing. He grasped that she was returning to reality from her innocent daydreams when, in reality, the girl knew as well as he did that she could not set foot on shore. Again he felt the contradiction.

Harry looked in surprise at the rude interruption. They had only been chatting. Was William perhaps jealous? It could not be denied that he liked the girl. But it was not possible to make more of it, for her connection to the boy was so strong that nothing could tear it apart. He didn't know what to think about William's irritated bearing.

The boy sat down at the foot of the mast. He put his face in both hands and sighed. "I can't bear this imprisonment any longer!" He looked up and met the gaze of the girl. Susannah looked back sullenly, and after a few minutes looked away. Then she met his eyes again and musingly said, "Shall we escape, Willy?" "Yes!" William said the fateful word with all his strength. "Don't be angry with me, Susannah – I am so tense. But I cannot stand staying here for even a minute longer!" "Me neither... and I'm not angry with you. I've no reason to be. I know what you're thinking. I shouldn't have talked about freedom with Harry while we are still being kept here until who knows when. It was my mistake!

The sailor looked at them with astonishment. Earlier, they had shown signs of perfect understanding of each other. The two youths, escaping death, looked bravely to the future. As if they knew that apart from their lives they had nothing to lose... Harry felt that not by interrupting but with persuasion he might be able to give them some advice.

"Listen to me!" The two young people turned their glance on him, in which there burned a wild, instinctive courage to be free of their cage. "If you run, where are you going to start? Without money you're going to die of hunger." "We'll take ourselves into the forest." said the young maid so calmly that it was as if it was going to be an excursion with first-class accommodation. Harry was totally stunned, and it got worse with the boy's next words. "The forest has everything. We won't suffer for lack of anything." "But you have no weapons!" "There's everything in the captain's cabin." "What kind of weapons? Flintlocks?" "No. Dagger, arrows, bow." "What? You want to live among the hills with those toys? And what if wild animals attack you?" "I can handle a bow as swiftly as a pistol" William replied sharply, because he didn't like Harry being so dismissive of such fine hunting weapons. "Do you know what waits for you there?" asked Harry. "Slavery!" cried out the boy, his brow twisted in torment. "What did you say?" asked Susannah and Harry together.

"It happened yesterday... I just went up on deck for some air.

It was very early. At the front of the ship I went to the rail. Suddenly my ear caught some words of a conversation. The captain and that thug Donald came out on the steps. I jumped behind a water barrel. The two went out beside me while they talked. The captain was trying to persuade the convict not to sell us into slavery. But Donald insisted that some acquaintance had requested we be locked up today. He is selling us as white slaves to a plantation-owner! He put it to the captain that they will get a good price for us, a price they can split 50-50! He laughed coldly, and they started to speak more quietly when they got closer to the steersman..." the boy finished with blazing eyes.

"That damned bandit!" shouted Harry. "I'll kill him if he comes anywhere near you!" "That's just what I don't want! That's my revenge, wherever he should be in the world... But we didn't want to embroil you in trouble. You've already taken enough risks for us." With that William related his plan. "We'll do it as if we'd attacked you. You lie unconscious on the deck, with your hands and feet tied. I creep into the captain's cabin. I take the weapons and we jump into the sea. Over there, where there are not too many people, we swim to the shore, and we disappear into the forest..."

However, the sailor had a better idea. "First we must get the captain away from his cabin, so that you can get the weapons. I have a simpler idea! Hide away on deck..." With that several bits of preparation were sorted out, and he went down to the captain's cabin. He quietly knocked. "Captain!" "What do you want?" asked Captain Reid, looking up from his work. "I locked up the captives, a half hour ago, in their cell. I bolted the door!" he said this emphatically. "Get to the point, I've got things to do!" said the captain sullenly. "Yes, sir!... So what I'm saying is... that is..." "Spit it out, Harry!" "Sir! The captives have disappeared!" "What the hell?..." Captain Reid jumped up, and, alongside the sailor, ran onto the deck companionway. The cabin door was forced, and slightly open. No one anywhere!... "Blast!" snarled the captain angrily, but in his heart he felt relief. At least he would not have to feel any pangs of conscience now with this unexpected turn of events. "Maybe they heard something from one of my quarrels with Donald..." he added, half to himself. "Or maybe someone informed them in time!" and he looked significantly at Harry, who didn't bat an eyelid. "But it's certain that Hawke will think I let them run." "What do we do, sir?" "For now we can do nothing.... They'll be too far gone by now..." Screwing his eyes up he scanned the sea and the coast. Then he shook his head and went back into his cabin. Stepping in through the door, he didn't notice anything missing. He sat down and continued his work.

Outside, William and Susannah crept out of their hiding place and took their leave of the sailor. They said nothing, but their faces were full of feelings for each other. They waved their last farewell, picked up their meagre parcels for the journey, and jumped over the rail.

There were two splashes in the water, and the waves died away over their heads. For a good stretch they swam under water. Afterwards they swam among the waves, moving at a good pace, and got ever further from the ship.

Harry, lost in thought, watched the two daring teenagers. Then an unexpected sound happened behind him. He turned round and his glance met with the hate-filled stare of Donald.

"...And now you die, you piece of filth!" Donald hissed between his teeth, and, pulling a sharp knife, lunged at the sailor. The quick attack surprised Harry, and he fell with the first blow. The huge blade glinted, and there was no time to be dazed. With a great spring to Donald's hand, the murderous weapon flew across the deck. With a massive left hook Harry knocked the villain to the floor. But the convict hadn't come alone. Two men armed with muskets stood on the bridge and, seeing the struggle, came to help.

"The captives got away!" spat Donald, and pointed the two new arrivals towards the swimmers approaching the coast. One thug jumped on Jackson, while the other raised his musket to his shoulder and shot after the escaping pair. William felt the first musketball whiz right past his ear, and knew there was trouble. Turning, he could see the disturbance on deck. He spotted the two newcomers too. More shots hit the water beside them. Again they dived under the water and swam for a while without coming up. They had to get further from the ship because the weapons had a long reach, and they were being hunted. They could both imagine the misfortune that had come to Harry.

Mariners on deck were alerted by the lethal disturbance. It quickly became obvious to them that the sailor had helped the young couple escape. But the good-hearted Harry paid dearly for this! The man who had shot at the couple had just pushed Harry's enraged attackers aside and shot him from close up. The world darkened before Harry. Slowly his life began to leave him. A thin trickle of blood came out of his mouth, running down his muscular chest. He muttered something hoarsely for a short while, then his gaze became fixed somewhere in the sky. His eyes became glassy and his soul left him. The sailor left behind on the deck a lifeless body – bait for the sharks.

While this drama was being played out, no one could intervene. In the meantime, Susannah and William reached the shore. Looking back at the ship they saw that a group of people were standing with caps lowered. Harry Jackson was no longer among them...

Susannah's eyes filled with tears, welling up with feeling for the superb young man. Perhaps destiny had decreed that Harry should finish his life, should leave this world, as a hero. He had fought to his last drop of blood to allow the two youngsters to live!

The cold-blooded murder weighed everyone down. Donald, now bloody, struggled to his feet and gave the sailor lying on the deck a savage kick. The two slave-traders, as if nothing had happened, packed up their things and left the ship. Soon they were mingling with the evening crowds....

Escape

William and Susannah could not spend much time on the shore, since they had to put enough distance between themselves and their pursuers. With nightfall the ship's bulk could only be seen as a black silhouette on the water.

"We have to go!" William insisted to the girl. The tears had not yet dried on Susannah's face. She wiped her eyes with the back of her hand, which had become stained with dirt. Without talking they walked away, not knowing where. Within half an hour only one or two houses appeared around them, showing that they had reached the outskirts of the harbor town. With their feelings of hunger growing, they distanced themselves ever further from the mournful scene. Slowly, tiredness began to take effect. As they reached the first sparse groups of trees, William began to search for a suitable place for them to spend the night. They prepared a sleeping place from heaped leaves and grass, then lay down. Glancing out at the chilly night, they huddled together for a while and fell into a deep sleep.

In the morning, William awoke first, to the sound of cheerful birdsong. He didn't feel as if he had rested: his limbs seemed to be made of lead. He looked around carefully. They had slept in a sparse thicket on a high spot. It was just as well they had not lit a fire the night before: from here, it was very possible that the light of the fire would have been visible from the ship. His glance strayed to the peacefully breathing Susannah, and the sight went straight to his heart at once. With a lovely creature like her, he felt he could go to the ends of the earth. Joyfully, he looked at the girl's figure. Her modest little dress was now seriously torn, and in one or two places it would not have maintained propriety. The Papuan village where he had made love with the native girl came into his mind. He and Susannah had never had physical relations; it was true there had not been a peaceful opportunity for that until now, but on the other hand, he had not had the courage to bring the girl's attention to it. Again his attention was drawn to her as she slept, and her body became ever more desirable.

Leaning over her, he kissed her full red lips. She slowly opened her eyes, then reached her arms out and pulled William's body closer to hers. When they had finished the "sweet kiss" so often mentioned in songs, they smiled at each other.

"What did I do to deserve such a lovely awakening?"

"We're free! The world is ours! We don't need anything, except... – " his stomach rumbled " – something to eat!" They both giggled. "Are you hungry too, Suzy?"

"I'm absolutely famished by now – haven't you noticed?" laughed the girl.

"Then I'll run and get some food." The boy jumped to his feet. They gave each other one more fleeting kiss, then William disappeared among the trees.

While our hero searched for sustenance, Susannah tidied herself. A stream gurgled past in a nearby clearing. The water ran into the sea not far away. At one point it widened where a twisted old oak crossed its banks, and here the water was deeper. Susannah chose this place to bathe. She stepped out of her worn little dress, and, shivering, immersed herself in the crystal-clear water. With small strokes, she took pleasure in moving through the water. When she stepped out on the bank, she lay on the trunk of the oak to dry in the blessed warmth of the sun, gently stroking her arms and legs.

Stealthily, she looked around. She was alone in the clearing, with only the birds twittering above her head without pause. She laid her head back and a stray morning breeze tousled the locks of her hair. The girl was exquisite, with every tremor of her Amazonian body proclaiming its perfection. The way she moistened her lips with her tongue and, holding her body proudly, turned her face to the sun, would have tested even a priest. When her body was warm and dry, she slipped her dress back on and walked back to their sleeping place.

William had just been lighting a small fire. Next to him on the ground lay a mountain goat. When the fire took hold, William pulled the goat apart. The heavy scent of cooking meat filled the air. With nostrils flaring, they watched the meat eagerly. As it cooked they gazed at it greedily, as if they had not eaten for a week. They fed each other the tastiest mouthfuls. After eating they carefully put the fire out, then gathered themselves together and moved on.

While they were on the Cambridge, Harry had told many tales of this continent. He used to show them maps of the South American interior, and now they tried to find their way from memory.

"It's best if we head for the hills." said William, thinking aloud. "Behind them are the big forests, where we can pitch camp." They could not know that the "big forests" were still hundreds of miles away. In between, they would have to cross the sky-high Andes mountain chain. Only after many months' difficult passage would they have descended into the sprawling forests of Gran Chaco. But perhaps, even if they had known all this, they would not have decided otherwise. Their only goal was to put as much distance as they could between themselves and their enemies.

For days, they walked towards the hills. The appearance of the countryside around them changed very little. They had to walk through scrubby little woods. Here and there, grassy plains stretched monotonously in front of them. One or two sections of steep hills rose to the sky. The bare peaks with white limestone rocks created the visual impression of bald giants slumbering on the grassy plains. The country was not completely deserted. Herds of animals grazed everywhere, noisily running away at their approach while looking back at the troublesome trespassers. William was happy at the abundance of animals, which meant they were always assured of a food supply.

At dusk they struck camp on a rare high point. Again, the boy did not want to light a large fire in case it could be seen from a distance. But after eating, they tiredly and wordlessly stretched out near the fire. Susannah fell asleep, but William remained deep in thought by the embers for a long time. Something would not leave him alone. The slave traders! What could have happened back there that allowed them to get away so easily? Had Donald Hawke resigned himself to leaving them to their fate, probably to be finished off quickly in a strange continent? The flames of William's wild thirst for vengeance had burned lower and lower the further they got from Valparaiso. He wondered whether there would ever be a time for a proper reckoning if they now plunged into the unknown, from which there would probably never be a way back out. New Holland was now very far from them -- many, many thousands of nautical miles from here. Would they ever see the land of their birth again? Was it worth going back there, now that there was no one back there waiting for them? No family or friends, just charred remains deep in the forest. Their parents had still not been buried with dignity. The predators of the forest had scattered their bones asunder, and on moonlit evenings they would light the night with ghostly glimmerings while they could not fade into the past, and were absorbed into the humid bed of the rainforest. But their souls would never find peace until they had been laid to rest in graves. A lump swelled in the boy's throat at these thoughts. In the embers of the fire he tried to find a solution to their future. But in every direction, his attempts were ineffective. Their future lay wreathed in storm clouds, which were often split by flashes of lightning.

Clouds coming from the west slowly obscured the nighttime lights of the stars and the good old moon. Stray currents of air smelling of rain arrived, which brought them closer to the ashes of the fire. A knot in one of the branches in the fire gave a loud crack, sending a shower of sparks into the night. William's gaze followed the biggest spark, whose trajectory made a large curve before it reached the ground. The light remained for a moment, and then was swallowed by the night. In the far west the sky turned grimmer. "There's going to be thunder" – thought the boy casually, turning towards it. He thought it through as he lay there, since they had to find shelter before the rain came. But this thought rang strangely hollow. He felt tired and helpless. Something would have to happen to rouse him from his apathy. Rain didn't give sufficient reason for panic. The newly darkened sky sounded as if it was coming closer. Suddenly, lightning split the dark night. After a short wait, an enormous roar of thunder followed. The enormous sound stabbed into William's listless muscles like a knife. He turned towards it and his blood slowly froze. On the neighboring hilltop, the lights of a dozen torches appeared. The howling of dogs on scent also travelled on the western wind. Bloodhounds, sniffing fresh traces. And as they sniffed each fresh scent, they became more impatient. William leaped to his feet, his nostrils flaring at the danger nearby. The slavers had picked up their trail!

"Susannah!" he shook the sleeping girl awake. "Wake up! We've got to get out of here!" The startled girl came to her senses. They didn't have a minute to lose. William kicked stones and dirt onto the fire. But they had already been given away. A shout sounded in the distance.

"They're over there! Release the dogs!" Three huge bloodhounds were let off their leashes, and raced towards them with terrifying howls. William shot the fastest one with an arrow at fifteen paces. The mastiff fell and helplessly pawed the stony ground. The arrow stood straight up from its body. The other two bloodhounds ran to their companion first. This gave the boy time to turn the second animal away. But the third raced to William and bit him in the shoulder. William yelled and reached for his dagger, but it was not there. With empty hands, he turned to face the beast of prey. Susannah tried despairingly to find a weapon in the darkness. Over their heads the storm clouds rumbled, and lightning zigzagged everywhere, its violet flash splitting the darkness of the night. Losing his balance, William fell. Looking for a new grip, the bloodhound went for the boy's throat. At that moment he had just enough time to kick the animal away from him, and it fell on the still-glowing embers of the fire. The dog struck them and its fur caught fire, whereupon it threw itself to the ground and rolled around. William found the knife and gave the animal a merciful blow to finish it off. Suddenly, Susannah screamed, "William!" The boy glanced at the girl, who with lance raised high stabbed the first slaver to reach them. Then suddenly, the downpour began. Their enemies' torches were extinguished instantly. A newly embittered struggle broke out in the hellish darkness. Here and there, curses rang out following the firing of muskets. But the musket balls whistled past their ears. A familiar voice shouted: "Don't shoot, their lives are worth money!"

William struck at the surrounding villains with his fists. Then he stabbed anyone he could reach. But when he heard the hateful voice of Donald Hawke, superhuman strength came to him to try to break free of the human ring around him. He wanted to ram his dagger to the hilt in the chest of that evil man, the cause of all their misfortunes. But behind him, a scream rang out from Susannah. By the light of the next flash of lightning he saw that the girl was already a captive. A pistol barrel was held against her temple. Raising his hands, the boy gave himself up. Rough hands seized him. His knife was twisted out of his hand and he felt a huge blow from behind, on the back of his head. He heard Susannah's despairing shriek, but as if from far away. He lost consciousness.

He had no idea how long he had been unconscious. When he woke up, he realized he was tethered tightly to a tree. The cords cut deeply into his flesh. Again, a wave of dizziness washed over him. Turning his head, he looked for Susannah. She was tied to the next tree. Her head down, she slept motionlessly in exhaustion. The rain had stopped by now. Somewhere at a distance from them a fire burned, with shadowy shapes sitting around it. They talked noisily, swearing at each other.

Fourteen of them had come from Valparaiso to hunt down the two young people. Two of them died. Four of them, however, had been injured by the boy in his wild rage, and were now occupied in binding each other's wounds, while casting hateful and amazed glances at the captives who had disfigured them so much in the struggle. William tried furiously to free himself, but the straps held him tightly. Gasping, he gave up his futile efforts. His head dropped and he fell into a dull stupor.

A mug of cold water and a kicking were directed at him. A cold morning had dawned, and the bandits stood ready for the road. The boy's glance sought out Susannah's. Pale, with tired eyes, the girl looked at him with a tormented face. William read mild reproach in her look, but it was possible that his tortured imagination was playing tricks on him. Compassion welled up inside the boy on seeing the state of his companion, and he hung his head miserably and gazed in front of him. It was his fault they had been recaptured; he had not been careful enough. But how could they have shaken off the bloodhounds that, for three days, had been reading their tracks like an open book?

The cords were loosened so they were able to start on the journey. Donald Hawke rode at the front of the group. He was with his convict companion. Clearly, he was not in the mood to strike up a conversation with the struggling youths during the journey. Their companions were waiting in the harbour town for their return. Susannah and William were the only evidence left of their dark past, and because of this Donald wanted to send them somewhere from which there would be no return – somewhere such as three hundred miles from here, deep in the endless pampas of Argentina, on the estates of Alfredo Garcia. This landed gentleman and immensely wealthy trader dealt in cattle breeding, but his ships, stocked with goods, travelled all over Europe. Donald Hawke had looked him up in his castle at Valparaiso and recommended he buy the two youngsters. When Garcia heard the ex-convict offer two healthy youths, he agreed to the bargain. They made an agreement and he gave Donald a bag of gold as a deposit. Then came the hiring of the seven slavers and two trackers, who, on their fast horses, soon picked up the district where the youngsters were hiding from the traces of their first campfire. Afterwards, with bloodhounds and good trackers, it was child's play to find them.

Alfredo Garcia had remained in Valparaiso for several more days since he hoped to have the two youngsters handed over to him before he travelled. He could make an excellent cowboy out of the boy. The girl, however, he would keep as a concubine as he had heard of her rare beauty. When she fell from his favour, he would put her to work on the farm.

By evening they had reached the camp where some of the headhunters had been left behind. Here everything stank of horses, and a day later they set off on the busy road to Valparaiso. Breaking the journey, they came to an enormous grey stone house. They gave the horses and the frontrunner to the staff, and the huge double gate, behind which Alfredo Garcia's Valparaiso palace was located, closed behind them. Susannah and William were locked in a windowless room. The two convicts, meanwhile, dismissed the slavers with pay, and entered the millionaire's reception room. Freed from his bonds, William cast his eyes around the place Fate had brought them to. In a couple of corners of the room, tar-smeared torches burned, giving dull light to the walls. Nowhere was there a window or an air vent that could have enabled escape. The only door, through which they had come, was made of heavy oak held together with strong iron bands, and looked unbreakable. Perhaps a small barrel of gunpowder would have been enough to blow it open, but there wasn't the slightest whiff of the stuff in here and no chance of getting any. There was no way out.... They would soon be handed over to a new host, and for years destiny would stamp their lives. Susannah crouched shivering in one corner. William walked countless paces around their confined space, looking for a crack to give them new hope, but he found nothing. The castle had been built for military purposes a hundred years before. It was carved from huge blocks of stone, fitted together precisely so there would be no way out through any wall. William finally gave up the scrutiny as pointless and slumped beside the girl. In silence, they waited for their fates to unfold.

On the first floor of the palace, Garcia had admitted Donald and Santiago. They greeted each other as old acquaintances. Over a bottle of vintage red wine, they soon concluded their business. Donald put a heavy bag of gold coins in the waistband of his shirt, and was able to follow their host for a look at the captives. The massive door creaked open. Garcia's men held their torches high, keeping their swords in front of them pointing at the boy. William looked at the space through the opened door like a wild animal lusting for freedom. Wild hope sparkled in his eyes but he did not move. Garcia stepped forward slowly and with dignity to have a better look at them. Susannah looked at him, her eyes wide with terror. William stepped slowly and protectively in front of the girl.

"Señor Garcia! This wild young stallion is the one we have to break in first," said Donald sarcastically. William glowered at the depraved man.

"Tie the boy up!" Garcia ordered his men. William didn't resist – against this group it was impossible to do anything. They tied his wrists together and attached them to an iron ring above his head and they pulled his rope up. His feet just reached the stone floor. Garcia then stepped over to the girl, stretched out a hand and stroked her face with it. Startled, the girl pressed herself against the stone wall. Her eyes were filled with fear.

"Watch out, Señor Garcia! This pretty little cat has sharp claws," boomed Santiago in his deep, hollow voice. He shifted his tobacco to the other side of his mouth and spat on the floor. "She stabbed one of our headhunters so fiercely when we found them that the devils took his soul straight to hell."

"Everything will be in order, Señor!" Garcia answered slowly. "When we put her into fine clothes, when we bedeck this fiery-blooded kitten in jewelry, she'll soon purr peacefully in my bed."

"Don't count on it, scoundrel!" howled William, straining helplessly against his bonds.

"And on the other hand, with breaking in this wild horse..." said the lord of the manor menacingly, turning to William, "we can't start soon enough." With that, he motioned William towards him. As the first whiplash cracked against William's back, the boy gritted his teeth. He had decided he would rather die than let them hear him screaming in pain. The lash cracked again... And again... His shirt was soon shredded off his back and blood began to flow. Susannah fell on her knees in front of their stone-hearted captor.

"Please, sir, have mercy on William!"

"Give him twenty lashes! And you had better watch your mouth. Afterwards, take him to the stable boys. Give the girl to the servant girl. Wash her and get her some suitable clothes. This evening I'm going away, but I'll be back in five days. After that, we'll see why I paid three times the normal price for this one!" With that he chuckled cheerily and left the room in the company of his guests.

William watched as they seized Susannah and took her out. After the fifteenth lash, he lost consciousness.

He came to in a hayrick. Apprentices and servants bustled all around, but no one gave him a second glance. Foreign words struck his ears. Everyone spoke Spanish. He moved slightly. The skin on his back felt as if it had been cut into a thousand pieces. Blood was still flowing from his wounds. The pain was intense. His face began to burn, a sure sign that the flames of fever were beginning to lick across his whole body. At the same time, however, his teeth chattered with cold. He buried his head in the hay and feverish thoughts of Susannah whirled around. When the image flashed through his mind of the villain lusting for the girl his hands clenched into fists and tears of rage came to his eyes, but now he could not bear to move. He lay still in the straw, and the world around him slowly ceased to exist.

Susannah's guards took her to the first floor, where they entrusted her to the chambermaids. Everyone spoke Spanish, so it was only with gestures that they could communicate what they wanted of her. They took her into a bathroom, where a huge bathtub stood. The bath was built of marble, and it was surely a wonderful thing to slide into the cool water on hot summer days. But now the girl nervously looked around the chilly room. Then the maids started a fire in the fireplace on one wall of the room, and Susannah could soon step closer to the cheering warmth of the fire. One girl brought clothes and laid them on a bench. She smiled kindly and then put her hand into the water to show that Susannah should bathe. With that, they left her alone.

With a mixture of fear and wonder the girl looked around and slowly undressed. She slipped into the water, which caressed and soothed her aching limbs. The bathtub was so huge it was almost possible to swim in it. Gently, slowly, Susannah changed position and moved cautiously. Hearing steps, she ducked under the water and then raised just her head. But it was only the chambermaid returning. She put a huge tray, loaded with food, on the edge of the bathtub. A finely wrought silver pitcher was on the tray, with a tin cup. Susannah was thirsty and sniffed the beverage. A rich fragrance emanated from it. She wrinkled her nose. She poured a little into the cup. To her enormous surprise, the liquid was blood-red, and the sight filled her with the greatest reluctance. Yet her curiosity and thirst were greater, and she tasted it. It had a fine aromatic flavor and slipped warmly down her throat. She drank the contents of the cup in small sips, then reached again for the tray, on which were slices of meat and a plate of fruit. She carefully took small bites and then, emboldened, began to eat hungrily.

Drying herself in front of the fireplace, she turned towards the new clothes. She felt the fineness of the fabric when she touched the first dress. It was made of an exquisite crimson silk. Gorgeous designs were embroidered in gold thread around the shoulders and neckline. Susannah had never seen such beautiful clothing. The other item was a thick dressing gown, which on cold evenings would surely keep the wearer warm within the chilly stone walls. In front of the bench were two pairs of shoes made of finely worked leather, also richly embroidered. Susannah stole a little look around and slipped into the red silk dress. She tied a belt thickly decorated with pearls around her slender waist, then put on the shoes. She twirled on the spot and the thickly rippling silk dress billowed around her like flower petals, rustling. Susannah wanted a mirror to stand before in her storybook dress, and this desire was soon fulfilled. The chambermaid came back. She took the girl's old clothes and beckoned for Susannah to follow. Soon they arrived on another floor. Here, thick, heavy fabrics were draped everywhere. It looked as if the lord of the manor did not merely allow, but actually enjoyed, luxury that would have satisfied the standards of kings. The chambermaid brought Susannah into a big bedroom furnished with a huge four-poster bed, a dressing table with a mirror, and several elegant chairs. On the floor, animal furs of every type lay everywhere like a giant patchwork. A shield was mounted on the wall and decorated with an ancient coat of arms. Below, on three shelves, were several swords and spears. The girl flashed a quick look at the weapons and then turned to the chambermaid. The servant girl made the bed and then, pulling back the curtains, lit several candles. Gesturing a friendly farewell, she left the room.

The door shut and Susannah heard bolts and latches outside slide quietly into position. She was left to herself. She paced around the room, looking over every nook and cranny. She walked over to the mirror and saw how much she had changed after putting on the strange clothes. Stepping over to the curtains, she looked outside. She could look into the courtyard of the palace, where a crowd of people swarmed to and fro at the main gate. With yearning eyes she looked for William, but saw him nowhere. She needed to wait; she had absolutely no idea how to find the boy. She knew her companion was a bright boy and understood that an opportunity would offer itself. She sat on the bed. Drawing her legs up, she rested her head on her knees and closed her eyes. The silence and the loneliness were terrible. She missed William's smile, his hug, his consoling words that had so often helped them through the greatest dangers. She was alone. In the house, the quiet intensified. Susannah started to doze as she sat. The candles slowly burned down, then a few went out in a wisp of smoke. Darkness enfolded the room.

The harsh chill of dawn brought William around. Slowly he moved in the rustling straw. On his back the fresh scars were uncomfortably swollen, but gradually his vitality was returning to him. He lifted his head and looked around. He had awoken on a hayrick in the corner of the stables. On his left leg they had fastened a thick iron chain, which he would not be able to get accustomed to. But it was long enough to allow him to reach the rim of the well, in which he found water in a wooden bucket. He drank long and eagerly. His stomach knotted from the cold water, but he could not find food anywhere. Not far away, the stable boys slept on a small pile of hay sacks. Apart from them, there was no one. He went back to the hayrick and waited. In the end, the first person he was able to exchange a word with was an old sailor. A rickety, clattering old wagon approached. A bearded old man in a sailor's outfit got down. He went around to the back of the cart and lifted a dirty flap of canvas. Behind it were several boxes. He took down the boxes and brought them to the wall of the stable. The contents clinked against each other. They were bottles of wine. When he had finished his work, he ambled over to the well to quench his thirst. He stood beside William, glancing at his iron chain and bloody clothes. Turning his head, he muttered:

"Those scoundrels gave you a battering! What did you do to deserve this kind of punishment?" William leapt up and spoke to the newcomer.

"You speak English?" The older man turned and looked at the boy from head to toe.

"English is my mother tongue, lad! I be a Yorkshireman from England, though I haven't seen my home for twenty years."

"What kind of place is this?"

"This is the palace of Alfredo Garcia, one of the richest and cruellest traders in South America. He's travelled the world, but he's very dangerous. They say that he ravages the seas with his pirate ships." The old man chuckled, but kept his hand in front of his mouth. "But you didn't hear this from me. What brought you here?"

"They sold me into slavery," answered the boy slowly and hung his head. The old man stood in front of him for a long time.

"That's not good. Escape as soon as you can, because Garcia's men don't have long lives."

"I'm not alone."

"Who else is there here? Your father? Your mother?"

"No, they died not long ago. A girl is with me. They took her away yesterday and I haven't seen her since."

"The lord of this place left last night by post coach. If you want to find the girl you'll have to go into the castle garden. The women from the castle can only go there during the daytime."

William grimaced bitterly and held up the chain.

"And with this?" He dropped it back on the ground.

"Every lock opens once; you just have to use your brain! Escape as soon as possible. If they take you to the ranch from here, there's no way out." He opened a package. He took out bread and a piece of hard cheese and pressed them into the boy's hand.

"In three days' time, the next slave transport starts from here to Argentina. You've got three days!" he finished emphatically, then went back to the cart in front of the door. He got back on and gathered the reins. The sound of horse hooves started to clatter on the cobbles. The cart turned in a wide curve and slowly trundled away from the palace...

With an appetite, William ate the food he had been given so kindly. In the meantime, the castle slowly started to come to life around him. Here and there stable boys hurried past and serving maids appeared with pails of milk and baskets of vegetables. At this point a decoratively dressed gentleman entered the stable accompanied by two muscular keepers, and walked over to William.

"Stand up!" he squeaked at the boy. William leaped to his feet and took a step backwards.

"Take the chain off him!" With the tools they had with them, the two helpers cut the rivet connecting the metal bands together within a few moments. The heavy chain fell off noisily. After this, the new arrival turned on his heel and motioned to William. The boy offered no opposition and followed. After the heavy chain, his steps felt feather-light. They went behind the palace, looking for the left wing. Here, staff were unloading hundreds of boxes from about twenty wagons standing in a line. William was also set to work carrying loads. Out of the corner of his eye he saw that armed guards protected the three gates of the square. Without a word, he carried on working.

The same chambermaid who had brought Susannah to the bedroom came to visit her in the morning. She brought something to eat and a big mug of hot coffee. Slowly it dawned on the girl that the door had been left open. Curiously, she stepped into the corridor and went down the stairs. She found the main entrance of the palace locked, but one of the back doors was open. She walked into the open air. She found herself in a park filled with thick, flowering decorative plants. Several women, a girl, and an older woman with a veiled face walked in the park. They chattered with each other and laughed cheerfully. Susannah called to the woman on the first path, but they could not understand a word she said. A second girl came and led her to a bench on which an elderly lady was sitting. She said a few words in Spanish, laughing cheerfully, and went away. Susannah spoke.

"My lady, do you speak English?" The woman turned to face Susannah. She pulled aside the black veil over her face to get a better look at the girl.

"You are the new girl who was hunted down by the human trackers?"

"Yes" sighed Susannah, and her gaze sank to the ground.

"Who is given to Señor Garcia?"

"... That is a long story..." replied the girl, and lifted her sad gaze.

"We have time enough, my child. My name is Eloise. I'm of French descent on my mother's side. But my father was an English officer who spoke many languages. When I was 18 years old, I was as exquisite as you. My father wanted to give me in marriage to a rich old banker who was already more than sixty. They were in debt and the old skirt-chaser was pressuring them for swift payment on their bills. The night before my wedding, I ran away from home. I became an actress. One day I came to know the love of my life, Jean-Claude, who was a member of a well-known company of actors. I joined them. Then we reached London. Life was wonderful and light-spirited. Three months later we travelled to Italy. On the Mediterranean, Arab piratcs took our ship. They killed everyone on board except the young women, and they took us to the slave market. An Argentinean rancher bought me. That's how I arrived in South America. I've spent thirty years here! The owners have changed three times since then. As I aged, my price decreased. Four years ago Señor Garcia bought me to teach his children English and to be their governess. He abused me like none of my previous owners. This spring the children were sent to England to attend school. I'm being packed off to the ranch."

"I heard I'm going there too," whispered the girl.

"Life is hard and merciless there. But tell me how you got here."

Susannah started her life story. The old lady listened sympathetically to the unusual tale. By the time Susannah approached the end, an hour had passed, and she took both the girl's hands, her eyes brimming with tears.

"My poor child! More bad things have happened to you in less than a year than happen to some people in a lifetime. Where is your friend?"

"After we arrived yesterday they flogged him and since then I haven't seen him."

"I'm free to go anywhere. I will look for the boy, and.... if possible, we will escape together!"

Susannah, with passionate gratitude, clutched the old lady's hand and covered it with kisses.

"Enough, enough, my girl!" the woman hushed her. "Believe me, if I were younger I would not dare. But I am too old now for a life of working 14 hours a day in the hot sun. If they send me to Argentina, I'd rather die first than be destroyed there by privation! Now, come with me, my child. I'll tell you what you have to do, and if God is willing, tomorrow night we will be free again!"

They stood slowly and the main entrance of the palace engulfed them. In one of the back corridors Eloise pulled up a wall-divider which covered a narrow door. Stealing a look around, she opened it. A musty, damp cellar smell came out through the door. Susannah gathered up her dress and entered behind the old lady. The stairs first spiraled down, then went straight to one side. Eloise turned left here. On the wall a torch burned. Underneath it, a dozen others lay in a box, unlit. Taking two, she lit one and pressed it into the girl's hand. Without a word, they went ever further and ever deeper. Susannah started to suffocate from the lack of air. Suddenly they came to another bend. A salty, nose-stinging stench of shellfish and rot hit them. Between steep rock walls, they arrived at a secret opening to the sea. A rowboat lay there, pulled up because of the low tide, with two oars in it. The opening in the rock was so well hidden from the sea that no one would ever find it unless they knew exactly where the opening was. Eloise turned to the girl.

"This is the only way we can escape. Of all Alfredo Garcia's people inside, no one knows of the pirates' way out. Here he swaps goods with pirates under cover of the night. Will you remember the way we came?" Susannah nodded. "Now we look for your companion and find where he is being held prisoner. I'll get some men's clothes for all three of us, and some food and weapons. I can go freely to every part of the castle because everyone knows me." She walked into a rocky hollow, and showing the girl, said, "Tomorrow night at eleven, be here with the boy. If I can't get back here in time, you'll find everything here. If God is willing, I too can win freedom in my final days."

"We will wait for you, Eloise! We won't leave without you!"

"You can't waste too much time! You must row far from here before dawn. They will look for you on land and at sea, but you mustn't believe in dreams. You must be careful!"

"We'll stay together, you'll see! After all this, we three will find happiness! You're experienced in everything, we will surely find the way out." The girl trustingly held the old woman's hand and squeezed it.

"Let it be as God wills, my child!" she whispered, and with that they turned and disappeared into the rock opening. Only their steps echoed slightly amid the stone walls. Afterwards the sound of the crashing sea was the only noise.

William worked the entire day with the other servants. About noon he got a little food and fresh water. The boy waited uneasily. He had still received no news of Susannah. As evening fell they were herded into a big hall where all the entrances were covered by armed guards. The hall was approximately thirty feet high. The roof had been cracked, perhaps by musket fire. Through the crack William could see the starry night sky, radiating a sense of freedom. In the middle of the hall a big fire burned. Several enormous spits held roasting meat. His mouth watered. He was hungry. He sat close to the fire and comfortably felt the radiating warmth. Some smaller stable boys took pieces of meat off the spits, and others followed their actions with close interest. Eventually a piece of meat cooked on the spit came to his hand, too. He wolfed it down. The fatty meat had a decidedly smoky smell to it, but he ate it all, to the last mouthful. With a full stomach, he lay on the ground. A dream came to him. When, around midnight, he began to doze off, he felt as if somebody had clutched his arm. Fearing an attack, he instinctively grabbed the person disturbing him. The newcomer was in a dark cloak hiding the body from head to toe. Now the stranger leaned towards the boy and whispered just one word.

"Willy!" Joy ran through the boy like a flame. Susannah was his nighttime visitor. The girl took his hand and led him after her, being careful to go around the sleepers. At night they locked the main door on the outside, but Susannah didn't go this way. To the left of the main door a narrow corridor was carved from the stone, which a narrow iron door sealed. She groped her way towards this and closed the iron door after them. About fifteen paces along, a torch burned on the wall. At the end of the corridor another form shrouded in a dark cloak appeared. It held a torch in one hand. Gesturing urgently at them, the form disappeared behind a door. William followed the girl curiously. When they found each other in a small room at the end, the two took off their cloaks. At last, William again saw the beautiful visage of Susannah. Beside the girl stood an elderly and dignified-looking woman who examined him searchingly. The first thing William did was to embrace Susannah's slim body and kiss her passionately on the mouth. Eloise broke the intimate silence.

"My children! We don't have much time! The change of the guard will be here in 15 minutes." Still holding Susannah tightly, William turned to face the lady. In a few minutes Eloise outlined the plan for the escape the following night. The boy listened with eyes wide, then took hold of the lady's hand and covered it with kisses. Eloise smiled.

"Now I understand, Susannah, why you want him with you! Your young knight knows how to charm a lady off her feet!" She took her hand back, then put it down the front of her dress. She pulled out a key and pressed into the hand of the amazed William.

"This is the key to get this far. Tomorrow night, we leave this way. Susannah will wait for you here. She knows the way to the dock now. I will wait for you both at the boat. The guards change every hour. But don't start for a while, because you'll find yourself face to face with the new guard when they come this far. Now, my girl, say farewell to your knight and we will meet again tomorrow night."

William kissed the lady's hand and hugged Susannah to him.

"Be strong, my love!" He pressed a quick kiss to the girl's mouth and slipped back through the door. The girl and the old lady changed back into their cloaks. They went in the opposite direction to the interior of the castle, and soon vanished around the curve of one of the corridors. The torches flickered monotonously, sending sooty smoke against the grubby walls. The creaking of a door sounded. The flames sprang up with the draft. The clanking of weapons disturbed the silence. The changing of the guard's had arrived.

William stole back to his sleeping place. Listening carefully, he looked around in the darkness. No one had woken among those sleeping all around him. Melancholy wheezing filled the room. The boy stretched out on the stone floor. He tied the key to freedom in the waist of his shirt. He heard the guards approaching. The change had happened just as the old lady had warned.

"Tomorrow!" The thought rang through him. He looked at the scrap of velvety night sky visible above. The stars twinkled more and more invitingly. The light of freedom again sparkled in the dark tunnel of death. He watched the dream unfold behind his eyelids, which were slowly closing. Before his wondering eyes floated Susannah in her dark veil, and the girl's beautiful face appeared. The beautiful lines of her mouth broke into a smile and she held the boy's face with her graceful hands and lovingly kissed him, kissed away the countless sorrows of this world, and the blood in his dripping wounds no longer boiled, healed by the magical power of pure love.

The next day was uneventful, but the torment of waiting was intense for both youngsters. True to her promise, Eloise smuggled the necessary clothes, food and weapons under her broad skirts to the opening in the rock face. The elderly lady was approaching the end of her strength as the day began to reach dusk. In a fit of dizziness, she took to her room. She had just enough strength to put on some men's clothes from underneath her pillow that she should have found time to put on earlier, then she sank onto the bed. Her face grew pale and she panted for breath. With her heart beating heavily, she collapsed and lay down. Dark shapes danced in front of her eyes and suddenly everything went black. Her face turned a deathly pale color and she lost consciousness....

Many times during the day Susannah prayed to the heavens for success in their escape. For today she had collected a small package with several slices of meat in it. From the wall she took a dagger and a short sword for defense. The hours crawled by at a leaden pace. When the big pendulum clock in the corridor chimed ten, tension surged through her. Eloise had promised she would open the door an hour before they left. She went to the door and tried the handle, but the bolt from outside would not budge. She put her ear to the door and waited. There was silence on the other side. Her head began to spin feverishly. Something had gone wrong! When the pendulum clock sounded eleven she went back to her room despairingly, wringing her hands. No one had arrived to help her escape. Minutes went by with horrible slowness. Susannah saw that the candles had almost burned down, and then she would have to wait further in complete darkness. Outside sounded the noise of the midnight change of guard. The pendulum clock slowly sounded out the hopeless midnight hour. A quiet scratching and fumbling sounded on the far side of the door. With a careful hand she tried the handle and there was a small, squeaky, sliding sound from the other side. The door creaked and opened slowly. Susannah gripped the dagger, turning deathly pale, and stood by the wall. The dull light of the candle revealed a nighttime vision to her. It was William. The load falling from her heart was so immense that she heard a rumbling sound, literally from her own blood pressure as she almost swooned. She hugged the daring youth, and held him to her desperately.

"Where is Eloise?"

"I don't know. She should have been here a long time ago. Something bad must have happened."

"Do you know where her room is?"

"No! But we can't start without her!"

"Susannah! We've got to go!"

"We can't go, Willy, maybe tomorrow..."

"There's no time! The slave transport starts at dawn! I heard them in the evening giving duties to the soldiers."

Susannah ran back to her room to collect her supplies for the journey. Afterwards, she ran to the boy, who was slipping out of the door. They stole to the end of the corridor, down the staircase and into the tunnels. Here, Susannah took the lead. In their agitation, they took a wrong turn twice, thinking themselves at the smugglers' entrance. Not daring to light torches, they went to the end of the corridor in total darkness. They both felt these to be the most tortuous moments of their lives as they found themselves again in the narrow passage. When at last the salty scent of the ocean reached them, they quickened their steps. It was a beautiful moonlit night. Running to the water, they found the boat at once. With the tide high, William pushed it easily into the water. Susannah ran to the rocky hollow. She whispered several times and repeated Eloise's name, but the elderly lady was nowhere. Susannah found the equipment and clothes Eloise had left for them. She gathered up everything she could and took it to the boat. In three runs, it was all finished. William packed away everything and looked at Susannah expectantly. The girl took off her red dress and put on men's clothing. She put everything into the boat and went to the boy. William climbed into the boat and loosened the mooring. He thrust once and then spread the oars. He began to row. A form carrying a torch appeared in the pirates' entrance.

"Eloise!" cried Susannah. William sprang out of the boat and onto the shore. It was indeed the elderly lady in the entrance, dressed in men's clothing. But what a state she was in! She had just enough time to press the torch into the sand and collapse senselessly into William's arms. William carried her in a faint and put her in the boat. Susannah helped Eloise to lie in the boat with them. When she took her hand away, she realized with a shock that Eloise's blood was sticky on her fingers. William again pushed off with the oars and they moved out onto the water. After several minutes, the waves of the open sea rocked them. They followed the shore and turned northwards. Susannah laid the head of the unconscious Eloise in her lap and bent over her protectively.

Only the curious moon bore witness to these daring deeds. They were free again…

Free Again

The reddish glimmer of dawn broke the dark sky above dry land. The moon had long since sunk into the ocean surf. The stars began to dim, then faded into the dark blue of the horizon. Suddenly, like pillars of flame, the first rays of the rising sun broke from behind the hills.

A tiny rowboat pushed through the water, three-quarters of a mile north of the shore. The oars rose, the blades sparkled in the water, then back down to give the rowboat another push forward. Straining with all his strength, William pulled on the oars. A fresh wind blew up, chilling the sweat-drenched youth. The waves became bigger, and the little boat began to shake dangerously. Susannah found a carved wooden scoop under the seat and used it to bail out the water sloshing over the side. In the morning light, they could at last take stock of Eloise. The elderly lady had not yet recovered consciousness. Worried, the girl bent over her chest, listening for her heartbeat. She was still alive, but there had been no improvement in her condition. Susannah tore a strip from her shirt and used it to absorb some of Eloise's blood. With a sudden start, Eloise opened her eyes.

"Eloise!" cried Susannah, and tears of joy rolled down her face. William came over, and together they tried to breathe some life into the dying woman. The boy poured several sips of wine into Eloise's mouth. She drank, but suddenly hacking coughs shook her body. She recovered herself slowly and raised her gaze to the two young people. The hint of a smile touched the corners of her mouth. The girl leaned over her.

"We're free, Eloise! This miracle happened thanks only to you!" The elderly lady's eyes moistened, and she opened her mouth to speak.

"I was never dissatisfied… I was resigned to my fate… I see now I made a huge mistake… We will have to fight for our freedom…" She began to cough again and a trickle of blood seeped from the corner of her mouth. "I lived as a slave… but at least I can still die free," she cried. Her eyes were swimming with tears. Susannah was shocked.

"What happened to you, Eloise? Who wounded you?" asked Susannah.

"The knife! I fell down the stairs. The knife hidden in my dress cut me… How could I have done something so stupid? I'm so sorry, my children…."

"We will cure you, Eloise! You will see. Everything will be all right!"

"I will stay with you, children! I will always watch over you from heaven. But my time on earth is slowly coming to a close." She reached her neck and took off a medallion and pressed it into the girl's hand. "Here is the only treasure I have ever owned… Maybe one day my secret will be revealed." Her gaze again misted over. She turned her head in the direction of the rising sun. The sun's rays filled her hair with a golden light. Her body stiffened, then slowly relaxed. A long sigh came from her mouth, her lips trying to say something, but it was too late. Her eyes opened wide, then glazed over. Fresh blood flowed from her mouth, then her head drooped. Susannah broke into heavy sobbing. William looked away, then spoke.

"We've got to put into land!" Again he worked at the oars, forcefully pushing them into the water, then pulling on them. The directionless, rocking boat began to glide again, but this time with a strong wind behind it towards the shore.

In the soft sands of the beach, they dug a grave. William arranged some stones into a pile to mark the spot. They bent their heads for a few minutes, then paid their last respects. Susannah mouthed a prayer for the salvation of the departed soul.

In the meantime, the sun climbed high, and lit the entire coast with daylight. William pulled the girl away from the grave. They pushed the boat into the water and the boy again plunged the oars into the water. Susannah kept her head turned and for a long time gazed searchingly at the shore, where the grave mound slowly faded with distance into the sand of the beach. She wiped her tearful eyes and looked at William. They boy smiled at her reassuringly. Before them stretched an endless expanse of water, behind them the rocky shoreline. William breathed in the fresh salt air. Above their heads screamed the ever-hungry gulls as they swooped for prey. The boat occasionally veered back towards the coast from the force of the waves. Again, they managed a distance of almost a mile from the coast. Rowing until dusk with brief rests, they again drifted towards the shore, carried by the waves. William steered them into a small bay, then beached the rowboat on dry land. He carefully brought them in towards the rock in case the rising tide should smash their precious vessel. They tossed everything out of the rowboat and wearily spread everything on the soft sand. They didn't try to light a fire, though the foresighted Eloise had packed a tinder-box lighter.

Generally, it took half an hour for the boy to kindle a fire. Now, however, they gnawed some slices of cold meat, drank some wine and went to sleep. They only woke from their exhausted dreams the next day in the late morning hours. To keep ahead of their pursuers, for several days they only rowed from dusk until dawn. Then, perhaps, a chance would come for them to reach the forest and then the hills.

During their resting hours, William labored at making new weapons in preparation. He made a strong bow with good arrows and a couple of spears as well. Susannah worked at altering the clothes, which were too large for her, having been designed for men. They decided that she would remain dressed as a man. Her long hair was hidden under a wide-brimmed hat, so from a distance they looked like two boys. William decided that from this point on they would be much more careful in their journey. Each time they finished their work they would lie on the soft sand of the beach. The days passed quickly. But after this long month since they had won back their freedom, they were to lose it again cruelly.

The striped weals on William's back still smarted from his whipping. Like a guardian angel, Eloise had hurried to help, and just as quickly, they had lost her again. What kind of heavenly powers could have played this evil trick on them? Both were still lamenting that the spirited Eloise could not be with them still. The thread of her tormented life had been cut before she had reached her goal. Now she would never taste the honeyed nectar of living free, after so many years of forced service. The only value her life had, in the end, was to save the two youngsters from being consigned to slavery. Saving two lives was the price of her own life. She could only wait for the deserved culmination of her heroic sacrifice from the stars. Her bones crumbled away in an unmarked grave on a nameless shore.

Again, at dusk, our friends took to the water. A wind blew up and at first this impeded their progress. But it blew from the south, forcing them into open water so that they felt as if it was playing with them. The stars shone in greeting. Next to the Southern Cross, Susannah found the small astrological house where, so many months before, they had pinpointed that falling tiny star. That was the night when she had the first kiss of her life, and also when their lives had gone astray, when they had been orphaned. She looked at the boy, who pulled evenly on the oars, and who was perhaps thinking of just the same things as she. They were just playthings, sailing towards their unforeseen futures in a little nutshell, which the now kind ocean might swallow up tomorrow.

The wax moon coated the endless water in silver phosphorescence. Around them, the water splashed even more. Swift flying fish flipped themselves out of the water. Then, with a bigger splash the waves swallowed them up again. William took a rest from rowing. His arms were knotted with cramps, and he tried to knead the tension from his muscles. They changed places. Susannah rowed further, so that the boat would not turn sideways where a cross-wave could easily have turned them over. William washed himself, so that the sleepiness stealing over him would not cost them their lives. He gave the girl a piece of meat. Then he took several bites himself. He took his place again at the oars, and, refreshed, started them on again.

Then the night clouded over, and the boy thought uneasily that from now on they could no longer keep a northerly direction. Because of this he rowed only for another half hour, then put down the oars and looked around. The waves slapped the side of the boat restlessly. Stormy weather was brewing. Within a few moments, a hellish darkness fell over them. Then, the first lightning flickered in the distance. They nearly gasped with surprise. A huge, three-mast sailing ship lay close to them. In the meantime, the wind blew up and around them, and the sea started to chop and heave restlessly. Soon lightning cracked and a terrible thunderstorm raged. William realized with horror that they had gone too far into the open sea and now there wasn't enough time to get the rowboat back to the shore. The wind, in gusts, wrestled with the boat, and pushed them towards the dark schooner. Its huge bulk loomed temptingly over them. Not a soul stirred on deck. One or two ship's lamps swung at the prow and stern. William saw that in a few more yards their rowboat would be under the prow of the ship. Perhaps they would not be noticed. But at just that second, a shout came from the deck.

"Ahoy! Who are you?" came the shout in English, and several lamps shone at the ship's rail.

"Shipwrecked castaways!" William tried to shout above the booming thunder, cupping his hands together. Lightning flickered above their heads and in their midst. It seemed the sailors wanted them to come on deck. William quickly got up and stood on the rowing bench. Strong arms pulled the little lost soul to the side of the ship. Someone let down a rope ladder. The boy sent Susannah first, quickly tying their packages together for the sailors to haul up. Finally, William also took to the rope ladder. The waves tossed the rowboat like a chip of wood into the hull, making the impact ring through the timbers of the ship, before the pieces disappeared into the churning water.

"At the last moment!" cried the boy above, as helping hands hauled them onto the deck. He appeared soaked from the rain, and whipped by the wind. The deck was drenched by angry waves at every turn. The sailors showed them into a cabin. The door slammed shut loudly behind them. In the warmth and light spread by large candelabra, they held each other. Outside the ocean storm raged. Now, outside, the dance really could begin!

Behind a broad desk, a distinguished-looking bearded man stood.

"Welcome on board the Iron Cat. My name is Captain Stanley Briggs."

"William Anderson. And this is my younger brother, Daniel." The boy gave a small bow. The captain, with a slight smile at the corners of his mouth, took a better look at the two of them.

"You don't look like you've seen much of these parts!"

"No, sir! We came here from New Holland. Our journey has been long and not long ago we suffered a shipwreck. Only the two of us, Daniel and I, escaped."

"Yes, yes," the man walked around them in a circle, thinking, then came to have a better look at the younger boy, who kept his cap on throughout.

"I see that there are just the two of you. It is madness for you to be at sea at a time like this. But I think it was through necessity, big man! Perhaps you haven't told me everything completely honestly, my young friend?" And at this, he looked searchingly into William's eyes. "Methinks your story limps a little somewhere." He picked up a three-branched candelabra and held it closer to the smaller boy's face. "I would say Daniel might be better named Daniella!" With that, he snatched off the cap. Susannah blanched and took a step backwards towards the wall. Her thick hair tumbled down around her shoulders. Reddening, William tried to apologize, but the captain waved him to silence.

"No need to explain, my friend. My men can keep a secret. But we have to trust each other or all will become known. Nobody talks about the past if they don't want to. Nor does anyone have permission to blab about the present. This is the only condition for our survival!"

With measured steps, he went over to a large chest covered with copper studs and took out a dark roll. He held the two corners and released the package, which tumbled open. Before their eyes, a black Jolly Roger flag unrolled softly. The captain watched their reaction keenly. It was certainly not the first time he had seen surprised faces when he revealed the ship's outlaw status to strangers. He rolled up the flag again, put it back in the box, and turned to them with arms folded.

"Tomorrow we'll talk some more. Now it's time to rest." He took a bell from the desk and rang it. Two sailors entered at this signal. They had obviously been waiting outside the door all this time. The two youngsters followed them, and soon found themselves below in the lads' quarters. Two hammocks were hung for them so they could sleep. One of the sailors escorting them gave William a friendly tap on the shoulder.

"You found yourself a good place, lad! We carve up anyone who mucks about with helpless innocents!"

The two youths took to their hammocks. Only a single lamp flickered, and beyond that everything was enveloped in darkness. Groaning, the bulk of the ship swayed back and forth, but it didn't seem to disturb anyone. The rocky, reef-lined shore was far enough away to keep the ship from harm. After raising the anchor the sails were only let out as much as was needed to make the ship navigable. The watch on duty waited for dawn. The Iron Cat clearly had a pressing reason to stay in one place for an opportunity. But this hardly concerned the couple. They had taken refuge with a higher power, and could feel themselves totally safe from their slave servitude on such a ship, a ship itself outside the law.

William reached over to the neighboring hammock and stroked the girl's face.

"Good night, Susannah!"

"Good night, Willy!" They wrapped themselves in their blankets and spent the rest of the night in grateful, heavy sleep.

The next morning they awoke to heavy pitching. Both went on deck so that they could better see their new home. The Iron Cat was a 450-ton ship. Through the constant work of the hands on board, with craft and labor over a long period of time, it had become faster and nimbler than other ships of its class. It was designed for fourteen cannons, but actually boasted twenty-seven.

Its gangways were raised higher. Its booms were longer than usual on such ships, and they could raise more sails. Because of a prow that extended further forward than usual, it was more maneuverable. Due to a weak rear wind, it was still standing off the shore. The sky was covered with slate-blue clouds, but because of the proximity of dry land, the coast sometimes disappeared behind wisps of fog. The sailors greeted them in a friendly way, but never stayed with them in their room for very long, as if ordered by their superiors not to get too close to them. Briggs' disclosure of their pirate role had already troubled William enough. He didn't want to put Susannah into further danger with any possible conflict. He heard enough from their conversations to know a little of the life of pirates, but for now this place still seemed safest for the two runaways. They walked on deck while some of the sailors were busy. But this quiet was only the calm before the storm. A yell came from the lookout's nest.

"Ship in sight!" Like lightning, the deck came to life. Armed soldiers took up positions, and even the sailors handling the sails grabbed weapons. Briskly they climbed the rigging, and in minutes, crowds infested the sails and masts. The bulk of the vessel moaned and juddered several times, then turned into the lee of the wind. The changing west-southwest wind caught the sails, which filled with loud clicking sounds. This took several tense minutes.

On the upper deck the powerful silhouette of Captain Briggs appeared. At his side was a decorated sword. His loose, black cape snapped in the wind, tauntingly showing its crimson lining.

At that moment, a sluggish, broad cargo ship came through the patchy fog. The Iron Cat momentarily lost sight of it and the other ship sounded the whistle so the two ships could avoid colliding. As a strong wind started, frantic scurrying began on the Iron Cat's deck so they could catch the wind in the sails. Just as quickly, the cargo ship vanished into another patch of fog before their eyes. The fog alarm was sounded on the deck of the Argentina. Its men were gripped by the superstitious fear of again losing sight of the spectral ship in the fog. Several minutes later, to general surprise, it seemed that a ship appeared on the far side of the Argentina, then vanished again into the fog, leaving the men of the Argentina filled with dread. Old, experienced sailors made the sign of the cross. The speed of the new ship was almost three times their speed. The captain of the Argentina cargo ship knew that he was being pursued by a boat. He ordered the men to shoot the cannons at the intruding vessel. Dull, booming sounds erupted into the emptiness. The terrifying silence was broken.

"Open the spare sails!" roared the voice of the quartermaster on the Argentina! The deck drummed with the sound of agile feet as more canvas was unfurled into the ever-strengthening wind. The prow of the ship cut deeply into the water from the increased force, and the whole of the deck swayed from the waves. The joints in the hull groaned, and the huge boat whined and creaked. Then a fierce wind blew up as if the thunderstorm were restarting. Side waves started striking strongly enough to tip the center of gravity deep inside the cargo ship. The captain then realized what a blunder he had made, and ordered the hands on deck to dock some of the sails, but it was too late. The massive force snapped the rigging and the main mast came down. The hull tipped and became impossible to steer. Huge waves smashed over the deck, ripping away everything that could move. Several sailors had fallen into the water at the moment the mast snapped, and now others followed. Yells of despair rang out, but there was no help. Those left on deck were only thinking of their own lives in those seconds. More ropes snapped. The front and back sails tangled together and came down quickly, one after the other. The waves toyed with the devastated deck. The captain ordered the remaining cables to be cut, and the whole deck to be cleared. They began bailing, as more water started entering the hold. This took hopeless hours as the hull drifted further into the open sea. The gale-force winds held off and the first rays of sun broke through the cloud. The first thing their eyes saw was the phantom ship. Undamaged, proud, it was moving at an astonishing speed. It was within cannon-firing distance, with its side turned towards them. The gaping mouths of the cannons appeared. From the main mast flew the dreaded flag - the skull and crossbones.

Those left standing on the deck of the Argentina looked on in horror. The Iron Cat let down pursuing boats, which swiftly reached the neighboring ship. The captain saw that resistance was futile, so the Argentina, Alfredo Garcia's largest trading ship, gave up without firing a single shot.

The transfer of the cargo took until late afternoon. Captain Briggs kept to his word and allowed the trading ship's crew to go free with the rest of his men. Rescue vessels still remaining on the trading ship were left for them to use. The despondent crew started to row towards the distant shore. They were now completely broken men, and had lost everything they had without a fight.

What was left of the trading ship had sunk within two hours. The Iron Cat waited for this, then again broke sail, and its mighty, powerful form disappeared into the night.

This was Captain Briggs' secret goal. Weeks ago, his spies had gone to town gathering information about Alfredo Garcia's trading vessels. He had learned that the 500-ton Argentina was being readied to sail for Europe, offering itself temptingly. There had only been the issue of the two English warships in harbor, ready to see the Argentina through the deadly South American waters. But this never happened. Alfredo Garcia believed false information from spies that England's Royal Navy had sunk the Iron Cat off Venezuela two months before. It was members of Captain Briggs' crew that brought this false information to Garcia. The goal was achieved. The hold of the Iron Cat was bursting with the legendary riches of the Argentina, strong spices and bales of silk. At the same time, large quantities of jewelry and gold coin had fallen to the crew of Captain Briggs' ship.

The clever use of subterfuge to seize the ship without a fight showed the superb seamanship of the buccaneers, and the boldness and cunning of their leader. Among his men, he had long been known for terrifying his enemies, his intrepid tricks making them despair. Lacking the fortitude to confront him, they would turn and run. Changeable, stormy weather had presented the opportunity, and it worked, calculated down to the last detail. Gales overcame the trading ship and delivered it up to them.

On that evening, the captain treated Susannah and William to dinner. Here the boy was able to greet an old acquaintance. This was the old sailor who had talked to him at Alfredo Garcia's palace, and who had so kind-heartedly shared his simple breakfast with him. William saw at once that there was no need to hide the truth. He openly recounted the unbelievable adventures of the last year. His listeners paid close attention. At the end, Captain Briggs spoke.

"I believe that after adventures like these, the cleverest thing you can do is to stay with us! I promise your destiny will not be a bad one. If one day we fall into the hands of the Royal Navy, we will cling together and the mighty wind will blow under our feet!" So much laughter roared out that the very walls of the ship shook. William took the offered hand in friendship. Again, their lives took a new turn.

The Iron Cat went sharp west into open waters. Only 72 hours later, they turned north again. They wanted to evade the fleet patrolling the shore, because after the news of the Argentina's raid the buccaneers moved fast. The Iron Cat had to avoid a skirmish. Its speed and maneuverability were significantly reduced because its hold was now heavy with booty. Their journey took six weeks.

During days of wild storms, Captain Briggs' men made a superb seaman out of William. The captain arranged a separate cabin for Susannah, gave her nice dresses to wear and treated her like a lady so that the boy often saw the girl only at suppertime.

The heat increased the closer they got to the equator near the coast of Ecuador. One hot, humid morning sails were spotted in the distance from the lookout's nest. The ship's crew heard the news with trepidation. They wanted some action after a month and a half of inactivity. When the unknown vessel clearly remained on their trail, Captain Briggs appeared on deck. He viewed the approaching ship calmly through a telescope. He summoned his first officer.

"Mr. Hobart! Pull in the sails, but keep the men ready!"

"Right you are, Captain!" The command went out and the Iron Cat's sails began to be furled in the glittering light of the open ocean. The other ship also reduced speed, and stopped, within good cannon-firing distance. From its main mast hung the banner of England's Royal Navy, in full glory. In answer, the Iron Cat hung out the English ensign. As a sign of respect, both ships fired off a greeting shot. The other ship let down rowboats on the facing side. Four pairs of rowers and a dark-clothed man got in. Captain Briggs looked over the arrival, whose wide-brimmed hat was particularly noticeable. The rowers quickly covered the distance between the two ships across the choppy water.

With ropes they brought them next to the side, and the newcomer climbed the rope ladder they let down with agile movements, soon arriving on deck. Taking off his hat, he extended a hand of greeting to Captain Briggs. The captain immediately stepped closer and extended his arms to the new arrival with a smile.

"Welcome, Richard! You've become a man since last I saw you!"

"Nine years is a long time, Uncle! Unfortunately, three weeks ago our ship sprang a leak, and the repairs took ten days. Otherwise we would have been several days ahead of you."

"The traders will be there at the meeting?"

"Just one will make the journey. The others are worried about the patrols."

"What a cowardly lot!"

"The Bold Eagle will be at the meeting in a week. They promised they would take everything and pay in gold!"

"One week..." murmured Stanley Briggs to himself, as he showed his guest into his quarters. The crew recognized the fellow ship, and cheerily welcomed the rowers on deck. They greeted each other loudly, and were soon toasting each other over rum.

Down in the cabin, talk became more serious. Richard was the first officer on the Fairchild, whose captain was Johnson Briggs, his father.

"How's my brother Johnson?"

"Father's in Jamaica. In his last engagement, he was injured seriously. This was five weeks ago. His condition's not shown any improvement. A group of three ships from the King were sent to destroy us."

"Stevenson's ship?"

"Sunk. Only the Fairchild was left."

"...and the Iron Cat!" said the Captain, deep in thought, energetically pacing up and down the cabin.

"A patrol of three ships?" He turned again to his nephew.

"Yes. All three heavily armed, with good crews, it seems. According to our information, Alfredo Garcia organized two fighting ships also. If they meet up with the other three, nothing can stop them!"

"I know. But I also hardly believe they're working together. Garcia is too greedy to feed the King's navy out of his own pocket. The sooner we're free of our cargo the better, because carrying this kind of load we're a sitting duck."

"Where do we go later, Uncle?"

"Back to Jamaica. There we wait for your father to get better. We must obtain a third ship, too, somehow – not to mention a crew."

"Wouldn't it be better to take a break and go back for a while?"

"Alfredo Garcia is the reason your grandfather died. While he lives, your father and I will have no peace!"

"I know, but they're stronger than us right now, Uncle!"

"Before the Briggs family name sinks to the bottom of the ocean deep, the Garcia family name will burn to ashes, lad!" shouted Captain Briggs with flashing eyes. Richard recognized his father's passion in those words. He knew it would be pointless to argue further.

The secret slowly leaked out, even to our heroes William and Susannah. It was fifteen years since the feud had begun between the two families, the Briggs and the Garcias. Henry Briggs had a trade network of good repute that linked from Liverpool through Europe, as well as the southern countries. He first met Alfredo Garcia in Rio de Janeiro. They shared views on business, and soon agreed on a major deal together, through which the two traders built up a truly solid friendship. But during this friendship, Garcia had kept his real interests hidden. After Henry Briggs put him in contact with his customers in Europe, Garcia had no need for a middleman. He had Henry Briggs brutally murdered.

However, Briggs' three sons began to investigate the cause of their father's death. Within several months, it became obvious that Garcia had stolen their father's clients. In just under a year, their trading network collapsed. At auction, the once friendly newcomer, the Argentine millionaire, purchased the trading business for one fifth of its value. Stanley, until that time a naval officer, left service in the Royal Navy, and armed the Iron Cat from his own resources. The first ship he sank would have taken Garcia back to Rio. However, an informer warned Garcia in time and he boarded a different ship in disguise. Soon the other two brothers followed Stanley into the family feud. They were outside the law, with warrants against them from their own country. That was fifteen years ago. The decisive engagement, so many years later, would soon be unavoidable.

Captain Briggs kept his nephew on the ship the entire day. For dinner, however, they went to the Fairchild. News spread like wildfire round both ships that five armed vessels were hunting them down. Captain Briggs gloomily waited for the offloading one week away, when the ship would be rid of its heavy cargo. The crew was on fighting alert. Guard was doubled on both ships. Every available weapon was carefully tested, cleaned and made ready for use. William felt burdened by the knowledge that their lives were going to be in greater danger than ever. They could be taken captive again, and with a worse end, quite possibly the gallows. He would never have retreated or acted cowardly, but he felt that this family vendetta could not be their destiny. Yet all around, they were surrounded by the endless ocean. There was nothing they could do. They didn't have enough seagoing knowledge to use a compass and a rowboat to strike out across the ocean. During this time, it was possible for him to be together with Susannah. They talked a lot about how they could win back their freedom, independent of anybody. But they never spoke these thoughts loudly, lest they lose Captain Briggs' trust.

On the fifth day, the Captain issued the order to set sail. The deck of the Iron Cat came alive. Running feet drummed all over the ship's decks. The mast was soon swelling with canvas and the ship headed east. The Fairchild followed slightly behind as protection. Every eye scanned the far distance. The heat grew, and the sea still swelled angrily. Each day, increasingly, fierce downpours drenched them while the two ships moved steadily towards their destination.

At sunset the next day, the lookout signaled sight of the coast. They reached the designated location for the meeting with the traders at midnight. The two ships dropped anchor about two miles off the coast, sheltered by a peninsula. All lights were extinguished on deck, and with jangling nerves they waited for morning.

As dawn came, the trading ship appeared on the horizon, coming from the north. From a distance, they used flags to signal friendly intentions. The waves calmed a little to allow the two ships to approach each other skillfully. The transfer of the cargo began.

During this time, Captain Briggs entertained the captain of the freighter and his officers in his cabin. They organized the payment details. The Bold Eagle would not be able to buy everything, so it had planned to stow the remaining cargo onto the lighter and nimbler

Fairchild. The Fairchild would then follow the Bold Eagle to Colombia, where, after unloading on shore, they would receive the extra payment in gold. This arrangement was not to Captain Briggs' liking. In unfriendly waters, he did not want to lose the company of the Fairchild, the only fighting ship that could protect them. However, he could not take their advice to follow the two ships to Colombia. The distinctive Iron Cat, recognizable from a distance, would now be known to the patrol ships. Therefore, he decided to remain where he was, off the coast of Ecuador, and wait for the return of the Fairchild.

By evening, the hold of the Bold Eagle was filled with cargo. In the meantime, the Fairchild had taken on the spare freight. The two ships left in different directions so as to throw off any pursuers. The Bold Eagle had a trading license, and wanted to hide the fact that it had traded with pirates.

By morning of the next day there was no trace of either ship on the horizon. The Iron Cat was now forced again to spend three weeks standing by. But this hanging around didn't sour the crew. They passed their time in different kinds of games, wrestling, swimming, fencing and fishing.

William and Susannah filled their time learning all sorts of skills. They had started to learn Spanish and Portuguese, among other things. At the same time, William was learning about the stars and how to navigate by them, and using naval maps and a compass. They spent long hours in the company of Captain Briggs, who was soon persuaded that his special guests far exceeded most of his own men in intelligence. In turn, the thought had occurred to the captain to take the two youngsters with him, later on, and if a chance came to return to England, to give them an education. They spoke a great deal about their memories of New Holland. But they could never answer what had happened to their parents long before. Uncovering the past often brought back bitter memories, and tears to Susannah's eyes. At these moments, Captain Briggs would hurry on to another topic.

They progressed well with their language lessons, which cheered the crew with their mixture of mother tongues, since it meant they could communicate ever better with the two youngsters. William went everywhere help was needed. He would take part voluntarily in the heaviest work. He made enthusiastic efforts to learn the mysteries of working the sails, as well. He spent a lot of time, even with Susannah, in the lookout's nest. There, far above the deck at that dizzying height, they could be completely alone together. They could talk freely on any topic without fear of an informer listening in. Tirelessly, they would scan the coast or the vast distances of the ocean with a powerful military telescope.

In the third week of waiting, they were in the lookout's nest when a point at sea attracted William's attention. After a slight wait, two more appeared from the northwest; they were increasing in size, thus clearly approaching. William jumped onto the rigging and climbed swiftly down to the deck to tell Captain Briggs in person.

Susannah had a curious look at the tiny dots. Suddenly she went white and dropped the telescope into her lap. She began to shake. She hurried after the boy and waited for him to return from the captain's cabin.

William knocked on the cabin door, and after being called in, stood in front of the captain. He found Captain Briggs bent over calculations, with a group of men laying out naval maps. Stammering, he announced the reason he had come. The captain strode out to the deck and with an agility shaming his men, climbed the rigging to the lookout's post. At length he studied the three small dots, which were growing in size. Back on deck, he looked at his assembled men. With his brows knitted in a hoarse voice he summoned the first officer, the armed company, and William. They all went to his cabin. The crew left behind waited silently for their return.

In his cabin Briggs went straight to the map, and touched the parchment at the coasts of Ecuador and Columbia. He thought at length and then turned to address the men waiting there.

"What I feared has happened! The Bold Eagle has given us away to the royal patrols."

"What has happened to the Fairchild?" asked Mr. Hobart, the first officer.

"Either they are captured or they are at the bottom of the ocean depths. I know my nephew. He would never give up his sword. Non of the Briggs will ever give in!" He looked at those around him with flashing eyes. "The patrol ships were given the exact coordinates. Turning back in a southerly direction would be our only way of escape. But the Humboldt current from the south has strengthened. That only leaves us a route out due north - towards Colombia, which is probably where Alfredo Garcia's ships are waiting for us."

"What can we do, Captain?" asked William.

Stanley Briggs looked slowly around the cabin. In one corner of his room was an ornamental chessboard. An Italian craftsman had carved the pieces from ivory in Rome. The old game of strategy was one of Briggs' favorite pastimes. He had taught William a little in the last few days, but with no better opponent, he would play against himself. Now the board was cleared, and he put just the black king back on the board in the lower right-hand corner. Then he put white pieces around it. He made a few moves, then turned to William.

"Look at this position, my young friend. Do you think there's a way out?"

William looked at the pieces carefully. The black king could only move in two directions. But the attacking white queen could easily cut him off.

"Well?" Captain Briggs looked at him urgently.

William went on, "Two moves… and checkmate!"

"Yes my friend! Checkmate! But can we really allow ourselves to fall into their hands?"

He looked slowly around at the men. The lieutenant took out his sword.

"We'll fight to our last drop of blood, Captain!"

Briggs also took out his sword, and a rare light came into his eyes. "We'll fight to our last drop of blood!" With that, the captain whisked his sword. The black king was left headless on the chessboard, but the body of the piece did not even quiver.

"Mr. Hobart!" He turned to the first officer, "All men at arms!"

"Yes, sir!" Hobart clicked the heels of his boots together, and strode out of the cabin. From outside came the thudding of a drum, and the pounding of feet shaking the deck. Soldiers and sailors took to their designated posts. The sails broke out, the timbers of the Iron Cat started to groan, and the southern wind filled the sails. Fierce waves rocked the deck. Every mouth repeated in whispers: "To the last drop of our blood! To the last drop of our blood!" By now, raw throats were shouting the words and swords were raised into the air. Sinister thunder rumbled. From the mast flew the black flag, which had filled so many faint hearts with fear over the last fifteen years. The Iron Cat surged into the waves. Water washed into the portholes and over the red-painted cannons on both lower decks. A deadly silence fell on the ship, with determined looks from men at the three warships from the royal force approaching across the water.

From the far distance the roar of cannon sounded out, to which another answered at once. Before their frozen eyes another two patrol ships appeared in the distance. On the upper deck of the lead ship stood Alfredo Garcia, and he never took his eyes off the hated form of the Iron Cat. On his face now was an evil smile, seeing the ships of the English Royal Navy falling into line behind the pirate ship. "No way out for the pirates! No climbing out of this one, brigand!" he hissed through his teeth, and shook his fist at the pirate ship. His thick voice suddenly shouted: "For fifteen years I've waited for this moment! The three Briggs brothers caused me so much harm, but Stanley Briggs is the most brazen and the mastermind of them all. Whoever takes him alive gets 200 gold pieces from me! 100 pieces just for his head! Death to the rebellious scum!" and he pulled out his sword. He roused his men to cheers. Meanwhile, he returned to his post, giving haughty commands to raise the rest of the sails. Only the first officer was worried for a moment.

"Señor Garcia! The gale will be on top of us in a moment!"

"Even better! I don't want to win this fight too easily. I only want one! The brigand will be fed to my dogs tonight!"

The strengthening wind covered them with grey thunderclouds. Daylight glimmered dully in the distance. Up in the sky, an albatross circled. A few old sailors looked up superstitiously. The appearance of the huge bird signified earthquakes, tidal waves and huge hurricanes, according to ancient sea lore. One of the oldest, the ancient gaffer Thompson, studied it for a long time, then turned to William.

"The end is near! The Iron Cat won't see another sunrise, I reckon." He lifted a gnarled old hand and ripped the collar of his shirt. On his enormous tattooed chest hung a thick chain, holding a big iron cross. He grabbed the cross and muttered to himself in the fierce gale, "The end is near! God give me a quick death!"

Again the sky rumbled, and the first lightning crackled down in the western sky, followed by an earsplitting crash. Panic began to break out on the three patrol ships – all hell broke loose. They ran into the hurricane with full sails open, which hit them so that the sea seemed to turn into a boiling cauldron beneath them. The whirling wind whipped up the waves from many directions. The three patrol ships tried to cut in the way of the Iron Cat, but it slid between them like a snake. At a short distance, Captain Briggs let loose a fusillade at the nearest ship. The destruction was unbelievable. The Iron Cat's cannon masters knew their craft. The neighboring ship lost its sails, and its tangled rigging fell into the sea. There was still time to fire the cannons, but the cannonballs did not cause any serious damage to those on board the Iron Cat. The no longer navigable royal patrol ship became a plaything of the waves. Captain Briggs stood on the upper deck, roped to the ship's wheel against the waves, and helped keep direction lest they capsize.

Now the other patrol boat came alongside and fired its guns at them. The Iron Cat answered with another fusillade. This attack had been better aimed, and the first cannonballs hit the pirate ship. The front sail heaved in tatters. Several seamen lay dead from the impact.

William and Susannah waited in the gangway in front of the main mast for their impending deaths. After several exchanges of fire, the Iron Cat sent a second patrol ship to the depths.

A short distance before them, the other two warships were also struggling with the gale. On the upper deck of the leading vessel, Alfredo Garcia howled orders in quick succession. With a ghastly smile on his face, he gazed at the Iron Cat with the last patrol ship on its heels. The four ships exchanged fire between one another at short range. The hurricane was now at its peak. A ball of lightning suddenly followed and with horrible explosions, it hit the ships. Garcia, in his rage, so wanted to see the destruction of the Iron Cat that he was spitting orders at the skies. One ball of lightning hit the upper deck and a sea of flame covered the deck. The fire quickly spread and ignited the gunpowder stowed in the hold. An explosion bigger than any yet blew Garcia's ship to pieces. Pieces of ship, human body parts, blood and excrement splattered over everything left in the vicinity of the struggle. The three remaining ships collided. Our young friends kept their heads down in the empty part of the hold during the fight. Through a tear in one wall, water began to pour into the hold. William quickly grabbed a coil of rope and tied two empty water barrels together. Within minutes, the water was up to their chests in the hold.

Up top, the embittered battle raged on. Acrid black smoke mixed with the clouds. Blood combined with the salt water of the ocean. Planks were broken, and sails were burning. Swords and axes flashed, men's death screams chilled the hearts of those still living. More and more cannon fire competed with the thunder. Explosions made it impossible to see anything. In bloodcurdling sheets, newer lightning commenced, and then came the sudden silence of death.

It seemed after this fight to those left living that only the storm had won. Victory and defeat had been swallowed up equally.

Inside the hold more creaks and crashes sounded, as the planks of the side wall gave way and the hull started to leak water seriously. Susannah screamed and swam towards William. The boy had enough time to get one end of a piece of rope to the girl and loop it around her wrist, and for the two of them to take a deep breath as water covered everything. When the pressure equalized, William pulled Susannah and the two barrels after him towards the opening, and they swam into the open water. The hull slowly creaked as the sea swallowed it. The two youngsters, using the last of their oxygen, barely made it to the surface. The two barrels were a huge help, as they too broke the surface. After a moment of heavy silence, the furious hurricane caught up with them. The spinning wind and the waves tossed and rolled them. Pieces of ships floated in every direction, the final result of the battle. The pirate captain had been right after all. The Briggs family name had not sunk to the bottom of the sea until that of Alfredo Garcia had burned into ashes!

The albatross was already above the clouds, continuing its journey. It was a bad omen that had proven to be true. Its appearance supported the legend of centuries of sailors' superstitions. Would any survivor tell, one day, of what passed here? Would there be anyone to strengthen the legend? The albatross had never been a blessing for mariners – it had brought only trouble and destruction.

The towering waves washed the remains on the surface for three days in a northerly direction. The sharks in their deep homes could have noted this rich feast day in their calendars. After the stilling of the storm, a quieter western current took hold. The wreckage of the ships washed closer towards the far continent.

Flocks of gulls marked the watery graveyard. With shrieks, they dived and looked for food, flying in circles around every floating piece of waste. The braver ones landed on pieces of flotsam to rest. One of them looked with interest at a small fish head on a scrap of canvas. The gull quickly waddled over and snapped at the tasty morsel. The bird could not have known that the food was bait in a trap. One twitch, and the snare closed on its leg. It writhed in despair, trying to escape, but its destiny was sealed. The sun sparkled on the blade of a knife and the headless gull fell. With a loud clacking noise, William quickly clambered up over the remains of the main mast. Turning back, he hit the hungry shark right behind him. The shark was ready to butcher him with its razor sharp teeth. The water was starting to boil around him. More sharks appeared. They were biting each other as well, just to get closer to their prey. The water churned. More sharks appeared, each trying to push the others out of the way. William hung on above, and tied together some of the wreckage. He looked around worriedly. Since the previous day, the number of sharks had multiplied. But until now, they had kept away from the weak survivors.

With quick movements, he ripped the feathers out of the gull's skin. He hungrily wolfed down a bloody mouthful, and lifted a piece of sail. Underneath, the haggard-looking Susannah slept. With her sun-baked hands, she reached out shakily for the offered scrap of meat. In three days, they had not eaten or drunk anything. The tropical sun began to herald the morning with its rays. In agony from their wounds, washed with salt water, they waited feverishly for night, which might again bring a few hours of relief. They picked every scrap of meat off the gull. William flung the bones far into the water. A dozen tiny fish sniffed around the remains of the bird. William squinted up at the merciless blue tropical sky. The two retreated under the canvas, away from the waves of heat from the sun. They took refuge from the heat in sleep.

Beside them in the water bobbed their life-saving barrels, which they still had tied to their wrists. In the sky, there were many curious birds, which signaled the proximity of land. Yet our friends were on the verge of total exhaustion and did not notice the good news. Gasping feverishly and trembling, they lay under the sailcloth, and could only hope that their shelter would not soon fall apart. They no longer had enough strength to swim.

The coast slowly appeared in the misty distance. They only reached the coast by night. The rough, uneven waves moving toward the coast overturned their refuge and flipped them into the water. Struggling, they tried to stay on top of the water, and they thrashed to reach the life-saving barrels again. Six-foot waves rolled them, but then the benevolent tide tossed them far up the beach, and sent their barrels smashing to pieces on the rocks. By now the two youngsters felt no pain from the sharp stones. They crawled on all fours out of the waves up to the sandy area of the beach, where they flopped together like two straws. In their resting place, the sound of the waves still crashed. They felt as if the sandy beach were pulsating and crumbling and they were both falling into the black depths – but this was just a trick of their tortured imaginations. They had reached the coast, the end of their long, stormy sea passage. They would remember the last three days as long as they lived. Without food or water, they had been tossed around in the gale, but they had reached dry land alive.

A miraculous higher power had again saved their lives for a purpose known only to those who have things left to do in this world.

The New Land

William gradually came to. He felt horrible heat all around him. He moved. Pain cut into his body. He opened his eyes, and the first thing he realized was that their life-saving barrels had smashed to pieces. Pain shot through his head. Dully, he gazed towards the coast. It was low tide. The hot tropical sun had left a thin layer of salt in the gravel of the shore, where it harshly dried every last drop of moisture that the retreating sea had left behind. Above his head, coastal gulls shrieked harshly. Unwillingly, he turned in the direction of the sun, which now stood high, crowning the tops of the thick jungle. William carefully raised his hand in front of him. His skin was covered with small bruises. Sharp pain seized his left foot. They would certainly remember the last three days as long as they lived!

"Susannah!" he cried, in a sudden rush of memory. He stood and squinted towards the ends of the beach. The girl was not far from him, having drifted along the beach during the night. She had abandoned herself to a sleep of total exhaustion. William wanted to shout, but his swollen tongue was caught in his mouth. He coughed dully and quickened his limping steps. Several gulls in their nests rose, agitated, as he approached, but he wasn't coming for them. Reaching the young maiden, he knelt beside her. The girl gasped feverishly in her sleep. Some of her hair obscured her face; the rest of it was covered with grains of the fine beach sand. She still clutched the rope of the barrel that had saved her life on the stormy sea. William lifted the girl, and then started for the nearest group of palm trees. He flopped down in the shade, and carefully laid the girl on the sand. Life slowly returned to Susannah's face. She opened her eyes and gazed at William.

"Water!" she whispered, and two weak arms pulled at the boy's neck. William tearfully kissed her, and then broke free of her embrace. He stood and looked along the coast in both directions. He had to find water soon, and food to keep them alive. He fumbled at his belt. With enormous relief, he found that his knife was still in its leather sheath. He removed it. The salt water of the last few days had pitted the shining blade with rust. He quickened his steps towards the densest clump of forest, which was a few hundred yards to the south, extending clear down to the sea. He knew there had to be fresh water there. He pushed back the obstructing branches to make his way into the jungle. Then he let out a loud yell. Trees loaded with fruit - bananas, coconuts - were his for the taking on all sides. And most important, a small stream trickled through the undergrowth. Thick green foliage covered its banks, crisscrossed by animal tracks. William packed the bottom of his shirt with fruit, and then filled two empty, dry pieces of coconut shell with water and took them back to the girl. After he made Susannah drink, the girl immediately felt some strength return, and sat up. Hungrily, they fed themselves with fruit.

Their hunger satisfied, their curiosity returned about where fate had brought them. They went down to the water's edge. They were in the centre of a huge bay. The coast stretched into the horizon in each direction. On this coastline, fringed by thick rain forest, there was no trace of any people apart from themselves. About a quarter of a mile in one direction, the waves had washed up new pieces of wreckage on the beach. Immediately they made their way there, in case something useful had come in with the flotsam. Susannah found just one treasured little item there, apart from the knife William still had. It was a precious gift from her mother, a mirror with a mother-of-pearl frame that had burst out of the lining of her dress. Nothing else remained. Taking stock of the gifts of the sea, William collected some pieces of wood from the mast, some larger scraps of sail canvas, and some pieces of rope that the ocean had brought in. They also found several items of clothing scattered around. They piled everything carefully into a bundle, so that they could check through it later for things they could use and things they could leave behind.

The first thing William did was to rig a small tent from pieces of the sail canvas that had emerged from the waves. This was a good idea, since in the afternoon there were several brief but heavy rain showers. The evening tide brought yet more flotsam onto the coast, and because of this William suggested that they should wait here a few days in case a survivor from the Iron Cat somehow washed up too.

As they had thought earlier, this area seemed totally uninhabited. There was no trace of human activity anywhere. As it does along the equator, full darkness fell within a few moments of evening taking its leave of them. The stars came out at once. It occurred to both of them to look for the constellations they knew, but in their place, other, unfamiliar constellations filled the night sky. This meant that they had crossed the equator and were now in the northern hemisphere. The boy started a fire, over which they cooked several skewered fish that they had found earlier in the shallow water. They ate huge servings of fruit, and drank and drank. They could not tire of the taste of fresh water after their long thirst. After this hearty feast, they stretched out wearily beside the fire. They both fell into a heavy sleep. They lay luxuriantly in the soft sand as if in the finest bed. The fire slowly dimmed and went out. Quiet covered the coast. Only the rhythmic sound of the ocean waves was unceasing.

Breaking through the clouds, the waxing moon showed itself. Its pale light transformed the sandy shore. Its light was not strong enough to penetrate the thick blackness of the jungle depths. The moon looked down curiously at the two exhausted youngsters as it climbed ever higher above the sleeping land. It had to hurry, because it was only a few hours until morning, when the flaming shafts of the mighty sun would burst forth and bring the moon's reign to a close. The blackness of the sky slowly faded into dark blue. Once again, the moon would have to flee to the other side of the earth, taking refuge from the sunlight, but until then remaining as if in waiting.

The youngsters woke in the sizzling heat of the tropical sun. Cheerily, they ran down to the blue waters of the ocean and plunged into the refreshing waves. The bad memories of the last few days that the water brought back were not worth returning to. Their youth and will to live helped them in stages. Here they were, on the edge of this tropical paradise. Soon enough they would set out again to further discover the place that they could one day call home. They did not know what pushed them further and further, just that the real goal in their future was not this deserted coast. They still had to pick up the broken thread of their lives, and follow it wherever it might lead them.

They spent three days on the peaceful coast, to regain their strength and equip themselves as best they could with tools and accoutrements. William made new weapons, a bow, arrows and a spear, so that they could hunt, and perhaps defend themselves against wild animals if they had to. To gain some experience, they went into the rich, wild forest along the sea's edge. This teeming wilderness attracted predators in large numbers. One morning, they took a short explorative journey in the surrounding area. They climbed a three-thousand-foot mountain. From this peak, they had a good view of the countryside. To the east, they spied a high chain of mountains stretching into the misty distance, with snow on their peaks. The mountains were at least a ten-day walk from here, about seventy miles away. William voiced the view that from the heights of those mountaintops they would be able to have a much better idea of the interior of this land. At last came the time when they packed up their things. Inside them burned the desire to know this uncharted wilderness. Susannah, now that they had reached a place far from their enemies, was full of confidence at the boy's side.

That night William again made a big fire so they could have some protection. Again during the day, they had had to collect firewood everywhere because of the showers that kept breaking out. After a full dinner, they turned in happily. During the night the boy awoke once, hearing the angry growl of a jaguar. The animal was drinking at the stream nearby and had realized angrily that strangers had made a path at the edge of the forest. William put kindling on the fire, which blazed up and the predators of the night quickly retreated into the protection of the rain forest. The crackling of the fire woke Susannah from her sleep. "What's wrong, Willy?" "Just go back to sleep, sweetheart! The fire is guarding us while we sleep." William stroked the girl's hair lovingly, and with a smile on her face, she slipped back into her sea of dreams.

The first rays of the sun made them jump to their feet. They ate more fruit, picked up their belongings, and in a moment the thickness of the jungle had swallowed them up. With a spring in their step, they followed animal tracks east towards the big mountain chain. William had to use his knife frequently to cut a path through the thick vegetation. They came upon several marshy areas infested by clouds of mosquitoes.

The first night after encountering the mosquitoes, they made camp on a small rise. They had to get out of the valley as quickly as they could, since there were so many midges. With a great deal of difficulty, William was able to light a fire. When the first flame finally sprang up, he threw some wet branches on the fire. Thick blue smoke billowed up, and finally cleared the air of the torment of the bugs. Near their camp, the boy brought down a small tapir, so they now had a good share of meat cooked for dinner. After they fed themselves, William sliced and smoked the meat they had left, so they wouldn't have to spend all their travel time on hunting.

For several days, they forged on tirelessly through the rain forest. Finally, one afternoon, the jungle thinned and they came upon stony land dotted with scrub brush. They had eaten all their meat, so William started to hunt after setting up camp. But however quietly he tried to move, his footsteps echoed loudly on the stony ground. Now he realized it would be hard to get anything on the hilltops. There were plenty of animals in this country, but they were all at a distance, running away before he could get close. Clearly they already knew about people, and they knew to keep their distance. A bare outcrop of rock now appeared in their path. He decided to climb it, so he could better see from the top which way to take from here. Arriving at the top, they finally had a good view. Down on the far side was a marshy lake. It was probably one of the places where water collected during the rainy season, and for several months of the year served as a watering hole for animals. Enormous boulders marked the water's edge, but thick pastures spread all around. Most importantly, there were herds of grazing animals everywhere.

William paid close attention to the sight spread out before him. Not far away a large herd was scattered, from which dozens of animals were going to the water to drink. Next to the drinking animals, a group of smaller forms were spread out in the trees. Then suddenly, something unusual occurred. The thirsty animals suddenly darted and tried to retreat to escape the danger. Then he saw the source of the danger. A jaguar sprang down on the ruminants from an overhanging tree branch. A young animal, several months old, was the victim. The jaguar sunk his fangs into its neck, and then dragged the animal into the undergrowth. The startled herd stood and craned their necks curiously.

Several minutes later, their thirst won and drove them back to the watering hole. It seemed that they knew that, just for now, no more danger would threaten them. By now, William had seen everything that had unfolded. He descended into the vale, and keeping downwind, approached the herd in the long grass, crawling. Like the jaguar, he picked out a young animal for himself. He pulled his bow and aimed it, then let the arrow fly on its mission of death. The animal jumped into the air when the arrow pierced its throat, then collapsed. Its companions twitched uneasily and sniffed in its direction, but failed to understand what had caused its death. When the boy appeared, they fled like the wind with a loud sound. William went over to the animal. He had never seen one like it. It had a long neck, but its body was furry. Its weight was more than he could drag, and it was clear that he would have to strip the carcass there and then and take back with him not just the meat, but also its useful warm pelt.

When he got back to their camp, his body was bathed in sweat from his exertion. Susannah was overjoyed to see him back. He had been gone a long time. She helped him cut the strips of meat, and built up the fire. While the meat cooked, William washed himself with a pot of water. As they filled their stomachs, the boy related what he had seen of the country. He also warned the girl about the dangerous predators who were their neighbors here. It struck him how casually he had left the girl back at the camp, without weapons. They decided that from now on, they would hunt together.

After dinner, they slept on a rock in the lake. William made a fire that they kept burning all night because of the wild animals all around. Turning in, Susannah soon went to sleep, but William could not rest for a long time. Each hour he had to put kindling on the fire for their protection. When the night was almost over, he dropped into the deep sleep of exhaustion. The fire guarded their sleep with a light that spread around their little camp.

Early in the morning, a chilly breeze came over everything. They woke in a cold, clammy world. By now the fire was no longer burning, but William found some embers in the ash, and soon had flames blazing and glowing again. They ate some bites of cooked meat, then packed up again and moved on. The sky was blanketed with thick rain clouds. They might not see the sun again any time soon. They walked a little faster to warm up by moving more briskly. For quite a while, the terrain did not change. Areas of scrubby forest and tall grass alternated with each other. In a few places they discovered large boulders in their path that took time getting over and around. In the cloudy, overcast conditions it was hard for William to keep to his east-northeast bearing. They were lucky that the land was elevated so that they could see in an easterly direction.

In the afternoon, the inevitable finally came. Rain began at first with a few drops, and then suddenly streamed down as if it were being poured from a bucket. They ran for shelter among some trees, but they could only rest there for a few minutes. This was when the pieces of sail canvas would have been useful, but they had been too heavy to drag this far with them. They shivered from the rain because there was nowhere they could rest. At nightfall, they still had no refuge. They could not make a fire - it was still raining. William spotted a big tree in whose forked branches they decided to spend the night. He helped the girl up. They got themselves into the tree and then pulled up the animal skins. Shivering with cramps, they clung to each other and tried to rest. They covered their heads with the animal skins. Above their heads, the rain drummed monotonously. Only through sheer exhaustion were they able to sleep a little before morning.

As it became light, they continued on their way. Susannah was limping alongside the boy. "What's wrong with your leg, Susie?"" I don't know. My ankle is a little swollen." William thought hard. He knew that he must do something. They had to find refuge until the end of the rainy season, or they would soon be finished. Since morning, they had traveled only one mile, and now they felt as if they were at the end of their strength. "Show me your leg!" Susannah took off her shoe and lifted her foot into William's lap. The ankle was swollen, a bluish-red color, and touching it caused shooting pains.

"You cannot go any further with an injured leg. We must stop here a while so you can rest it. We must make a fire in some protected place, but where?" He prepared a comfortable place for the girl to rest. He then picked up his weapons and looked around the area. He did not go too far for fear that something would happen to the girl. He checked the rocks, looking for a space where they could withdraw from the rain for a few days.

Then a stumbling young animal, perhaps only a few days old, attracted his attention. It was that long-necked, furry species which he had killed one of a few days earlier. The urge to hunt suddenly welled up in him, and he quickly decided he would try to capture the animal alive. He moved in, but even on its wobbly, ungainly little legs, it scampered nimbly out of the way, disappearing behind a bush that grew beside a high rock wall. William crept up to the branches and was more than a little surprised to find, behind it, an opening into a cave. The way in was narrow, but further in it was possible to stand up. Close to the mouth of the cave grew some dry grass, which he gathered for striking sparks, and then he ducked into the cavern. Having made light, he saw his little captive, who stood shaking at the far side of the cave. It had nowhere to run, since the cave had no other exit. Smiling, William looked at the unlucky little animal. They did not have much meat left, but he could not lay his hands on such an innocent little newcomer. He backed out of the cave and put thick branches over the entrance to close it off. He cheerfully went back to the girl and told her the good news.

They collected their things together at once and set off for their new home. The boy really had found a cave suited for living in. Fifteen feet long inside, it was approximately nine feet wide. In the middle, it was a little wider. Grit covered the dry soil. The boy carefully advanced on their little captive, holding a bunch of grass in his hand. He could not have been more surprised when the animal walked towards him and began to eat. Susannah happily greeted their new little friend and gently stroked its silky fur. With a leather strap, William tied the calf's leg near the entrance. Turning back, they had another look at their future home. The walls of the cave were smooth, and because of this it was easy to clean them of bugs. Then they found a large grey snake in a small cavity in the cave wall, where it was curled into a ball. Susannah shrieked with fear and ducked behind the boy for protection. William used fire and smoke to drive their unwanted guest from the cave, and finally they took possession of their new home.

The first thing William did was to start a real fire as soon as possible. He built a simple fireplace of pieces of stone arranged in a ring and made a fire within it. He also stacked lots of kindling in a corner of the cave. He cut away the bush blocking the entrance to let in more light. This also allowed some fresh air to circulate. They cooked the meat they had left, and ate hungrily to get their strength back as soon as possible. At night they brought in their little protégé, and made a place for him in a corner of the cave to keep him from becoming dinner for a predator. Before lying down, William again fashioned some screening out of the thorny foliage to shut off the entrance to the cave. Then, finally, they could embrace each other in peace and safety beside the fire. The glowing embers radiated benign warmth, caressing their limbs. Susannah put warm skins around her legs, then let her head, crowned with her glorious hair, lie in William's lap. She made herself comfortable. Wordlessly, they gazed long into the flames.

This was the first evening in a long, long time that they had had a solid roof over their heads. William stroked the smooth locks of her hair, then reached for her hand. Susannah fit her graceful hand into the boy's palm. Their fingers delicately played with each other. The girl lifted her head and looked at the boy. William smiled, and then leaned over her. Opening his lips, he sought her mouth to kiss. Susannah lifted her mouth to his, and he kissed her gently like a bee touching the petals of a flower. Their kiss was long, and sweeter than nectar. Neither of them wanted it to end. Once, they stopped to take a breath and every beat of their hearts throbbed with the passion of youth. After this, Susannah nestled her head into the hollow of William's shoulder and closed her eyes. She stretched out a hand beside her and drew in the sand idly. She let the grains of sand trickle between her delicate fingers playfully. She waited hesitantly to see what would happen. William gently caressed the length of her body. Susannah shivered slightly and sighed. Slowly, she broke out of the boy's hold and stood up. She put her hands on her shoulders. She lifted her dress to her chest and pulled it over her head. She slipped the straps off her arms, then removed her underdress from her slender body and let it fall to the ground. She stepped out of it and, a little unsteadily, approached the boy. She leaned towards him, kneeling, and then lay down next to him. William, on his elbows, slowly leaned over her. He covered her body with a wave of tender kisses.

Shuddering with a fever of desire, Susannah pulled the boy to her. The sky growled, and lightning flickered across the western sky. The wind picked up and brought raging rain to lash the forest. The flames of the fire flared up, and the sparkling embers sizzled. The fire made little dancing patterns in the ash, then a big gust of wind raised the fire again, and the ashes covered the flames thickly, extinguishing the fire, bringing soft darkness to the inside of the cave.

A cloudy day dawned. Heavy, grey rain clouds covered the sky. Weakly, the sun tried to break through the cloud. Its form showed sometimes, like a pale silver disc, then it was buried again in the dense cover of the thunderclouds. The inhabitants of the cave woke slowly. Pressed tightly against each other, they looked at the damp outer world. The fire had long since gone out, and they would not willingly leave its warm ashes for the chilly morning. William got out first from underneath his clothes and skins. First, he lit the fire again. Only when the flames were cheerily crackling would he let Susannah get up. He led the young animal captive into the open, and fashioned a longer tether for it. Turning back inside, he collected his hunting tools and said farewell to the girl as he set off to hunt. Susannah carefully blocked the entrance after him and prepared a sharpened spear, in case she needed it for protection. While waiting for the boy to return, she put together some warmer clothes. She made a needle from a splinter of bone and some thread from animal gut. Her work went very slowly. Hours had passed since the boy had gone. She heard sounds, and now peered out of the opening curiously. Tied on his leash, their little guest began little beseeching whimpers. Susannah could not imagine what might be the trouble. From somewhere beside the cave, heavy steps sounded. Susannah took the spear and rushed to the protection of the little calf.

Coming out, however, she realized who the new arrivals were. Dozens of grazing animals gathered around the tethered guest, from the same species. At the sight of her they lifted their heads, but they didn't go away. Slowly, they wandered further, craning their necks curiously. However, one of the animals stayed with the calf. It was his mother, who was now suckling him. Susannah smiled to see them. Just then, William returned from the hunt with meat and fruit. The girl went to him and helped carry in his provisions. William also noticed how tame the mother animal was, not running away when he approached. He threw some fruit at her feet, and then returned to the cave. After eating, they tried on the newest bits of clothing. As they gained altitude and the weather turned colder, wrapping themselves in fur would be a good idea if they had to go for firewood or hunt somewhere at a distance.

In the afternoon, William caught another sight of the mother animal's remarkable tameness. After she had fed her little one, they grazed at a distance together on the tether. This gave the boy an idea, which he conveyed at once to the girl. He thought that on their later wanderings, pack animals might be useful. If these two creatures stayed together, he was sure they would make each other tame enough to be saddled. They saw many things together at once. During the rest of that day, they fashioned a saddle that they tried the following day. They worried that the animal might be driven wild by the unaccustomed saddle, but as soon as it was fitted over its head, it stood quietly and allowed the reins to be adjusted. Susannah was the first to try out their new steeds. William helped her into the saddle, and then holding the tether, walked alongside her and the animal. The girl led the animal off and, speaking soft words, stroked it. The extraordinary tameness of the animals was still a mystery to them, but they soon worked it out. When Susannah urged the animal to faster steps, she held onto it by its long fur, laughing.

Then she discovered in the fur a thin set of reins, noticeable once you looked. She shouted out her discovery to William. "We are not alone!" The boy came over to have a look. He suddenly felt the fire of a pair of strange eyes. There was only one answer to the mystery. The animal was an escaped possession of a nearby native tribe. William decided that when the weather was a little better, he would look around the area more carefully. They had to find out who their neighbors were. Were they enemies or friends? In any case, he broke off the walk and they went back to the cave.

William began to worry seriously that one day a wild animal or an enemy would come for Susannah when he was not at home. He decided to teach the girl how to use the bow. He made a smaller bow, but it was almost as strong as his. He also made light arrows, which he tipped with palm splinters hardened in fire. Since the girl was not used to the bow, the first arrows did not go near the target but at least they flew, to the joy of her teacher. After three days, the first arrows went into the target area they chose at a distance of thirty paces. William explained and showed her the correct use of the bow and how to raise the arc to hit something at a distance. Susannah was a good student.

Two weeks later, she brought down a mountain goat for supper. Of course, her eyes filled with tears at the sight of the dying animal, but William was filled with glee. From now on, the girl could protect her own life if necessary! They went home cheerfully. While the boy cut up their prey, Susannah made a fire, and soon the tempting scent of cooked meat was filling the cave. They ate as if they had not eaten for days. Sometimes they smiled at each other. Often there was no need for words. The cave gave them their first protection, their first refuge from the rain. The warmth of the fire radiated the feel of home. With full stomachs, they happily turned in for the night under the covers.

In the last few weeks, William had built a neat little wooden structure next to the entrance to the cave, so that their domestic animals had some security from predators. Often, the roar of a jaguar sounded near the pen when he scented the odor of the animals inside. Hearing this, they simply put more kindling on the fire, and the blazing flames quickly drove off their uninvited intruders.

Susannah's leg improved, and they were counting the time left until the end of the rainy season. They wanted to trek further, as far as time would allow. They talked often of what might await them on the far side of the mountains. Was it worth going further? Should they stay here in the cave? William felt that in the course of exploring further they would find the place that was right for them, rich in wild fish and fruit. There they would build a bigger house, and live in comfort. But until then, this cave fully satisfied their needs. Several days later, when the rain clouds were breaking apart a little, they started to check out the surrounding area. Curiosity still burned in both of them to know how far away the first people, the natives, lived.

They took two carriers with them on their journey, and the calf was already strong enough from the past weeks to carry a small pack on his back. They proceeded slowly, deliberately, to check each important point of the district. They didn't want to blunder and lose the safety of the cave. As they went further, the land rose. The distant hills were already snow-capped. There was only sparse scrub in the land by this point. Over the stony soil, patches of tough, dry grass were scattered. Fewer and fewer animals came into their path, perhaps because of the lack of water. In a few places, mountain goats sprang from rock to rock. But they ran away wildly. Clearly, they were already familiar with people. The morning again brought cloudy weather, but several hours later there was a break and the sun shone palely through. They looked around at the mountaintops. East and west, the chain of peaks stretched as far as the eye could see. Under one, the dark strip of a river stretched out. Going further down was not possible, though. Disappointedly, they turned back to their camp and packed up.

Their way back went quickly, since the slope was downhill this time. In the afternoon, they took a short break. Sleep overtook Susannah. William smiled to see how tired his companion was. But when, a good hour later, she began to wake up, she had a severe headache and tried unsteadily to stand. William put her in the saddle at once and they quickened their pace. It already appeared that it was not a good idea for the girl to spend the night in the open. The girl assured him palely that it was just a bad spell. William had lost some weight over the last few months, becoming more sinewy, but his face was tanned and it was clear by now that he was not susceptible to fever. Susannah, on the other hand, had lost the tan from her face. Her paleness was only becoming apparent to the boy now. He did not know the reason, but he felt the start of something worrisome. He led the two animals after him nimbly.

He hoped that by tomorrow noon they could reach the cave, and there the girl could avoid becoming worse. However, by evening what he had feared had begun. The girl became feverish. William hoped it was just a normal chill. But Susannah was delirious around midnight and tossed uneasily in her sleep. He wrapped her tightly in furs and tried to make her drink water. What little food he had forced her to eat earlier the girl vomited. She floated ever weaker on the sea of fever. The boy had no idea what to do. He kept vigil the entire night beside the patient. He burned the fire high to keep the girl warm. As morning arrived, he hurried to break camp and get back on their journey. In the early afternoon, he caught sight of the cave's familiar rocks at last. He took the girl in and laid her down. He wrapped her carefully and made a fire. With no appetite, he sat beside Susannah, watching her deathly pale face. Slowly, an understanding took shape. If the girl died, he would be alone! He must find help, but from where or from whom? He sat up with the sick girl another night. By dawn, his head was drooping. He knew he could not let himself sleep. Now that it was morning, he must go for help. The girl's face still burned from the heat. Sometimes she moaned or muttered something in her fever.

Finally, in the early morning, she relaxed and went to sleep. William wobbled exhaustedly into the fresh air. He washed. The cold water brought him back to himself. Filling one of the goatskin bags with fresh water, he went back into the cave. Suddenly hunger raged. Starting the fire again, he cooked some slices of meat. He made some for Susannah too, though he didn't have much hope that she would eat too. He woke her. The girl pushed away the hand holding the meat and only reached out for the water. After several gulps, hacking coughs began to shake her whole body. Weakly, she flopped back onto her makeshift bed and her eyes closed. William carefully tucked her in and then wrapped up some food set aside for her, and put it in a leather bag. He changed her hot bedclothes. Stepping into the open, he got the pack animal ready and then blocked up the cave entrance again. With several worried looks back, he set out. He had decided to look for people in the northwest.

From a bigger clearing, he picked out a distant high point, and then took himself down into the forest. He roamed for a long time. On this route, the vegetation grew thicker. Several times he had to cut himself a path with his knife. But he kept heading for the high land that he had seen earlier. Tying the pack animal to a nearby tree, he climbed the nearest cliff to get a better look. Out of breath, he reached the top. He looked around carefully. A long way off, he could see a low cloud. Patiently, he scanned the country below. He was looking for signs of people. He began to feel increasingly hopeless. To the west, only the green crowns of the trees spread out. There was nothing there. Or was there? A strange strip of mist caught his eye. The strip was bluish, like the rest of the mist, but it was not horizontal; it was vertical. Could it be smoke? New hope sprang up in William. He looked again, more carefully. After ten more minutes of looking, it seemed more likely that it was smoke. He made up his mind that either he had to cut his way through the forest to get to the unknown target or return to Susannah, who now needed him desperately! Hope grew stronger. He must get help! He climbed down from the rock and went further. He oriented himself and set off immediately on the first track into the dense undergrowth. He moved forward ever slower with the increasingly dense foliage. Branches and thorny bushes scratched his face. Dozens of biting insects inflamed his skin. Above his head, swarms of mosquitoes followed him. But he did not stop for a moment. He was now unstoppably pursuing his unknown goal. The sun was already well behind the trees when he felt he was nearing his destination. He knew that he had to bring help to the girl by tomorrow morning. Finally, the brush began to thin out. He found himself on a broad path. No branches reached across the path, and it was clearly a path used by many, without obstructions. He started left on the path, carefully marking the point where he had emerged from the scrub.

Several minutes later, little covered pyramid-like structures, huts, popped up. It was an Indian village. The settlement was in a cleared section of the forest. He could not know that his every step and movement had been observed by uncertain eyes since he stepped out of the scrub. The members of the Tonga tribe working their fields had already learned from scouts of the arrival of the stranger. The whole tribe curiously gave their attention to the youth who had stepped from among the trees in such a weather-beaten condition, leading a llama loaded with carrying packs. Even greater was their surprise when the tribal chief recognized the llama ambling peacefully behind the boy as his own. Of course, William had no idea of any of this.

Stepping out of his tent, tribal chief Kaiva came and stood in front of the boy. His men obediently opened a way for him. With a few steps, the chief came to a stop in front of him, and looked at him with close attention. William pulled himself up to his full height and looked openly into his eyes. The stern gaze of Kaiva then softened and he raised his arm in greeting. The boy returned the gesture. The chief then spoke a couple of words. Several women hurried towards the huts to bring some food. At a gesture from the chief, they put the food they had brought at William's feet. William bowed in thanks at the hospitable gesture. He had nothing with him that he could give in return as a gift, so he put down his weapons before the tribal chief.

Kaiva took up the bow and looked at its construction with great interest. Then, smiling, he gave it back to the boy.

The tribal leader wanted to know what had brought the young hunter alone across such wild country. With gestures, they tried to communicate with one another by making drawings in the dirt. William soon began to see, however, that he was unable to explain his real goal. At this point, he stepped over to a girl, took her by the arm and pulled her in front of the chief, who waited to see what was going to happen next. William tried to mime high fever, putting his hand many times to the girl's brow. The chief nodded understandingly and then brought his brows together in a frown. Finally, he gestured with empty upturned hands to show that he did not understand what William wanted of him. William's world collapsed. At this moment, a combination of exhaustion and bitterness at his wasted journey came together and he collapsed on his knees in front of the chief. Kaiva took the exhausted boy into his own tent to rest from the exertion of his journey. Outside, Kaiva's adviser came over to him. He whispered several words in his ear, and the chief's face gradually cleared. He barked out a few words and at once his men got up and hurried down a bend in the forest path.

This had happened the summer of the previous year. One morning, out on a hunt, hunters of the tribe found a young man in the forest. The unconscious man had no weapons. Although a gun lay next to him, the Indians did not know what it was for, and left it there in the brush. They brought the stranger with them to the village. After several weeks, realizing he had nowhere to go, the hospitable tribe took him in. Now he lived with them, and the chief's adviser had just thought that perhaps he could understand the new arrival. When

Davis Franklin knew that a countryman of his had come, he ran back to the village at once, with several companions. He arrived around midnight and woke William. Davis spoke to him in English and to his shock, the boy replied in a pure Yorkshire accent.

Franklin had learned to speak the Tonga language reasonably well the year before. As interpreter, he was able to explain the reason William had come. The Indians diagnosed the girl at once as having malaria. This terrible illness was spread by mosquitoes mainly in the rainy season, and the Indians living here suffered from it greatly. They cooked several types of plants with which they could cure themselves of it. But they also knew that the best cure was much better than these. The best treatment for malaria was quinine! When Kaiva understood that William's woman had malaria and that he had left her on her sickbed in a cave several miles distant, he collected his men together at once, and gathering their torches, they set out on the road to find Susannah.

The muscular heroes of the tribe took turns cutting a path before them through the thick foliage, so that the bigger group could easily move forward. They took with them herbal infusions, lots of honey, milk, meat and fruit for the little sufferer. William was so worried about Susannah that he felt his heart might break for yearning. He did not know what state they would find the girl in. The deadly fever might have wrought fatal damage in the meantime.

The boy felt that their journey was taking forever. Davis went with him, hardly able to keep up with the boy who in his despair had superhuman strength. Davis, with fascination, nagged William with questions about what had brought him to this land. Although the boy was hardly in the mood to answer, he told of his adventures, sufferings and strivings so far. William's words struck Franklin to the heart. But something would not leave him alone.

"But tell me, what was the name of the land you come from?"

"New Holland."

"But what took you there?"

"I don't know... I was born there," the boy answered sadly. Davis listened. He saw how much the uncovering of the past was painful for William. At sunrise, they reached the outcrop of rock where the boy had climbed earlier and spotted the smoke in the distance. From here, the road led through easier territory and they moved faster. William looked around a little proudly at the little army he had brought back with him to the girl.

When at last the familiar rocks of the cave came in view, he ran in front. Hurriedly, he threw aside the obstructions at the cave entrance and rushed in. With a desperate look, he took in the results of yesterday evening's fever. In her delirium, Susannah had thrown her bedding off and rolled onto the rough floor. She had knocked over the wooden water container. She lay there unconscious, but alive! Her pallid, hollow face bore the deep imprint of the destructive illness. William leaned over her in silence. Holding her in his arms, he lay her back carefully on the bed. He rearranged her sleeping place, then took the quinine from the hand of the arriving Kaiva and carefully gave her a dose. There were still a few sips of water in the water container. He used this to give her the life-saving medicine. The water brought Susannah around, but the bitter quinine made her grimace. She gazed lifelessly at the boy with unrecognizing eyes. William's face was streaming with tears, and he held the girl desperately to him.

Anxiously, he scanned her face. The girl's mouth moved, as if she wanted to say something, then her head fell forward. "She's dead!" shouted William in complete anguish, but Davis, kneeling beside him, soothingly grasped his hand. "It will be all right. The quinine will do her good. She will live, you'll see." The words were some relief to the boy's despair. But he would not move from the girl's side. Again and again he looked at her agonized little face, which always used to smile at him so cheerily. Now there was, at least, still life in her. Davis again quietly spoke to him.

"Come, let the girl sleep." With this, he stood and left the cave.

Outside, the Indians curiously waited for developments. Davis reassured them that they had arrived in time. Chief Kaiva called William to his side, and spoke to him through the interpreter.

"The white hunter now has no need of me. I go back to my village. I leave four warriors here to help you both with meat and fruit while the little flower recovers. The gates of my village are open to you. I will build a separate house for you. If it is good for you, you can become members of my tribe." The noble offer from the good-hearted Kaiva astonished William.

Bowing in thanks, he said: "I thank the mighty chief for all your help so far. You have saved someone who is more valuable to me than my own life. You offer us a home, which shows your deep kindness. But I cannot make this big decision today without talking to my companion." Davis faithfully translated every word. Chief Kaiva listened, then bade farewell.

"Let it be as you wish, white hunter! I await your answer."

Taking their belongings, they bade farewell to each other. Within moments, the forest swallowed Kaiva and his men. As the first task, William went for fresh water. The four natives went off to hunt. Davis stayed alone beside the girl. Coming back, William went straight to Susannah. He moistened a piece of cloth and wiped the girl's face. Then he took her weak, dainty hands between his palms and stroked them gently. Susannah slept peacefully. It was easy to see how much the disease had taken out of her. Malaria is a fast-developing illness, lasting from three to six days. The climax is the most dangerous, generally when the fever reaches its highest pitch. With an already weakened constitution, it can be fatal. Davis sat wordlessly beside the boy and watched his anxious fussing.

When the hunters came back, they started a fire and cooked the meat. They all ate hungrily, having been on the march all day with no time to eat anything earlier. Stomachs full, they lay down wearily before the cave. Susannah didn't eat anything this evening either. William took great trouble to make sure that she had at least her quinine and some water. Only for a few moments did the girl come to her senses, then again fell back into a stupefied fever. William had another night of stress. Sometimes the girl called out in her sleep, and repeated her parents' names in the darkness. And sometimes she stared in front of her with half-open eyes, while her body swam with sweat. The superstitious Indians sometimes looked in nervously at the girl, surely at the mercy of the fever demon, which they believed had superhuman strength. William whispered soothing words to the girl the whole time, and lay her back down. He covered her carefully again and again. In the early morning, everything was quiet. Davis suggested they try to rest. He reminded the boy that this was still not the climax, the real crisis. Probably the next night would be the most difficult. Until then, they slid into deep sleep. Outside it clouded over and rain began to fall again. The monotonous sound was even better at lulling the tired people in their sleep. The day was spent in uneventful waiting. William was overjoyed when once in the afternoon Susannah opened her eyes and could take a little food at last.

"Do you feel better, Susie?" The boy managed to smile at the girl, who looked as if she had recently returned from the grave.

"Yes, I'm absolutely fine now!" came her weakened voice.

"Where were you yesterday?"

"I went to bring help."

"And did you find any?"

"Yes. I chanced on an Indian village. I got quinine from them. That's the miracle cure that's going to make you better!"

"It's bitter!" The girl wrinkled her nose. "Of course, but you see, it'll do you good."

"The Indians are here?"

"Four hunters and an interpreter."

"Willy!"

"Yes?"

"I'll never forget you..."

"What?"

"That... that you saved my life!" the girl whispered with tearful eyes. William stroked her face.

"I couldn't live without you!" he said. "Oh, you're so sweet, Willy! And I couldn't begin to live without you, however I tried!"

"What would you do?"

"I'd die!" Susannah clung to the boy's neck. "I feel so strange. As if I've been lying here for weeks. It will be so good to be on my feet again. To breathe fresh air under an open sky... but... I don't have the strength to stand."

"And I wouldn't let you get up. You must rest! Tonight comes the worst part of the fever. By tomorrow we'll just laugh at the whole thing."

"Don't leave me alone! I'm afraid! I had such horrible dreams... I saw death approaching!"

"Don't talk nonsense. There's nothing to be afraid of. I will be here beside you. I won't move from your side even for a moment."

"Oh, thank goodness."

William tried to feed the girl several bites. He made small pieces so that the girl could eat more easily. The patient ate a little but with no appetite. Still, she forced down the food, knowing that soon she would need all her remaining strength to last through the renewed fever. But soon she pushed away the boy's hand offering more food.

"I can't eat any more!" William made her drink some honeyed tea, which the girl gulped down thirstily, lying back on her bed afterwards. The boy spoke encouragingly to her.

"When you wake up, I will be here beside you. Now try to sleep, and conserve your strength!"

Susannah languidly did as she was told.

Outside, the night came. The girl slept peacefully for a while. Then the fever seized her again. Her whole body began to shake. Again William covered her body to try to keep her warm. Soon the girl's face began to burn. Her body was drenched in sweat. Desperately she tried to get up, but each time the boy laid her back in bed and covered her again. William changed the cooling cloth every minute. The girl's condition became ever worse. She raved, and many times tried to escape from something or someone. Perhaps death was beckoning to her? At these moments, the presence of the watchful Davis was helpful. The boy began to lose hope in his heart as time passed. Towards midnight, Susannah relaxed in sheer exhaustion, and fell into a deep sleep.

"Now I'm sure she will live," said Davis reassuringly.

"The full fever won't come back. We can go to sleep now." Davis recommended the appealing idea of rest, but the boy refused. Again, he gazed on Susannah.

"I will still watch over her. She might wake up and need something from me."

Davis shrugged and went to a free space in the cave to sleep. William remained awake around all the sleepers, and stayed alone with his thoughts. He mulled over how their destinies would continue. He felt it would be wise to take the offer from the tribal chief. They could build a home of their own in the village if they could stay there. Many good things could follow if they decided to do this. They would not be alone and solitary. Whatever help they needed would come from the good-hearted Indians. They could spare themselves the dangers and deprivations of further uncertain wandering. What was most important, they would have found a home.

Slowly, weariness sapped his strength. His eyelids began to droop and close more often. He nodded and then his head dropped. He fell on the edge of Susannah's bed and dropped into a deep sleep.

Early in the morning, the movement of the Indians woke him. He looked at the girl immediately. Susannah was still deeply asleep, which was a sure sign of improvement.

Just as Kaiva had said, the girl was given quinine for several more days lest she relapse, with William waking her and giving her the next dose. Susannah's eyes had improved visibly, but she was still too weak to get up. William pleaded with her to eat some food, though she still said she had no appetite.

"Are you better?"

"Yes, I just feel very weak."

"You're not tired? Do you want to sleep?"

"No!" came the objection. "I've slept enough in the last few days. What's going on in your head, Willy? I feel that you want to say something important," said the girl slyly. William smiled. He couldn't keep any secrets from Susannah!

"If you want, I'll tell you what happened while you were ill." Susannah nodded with keen curiosity.

William started the story. When he got to the part where he explained that one of the members of the Indian tribe was a white man, Susannah's eyes flashed.

"Who?"

"It is I, young lady." Suddenly entering the cave, Davis spoke, catching the end of her remark. He stepped over to the girl.

"Allow me to introduce myself, young lady. I am Davis Franklin."

"Susannah Gredford." the girl extended a hand of greeting. To her amazement, Davis kissed her hand. Speechless, she reddened and took refuge at William's side. Franklin chuckled.

"I see, young lady, that you are not used to English manners. But here -" his voice became a little sadder for a moment "- they are not necessary. Please excuse me for bursting in on you both." With that he retreated, bowing.

"Please don't go!" cried Susannah. "William wanted to tell me something important, and I do believe it concerns you."

Davis looked questioningly at William. The boy thought hard for a few moments, then answered.

"The Tonga tribe's hospitality towards us is so great that Kaiva has offered us a home! He suggested we move to the Indian village and live with them."

"So that's what it is!" cried Susannah in surprise. For several minutes William and Davis looked at her, but could read nothing in her face. A deep silence fell, and then after a short time she looked up.

"I will follow you, William, wherever you wish! What is good for you is good for me!"

"Thank you! It's my belief that with the community we grew up in, and that which is now open to us... that there we should continue our lives. Because of this, I believe the best thing we can do is move to the village. I hope we won't be a burden to them."

Davis joyfully hugged the boy.

"You are wise, lad. I know you won't regret your decision."

The busy Indians came in side when they heard the rejoicing. Davis, speaking the Tongan language, explained to the four men how things stood. Their bronzed faces were visibly gladdened by the news. They quizzed Davis on when William and Susannah planned to start back. Franklin conveyed their question.

"It will have to be at least two days before Susannah can stand the journey. Before that, we cannot go!"

The answer dampened their moods a little, since they wanted to be back with their families. Their voices conveyed uneasiness. Then William suggested that they turn back home, and he would follow with Susannah several days later.

Davis did not endorse this. He knew Kaiva, the leader, who would just send the men back. They would have to wait here. The hunters understood Davis's difficulty and stayed silent.

The next morning Susannah was able to make her first effort to get up. With William's help, she stood up. Supporting herself around his neck, she walked into the open. The girl was still very weak. If it had been up to William, they would have waited two weeks before attempting a journey. But the Indians probably could not understand this, and wanted to be back home. Outside, Susannah could breathe some fresh air. She felt it had been an eternity that she had been ill. Gradually, however, the strength returned to her limbs during her walk. When she was tired, they returned to the cave. During this time, the Indians had prepared breakfast. Cooked meat and fruit awaited the hungry company. Only Susannah, still with no appetite, nibbled like a bird.

With nothing else to do this morning, they began packing. Their hearts were a little pained that they were leaving their solid home here which had seen them through so many vicissitudes. The morning preparations did not require a great deal of work. The saddles were prepared for the journey. Susannah pleaded to William while they saddled the two llamas, so they rode out a short distance into the woods. A huge herd of llamas grazing there looked at them curiously. These were wild creatures, and perhaps it puzzled them that their fellow llamas carried strange beings on their backs. Then a loud noise sounded and with a clattering of hooves, the animals disappeared into the thickets. The young couple went further and found that a massive old tree had fallen. They got off and rested for a while. The forest was deathly quiet, not even a bird singing. With this cloudy weather, it seemed that not a single one was in the mood to sing. Looking up, they could see that the sky was turning lead grey. William turned back without hesitation, anxious that Susannah might get soaked if it rained.

Within half an hour, they were back at the cave. At the very end, just as they had almost reached home, the first drops started to come down. After this, it started to pour without a break. Inside, Davis and the Indians sat around the fire. They made a place for William and Susannah so they could dry off. William took a jaguar skin and spread it out. The girl thanked him for his thoughtfulness, and wrapped up in the warm skin. Then, because of the language difference, a rather one-sided conversation took place. William said that if it was not raining in the morning, they could start moving.

After sunset they soon turned in to rest, staying close to the fire, which the Indians took in turns to keep burning all night. The rain did not last the whole night, having completely drenched the surrounding area. In the morning, there was a break in the cloud cover, and at last the sun with its twinkling rays began to revive the dampened wilderness. With the first rays of the sun, our heroes were on their feet. They packed up the animals and started at once, because the Tongans wanted to be back at their camp.

In the depths of the rain forest, clouds of mist wreathed them, dimming the light under the foliage. The lively Davis pressed on, with two Indians at his side. They cleared a passable path of obstructing vegetation before the loaded pack animals. They didn't stop even when they were hungry, but ate bites as they moved.

In the afternoon, they came upon the path leading to the Tonga village. Davis sent an Indian ahead to let the chief know of their arrival.

This was unnecessary, however, because the scouts had spotted them and told Kaiva several minutes before. Tongan observers watching from the heights had known of their imminent arrival from several miles away, and had hurried with the news to the village. There, everyone was excited immediately. The chief sent out orders for a house to be built. He wanted to build the finest hut for his guests, prepared by skilled hands, and most of this had already been done some hours before. Kaiva put on festive clothing, and set out to receive the young couple. His son Kind escorted Kaiva. The chief's son met William today for the first time. Kaiva had warned his son not to gaze lecherously on the white beauty or he would face his father's anger. Kind could see with his own eyes what his father's words had meant. William and the exquisite Susannah belonged together and if it had come into any man's mind to lust after the girl for himself, it was now erased from his memory. They simply did everything they could for the white-skinned beauty. And everyone adored her. Upon being introduced, they touched her hand as if touching the hand of a goddess who could protect them from every evil.

In the moments after the joyful meeting, Kaiva sent orders for a procession into the village. Susannah and William were very moved by the hearty reception. They could see Davis's words were true when he said, "You will not regret your decision!"

On the outskirts of the settlement, they met the first women and children coming out. With great celebrations, they arrived at the main square before the chief's tent. A short time later, fires were burning, and the women were preparing a celebratory lunch. Kaiva moved the young couple into his own tent while their own house was being finished. Then Susannah was able to sleep after the exertion of the journey, while William walked around the village. Everywhere he turned, he met friendly faces. Cheerful shouts and waves were all around. At the other end of the village, in a small clearing, their house was being readied. The Tongans clearly did not like high-density living. Between all the huts was a clear grassy space. The frame of their house stood ready and soon the roofing and walling would start. William and Susannah looked at each other happily. Perhaps they were now, at last, soundly blessed. They would have a life without struggles, with much joy and happiness.

They looked forward to the quick completion of the house. Lunch had been prepared in the meantime, and runners came to fetch the two young people. They took them by the hand and brought them back to the main square. Kaiva was already sitting before the place settings for the feast. Kind, his son, sat at his left. Beside him sat Davis. To his right were his Tongan relatives. The celebratory feast was not ostentatiously overloaded with food. But its simplicity, and the fact that the residents of the village had put out everything they had, won the hearts and esteem of William and Susannah.

After eating, drumming and an irresistible dance began. At the table of the chief, special intoxicating drinks were served. Susannah and William accepted out of obligation and gratitude, but only drank moderately. Davis introduced his Indian wife, a gentle-looking and sweet-natured young woman. They had no children yet.

The celebrations lasted until late afternoon. Then Kaiva officially announced the arrival of the new Tongan tribe members. The residents of the village cried out joyfully at the news. Davis dutifully interpreted Kaiva's ceremonial words. When the speech was over, the whole village started out to have a look at the new house. Before the door, the chief stopped and gestured with his hand. Davis interpreted as he summoned the young couple to take possession of their new home. And on top of it all, inside they found gifts, showing the village's humble goodwill.

William said several words of thanks in both their names, then expressed their intention to serve the good of the village with all their might.

Inside, they looked at the presents piled high, which were mainly items of furniture and useful utensils. The walls were decorated with the skins of various predators. In the middle stood a weapon holder. Inside there was a completely new spear, a skillfully carved and decorated bow, and arrows in quivers to go with it. Next to it laid a shield decorated with the symbols of the tribe: a rising sun, and a crossed bow and spear. There were also clay dishes, mugs, and every kind of food and drink. At the back of the hut was a big hammock, also decorated with skins. Beside the bed was a fireplace. For smoke fumes, there was a hole in the roof that could be closed in case of rain. Everything was wonderful here. From one moment to the next, their dreams had become reality.

Because it was a little chilly, William went behind the hut, where helpful hands had piled a stack of firewood. Soon a cheerfully crackling fire was burning and they could embrace each other beside it. Touched, Susannah looked around. "I'm so happy here with you!"

"We'll be safe here, you'll see! Get well as soon as you can, and tomorrow we are Tongans!" William said cheerfully.

"That sounds wonderful, my knight!" said Susannah, stroking the boy's side.

"But young lady! In keeping with English etiquette, you can't lay a finger on the pantry goods. The diet is strict. Only bitter herbal tea, and a dose of quinine!" laughed the boy.

"Promise me you won't make me take any more quinine, and then you can kiss me!" teased the girl in return.

"But my dear! In your condition?" Susannah pressed her mouth to the boy's, and they kissed, and kissed.

Outside the sky turned to night, and the moonlight caressed their new home. From outside, tinkling laughter and whispered loving words could have been heard in the hut, but the moon was unconcerned. It glided higher in the night sky, and its silver light glittered on the descending drops of dew.

Almost The End

Forcing themselves out of the tempting softness of the bed, they left the hut and went in the direction of a small stream. The morning was chilly, so they washed themselves quickly, then raced back to the warm embrace of their little home. On the way back they met some Tongans, and cheery greetings were exchanged. They reached home shivering, but with powerful appetites. They had a wide range of things to eat, because the hunting had gone well. After a simple but filling breakfast, William thought they should go to the chief's tent to see if there were any tasks or responsibilities they should perform on behalf of the tribe. By now, the village was up and about. Many men had enormous bows on their shoulders, meaning that they were going to start on a hunt soon. Arriving in front of the chief's tent, they looked around for Davis. He was three huts further along, where he walked out the door and gave a friendly wave. He was loaded with weapons as well.

"Good morning, Davis! Can you give us some help? We'd like to have a word with Chief Kaiva," said William.

"There's going to be a big hunt. Kaiva already asked me to let you know."

They stood in front of the tent and Davis asked permission for them to enter. Kaiva received them at once. With a beaming face, he invited William on the hunt. They boy happily accepted the invitation. But Susannah wasn't enthusiastic about the idea.

"Don't go!" she whispered to the boy. "I'm afraid!"

"I must go! Otherwise, they might believe that we only want to be by ourselves. I must do my part for the work of the tribe. Just go back home and get something ready to eat for when I get back."

"All right, darling!" They shared a farewell kiss. William sent Susannah home with a reassuring wink, and took his place among the hunters.

Susannah went home. All day she cooked, cleaned and mended, never noticing how quickly the time passed. Sometimes she could hear the cries of children playing outside. She began to think how good it would be for her to have children too. After all, she was already sixteen. She daydreamed a little, lying on the bed. Several minutes later, sleep overcame her.

She had no way of knowing how long she had slept. The first thing she seemed to hear was a sharp roaring sound. The sounds came from outside and were coming closer. By now she knew, through a fog of sleep, that she had to wake up. She opened her eyes. It was dark in the hut, and she could hear rain drumming on the roof again.

"William!" The boy suddenly came to her mind. "He's not home yet!" She jumped up and ran from the house. From a distance, she saw running figures with burning torches. Someone was being carried on a stretcher. With an anxious heart, she hurried towards the lights.

In front of Kaiva's tent, a large crowd swarmed in the pouring rain. Inside the tent not William, but Kind, lay on a wide bed. He was bleeding from several hideous wounds, and his left forearm was missing. Around him, attendants tried to stop the bleeding at the stump. By now, the young man's life was in the balance after losing so much blood.

One young woman tried to make the half-dead patient drink some herbal tea. Susannah frantically ran through the crowd looking for William. Glimpsing him, she cried out with joy and rushed over. The boy had a few injuries, but luckily his wounds were far less severe than those of Kind.

The horrible tension locked inside Susannah burst out, and horrified at what she had seen, she fell into the boy's arms sobbing. Seeing the girl's state, Davis Franklin sent the two of them home with no further delay. He asked them to come back in the morning, because the chief wanted to see them. The boy nodded, and left the tent with the girl clinging to him tightly.

They plodded home mutely in the rain. At home, William spoke first. He called the girl to his side and wiped the tears from her face.

"It all started so well....We set off in the direction of the hills. Kind wanted to win the heart of his future wife with a leopard skin. Four hunters were constantly going ahead to signal if any game worth catching should show up nearby. On several occasions, we were able to surprise whole herds of animals, and bagged a good many of them. We had enough in the bag by early afternoon to turn back quite happily. But Kind didn't want to return without a leopard skin. He was an experienced hunter, but if there was any suggestion of a big predator, he went ahead for the kill. He didn't let anyone go with him to help."

"By now, it was late afternoon. We would have liked to turn back. And then, at that point, his luck ran out."

"What turned out to be a huge female leopard appeared a few hundred yards off. Again, Kind set off alone."

"We were skinning the animals we had already caught, and finished getting them ready to bring back. We were sure he would succeed... But several minutes later, we heard a horrible scream. It was a human voice."

"I was the closest to the forest into which Kind had gone. Without a second's pause, I sprinted into the bush towards the sound of the screaming. In a clearing, I laid eyes on a terrible sight. Kind was lying on the ground..."

"After successfully killing and laying out the game, he was skinning the animal in complete peace when the animal's partner appeared and jumped upon him from behind. Kind had no time even to use his knife. The massive male knocked him down and started to maul him in a wild rage. That was when I got there... I knew I could only save his life if I could draw the animal's attention away from him to myself. I shot an arrow, but my aim was bad, and I only wounded it. But I managed to do what I'd wanted. The beast turned in my direction and threw itself at me. I finished it off with my knife. Quickly, the other hunters arrived too, and rushed to help Kind. He lost a lot of blood, but his life was saved."

Susannah listened to the account with her eyes wide. Now she stood and hurried over to the water container. Wetting a piece of cloth, she went to the boy to clean his wounds. She bound the cuts carefully, then stoked the fire and heated the food. They sat together and ate in silence.

After dinner, William heaped praise upon the girl, saying how invitingly decorated their home was, obviously the result of dedicated work. But Susannah turned her head away, upset.

"What's wrong, Susie?"

"I let you out of my sight once, and immediately you're in trouble!"

"But I didn't get into any trouble!" countered the boy.

"It wouldn't have taken much for you to be lying beside Kind!"

"Are you angry with me because I helped Kind?"

"There were others there, not just you!" said the girl defiantly. "Don't you understand? We are both together, and we will be after this too! It can't change anything that we've moved in here with the tribe. What is going to happen to me if you're always looking for danger and one day you don't come back?"

Listening, William took the girl's outburst thoughtfully. Now he understood everything. Susannah had the same dread as when he had left for several days during her illness. She would be alone if her companion died. But what could he do? Danger could take them by surprise from anywhere. He could hardly spend the whole day hiding behind her skirts.

"I promise that from now on I'll take better care of myself. There won't be any trouble."

Susannah didn't answer. William could see that they needed to sleep after the day's events, and perhaps tomorrow it would all seem far away.

They dried themselves in front of the crackling flames of the fire, and then went to bed. They talked quietly for a few moments, and the chilly mood between them began to evaporate. They fell asleep wrapped in each other's arms. William was right. They really did need to sleep after the day's events.

A long sequence of truly peaceful days followed. There was perfect harmony between them. Weeks went by before something happened that once more disrupted their lives. Destiny targeted them again. A newer test awaited them, a new demand for a sacrifice.

Susannah woke each day and gave their Indian friends whatever help they required. Truly, the Indians needed the two youngsters as much as the two needed this wonderful, harmonious community.

One day Chief Kaiva received word that Moguvan warriors had crossed the border of the two tribes' hunting territories. There had been an often deadly rivalry with the Moguva tribe for a long time. Two years before, they had attacked the Tongans, but the Tongans had struck back and almost completely destroyed the other tribe's fighting force. Now they were allied against the Tongans with another tribe desirous of new territories, the Konva. With no declaration of war, the attack had come.

The Tongan village was electrified by news of the danger. There was a need for every man who could carry a weapon, in a fight against a group reported to be three times their size.

Chief Kaiva summoned William. By now, the boy understood the basics of the language, and for several weeks they had both been trying diligently to get to know the inhabitants of the village. William answered the chief's summons at once. By now, Kaiva had grown fond of the quick-witted lad. Of course, this was especially true since William had saved the life of his son Kind. Privately, he was a little troubled by why such an excellent young man could not be found within his tribe. He was even thinking of bequeathing his leadership to William. Kind, now much less able after his accident, could hardly lead the tribe after Kaiva's death.

But according to tribal law, a foreigner could not fill the top post in the village. Despite this, Kaiva secretly hoped that if the boy continued to show such sharpness and prowess, the villagers might choose him as their leader one day. He would not stand in the way of their decision, and could pass his chiefdom on to the worthy young leader.

William saw that worry was lining the chief's face. Kaiva didn't beat around the bush, and told William why he had summoned him.

"My Tongan subject, whom I accepted into my village as a guest, is satisfied with all that my people have offered him?" He raised his voice and looked deeply into the boy's eyes.

The question surprised William, but he answered in a calm voice.

"Yes, Chief Kaiva. We are happy with everything."

"Enemy tribes have trespassed on ancient Tongan land. Soon blood will cover the soil of our home. Our hospitality compels us -" and again he looked searchingly into the boy's eyes "- to instruct you that this war is not your war. If you wish, you may leave with the 'Flower of the Forest' and make a new home in peace elsewhere. If this mood of war among our enemies subsides, and I am again able to favor you with my former hospitality, you are welcome to return to my village."

William was at a loss for words.

"Now go and decide your future. Fight to the death with us, or leave this place."

With that, Kaiva gestured for the boy to go.

William left the chief's tent with his head bowed. Immediately, he hurried home. Once again, their peaceful life had been shattered! And the spring had covered the ground with such bright flowers. Yet the thunderclouds were gathering over their heads again.

Plagued with worry, he returned to their home, which they had made so beautiful during the season just past.

He found Susannah in the middle of cooking a meal. The maiden could sense grave trouble from the boy just entering. She went pale and her gaze fixed on his face. She wanted to hear the news as soon as possible.

"Susannah, the Tongans are getting ready for war. Tribes seeking power will attack our village soon, and everything here may be destroyed."

Susannah stared as she heard the horrifying news. For a moment, she couldn't bear to speak. William quietly related the alternative they had been offered. At the news that they would again be consigned to the dangers of the unknown, tears overcame her.

William furrowed his forehead and racked his brains. The irreversible decision took several long minutes to crystallize inside him. They could not abandon the Tongans! They must take part in their war. Honour would not allow them to turn tail like a pair of dogs. They would stay!

"Susannah, you know, this is our home now, and if we stay here we will be stronger."

The girl lifted her gaze to the boy. She knew William was right. Wordlessly she nodded, and in her eyes, determination now burned.

"We'll stay!" answered the girl. William pulled her to him passionately, and tenderly kissed her. With this, they sealed their decision.

They went at once to Kaiva, and told him of their decision. The sad face of the old chief broke into a smile at the sight of the two fine youngsters. He felt he could trust them to the death. He put thirty men under William's leadership. William's face lit up and he bowed his head at the honor of being entrusted with such a position.

Kaiva signaled his decision with his staff, and then William waited in front of the tent for further orders. The chief soon appeared in full battle gear. Everyone there knew just how much depended on the wise leadership of Kaiva. Their entire existence, the very survival of their nation, was now in danger.

Kaiva gave further orders, and not in his usual florid language. He planned to lead some of his men into the dense forest and into the trees. From there, they could attack the enemy with showers of arrows.

Another group was to act as a decoy and head off the main troops of the Moguva and Konva so that the main battle would not be in the village, thus not endangering the lives of the children, women, and old men unable to fight.

A third group was to attack the enemy from behind. The fourth group - the leadership of which was entrusted to William - was to destroy the rear guard of the enemy, which had set up camp on the border of the Tongan territory, where, if this attack plan succeeded, they would capture the chiefs of the two tribes. Kaiva put the greatest emphasis on this last plan. It could hardly be believed that the leaders of the other two groups would be victorious in the face of such overwhelming odds. But if the chiefs of the two allied tribes could be taken captive, and their warriors left without leadership, the Tongans might manage a victory. He knew well that an army without a leader was not difficult to outmaneuver. But for this exceptional and difficult plan, it was vital that William's talent and intelligence attempt the impossible with just a handful of men. Perhaps the future of this entire tribe would be in his hands.

William went out to select his thirty men from among the ranked warriors. Several he had already come to know well in the time since they had moved into the village. These men knew already the kind of abilities he had, and confidently consigned themselves to his leadership.

William went off with his men, and they had a brief war council. Several of them had brought strong rope good for lassos. They performed the quiet work needed to make them ready.

Soon, they set out towards a little valley where the Tongan scouts thought the leaders of the two enemy tribes were to be found. William sent two scouts ahead to locate the enemy.

A few short minutes later, the warriors ran back. The enemy approached. One of the scouts had torn off a tree branch, and put it in William's hand.

"The enemy number as many as the leaves on this branch!"

The boy knew at a glance that this meant they could be more than a hundred.

"Up in the trees!" he ordered his men. The tree-climbing took only a few moments, for the Tongans could climb trees with the skill of monkeys.

Quiet filled the forest. Even the birds went silent, as if waiting for everything to begin.

Shortly, the first of the enemy warriors appeared. They crept along, painted in black and red. It was visible from afar that they had not undertaken this journey happily.

They knew the fierce opposition they would receive from the Tongans. Maybe they only felt safe in large groups.

Slowly, in a long line, they proceeded below the Tongans quietly clinging to the trees above their heads. The cracking of a single branch would have been enough to have the multitude rush upon them.

William counted one hundred and thirty of them. When the enemy had moved out of earshot, they climbed hurriedly from the trees, and William ordered them to continue the journey. Keeping their bows ready to shoot, they stole along further. They were ready to enter into battle at any moment. Nerve-racking moments followed. The rainforest was so quiet that it seemed to be listening. It was as if each inhabitant of the forest knew that soon, bloody battles would break the silence. Even the birds huddled together mutely. They looked down curiously upon the forms of a handful of determined men. The monkeys nervously escaped to more distant trees, shrieking above them with undignified, piercing cries. Sometimes they threw one or two of the harder fruits at them, with mixed success in hitting their targets. The warriors ignored the angry monkeys. Their attention was fixed on something more important.

From the Tongan village, hundreds and hundreds of throats broke into screams of battle as the village was overrun.

William's heart tightened with thoughts of Susannah. He tried to brush his anxiety away. However, he had no chance to dwell upon it, because his scouts had again caught sight of the enemy.

"Two Moguvan guards are standing at the edge of the clearing. We couldn't get around them because of the rocks." said an old Indian, Menda. William stayed calm, because two hundred men might have been in their way instead.

"We'll take them out," stated the boy curtly. "Two warriors, come with me! The others, go with Goko and encircle the camp. Comb the area in case other dangers threaten us. We three will put an end to the guards."

"Right away, Chief William!" Goko answered cheerfully, as if he were setting out on a small hunting expedition. William smiled at the respectful address of "Chief". Then, with a clear signal, sent his men off. The three remaining men then started their dangerous task. In complete silence, they began to creep towards the guards. The wilderness swallowed up Goko and his men.

The two unsuspecting guards were quietly waiting at the edge of the forest. They did not notice the skulking forms nearby. Slightly louder whispering emerged from the foliage, and the two lassos flew out on their mission of death. The two loops tightened around the enemy's necks simultaneously, and with some powerful tugs they lay in the long grass. In a moment, the three were standing beside the two dead guards. Both stared at nothing. Their faces were frozen in expressions of horror. They had reached the ends of their lives. They were dead, and wherever their souls had gone, they now belonged to the skies.

The success of this small military skirmish encouraged them. They had only gone a few paces from the dead bodies when unexpected battle sounds reached them. Before their astonished eyes, Moguvan and Konvan warriors came into the clearing. With their bows, they loosed a shower of arrows on Goko's equally surprised men, who had been discovered by a guard watching from above. He alerted his comrades at once, a team of around a hundred who were waiting nearby. Within moments, their situation was transformed. William's hopeful mood sank, and when a spear slammed into a tree right next to him, disappeared completely.

Goko's smile with which he had set out on the manhunt began to fade. They fought bitterly against a tribe three times their strength. They knew they would not be able to hold out for long. But it was better to go down fighting than under torture from the two barbarian tribes. The battle was short. Although the Tongans fought like leopards protecting their cubs, they were overwhelmed. They killed forty of the enemy, but only twenty of the thirty Tongans were still alive. Among these, two were seriously injured and three more slightly wounded.

And now they lay next to each other, tied with rope. The thought that they would die soon completely shattered their rock-hard characters. They awaited death, and worried that their families might suffer a much worse fate.

William, miraculously, had escaped captivity. He killed two Konvas in battle. And when he no longer had his knife, he used his hands as weapons against his enemies. In the struggle, he chased two opponents onto a large boulder, and when he saw that his companions were all lying on the ground, he seized his opponents and threw them, with himself, off the edge. With a cracking of branches and death screams, then a dull thud, his head hit the ground and he lost consciousness.

The sun set in the thick of the forest, and the veil of night covered the aftermath of the bloody fight. William opened his eyes. Quiet reigned everywhere. He slowly groped around him. A man lay not far from him, dead. A little further, another body lay motionless. He felt his head and found a large lump. Now he remembered what had happened.

"Susannah!" The name jolted him painfully. "What happened to her? Was she still alive? Perhaps she was dying right now and he could not be beside her!" These thoughts pierced his mind like burning arrowheads. He knew he had to leave at once. He jumped up, and tried to find his bearings. Then the thick darkness swallowed up his form.

His companions were still alive, tied tightly with cords, quietly exchanging one or two words between them. Goko was still alive, though he was one of the seriously injured. A spear had pierced his thigh, and when he had broken it off, the point stayed in his leg. The young Tongan was enduring hideous pain. But still, he could keep himself together. For the first time, he realized that William was neither among the dead nor the captives.

"Where is Chief William?"

"I have not seen him since the battle," said his companion, Moloka, lying next to him. Quickly, it became clear that among the survivors, no one had seen William for a while.

"Is he dead, too?" Goko whispered sadly to his comrade.

"No! He cannot have died. I have not seen him laying with the dead or with the wounded." answered Moloka.

"He is very clever and bold! You'll see, he will bring help, and free us." said Goko trustingly, twisting his face against the continued pain.

"Help? From where? Truly, we cannot win against such a strong enemy. Only a few of them can have survived. Those who have survived the slaughter will be tied up like us!"

So said Damoa, who was lying a little further away, and had heard the conversation. His companions said nothing. But deep in their hearts, one last spark of hope still glowed. The fantastically capable young man would, perhaps, work some kind of miracle, even in their desperate situation.

Meanwhile, William had reached the edge of the Tongan village. The acrid smell of smoke reached his nose. The settlement was completely devastated, with huts still burning in several places. The Konvan and Moguvan warriors were still gathering captives and looting the village. Their huge number alarmed the boy, especially now that he was so close. Quickly, he saw that he was probably the only free one left. He must do something, but what? Under the cover of night, he could accomplish nothing. He would have to wait until sunrise and then start looking for Susannah. He saw that only a miracle could save the Tongans.

Sleeplessly, he held vigil through the rest of the night. When the eastern sky contained the first hints of the burning rays of the sun, he was on his way again.

First, he wanted to check the village to see if he could find any survivors. Each member of the enemy tribes had left, and nothing remained except ruins. William's eyes took in the signs of the terrible destruction caused by the barbarians.

The skillfully-made houses, huts, and tents all lay in ruins. Frames burned to cinders showed the effects of the devastating fire. Stunned, it sank into William's mind that not a single living person was left in the village. Looking around, he walked along the main path of the village. Total quiet reigned all around him. The conquerors had taken everything of value that they could carry.

Whatever was left had been destroyed by the fire. The silence of death covered the settlement that had flourished not long ago. Broken-hearted, William walked to the end of the path.

Dead bodies covered the ground. Blood and horror ruled this place. He recognized several Indians among the dead who had been good neighbors, helpful companions of the tribe. The smoke from the still-burning remains stung tears from his eyes.

Soon, he was standing in front of the wreck of his own house. Unconsciously, he scanned the ruins for Susannah. But he knew the girl could not have died; she must have been dragged away somewhere. He walked through the half-split doorway. Inside, everything was a mess. Here and there lay smashed utensils that the attackers had either felt no need for or had not noticed. Everything they had left had become food for the flames, and now exuded destitution and destruction. The boy looked over every inch of their fond home where he and Susannah had at last spent some time in peace and happiness.

But destiny had again taken everything from them -- home, friends, and now each other. Who knew when they would see each other again? Bitter rage flared inside William's heart. He furiously kicked a blackened piece of wood, which bounced away, throwing sparks. Underneath, he spotted something small. It was the mother-of-pearl inlaid mirror from Susannah's mother, which the girl had guarded so carefully. The boy bent down to the little treasure and picked it up. The mirror's glass was cracked, and the wooden carving and frame had been burned in places. However, it still conjured for William old times, carefree happiness, New Holland.

One last time he looked around the hut, which had served its purpose until its destruction, and walked out the door. There was no reason to stay here any longer. He had to do something to free his friends from the tribe. Something to free Susannah, who must be waiting for him! He had to go - he couldn't waste another minute. Every minute, the sufferings of the captured men increased. Now, for the first time in his life, the fate of an entire tribe lay in his hands! He had to act.

Hurrying, he ran from the village. The enemy's tracks were not hard to follow, since they had seen no need to cover their traces after the battle. They clearly believed that every living Tongan was in their hands. The rain forest swallowed up William's quick, quiet steps.

In the camp of the two allied tribes, there was an exultant celebration of the victory. Fires were lit in the late afternoon, and a festive dinner quickly prepared. It never entered their minds to do anything about their captives.

Yet by now, the captives truly needed help. Many of them were wounded, and could not treat themselves. Of all of them, only a few Konvan guards stayed nearby, but looking after the captives was more trouble than they could be bothered with. They had untied several women from their bonds so that they could see to the wounded. They brought water, washed wounds, and bandaged the men. But since there were only a few, they could not deal with everyone. The tribe, which not long ago had been so proud and strong, was now a sad and sorry sight.

About forty percent of the villagers had been wiped out when the enemy overran the settlement, not caring whom they killed - children, elderly people, women or men.

Susannah was busying herself among the wounded. Her ebony hair, matted, hung in her face. Her face was streaked with tears and smoke and marked with the suffering she had been through. She made her way around, carrying water. She felt that everything had ended. William could not be alive, which was the worst of all. Dead! Her pain made her indifferent to the misery of the others. Everyone was wrapped up in their own troubles.

They mourned lost lovers; they cried from the pain of their wounds. They were sunk in despair, unable to see a future for themselves. Because of this, Susannah went to all the bound captives and made them drink. Soon, she came to Goko. By now, the young man had fallen into a fever from his injuries, and he hardly recognized who was raising a drinking vessel to his mouth. He drank thirstily for a long time. His tired, troubled eyes slowly took in the form of the girl.

"Flower of the forest!" he whispered faintly.

"I'm here, Goko!" Susannah leaned over him.

"Chief William..." he began, but his voice faltered.

"What about William?" the girl was paying attention suddenly.

"William did not die! Chief William... away..." Goko choked out a few words and then lost consciousness.

Susannah's heart beat powerfully, hearing this unbelievably sweet news. The life returned to her body. But hadn't she just heard this from a feverish man in a delirium? Yet now, her heart was pounding joyfully at the fateful news. William would come for them soon and set them free! Once again, she would be enfolded in his strong arms, and nothing bad would happen anymore. Nothing would make her abandon this beautiful fantasy.

"William's alive!" She was exultant inside. With full devotion, she tended the sick, as if with each one her meeting could be brought closer. She put a skin under Goko's head and covered him with another. The fever from the wound was killing the man with its destructive heat, but his body trembled in the cool, damp night.

When the girl had emptied the water vessel, she set off to refill it. As she walked past, the Konvan guards watched the beautiful, white-skinned Tongan maiden with sharp eyes. They could not have known what life-and-death struggles they would have to fight with William if they wanted to lay eyes on his beloved. And they could not have known that a cruelly sharpened, glittering dagger now weighed their lives in the balance. It wanted their blood in exchange for the lives of so many innocents. God's true avenging angel approached the guards stealthily: William Anderson.

Before this, William had already had his eye on his first future victim. A tall, strongly-built Konvan, who had many defenseless Tongan lives lay on his conscience. William kept the dagger between his teeth, to keep both his hands free for movement. Like a snake, he slid towards his unsuspecting opponent. William was not consciously thinking that he would soon take a life. His rage and bitterness demanded blood! The Konvan's attention was occupied as Susannah came back with another water vessel. William's chance came just when the Indian was looking elsewhere. And if he had only known it was Susannah he was lusting after! Perhaps William would not have been able to control himself. But now there was no reason to wait. Like a leopard, he threw himself on his victim, and before the man could make a sound, William plunged the dagger up to the hilt into his barrel-like chest. Only a gurgling sound came from the man, and William felt warm blood begin to flow over his hand.

When the man's body had gone still beneath him, he pulled the knife out with a single wrench, and wiped it hastily on the grass. Soundlessly, he stole forward.

He knew there was not much time to act, because someone could come at any moment and stumble on the Indian's corpse. Hurriedly, he moved over the bound men. He had realized it would be pointless to free everyone, because some were incapable of moving. His plan was to collect only those men able to fight. He would arm them, and use them to try to occupy the enemy, once alerted, while the rest could reach safety. The only opportunity for this plan to work was the time the Moguva and Konva were enjoying themselves beside the fire. They had placed their weapons in a small pile, away from the fires, where they knew they were safe from the bound captives. William crept further and soon reached the first Tongan. It was one of his own men, Sagat. William leaned towards him and addressed the sleeping man.

"Sagat! Wake up, Sagat!" The man opened his eyes and turned towards our hero. A muffled cry came out.

"Chief William!"

"Yes, it's me! Listen to me. We don't have much time." With that, his sharp knife sliced through the bonds of the captive. "The ones we need are those who aren't injured. We have to find them soon, and with them we will get the weapons."

"I understand, Chief! I'm not injured, you can count on me!" Sagat rubbed his wrists with satisfaction; they had chafed under the tightness of the cords. He told William where he could find warriors who were still able to fight.

"Now lie down again, Sagat! If you hear three whistles, go for the pile where they've stored the weapons."

"Right, Chief!" Sagat carefully lay back in the grass, and tense with alertness, waited for the signal from their young leader. He could already imagine the events to come, when he would kill their captors. Pain tormented his heart and bitterness choked his throat. His wife, every member of his family, two beautiful children - all had been killed by the barbarians. He felt he had nothing to lose. They would pay for every outrage!

The allied tribes who were celebrating had no inkling of the assault being prepared. They felt completely safe next to their tied captives. They were sure of their power, secure in the superiority of their tribe. In their worst nightmares, they could never have imagined that they would soon lose that power!

In the quiet night, a bird call softly sounded. This meant little to the Konvan and Moguvan warriors. Nor did they have any idea that by now, there were no guards left in position. One by one, they had gone to their rest. Some with a single knife thrust in the heart, some with ten strong fingers around the throat.

In the area of the Tongans, though not a soul stirred, the grass began to move in waves. William had freed his men, signaled with a whistle, and sent them towards the weapons. He himself set out to look for Susannah. The injured sent him to where the dying lay. Here, Susannah worked tirelessly. With beating heart, William waited to meet the girl. Since those lying further away could not know the turnaround in their fortunes, it was no wonder that his unexpected appearance awoke hope in their hearts. They would have liked to press him with questions. But William's attention was now fixed on one thing only. He glanced at the girl's busy silhouette nearby in the flickering light of the bonfire. Now, he saw no one else around. Taking every precaution he could, he moved quickly over to the girl. Susannah was giving water to an injured man when a familiar shape appeared next to her. For a moment, she believed she was dreaming. The vessel dropped from her hand. Before she could say a word, William sealed the mouth of his loved one with a kiss. They didn't know how long the kiss lasted, but they wanted it never to end. For a moment time stopped, and all their troubles disappeared. They felt as if only the two of them stood in the clearing. They were lost in each other's gaze.

The boy was the first to speak.

"Are you all right, Susannah?"

"Yes, my knight! I missed you for so long!"

"I went back to the village first, to look for you."

"What now?"

"Stay here, near the fire, and hide. After the battle, we'll meet here. Tell me you love me and I can overcome anybody!"

"I love you, Willy!"

"Be strong!" William pressed the girl's trembling body tight against him. Then he disappeared into the long grass. The girl broke into heart-rending sobs. She could not, nor did she want to, hold back her tears. All day, she had been strong in the face of a series of ordeals. Now no one could see her momentary weakness.

With no major exertion, the Tongans got possession of the weapons. Although their number was tiny compared to the almost three hundred of the enemy, this time they had a chance at victory. They had the weapons of the Konva and the Moguva in their hands. William praised his men's readiness. He gave orders for the beginning of the attack.

From seventy throats came a terrifying war cry. And the Tongans, with their white leader before them, rushed upon their confused conquerors. There was unbelievable panic in the ranks of the enemy. At first, they believed the Tongans had found help somewhere. In horror, they scrambled for their weapons, but they had gone! One after the other they were cut down, almost without resistance.

Finally, there sounded a strange voice, that of a white foreigner ordering them in the Tongan language to surrender. The Indians had now lost their heads and without delay prostrated themselves before this unknown higher power.

Several who tried to escape got an arrow or a spear in the ribs. The Tongans quickly bound their captives. From the two allied tribes, only one hundred and fifty were still alive. The Tongans, thanks solely to William, lost only four men in the fight.

Afterwards, the former captives sat around the fire. The Konvan and Moguvan warriors were bound at the edge of the camp, but they were kept under strict guard. There was enough food for the weary Tongans from the leftovers.

The tribe sat out what was left of the night. There was nowhere to sleep. Only the exhausted children slept with truly sweet dreams, in their mothers' laps. On William's orders, the Tongans dug graves for the dead. Then they waited for the new day, to finish everything.

William went to look for Susannah. He found her crouched beside the fire, trying to get warm. Sheer exhaustion caused her to keep nodding off, but she could not sleep. William knelt and hugged her. The girl happily lost herself in his embrace. They didn't speak. Mutely, they stared into the hypnotic rippling of the flames. Without words, they knew what was in the other's mind. They were free again, but with no home. Again, the world was open before them to start a new life. William lowered his head, lost in thought. Susannah saw clear signs of pain on her companion's face.

"What's wrong, Willy?"

"We must go away from here! Far away! I couldn't live in a place with such terrible memories so close."

"What about them?" asked the girl, indicating the mutely mourning Tongans. The two were talking to each other in English, so no one understood what they were saying. "Kaiva, their chief, is dead. They have no leader. We cannot leave them now!"

"You are a truly sweet girl, Susannah. In the greatest misery, you think of them. But our future is also doubtful. Several months ago you said to me, when I saved Kind's life, that 'we are two and we shall be afterwards, as well'!"

"I admit, I was wrong," said the girl, with bowed head. "But how do you remember my words so exactly?"

"Perhaps that's why I noted it, because something told me that sooner or later you would see your mistake. The Tongans gave us a home, warm friendship, and they were loyal to us. And in return they obliged us to make a life with them."

"Don't be angry with me."

"I'm not angry. I would be despicable if I were angry with you."

Their quiet chatting continued into the next morning as the sun rose. One hundred and twenty-five Tongans awoke from their lethargy. The captives lay watching. They knew that soon a decision about their destiny would be made. They waited to hear what punishment the white chief would exact from them. The camp came alive. A group of hunters set out to supply the members of the tribe with fresh meat. The women arose, and with their children, searched among the stolen belongings to see if they could find their own possessions. Here they also came across several enemy huts that had been smashed and burned to ashes in the battle the previous night.

William collected weapons together. From among their home's furnishings they only had some leather clothing, some llama skins, and Susannah's little mother-of-pearl mirror to call their own. That was all that was left. The rest had been consumed by the flames. Susannah was overjoyed to get her mirror back. It didn't worry her that the glass was broken, the handle charred. Still, it was something that was a precious souvenir of her mother.

The hunters returned from their foray with meat. Soon, the delicious aroma of cooking food filled the air. Everyone had an excellent appetite for the freshly-cooked meat. After eating, William felt that he needed to say a few words to the tribe about their future. They could not stay forever in the clearing. They had to decide the fate of their captives, which was weighing on the boy. Now, indisputably, everyone looked to William. His bravery, and his leadership abilities that had become clear, obviously meant that he alone could become the chief of the tribe after Kaiva. No one said anything, but everyone expected it to happen soon.

William called every able-bodied person to gather around him. They waited curiously to see what he would say. It could not be about rebuilding the destroyed village; that would be impossible. Tribal law forbade disturbing the land of the dead. The razed Tongan village should be returned to the jungle, as belief stipulated, to bring back the dead, if green vegetation again occupied it.

All of them went quietly and looked at William expectantly. The boy looked over the tribe. By now, he was seen as one of them. Susannah slowly walked over to stand beside William, and the Tongans regarded her as their queen.

"Honorable Tongan people," the boy started falteringly, "you gave us a home. Now, you have avoided the extinction threatening your entire nation. I'm overjoyed that I could help you. But you have brought this victory to a conclusion. You look upon us as one of you. Because of this, I must ask you a question. Will you follow me to where I believe a better life awaits us?"

"Yes!" roared the tribe in one voice, from mouths that had been mute until then.

"Chief William! Be our new and eternal leader!" a weaker voice shouted this time. Every head turned. It was Goko who had spoken. His words did not fall upon deaf ears. The words spread from mouth to mouth. Soon, everyone was shouting.

" William is our chief! Wise, worthy successor of Kaiva!"

Our hero received the acclamation with a beaming face. Touched, he looked around him.

He felt that he could never deserve the trust of these loving people.

"I thank you for your choice! I would have loved it if the wise Chief Kaiva could have lead you on this road. But the Sun god, creator of all life, called him. He has given his command to me now, and in his place and in his name I must act. We must go on a great journey! Not long ago a bloody battle took place, and these disputes will not fade. There will never be more on this land than there was before now. We would never know when a conquering tribe might attack us again. We must leave here! Not as defeated refugees, but as the honored Tongan people. As a tribe that does this act of its own free will, not from necessity."

With the conclusion of his speech, an impressed silence reigned for a moment. The crowd was as silent as the dead for a short time. Then, as one, a joyful cry was heard, soon breaking into a celebration. William raised a hand as a sign that he wanted to speak again.

"I thank you for your trust! We must embark upon a great trek, where not everyone will be able to bear its trials and tribulations equally. Because of this, the tribe must remain together! Whether we are lucky, or whether we are in danger. We cannot know what awaits us many miles further. Now, the spring is still young, and I hope that by the time the rainy season comes we will have a solid roof over our heads." They listened... But in the course of listening, there were words of appreciation, too. Their new chief had foresight and wisdom, and only wanted the best for the tribe.

They could not linger in discussion on this point. They had to decide the fate of the captives as well. William did not want to hear any proposals that they all be killed. Slaughter repelled him. He only killed out of necessity. On the other hand, he did not want to free them, as this would earn the rage of the Tongans expecting justice and punishment.

Whatever he said, he had to be clear and forthright, lest the trust the tribe's members had placed in him start to waver. He didn't want to make an obvious blunder if there was a solution close at hand. But what solution? What could he do?

But his quick-wittedness did not desert him. A solution came to him. He wanted to connect the freeing of the captives to the way they had violated and pillaged the Tonga village. Yes, the Moguvan and Konvan warriors would have to ransom themselves.

They would ransom themselves for food, weapons, tents, animal skins, and other useful items. Whatever would be necessary on their long trek. Explaining the plan, he waited a little nervously for the reaction. He was pleasantly surprised at the reception. Everyone found the plan excellent. At once, they found old Tonam, who, as the oldest member of the village, led introductory discussions on what items to demand as the ransom price. Two young warriors helped the old man and escorted him to the captives. William and Susannah followed them, hand in hand.

"Are you tired?" William asked the girl mischievously, after she had stumbled twice in succession and only the boy's strong arms had kept her from falling on her nose.

"No! Just the grass is so long!" the girl returned, a little flushed in the face with annoyance, pleasing William since it showed he had succeeded in teasing her.

"Ah, these clumps of grass! Nothing better to do than to get in the way of my little queen when she misses her unsure steps!" smiled the boy, and dodged away when a cuff around the head came in his direction. The girl's eyes, ringed with sleeplessness, glared at him reproachfully.

"Oh, Willy! When will you ever be serious? And you have agreed to be the wise tribal chief!" They looked at each other and laughed.

The sun slipped out from behind a white cloud of tropical mist, and took an interest in the events happening in the forest clearing.

Paradise Island

And so our heroes' adventures continued. Continued, but it wasn't just the two of them anymore. An entire tribe now depended on them for guidance and protection, should any obstacle or danger present itself along the way.

It took three days to prepare for the journey, and during this time, the hostages were freed. Messengers sent to the villages of the Moguva and Konva rendered a full account of the Tonga's demands, and the villagers gladly agreed to them. The same day, hunting supplies and produce were delivered. William thoroughly inspected all the items received. When he considered them to be sufficient, he gave orders to have the hostages freed. The Tonga cut the warriors' ropes and in no time they and their ransomed family members disappeared into the thick forest.

On the fourth day, the Tonga tribe set out. With heavy hearts, the Tonga nation bade farewell to the land whose every species had contained so many pleasant memories for them during the past hundred years. A sense of abandonment hung in the air. It was no wonder, then, that many a warrior found himself secretly wiping a tear from the corner of his eye. What a disgrace! Only women cry! Nevertheless, even the men spared no tears that day.

The first night of the journey, they found themselves on the edge of the Tonga hunting grounds. They made camp early and built fires. The weary travelers gathered around the roaring flames and hardly touched their food.

The moon, the night's wanderer and guardian, already illuminated the sleepers with its pale light. Only the guards were still awake. The sound of their own low voices was the only thing that kept their eyelids from closing. Enviously they regarded their sleeping companions, dreaming now, perhaps, of a happy future.

As the sun rose from the thick forest, it found the Tonga ready to move on. They packed their belongings quickly. The sleeping children were wrapped in leather skins and mounted on pack animals. William led his people in a northerly direction, then gradually back toward the west. Unknown forests appeared before them. William and Susannah walked ahead, hand in hand, talking quietly.

"Where are we going, Willy?"

"I think the best thing is to head toward the sea."

"Why?"

"I don't know. I guess I just feel drawn to it." The boy grew silent, but Susannah could sense what was on his mind.

"I know why you want to go in that direction. It's about wanting to go home, isn't it?"

"Yes."

"I feel the same way."

"But it's impossible."

"Nothing's impossible if we really want it," the girl said dreamily. "All we need is a boat!"

William smiled at the naïveté of the words. "No, a boat isn't enough. We need more people. Knowledgeable people. The boat has to be sailed to New Holland, and nobody here knows anything about that. And anyway, where would we get a boat that could go that distance? And we have the Tonga to look after. What would become of those poor people if we were to just leave them? The first thing we've got to do is get a roof over our heads."

They continued on the arduous path toward the sea. With the pack animals, they progressed very slowly. Also, the fact that they numbered so many meant constantly having to look for food and, more importantly, water.

Around noon they rested. The heat had grown intense, and this caused the rain forest to exude a heavy, suffocating vapor. The trees absorbed the sun's burning rays, but there was no movement of air beneath their leaves. The exploration party returned to say that it had discovered water. The thirsty travelers set off in the direction they indicated. They knelt and drank greedily from the cool stream. The children bathed and filled the goatskin water holder they'd brought with them and hadn't had the chance to use until now. But fresh meat was needed as well, and the sound of their rejoicing had long since frightened away any game in the area. The hunters went in pursuit of new prey.

For those who craved a little peace and quiet, the chattering monkeys which suddenly surrounded them gave them little cause for rejoicing . The mischievous creatures ventured right up to the edge of the camp. The children were delighted. The monkeys grimaced at the strange newcomers. The braver ones climbed trees and threw fruit and dried twigs, shrieking all the time at the top of their lungs. This was their way of rallying the young Tonga to battle. When the shrieks grew three times as loud, the returning hunters put a stop to the game. It didn't matter -- the boys were just as happy to watch their fathers skin and cut their prey. It was exciting to watch. They also had to learn these skills, for the time was coming when they would undergo the trials of adulthood. Armed with only a bow and a few arrows, they would have to track and kill a leopard and return with its hide as a sign of valor.

After lunch, William gave the orders to move on.

Their journey had lasted twelve long weeks, owing to the summer heat. Not everyone had been able to endure the hardship. The "Jungle Spirit" had claimed the lives of a young woman, two elderly men and two children. The woman had been killed by a puma. The old men had succumbed to a fever brought on by the heat, and the children to venomous snake bites.

At the end of the twelfth week, they arrived at the coast. A sense of awe filled the Tonga when they laid eyes on the Pacific Ocean. This was the Great Water that Davis Franklin had often told them about. But Davis Franklin could not be with them today. He'd died in the battle, an arrow shot through his neck.

Cries of wonder came from the warriors. The women regarded the ocean with misgiving. The gently foaming waves terrified them. What surprised everybody the most was that the water was salty and undrinkable.

The children adapted themselves to this new environment in no time. Shouting loudly, they waged war on the "blue wonder". The sound of their laughter as they rode the waves lightened the mood.

Everybody was very glad when William announced that they would stay there for two days.

Their final destination was reached five days later. In one place, the ocean gave way to dry land. Only the highest areas remained above water. It was here that they came upon the little island that was to become the new village. It was joined to the continent by a long strip of land. This would make for a good defense against enemies invading from the shore, for the only way to reach the island was by canoe.

At first, the idea of settling on an island surprised the Tonga. William then enumerated his reasons for wanting to stay, and finally won them over to the advantages.

Everyone was pleased with the island. A nearby stream would provide all their water. Camp was quickly set up. Provisional tents were pitched to keep out the rain. Lush vegetation grew on the island, and a good many trees were also discovered which could later be used for constructing houses. That night, they celebrated with a feast. They toasted to their chief, William, who had led them to this island.

It was dark by the time everything had grown calm. William and Susannah took a walk along the shore. A splendid moonlit night lay before them, with thousands of stars sparkling in the heavens. Coming off the open sea, a salt smell mingled with the scent of wildflowers – this, too, might have had an influence on the young lovers' thoughts at that moment. They walked for a long time, then sat on the sand. The waves, pulsing with life, caressed their feet gently.

"This is just like that night… It wasn't so long ago, after all!" said William, breaking the silence.

"What do you mean?"

"Don't you remember? The seaside, the silence...We sit next to each other and I embrace you…"

"Ah, yes, I remember," the girl said, coming to life. "New Holland!"

"New Holland! Our first night together."

"Oh, it that seems like a hundred years ago."

"The only thing missing is a falling star."

"Falling star?"

"Yes."

"Do you remember that?"

"Do I remember? That was when I asked the heavens to make you mine!"

"Well, now you have me, Willy. You got what you wished for, only I'd say we had to pay a little too dearly."

"It was the hard times that made it all possible."

"If we'd gone to the 'dinner' that night on Donald's boat, our bones would be moldering to dust now in the savages' camp!"

"But Fate had something else in mind."

They would have continued on talking this way for a long time, had Susannah not yawned. She looked at the boy.

"The time has come, my dear chief, for us to sleep," she teased him. The boy smiled. "Tomorrow's going to be another busy day. We have building to do."

"Yes," he said, "and I hope for the last time. I'm tired of moving and running all the time."

"Me too, but at least we're not alone."

As they headed back to camp, the sand, smooth as a tabletop, absorbed the sound of their footsteps. Only the quartz dust below their bare feet squeaked ever so slightly.

The next morning, the whole village was awake to witness the first burning rays of the sun. Before breakfast, they all had a swim in the cool waves. It was a cheerful, carefree scene.

After breakfast, William divided the work. Half of the men were given the job of chopping and carrying wood; the other half were sent hunting, for meat was scarce at this time.

The women sat down to weave. The thick rush mats they made would be used to insulate and fortify the walls of the houses. The children helped wherever they could. This continued for weeks, and the hard work paid off. Houses popped up everywhere. Before long, every family had a place to call its own.

The life of the tribe returned to normal. With the help of the wise elders, Susannah and William adopted the customs and religion of the tribe, which centered on the Sun God. They learned quickly, so that by the time of the "Sun Celebration", William himself was able to prepare the village for the event. The Sun Celebration took place at the same time every year. It had been handed down to the Tonga by their ancestors and they adhered to it strictly. This also happened to be the day of the manhood ritual, the day on which the boys would have to prove their readiness to become warriors. And the following day, another outstanding event would take place: William and Susannah's wedding! Talmont, the medicine man, would preside over the ceremony.

The preparations for the festival took an entire day, but by sundown everything was ready.

The tribe slept little that night, especially the boys who were to become men. A great deal depended on their performance in the days ahead. They would either become warriors or remain "monks" (children) for another year.

By sunrise, the torches had been lit and there was a great deal of hustle and bustle. By the time the first rays of the sun had illuminated the east, the village resembled an anthill. Talmont instructed the boys: "You have three days to kill the leopard. Right now, there are eleven of you and pursuing so many leopards will require much time. The Sun God decides which of you will find your prey nearby, and which of you will have to travel far to find it. You are completely on your own. If trouble should befall any of you, the others cannot come to his aid. Use your wits and cunning. You know the laws of the wild – abide by them! He who returns with a leopard skin will be given the 'name'. He will be a 'konam', a warrior. But he who returns without a leopard's skin will remain a 'monk' for another year. Go. The Sun God be with you." With a wave of his hand, the wizard dismissed them. Cheering loudly, the young boys gripped their weapons and raced off the island. They all hoped to be the first to kill. On reaching the thickets they separated, as group hunting was strictly forbidden.

The boys' parents looked on anxiously, knowing that the task before them would not be without danger. They were to face none other than the regal beast, the leopard. They knew that not all of the boys would return from the forest of a thousand dangers, and that those who failed would die a gruesome death. There was no escape from the leopard's terrible fangs and claws!

The drums pounded in the main square. The Tonga waited in eager silence.

The tribal elders appeared. Behind them, in ceremonial dress, William and Susannah walked out of the chieftain's tent. A murmur of surprise ran through the crowd. Susannah, in her wedding dress of forest flowers, looked astonishingly beautiful. It had taken the village women two weeks to prepare the wedding garments. For Susannah's long black hair they had woven a garland of the most beautiful of the forest flowers. The raffia dress brought out her slim, lovely figure.

Her forehead was adorned with fire-red coral in which genuine pearls gleamed. The pearl necklace she was wearing rivaled the sun in brilliance. Her wrists and ankles were also decorated with pearls. These ornaments made her face appear no less fair. Even the searing rays of the tropical sun had failed to touch or damage her milk-white complexion. Her finely-shaped eyes now gazed proudly on their admirers. She was like a goddess, and the Tonga would have liked nothing better than to have bowed at her feet and worshipped her.

The wedding began. The customs had been "anglicized" a little, for a typical tribal wedding would have required days. William and Susannah's wedding, on the other hand, lasted a mere hour and a half. Out of respect, Talmont went along with all that William asked, insisting only that the couple be united in the name of the Sun God. He declared them man and wife. Everyone presented gifts and gave their blessing to the newlyweds. At the banquet, William and Susannah's faces beamed with joy. Their happiness was complete. They had these friends and a home, and marriage brought them even closer together. William embraced the girl gaily. Susannah looked at him and their glances met. He could see the future in her shining eyes. They sealed their vow of fidelity with a kiss.

The festive mood lasted far into the night, but there were other reasons for staying awake so late. They anxiously awaited the young boys' return. Apparently, the hunt was not going as smoothly as they had hoped. Around midnight, the village became quieted down. There were only the watch fires now, burning on the island and at the entrance, to light the way for those returning home.

At two o'clock in the morning, cheerful voices woke the slumbering village. Torches were lit and the tribe came out to investigate. Two boys appeared in the distance, waving. They were carrying leopard skins. In no time, the crowd had surrounded the young men with shouts of joy. The Tonga tribe had two brave new warriors.

They embraced the young men and examined them for wounds. Yes, there were plenty on both of them, but the important thing was that they were alive and two leopards dead.

William and Susannah, awakened by the clamor outside, dressed quickly and joined the celebrants. The chief studied the two young warriors and the wounds which bore witness to their struggle with the regal beast. He confirmed their manhood with the following words:

"Today two 'monks' have departed from our village forever, leaving their childhood in the wilderness. And two brave 'Konam' have come to take their places. From now on, you will be given your own houses, and if you have a bride in mind, you may marry. May the Sun God bless you both!"

The two youths were deeply moved by the praise they had received. William dismissed them, and the young couple returned home to continue sleeping. The excited crowd remained awake in the hope that more new warriors would arrive shortly.

The morning greeted the world with magnificent colors. The sun clothed the rain forest and the island in rose. The night was long gone. Its power was broken, and the sun climbed its celestial ladder to bathe the region in crimson light. Suddenly, every living creature came to life.

The birds continued singing the melodies that the brooding darkness had cut short. Trilling, chirping, cheeping, screeching in their own tongues, they informed the world that a new day had arrived. The four-legged predators went hunting. They listened closely for the faintest sound, because in the daylight it was not only they who were able to see more clearly – they, too, could be seen more clearly. Hidden dangers lay everywhere.

The new day rose on the nine boys who were still in pursuit of their leopards. After a night of terrors, they set out with new hope -- the hope that they could return home honorably.

By sunrise, the village was already at work. The celebration belonged to memory now, and again there was much work to attend to. That day, three more youths returned carrying the proof of their worthiness to become men. This made five who had returned to the island; nothing was yet known of the other six.

By midnight the next day -- which was the time limit -- there was still no news of the other six boys. The Tonga were becoming worried. A torch burned at the entrance of each house. Many people, especially loved ones and relatives, held an all-night vigil. William called together the leaders of the village to tell them that a small search party would be sent out at dawn to look for the 'monks'. He kept his word. When the sun had broken through the darkness, they started out. William himself led the team. They searched until noon without result, then stopped at a sparse cluster of shade trees to rest and eat. They lay in the grass for a short time to gather strength for the scorching journey ahead. Suddenly, human voices rang out. The men jumped to their feet and, taking their weapons, ran in the direction of the voices. A wide swath of beaten grass lead to the heart of the jungle. One of the warriors bent down and raised a hand.

"A leopard!" he whispered. The warriors fitted arrows into their bowstrings. Tracks in the grass showed that a struggle had recently occurred. Approximately 100 yards away, the men witnessed something simultaneously comical and terrifying. A good-sized male leopard was leaping constantly in an attempt to snatch a boy from a tree. The branch of the tree creaked dangerously lower and lower toward the ground. It didn't take long to understand the gravity of the situation, and in a matter of seconds two dozen arrows flew to end the predator's life. The boy was one of the tribe. With a cry of thanks, he jumped out of the tree.

The story he told the men was no ordinary one: "Yesterday I couldn't find a leopard anywhere. I searched all day with no luck. When it grew dark, I climbed a tree and spent the night in it. The next morning, I would give hunting one more try. I didn't want to return to the village a 'boy'. I must have been very tired because I had just awoken. I decided I would try to catch something for breakfast. I had just climbed out of my resting tree when I heard a threatening growl that made me stop. I knew instantly that this was the regal predator. I drew back my bow and followed the direction of the sound. Then the leopard suddenly leaped out of the bush where he'd been resting, and ran toward me. I shot at him but I was so excited I only struck him in the leg. That only made him angrier! I didn't have another chance to shoot, so I ran in the other direction, and the leopard chased me. Then I screamed for help, but there was no help in sight so I climbed this life-saving tree. And that's when you arrived and saved my life.

"If it hadn't been for you, the leopard would have had me for breakfast!" The young man had blushed while relating his story. He had gesticulated wildly. Now he was silent. With shining eyes, he looked up at the men expectantly. His words had made them thoughtful. The white chief was the first to reply.

"Although it is forbidden to help initiates, we were forced to make an exception in your case. The time limit has expired. You will return to the village as a 'monk' because you have failed to prove your valor." Saying this, William dismissed the boy with a wave of his hand. The boy's countenance became very sad. He would have to remain a "monk" for another year. Quietly, he asked: "How many leopard skins were brought back?"

"Five."

They parted ways. The men continued their search for the remaining five. Left to himself, the boy deeply regretted his failure. He could already see the mocking grins of his peers. He needed the independence. He already had a secret bride-to-be, Sagat's beautiful daughter Milla, and they had wanted to marry for a long time. All this time he hadn't touched the girl, convinced as he was of his success and that she would be his at last. If he hadn't failed, the pretty thing would be his now. Everything was ruined! He kicked a root that protruded from the ground. "I won't let anyone else have her!" he hissed between his teeth. And with vigorous steps, he set out for the village.

He was sure he could not wait another year to have Milla. A new plan began to hatch in his mind, and after thinking it through, the situation began to seem less tragic. He was feeling somewhat better now, but shame still burned in him like fiery coals.

William's team located another boy, but he was no longer among the living. His frozen gaze stared into nothingness. His body bore the leopard's enormous claw and fang marks. They buried the poor boy immediately, together with his weapons. And with this, the "weak" name disappeared forever from the Tongan community.

There was still no trace of the other four boys, but nothing more could be done today; the men had to be back on the island by nightfall.

The returning team was flooded with questions. They explained what had happened to two boys, but when asked about the other four, they gestured in the negative.

Susannah found William and they walked home together. After dinner, they climbed wearily into bed. They held each other close. Susannah didn't want to pester her husband with questions. In a short time, he was fast asleep. Susannah caressed his face, and snuggling close to him, drifted off herself.

The still night greeted the jungle. A little late on arrival, the old moon showed itself from its hideaway in the clouds. It rose higher and higher until its pale light cast a glow over the island.

Around midnight, the door of one of the smaller houses opened and a figure emerged. His cautious steps were swallowed by the night. A short while later, another door opened and a shadow appeared. It looked timidly around and hurried toward the shore. Judging by the way it moved, anyone would have suspected this to be a girl. It was Milla, Sagat's eldest daughter. The figure waiting for her on the shore was the unlucky 'monk', Pang.

The boy immediately recognized the person approaching by her walk. He hurried over.

"Why did you call me here?" whispered Milla.

"I didn't kill a leopard. We can't marry now."

"What will we do?"

"You'll have to wait another year for me."

"But that's impossible!"

"You mean you don't love me?"

"Of course I love you! It's just that I want us to be married and to have our own house."

"But that's against the law."

"Couldn't we do something to change it?" the girl asked, snuggling close to the boy.

"Only…if you were to become pregnant."

"What did you just say?" the girl asked, shocked.

"That's the only other way."

"I hadn't thought of that."

"Try to understand. It's the only other way we can be together!"

"When should we?"

"When should we what?"

"Well, you know."

"Now!"

Holding hands, they withdrew into a bush. Pang had prepared a soft bed of animal skins. Seeing the boy's "forethought" the girl blushed deeply, though the darkness concealed this. She was quickly out of her clothes, and in a matter of moments the lovers entered the realm of the beautiful. The curious moon was their only witness.

The next morning, the Tongan village had no idea of the "violation" that had taken place the night before, though the truth would come to light soon enough. Milla, whose loss of virginity had caused her much pain the night before, awoke delighted by the fact that she would soon be a mother. The "partners in crime" didn't confess immediately. They would continue to behave as if nothing had happened.

Another team was being sent for the lost youths. They prepared to remain away longer this time, although a number of them looked upon the search as utterly pointless.

William led the way again. They planned to be gone for two days in order to explore the more remote areas. If they failed to find the boys this time then, sadly, the matter would be out of their hands.

The fifteen men started on their way. They made haste, traveling a great distance in only a matter of hours. But in their random search of the vast jungle, there was very little chance of actually finding anyone.

It was well past noon when they found water, and they settled down for a brief rest. The heat was intense and sapped all their energy, but the cold water, which they had collected from a deep hole in the ground, refreshed them greatly.

In half an hour they were on their way again. They stopped several times to examine tracks, and often followed only to be disappointed. Finally, arriving at a wide grassy clearing, they set up camp. The great fire they built could be seen from afar. They killed some birds and small wild boars and gutted them. They roasted the birds and large chunks of the boar, gathering impatiently around the fire. When each piece had been roasted well, they ate to their hearts' content.

Half an hour later, their stomachs full, their bodies at ease, the men stretched out before the fire. The guard stood by, putting an occasional log on the flames. Each man slept with a weapon close at hand.

The night passed calmly. No heed was given to the noise of the nearby predators. The guard nodded off now and again.

When the sparkling starlight had faded and a faint glimmer had spread over the eastern sky, the guard woke his replacement and turned in for the night. This exchange did not startle the sleepers. They turned over and went back to sleep with the knowledge that morning was still far away.

On waking, they got a good start. William planned to continue the search until noon and then return. But as fate would have it, their journey had not been in vain after all. They encountered a narrow animal trail that facilitated their search. The trail was so narrow that they had to proceed single file. Sagat, who was at the front of the line, suddenly stopped. He bent, picked up something, and showed it to his companions. It was a worn-out moccasin.

"Somebody from our village must have lost this or thrown it away."

"We're on the right track," said William. "We'll know more very soon."

They increased their pace. After a long, even stretch they arrived at an open field crisscrossed with many streams. The water prevented larger plants from growing here. The men were in the process of deciding how best to cross it when they spotted smoke not two hundred yards away. This decided it for them. They would find out who the dwellers downstream were. They couldn't know if these were enemies or friends. They found a shallower stretch of water and crossed. With their bows drawn and ready, they stole toward the fire. They looked with surprise at the figures lying around it. The faces were, indeed, very familiar. One of them looked up. He had a disturbed expression on his face and perhaps did not even recognize them. Sagat was the first to approach. The people in question were, in fact, the four "monks", but they looked terrible. There was hardly any life left in them now. Mang, another of William's men, quickly summed up the situation. He picked up a leather bag, opened it, and removed a handful of the contents. Astonished, he showed it to his companions. They were little red berries, poisonous berries. Their sweet taste made them very pleasant to eat, but the poison killed within twenty-four hours. Mang and two others ran to find the antidote in the jungle. About an hour later they prepared herbal tea in a clay pot they'd brought with them. They made the boys drink it. The emetic brew produced the desired effect. By nightfall, the boys had been restored to health. Only their faces were still slightly yellow from the poisoning.

All four had succeeded in slaying a leopard. They had been looking for the road home when they met each other along the way. That had been the day before yesterday. They had set up camp in the place where the rivers met. The next morning, they planned to return to the island. But in the course of that night, a light but plentiful rain broke out. It caused spring floods in the nearby mountains which rushed down into the valley. The streams overflowed and swept away everything in sight. The boys took refuge in the trees and watched as all their weapons and supplies were carried away by the flood. In the morning, they were famished. They were at least a day's journey from the island and without a scrap of food. Looking for fruit, they discovered the red berries, and ate their fill.

Had the search team arrived a few hours later, they would have arrived only to bury them. The important thing was that the adventure had had a happy ending. It was better to return home late than never.

The men decided that it was best to settle here for the night with the convalescing boys. They wouldn't have found a better camp in the area anyway. Following a short but filling supper, with the exception of the guard, everyone dropped off to sleep.

Around midnight, the guard woke them up. The weather was changing. A strange murmur now filled the jungle. A storm was brewing. The air became heavy and suffocating. Not long afterwards, a wind arose. It was like the breath of someone ill with fever. The sky snarled and great drops of rain fell to the earth. The storm had arrived! Panic-stricken, they raced for cover. The warm rain lashed their defenseless bodies, and this was an almost pleasing effect at first. For twenty minutes, they were given a taste of a war of the elements. Then all hell broke loose, and the sky opened as if it would collapse on them. Enormous thunderclaps announced the beginning of the real storm, before which the thunder itself shook with terror. The warm rain became an ice-cold downpour with fist-sized hailstones. The hurricane became stronger and snatched away everything in sight. Now they had constant thunder to contend with in their rush for shelter. The Indians, superstitious when it came to the elements, regarded the sky fearfully. William, who had survived a few such tempests before, pulled a llama skin over his head to keep out the water that poured down in solid sheets. He crouched on the grass. The hail struck his back and the torn-off branches. He didn't let the pain affect him. He thought of home and the pretty girl who would be sleeping alone tonight.

During the night, they had no other choice but to take refuge in the treetops. New streams poured down from the mountains. The war of the elements raged until daybreak. The full summer storm had struck man and beast alike. Once the hurricane had receded, the Tongans climbed down from their fortress. Some looked pitiful, with heavy circles under their eyes. Nevertheless, they rejoiced that they had survived the night. Nobody had sustained any serious injuries. Their scratches and scrapes were mere memories of the preceding night. With everything still dripping wet, there was no question of building a fire. The many streams continued to surge. Coming to a narrower section, they threw a lasso around the branch of a tree on the other side and swung across one by one. As for their weapons, not all were found, but this wasn't the most important thing on their minds at the moment. They went forth with grumbling bellies, hoping to reach the island by nightfall.

William recalled how it felt to spend the night on the open sea. His last sea voyage was so vivid in his memory that it made him shudder to think of it. Mountain-high waves in the stormy night. Deserted, thrown back and forth in the ruined sailboat.

In the early morning hour, it was already burning hot. The vegetation steamed. A mist covered the entire forest so that it was almost impossible to see. Today they would make hardly any progress, often taking wrong turns because of the poor visibility. Also, the visibility distance necessary for hunting was missing. They had to make do with fruit they found along the way. That night they sat hungrily around a fire that had been nearly impossible to start. They waited until their clothes had dried, and then turned in for the night.

By morning, the weather had cleared considerably. They could go hunting immediately. They shot many fowl and small game. Nothing less than a feast would do for the starving men!

Around noon they were on their way again. The abundant food had brought back their strength, and they were making good time now. By sundown, they reached the place where they had rescued Pang. Though the ocean was not far away, they didn't want to be left stumbling through the dark. They spent yet another night in the forest.

The storm had caused trouble for the islanders as well. William had failed to consider that their water-locked village could be subjected to great danger in stormy weather. The ocean had found its way everywhere. Personal belongings lay washed up on shore. It was a good thing the houses had been built at the highest points. The elements had wreaked havoc on the island. Many roofs had been torn and the houses themselves flooded. Many villagers had to take cover in neighbors' houses. Packed like sardines in a can, they waited for morning to come.

When the Tongans emerged at sunrise, they were astonished to witness the work that the wind and water had accomplished overnight. Trees had been pulled up by their roots, bushes taken away, animal and bird carcasses covered the island. The islanders went to work immediately. They dumped the carcasses in the ocean. The sharks, drawn by the smell of blood, gladly accepted the free food. But even more than the thousand other worries plaguing them, what concerned them the most was the whereabouts of the search party.

Susannah cleaned gloomily in front of their house. Her thoughts turned constantly to William. "Something bad has happened to him," she often said to herself. The idea made her heart sink, but then she managed to find a way out of her despair. Shouts of excitement brought Susannah back to the present. The Tongans had gathered to look at the ocean. She ran toward them.

"Big canoe! Big canoe!" they shouted to her, pointing excitedly, gesturing for her to make haste. The immense stretch of water unfolded slowly before their eyes. Suddenly their cries caught in their throats.

A three-mast frigate appeared. It was listing to one side, which indicated that it had sprung a leak and was carrying a great deal of water in its hold. Its sails were in tatters. Of the main mast hardly a yard remained. The ship resembled the one that had brought them from New Holland.

"Could that be the Cambridge?" Susannah wondered. She strained her eyes to read the name on the ship, now less than 200 yards away, but this could not be done without a telescope. The unknown structure – due to a miracle or a hidden current – was being carried into the bay, approaching the sandy shore at an unstoppable pace. The Tongans outran the water and the giant toy it supported. The ship bore the unmistakable marks of last night's storm. Now the entire Tongan village had gathered on the south part of the island. They gazed with amazement at the approaching ship, about to run aground.

Suspenseful minutes passed. The Indians were more curious than bold at this particular moment. The boat swept in: with driving momentum, it cut a deep arc in the wet sand and glided over it.

Every joint on its large body creaked and cracked. Then it stopped. The waves gently slapped at its broad sides. There was total silence on deck. The villagers looked at each other in confusion. Nobody dared climb on board. Who knew what would become of the courageous person who tried it?

Susannah read the ship's name. Struggle was written in proud gold letters on the ship's prow. Minutes passed, and still not a soul appeared on deck. This gave a few warriors the courage to act. They climbed up the broken rope ladder. Then, to everybody's complete surprise, William's wife waded into the water and also climbed on deck. The warriors peered into an open door and entered. A room filled with marvelous, unfamiliar tools met their eyes in the captain's cabin. They fingered the objects with interest, not knowing their uses. Susannah entered the room. They looked at the brave girl with surprise.

"Come with me," she demanded. "We have to check for survivors." The men nodded in agreement, although they were a little sorry they could not spend more time in the room becoming better acquainted with its many curiosities. Susannah proceeded to the hatchway leading to the crews' quarters. There, in the semi-darkness, motionless human bodies were lying. They checked every one carefully, but none was alive. Starting to feel sick from the noxious odor that filled the room, the girl and her companions left. They went to the stern of the ship, where they noticed a new hatchway. This was the guests' quarters. They opened the door quickly. On opening the door of one of the decorated cabins, they glimpsed someone lying on the floor. He was whimpering faintly. Susannah signaled her people and they carried him to the deck. The girl continued her search, but there were no other living persons in sight. She thoughtfully climbed to the deck to get a better look at the survivor.

The man had grey hair and a beard. Dried blood covered his face. The girl felt as if she had seen this face somewhere before. The man weakly called for water -- in English! The Indians asked the girl what they could do for the white foreigner.

"Bring him some water," said the girl. The warriors carefully lifted the wounded man and, raising him on a board, carried him with cautious steps to the shore. Outside, the curious onlookers surrounded them. They sent a woman for water and she returned a short while later, bringing the invigorating liquid in a clay pitcher. The stranger drank greedily, emptying the contents of the entire pitcher. Susannah stared thoughtfully at the man, searching her memory to remember where she had laid eyes on him before.

The Indians prepared a stretcher and carried the now-unconscious sailor to the village. They took him to an empty guest house. Two women attended to him. Susannah went home, and it struck her again that William had not yet returned. She was heartbroken. She sat on the edge of the bed and tears escaped from the corners of her eyes.

By the time she collected herself it was late, but it was still possible that the boy would return that evening. And that meant preparing supper. She went to work right away.

Night had fallen so quickly that she had hardly noticed, busy as she was preparing the meal. It was ready now, but there was nobody to eat it.

More time passed, and Susannah realized she would be sleeping alone again tonight.

Bored with waiting to no avail, she decided to go and have a look at the castaway. She brought a clay pitcher of fresh water. She walked into the peaceful twilight and in a short time, she arrived at the guest house. She brushed aside the llama-skin door covering and entered. Two women were sitting beside the sickbed weaving baskets. One of them turned to Susannah and signaled for her to be quiet -- the wounded man was sound asleep. In the torchlight, she could clearly make out his haggard, care-worn features. The blood which had so heavily covered his face had been washed away, and his features could be seen much more clearly now. Susannah took a step closer. Her eyes widened. The blood froze in her veins. Her heart beat like mad and everything darkened around her. The pitcher fell from her hands with a loud crash. She recognized the wounded castaway as none other than the man who had destroyed their lives and was responsible for the deaths of so many innocent people -- the cruel, bloodthirsty, depraved Donald Hawke!

Holding back her terrified scream, she ran from the room. The Tongan women looked after her, astonished. Gasping for air, she ran home, took a dagger and threw herself on the bed. Her thoughts, quicker than lightning, flickered between hope and despair. She held the sharp blade up to her eyes. She watched the way the shining side glinted wickedly in the red light of the fire.

"What happens if that criminal wakes up and comes after me? What happens if William comes home and discovers who Fate has thrown in our path again? William! Where are you?! Why don't you come home and take me in your arms? Why aren't you here to protect me? WHY? WHY? WHY?"

Everything around her began to spin. She could feel her stomach heave. Jumping up, she went over to where a clay pitcher stood. She splashed water on her face, dried it on the sleeve of her dress, then screamed with horror at a shadow on the wall. But the shadow was her own. She was alone. She lay on the bed and placed the dagger beside her head, then buried her face in her hands and trembled. The fire crackled dully as her tortured imagination drew new and terrifying pictures on the wall in front of her.

Nightmares tormented her all night, not leaving her a moment's rest. She was afraid to sleep, but she was just as afraid to wake up.

As soon as she dozed off, she started awake, terrified, thinking she could hear the convict's heavy breathing.

"William, where are you?"

Late the next morning, she woke exhausted. The dinner she had prepared remained untouched. She picked at it, but she had no appetite. She was still deeply disturbed by the fact that destiny had brought them together again with that evil man. William had still not returned. There was nobody with whom to share her awful secret. The hours ticked by with endless waiting.

The villagers were starting to worry seriously about the missing men. It was terrible to think what would happen to them if they were never to return.

That day Susannah didn't dare visit the guest house, afraid that her behavior would arouse suspicion in the Tongans. She spent the day on the narrow strip of land that connected the island to the mainland. Imploringly, she eyed the jungle that hid from her sight the one man she yearned to see, the only one who could possibly help her.

Donald Hawke's condition improved considerably. His extraordinarily strong constitution had withstood the serious wounds he had received. It was the loss of blood that had caused him to weaken. By mid-morning, he had recovered his senses. He'd finished the plate of food set before him, then had fallen into a deep sleep. He would have liked to have known what had happened to his companions and to the ship, but he couldn't communicate with his nurses.

Finally, he resigned himself to his circumstances and remained silent. So far, he hadn't experienced ill will on the part of the Indians. He could continue with his plans as soon as he was well again.

He and his remaining companions had boarded the Struggle at Valparaiso eight weeks before. The few months they'd spent in the harbor town had been sufficient for them to squander the bulk of their fortune. But they still had more than enough left over to make two dozen Europeans rich. Donald mentioned his plans to go to England. His former inmates immediately wanted in on the deal. It didn't matter to them where the money was spent. Hawke established contact with William Stevenson, the captain of the Struggle. They quickly reached an understanding regarding travel costs. The convicts knew that Captain Stevenson was a true gentleman and used this fact to their advantage. They moved into their cabins, and the next morning the anchor was weighed. With the wind in their favor they left the busy city of Valparaiso behind, the place where they had rid themselves of more than half their gold.

For two weeks straight, a southerly wind drove them on and they traveled east at a good pace. Then came several windless days.

When one morning the wind strengthened again, they unfastened the sails of the Struggle and proceeded on their way. On nearing the Equator, it grew hotter and the crew grumblingly completed their work on the scorching deck.

It was the eighth week of the voyage when all luck abandoned them. The water supply was running low. The water remaining in the barrels had become putrid. It had to be boiled and cooled now before it could be drunk.

In the east, storm clouds had gathered. The sailors anxiously eyed the approaching danger. The storm broke around midnight and by the early morning hours, it was becoming a hurricane. Everyone was protecting the ship. The seamen had taken turns at the pump all night, bailing water out of the hold. By the next day, the storm had only worsened. The crew was filled with dread. Then, to make matters worse, a dysentery epidemic of unknown origin broke out on board. Within twenty-four hours, the men were struck down.

With a hurricane raging outside and the Struggle trying to stay afloat on the peaks of the waves, the crew and passengers writhed in agony on their beds. By some miracle, Captain Stevenson and Donald

Hawke remained immune to the sickness, despite the fact that neither of them had taken any precautionary measures. They climbed to the deck and tied themselves to the helm. As they were steering relatively close to the coast now, they had to take strict precautions not to run aground on a reef. It would have meant the bitter end of them. With mountain-sized waves threatening to snatch them from the deck, they tried desperately to stay on course. Captain Stevenson had already lowered most of the sails. What canvas remained in the air flapped madly in the wind. The ship proceeded at a dizzying pace. There was nobody left to lower the remaining sails. The crew members thrashed in their quarters, tormented by abdominal pain. The mainmast was the first to surrender itself to the raging elements. The canvas was already in tatters when the halyards snapped. The mast sagged toward the deck. Terrified, the two men wanted to escape, but by the time they had the tight rigging untied, the mast crashed down on them. Captain Stevenson was struck by one of the yards. He was tossed over the handrail like a doll, then swallowed by the churning ocean. His death cries were lost in the roaring hurricane.

Donald was left alone. He received a nasty blow to the head and fell over. He had managed to tie himself down, but a huge bottom wave nearly washed him off the deck. He succeeded at grabbing one of the ropes at the last minute. This saved him from certain death. Blood poured continuously from his forehead, mixing with the violent rain and the salt water. At a snail's pace, almost squirming, he managed to climb down from the deck platform and landed on the hatchway leading to the guest cabins. He remembered how the heaving motion of the boat made the door slam shut behind him. Everything went dark around him and he lost consciousness.

The ship lost direction and was free prey to the wind. It now sped in the direction of the Columbian coast. The waves still attacked the ship furiously. They tore down the broken and slackening mainmast and the ocean carried it off.

Not far from the shore, the Struggle collided with an underwater reef. This did much to slow it down. The giant blow it received resonated throughout the entire body, and sent the dying men crashing into the opposite wall. As more water filled the hold, the ship lost even more speed. By the time it entered the bay and floated toward the island, it was already half-sunk.

So much for Donald Hawke's journey from Valparaiso to the island, of which he was the only survivor. Losing hope, Susannah interrupted her walk and returned home.

Night arrived again, draping its black veil over the jungle. It entered into her heart as well, where hope was on the point of being extinguished. But the tiny ray of hope that had always flickered there continued to glow, and would not abandon her completely.

"This can't be the end," she told herself reassuringly, but with little success. "Maybe tomorrow," she thought. She sighed heavily and collapsed upon the bed. She was no longer afraid of Donald Hawke. Her soul assured her that the convict could never harm her again.

The pale light of the dying coals left the little home and the bed on which she lay dreaming. She gazed at the glimmering sparks. She didn't put any more wood on the fire. The night was warm anyway. Her face was lit with the faintly glowing embers, but her eyes were filled with the flames of youth.

When her eyelids had closed, she traveled to the land of dreams. She reached for William. The boy took her in his arms and gazed smilingly upon her. He spun the slim girl around and they threw themselves down on the silky grass. The girl's laughter rang out and the tiny ray of hope burst into flames.

The sun had hardly greeted the Tongan tribe when happy shouts shattered the morning silence. The people came out of their houses to see where the noises came from.

"They have returned! They're here!" came the loud cries. Soon, the entire village was surrounding William. The joy was even greater when they discovered that some of the lost boys had also been returned to them.

Hearing the commotion outside, Susannah dressed quickly. Two minutes later, William was holding her in his arms and she greeted him in a voice thickened with tears of joy. At that moment, everything around them ceased to exist. They could only gaze on one another. Hand in hand, they headed home. William looked at the house with joy.

"Home at last! Did you miss me, Susie?"

"Very much! I thought for a while you would never come back to me."

"Through hell or high water, I would always find my way back to you!"

"The nights were empty and terrible without you here. Tonight I can finally rest again. My knight has returned to his lady!"

And saying this, she curtsied. William knelt and put one arm around her waist.

"I won't ever leave you again, I promise," he whispered. Susannah kissed the top of his head.

"Are you hungry?"

"If you only knew how little we have eaten these past few days, you'd make me the biggest roast this village has ever seen! Want to hear about our adventures?"

"First, eat," said the girl, taking him by the arm. While William ate, she watched him with delight.

"You're not eating, Susie?"

"I'm not hungry. I had little appetite the entire time you were gone."

"But I'm here now."

"That's true. All right, I'll eat too."

After breakfast, they lay on the bed and held each other close. William recounted his adventures to her. He told how unexpectedly the storm had hit.

Susannah listened attentively, but inside her, another storm was raging. She was anxious for William to finish his story so she could finally tell him her secret. She knew that what she was about to say would come as a great shock to him, but that there was no way around it. Sooner or later, he would have to discover the truth about their unexpected visitor.

After William had finished talking, he waited to see what Susannah would say. He saw that something was troubling her.

"What's the matter, Susie?"

Susannah slowly lowered her pretty head. She couldn't quite bring herself to say it.

"Nothing," she said under her breath.

"Tell me the truth. I can see that something's bothering you." He reached out and touched the girl's face, causing her to raise her head slightly. She allowed it. She looked at him with tears shining in her eyes. William didn't know exactly what the matter was, but his heart was filled with pain to see her suffering.

"Tell me, what's wrong?' he urged softly. Susannah took a deep breath and began slowly.

The more she told him, the more deep feelings of bitterness, surprise, and anger gathered in William. When the name of Donald Hawke was pronounced, he felt the whole world go dark before him. He knew everything now.

He was filled with perplexity. He had the one man responsible for all their misery there in his grasp, and yet he felt he could not bring himself to repay the man with cruelty. The man's terrifying incident at sea, his having come so close to death had caused his hair to go grey. The dashing, arrogant, dauntless convict in his thirties had come to resemble a sick, broken-down fifty-year-old man overnight! What should he do – kill the man? Let him go? Take him prisoner? Starve him? Killing him wouldn't bring back their loved ones. On the other hand, could he let him go, just like that, knowing that Providence had delivered him into their hands? Could he let him go at a time when he had come close to believing that there would never be a way to avenge himself upon the villain? What should be done? William could feel his spirits sink under the weight of these unexpected troubles.

Susannah regarded him all the while, waiting for the final word to come from his lips. But William still didn't have an answer.

"It's like a bad dream," he whispered to himself. "That you can't awake from."

"Where are you going?" asked Susannah with a start.

"For a walk," the boy replied. He raised the llama skin. Pebbles grated under his feet, but the distance soon absorbed the sound of his footsteps. Susannah was left alone.

William walked past the house where Donald Hawke was lying. He walked to the shore and sat down in the sand. The cool waves soothingly caressed his bare feet. Doubts began to plague him again.

Donald's condition had worsened considerably during this time. He was running a high temperature. His head wound began smarting again. Due to the heat of the air inside, the house became stifling. He had great difficulty breathing. He would have liked to go outside for some air, but he was too weak to get up and there was no one around who would have understood his request. He was tormented with thirst constantly now. The Indian women, who had not ceased tending to their patient, were surprised to find that his condition had worsened. As they could not understand his feverish requests, one of the women finally went for Susannah. The girl showed neither joy nor disapproval. She followed the Indian woman back. She thought anxiously about having to talk to the man. She would most gladly have fled, but found the strength to continue.

Donald tossed feverishly on his bed. His large head wound had turned a ghastly color since the last time she had seen him. She approached the bed. Sensing that somebody was standing over him, he opened his eyes.

"What can I do for you?" asked the girl, her voice trembling uncontrollably. The English words surprised Donald Hawke. He tried hard to focus his eyes on the speaker.

"Who are you, young lady?"

"I'm English… more or less."

"What do you mean?"

"My parents were English."

"Then…how did you end up in this godforsaken jungle?"

"What would you like, sir?" asked the girl and involuntarily turned her face from him.

"I know that voice! I've seen you somewhere before! Who are you, young lady?"

"It seems you don't need anything," said the girl coldly. "God bless you, Donald, sir… That is, if you deserve it." Saying this, she turned and ran. A stifled cry followed her.

"Come back, young lady! Come back, I beg you!" But Susannah didn't go back. She ran home. She ripped the llama skin off the door and threw herself on the bed, sobbing.

Donald Hawke was left alone. He reflected on this unknown, yet strangely familiar girl. Had it not been for the fever he would have recognized the beautiful girl immediately. The fever had dulled his senses. The girl had known his name, which could mean that she was someone with whom he'd had dealings before. The name would have come to him had it not been for this horrible fever.

The animal skin was drawn aside again and this time a man, naked to the waist, with strong features, appeared before him. Fate had caught up with the despicable man and was about to deal him the final blow. Donald recognized Hull Anderson's son William immediately. A stifled rattle filled his throat and terror distorted his features.

The boy said nothing. He looked the man over for a while, both physically and spiritually. He tried to bring back Donald Hawke's scornful, cruel features. Something that would have justified revenge. But he found nothing of the sort. Susannah had been right. A grey-haired, broken-down old man now looked back at him with fear.

William glanced around the room. He looked at the bloody clothes beside the bed. From the pocket of the torn shirt protruded a familiar object. William removed it. It was the double-edged dagger that Donald had given to him so long ago. The blade was dirty and sticky from some victim's innocent blood.

A few days' journey from Valparaiso, when they'd been taken captive again, Donald had taken the dagger back from him. Now the murderous weapon was back in his hands once more. It could be used to deliver justice, to take advantage of the convict's vulnerable position. He also found the monogram D.H., for Donald Hawke, inscribed on the blade. He looked into the convict's eyes. They gleamed with feverish fear. He took the dagger and plunged it into the headboard. Slowly, he turned and left. He had no more business with the man. God was his judge. The outlaw, as far as he was concerned, had already got what he deserved.

He went home. Walking through the door, he and the girl exchanged glances. Susannah sensed immediately that something had happened.

"You went there?"

"Yes."

"And…"

"He recognized me. He recognized me right away!"

They didn't say anything more about the convict, although they had a sense of what was about to take place.

The meeting had shattered Donald Hawke. Fate had reunited him with two people whose lives he had destroyed. The tables were turned, and it was he who was at their mercy. It still wasn't clear to him how the youth had ended up in the Indian village. It didn't really matter now. He had no companions remaining and their treasure was long gone.

The evening tide receded from the shore and swept the "Struggle" into the bay. But it was too full of water to stay afloat for long. The ocean had flooded the deck, broken into the cabins, and filled every airless chamber. By nightfall, it had disappeared in a swirling eddy.

The convict was left with no other choice. It was death. He eyed the knife thoughtfully. He stretched out his trembling hands and wrapped his fingers around the hilt. He lifted the double-edged blade that glinted sinisterly in the light, then he closed his eyes, took a deep breath, and...

Fate granted him a speedy death. A few spasms shook his body. His countenance became glassy. Blood spurted from one corner of his mouth. His dark soul flitted from his body and descended to hell, where it belonged.

The news of the castaway's death spread through the village like lightning. The Indians gathered for a last look at the dead man. They pitied him, thinking that it was his infirmity that had caused him to put an end to his life.

But there were two people on the island who received the news with a sigh of relief. The ominous presence was gone from their lives. Justice had been done.

They buried Donald Hawke the next morning. It was William's desire that Donald Hawke be buried like a seaman, wrapped in bulrushes. Holding hands, William and Susannah, together with the Indians, watched from the shore as the canoe stopped a hundred yards into the bay. The rowers lifted the body, placed it on a board and floated it away. With dignity, the waves came together to form a shroud. A deep silence fell over the onlookers.

Another chapter in the life of the two young people had come to a close. The Tongans could not have known what the couple felt as they watched the corpse sink. Having survived so many adventures and trials, always managing to pull through, one would have thought that they would be happy now. They were free of their worst enemy! And yet they felt a kind of emptiness. Donald Hawke belonged to the past, and their parents belonged to their past. The convict had robbed of them of New Holland and their childhood and forced them to grow up too quickly in the course of so many hardships. Real justice would have been the ability to mend the broken thread of their past. But this was impossible. The dead couldn't be brought back, but forgetfulness would eventually cover the past with its merciful veil. Their futures stood before them now. They didn't know yet, and there was no way they could know, that the real trials and joys were still to come. That in the end, as in a fairytale, they would be given true happiness – as a reward for their steadfast love for one another!

Voyage Through Cape Horn

The Storm left Liverpool in May of 1796 and sailed for South America. Although a warship by design, its current task was of a different nature. The soldiers and weapons on board were for matters of defense. They were bound for the Colombian coast in search of gold. Indian legends spoke of rivers that, in fair weather, shone yellow from the gold dust they contained.

The expedition was commissioned by George Thomas, an English businessman. When his plans to expand his North American investments failed due to lack of capital, he relied upon the expedition to finance his dreams.

The Storm was an 18-cannon, 800-ton, 3-master frigate. It boasted a crew of two hundred and forty men, although the majority were trained soldiers who knew precious little about the sea. The sailors manned the ship while the mercenaries lounged on deck, biding their time until their arrival in South America.

George Thomas and the captain, Howell Harrison, had known one another since childhood and had remained good friends. When, one day, the businessman had called on his friend to ask if he would be interested in undertaking the voyage to South America, Howell had accepted the offer immediately. A mere two weeks before the trip they drew up an agreement and the captain selected his crew. At dawn of the prearranged day, they weighed anchor and set sail on the long voyage. A fair wind drove them forward and they quickly disappeared from the gaze of the curious onlookers.

Sailing past the Scilly Islands, it took them two days to leave the territorial waters of England and reach the wide Atlantic. Their first stop was Las Palmas, one of the cities of the Canary Islands, where they took on water and supplies. They remained in Las Palmas a week. Arriving at Rio de Janeiro four months later, they celebrated the successful Atlantic crossing over barrels of rum and beer.

Captain Harrison invited his officers to dinner at one of the better taverns in the area. He knew the tavern and its owners and in a short time, he and his men were dining in one of the private rooms. It was important to the captain that they be far removed from the noisy harbor crowd.

The dinner proceeded with everyone in high spirits. After the meal, the captain suddenly rose and locked the door. Returning to the head of the table, he looked at the expectant faces of his men.

"Men, I know this action has come as a surprise to you. But it is extremely important that we remain undisturbed. Many of you, in the course of our journey, have inquired as to our destination, and I was unable to answer at the time. I didn't want the information to be heard by the rest of the crew, who are known to gossip. But now the time has come for me to disclose the secret that is known only to myself and my employer, George Thomas."

Their stomachs full, the men had been relaxed and at ease until that point. The captain's words brought them back to wakefulness. Curiosity was marked on their faces.

"No need for any further questions. Our mission is to search for gold in the mountain country of the West Cordilleras in Colombia." Murmurs of surprise escaped those present. When they had calmed slightly, Captain Harrison continued: "My employer, Mr. Thomas, is in possession of several maps which mark the gold rivers of Colombia. The best way to proceed is from the Caribbean Sea to the Gulf of Darien and up the Atrato River. The Atrato is wide enough for our ship, and from that point we can proceed to the Cordilleras by canoe. However, the inhabitants would discover our intentions in no time and that would be the end of the entire expedition. They would butcher every last one of us before we came near the gold! For this reason, I propose the following plan: Circle Cape Horn and sail along the coast of Chile to Ecuador. There we will take a long rest, then continue north until we reach the Colombian coast. Here the population is very sparse, unlike the north. There is a much smaller chance here of finding trouble, and we can reach the Cordilleras on foot. It's only about 10 days from there."

"What happens if the Indians turn against us?" asked the first mate, James Bross.

"That depends on us and on the experiences the Indians have had before with white men."

"Are we at risk, Captain?"

"If things turn bad, we have 175 soldiers at our disposal. But a few gunshots should be enough to send the savages running for their lives. The question I'm going to ask will decide everything. Do you men agree to remain at your posts? If so, it will be up to you to let the rest of the crew in on our plans -- but only when we are at sea once more. Any of you officers who choose to withdraw will be left here in Rio de Janeiro."

His words were followed by a long silence as the men weighed the risks involved. But the thought of success and the wealth it would mean for them finally won them over. They had to succeed!

The men voiced their approval unanimously, and Captain Harrison brought forth the contractual agreements for each of them to sign. The memorable evening then continued downstairs in the tavern, and the men were very careful not to allow their secret to escape.

The following morning, Howell Harrison called the entire crew together. He informed them that they would set sail in three days for Cape Horn. This time, there would be no stopover.

Grumbles of discontent ran through the crowd on deck. Only four days of rest after such a long journey! But what could they do? The captain's decision was final.

The Storm weighed anchor again in the early morning hours of October 12, 1796, leaving the stunning harbor of Rio de Janeiro behind for that graveyard of ships, Cape Horn.

The days on the Atlantic passed slowly. Occasionally they met smaller boats and fishing vessels, and the members of both ships would greet each other with loud "hurrahs". Even the captains would exchange a few words via speaking tubes. When Captain Harrison informed one such captain that they planned to circle the Horn, the captain could do no better than to wish them all the luck in the world.

The further south they ventured the less predictable the weather became. By the time they reached Tierra del Fuego, more winter clothing was to be seen on board.

One morning, the first snowflakes appeared from a dark cloud. Captain Harrison spent much time poring over his maps and plotting the course. He debated sailing through the Strait of Magellan, but his officers were so strongly opposed to the idea that he finally abandoned it. Nearly all of them -- old sea-dogs like himself -- had had some experience with the Straits, and could remember the suicides and madness arising from the heroic attempt of a captain they had sailed with. Venturing into the Strait of Magellan meant putting all the eggs into one basket. It was exceedingly narrow and difficult, and usually only smaller vessels made it through intact. The Storm, a deep-draft ship, required much more room to maneuver. The Strait of Magellan began at the mouth of the Virgin Cape and wound on tortuously for 400 miles. It ended, to the great relief of all brave seamen, at Cape Thomar. Its most dangerous aspect was its tidal range, which could reach an average of as much as 50 to 70 feet. At high tide, the Atlantic poured into the Virgin Cape and headed for the Pacific Ocean. The powerful waterfall whisked away anything that crossed its path. The same thing happened at low tide, when the Pacific Ocean poured into Cape Thomar. Wherever this tidal rise and fall coincided, the range took on enormous proportions. Any boat unlucky enough to be passing at that time would be smashed to bits. For this reason, a captain had to know precisely where the ship stood in relation to the tides. A miscalculation of only a few hours could be fatal.

With all these factors in mind, the Strait of Magellan was decided against as a possible course. Yet in some ways Cape Horn, the cemetery of ships, was even less predictable than the Strait, except for the fact that it was always dangerous.

The Storm soon spotted the grim, rocky shore of Cape Horn as it sailed along the coast of Tierra del Fuego. The ocean's moods changed radically from one moment to the next. Now mountain-high waves attacked the boat from every direction. The wind grew fierce, but blew in opposing directions so that the boat was dead in the water for days at a time. Violent squalls, hail- and snowstorms came upon the ship so that it became harder and harder to maneuver. The frozen rain made the rigging so heavy that it often snapped, and the sails now required superhuman strength and skill to manage. They tried to remain clear of the coast, but the depth of the water also had to be taken into consideration. Hidden shoals, some 18 to 28 feet deep, lay in wait for an unfortunate ship to run aground on them. Captain Harrison often helped the helmsman and they worked together to steer the majestic ship clear of the deadly shoals. High waves lashed against the ship, often from many directions at once, attacking suddenly and flooding the deck. The crew frequently took turns at the pump. The joints of the deck let a constant stream of water into the hold. While the sailors remained aloft manning the sails, the mercenaries worked down in the hold with the pump. Although they were less than enthusiastic about the task before them, they wouldn't have traded places with the freezing, wet sailors for anything.

As the south wind howled in their ears, a gentle south-west breeze played to them the soft melodies of the Pacific. Three weeks passed, and Captain Harrison was shocked to discover at the end of his calculations that they'd hardly made any progress at all. He called in his first mate.

"Mr. Bross?"

"Aye, sir!"

"What's the cut of the jib? How do the sails look to you?"

"We trimmed every sail we could, sir! The wind tore them to shreds, and the yards can't take it."

"How do the sails look, Mr. Bross?" The captain repeated. Bross knitted his eyebrows but answered quickly.

"Only the middle sail is raised on the foremast and the mainmast. The mizzen sail is reefed and trimmed on the mizzenmast. But on the jib, only the storm-jib is raised, sir. The wind is blowing in two directions. We're going backwards as fast as we're going forwards."

"What would you suggest we do, Mr. Bross?"

"All we can do is wait. Maybe the winds will change."

"Wait? How many men are on deck?"

"Thirty, sir. The rest are in the fo'c'sle."

"All men on deck, captain's orders!" the captain interrupted him. "I'm taking over," he said, jumping out of his armchair.

"Yes, sir!" the first mate and bo'sun said, hurrying out of the cabin, and in a matter of seconds his voice could be heard booming: "Let's go, you lazy good-for-nothings! Faster! Faster!"

The pounding of feet resounded on deck. Captain Harrison wrapped himself in his cloak and went up to the deck. The wind nearly hurled the hatchway door in his face. The snow fell in thick flurries and crunched beneath his feet. The captain didn't waste a minute. He snapped out one command after another:

"Trim the foremast, mainmast, and middle sail! Fasten the stays to the weatherboard! Full fore-and-aft sails! Trim the middle sail! After-mast, latin sail: Haul! Haul the jib!"

At first, the ship came to a standstill, then as the fresh canvas came untied, it heeled windward. The sails filled, flapped shut, and filled again. The rigging tautened with a twang. As soon as a line snapped, another took its place. The after-mast creaked forward. The fore-sails pounded like drums, but remained intact. And wonder of wonders, the ship shot forward! At first, the crew eyed the spar with fear, but seeing that they were making progress against the wind, began to shout loudly with joy. Captain Harrison made some assessments, then turned to the first mate.

"Mr. Bross, reduce the watch by two. Replace the crew and the rigging every four hours -- either with middle sails or the entire rigging or without the middle sails."

"Yes, sir!" said the first mate, clicking his heels together. The captain returned to his cabin, leaving his first mate looking admiringly after him.

The captain went down to his cabin and spent a long time poring over his maps in the dim light of the swinging lamps. He made calculations and retraced the ship's present course. When he became too tired to continue, he made himself tea in the galley, and sat thoughtfully in his armchair for a while.

Later he went over to his sea chest, took out a set of jealously-guarded keys, and opened the locks. The lid was open in a short time. This was where he kept his most treasured personal and family belongings. As he often did when he had the time, he removed the gold jewelry box. He removed a medallion from it. The medallion was pure gold and ornately chased. In the middle of the medallion, framed in mother-of-pearl, was the image of a beautiful girl. She was Countess Elizabeth Raymond, that adventurous girl whom fate, along with the other thirteen "mutineers" on Captain Cook's ship, had been cast ashore at New Holland. Following that incident, she had became the wife of Lord Gredford and the mother of Susannah, the very likeness of her mother.

Captain Harrison knew nothing of these latter events. He and the Countess had been sweethearts many years before, but due to irreconcilable differences in their social standing, had been forced to abandon any hope of marrying. Elizabeth's father, a lord from a very powerful family to whom title and wealth were everything, would never have allowed such a marriage. Sir Thomas Raymond would never have accepted a sea captain as his son-in-law. Realizing that the situation was hopeless, Elizabeth gave the young man the medallion as a keepsake to remember her by.

Years passed and the news of Captain Cook's famous voyage spread. Harrison knew of the fourteen who had been put ashore at New Holland -- what was later to be known as Australia. He knew that the Countess had been among them, but he had never been able to discover where exactly they had gone ashore. Nobody knew. And the crew had scattered or had gone on to join other ships. Howell Harrison had never been able to find out the truth from Captain Cook. The foolhardy captain embarked on a few other voyages around the world and died soon after, far from his homeland, taking his secret to the grave. It was then that Captain Harrison, mainly at his own expense but with some financial help from his friend, George Thomas, took it upon himself to sail for New Holland.

This happened in May of 1772. Captain Harrison searched in vain for two years before returning to England in June, 1774. Still, time had done nothing to diminish his love for his Elizabeth. It did not matter that he was approaching his fiftieth year; it was impossible for him to give up hope that he would see her again one day. There had been other expeditions that had all, likewise, come to nothing.

As the years sank into oblivion, many believed the castaways to be dead. But Howell had still not given up hope that he would one day meet one of the castaways who knew of the Countess's whereabouts.

In the course of his career, he had never married and had lost all desire to do so. He had always been a lonely sea-dog, and there was no point in trying to change this now. The years were passing and soon he would give up his post to a worthy young man whom the Admiralty would select. This, most likely, was his last voyage. If they succeeded in finding gold and he was lucky enough to look upon England again, he could retire peacefully to his home in Bristol that had been locked up for many years now.

Harrison spent a long time gazing at the portrait, at the delicate, eternally young features that an artist with the initials "d.r." had done so well to immortalize. Finally, he sighed and placed the medallion back in the box, the box in the chest, and shut the lid. The lock clicked and the past was once again safely out of the reach of strange hands. Captain Harrison drank the remainder of his tea and approached the door with a thoughtful expression on his face. He wanted to have another look at the Storm before turning in for the night. The days had become bitterly cold. They'd sighted ice floes recently, and from that moment on, no one on board had had a moment's peace. The sailors had to be ready at the sails constantly to prevent a collision. The snow fell almost continuously. The squalls often turned into hurricanes and the cold grew so fierce that it hurt to breathe.

Bitter days lay ahead. Only with reduced rigging could the ship manage against the ever-strengthening winds. They progressed at a snail's pace.

A few days later, Captain Harrison became aware of something highly unusual. He went over his calculations several times to verify it. The figures were always the same. They showed that the wind was blowing predominantly from the south and the south-west – indeed, one of the great risks of sailing the Cape. But his calculations also confirmed that they had come upon a hidden current, one the captain had never heard of before, and that it was pulling them slowly but surely in a southerly direction.

Even the oldest of the mariners on board, despite having sailed the Cape a dozen times or more, had never heard of this strange current before. The sailors sent up prayers of supplication to heaven, and thought: "All this suffering, and now this!" To add to their trials and tribulations, an enormous ice field was now threatening to envelop the ship in an open wedge. The second mate sent for the captain immediately and tried to handle the situation as best he could.

"Replace the sails! Let go the line! Pull the sheets! First watch to the mainmast! Replace fore-sail!"

The frigate came to a standstill. A terrible tremor ran through it. As the wind caught the hull, the jib-boom plunged underwater. One after the other, the sails overturned. The ship tried to turn, but it was too late. The wedge slowly closed around the ship, checking its retreat. This was every Arctic traveler's worst nightmare: To be trapped in an ice field's deadly grip!

This happened on December 29, 1796. The "dead water" surrounding the ship froze in a matter of hours. They were right to think that if they were to sweep any further south in the frozen water, they were doomed. The boat would snap like a twig and all that would remain of the crew would be frozen corpses. Captain Harrison informed them what had happened. The officers themselves were aware of the gravity of the situation, but no one said a word. There was nothing to say. If they didn't find a way to escape within two or three months, they would all die.

The carpenters built a fortification under the deck hatch to help insulate the stokehold. After this, nobody left the cabins. They had enough fuel remaining to last a few weeks, but they would have to use it very sparingly. The cabin temperatures soon dropped to the freezing point.

The men greeted the New Year a little sadly, exhausted by their many hardships. They could only wish that the New Year would bring speedy liberation from the icy tomb.

Two weeks passed. They kept only the galley coals burning now. This way, they would at least have hot tea to drink, and could roast the frozen pork and beef.

When the weather permitted, they took small excursions onto the ice field. They did this partly in hopes of finding a way out, and partly to escape the constant monotony of cabin life. The exercise returned to the men some of their vitality and the strength to continue, in the hope that they would one day live to tell of their adventures in a warm smoky tavern over a cup of grog.

Taking measurements, they discovered that they were situated on the outer third of a 4-mile wide ice field. The current was still taking them south. Breaking through the mile of ice would do them no good, for the water would freeze again in a couple of hours. Then another idea occurred to the men. Using their vast supply of gunpowder, they could blow their way through the ice! But this, too, proved futile. Ten times their supply of gunpowder would not have sufficed.

To add misery upon misery, a new danger suddenly presented itself on board: A number of men began to complain of painful and bleeding gums. Captain Harrison immediately brought out a few crates of lemons, though it didn't take him long to realize that there weren't enough to go around.

By January 15, 1797, 42 members of the ship's company had scurvy. The captain was at a loss. He withdrew to his cabin and refused to see anyone. His cabin was the same as all the others on board; frost covered everything. He sank into his huge armchair and brooded on the present situation. How could he save his ship and his ailing men? Of course, the captain had no way of knowing that the answer to both these problems lay in nature itself.

On January 22, a new team set out to explore. Two hours later they returned, shouting excitedly to the men in the hold. A few of the men came out of their cabins and shouted back, annoyed:

"What do you want?"

"Seals… the seals have arrived!"

"Good for them. They're better made for the cold than we are," grumbled a young sailor, Jack Houston. He cast a questioning look at the bo'sun. The old mariner thought it over, then burst out laughing. He gave the greenhorn a huge slap on the back.

"We're saved, son, don't you see?" the bo'sun exclaimed, his eyes shining with mirth. But when he raised his hand to repeat the friendly gesture, Jack quickly stepped out of the way. He gave the old man an indignant look.

"What's Mr. Woodland talking about?"

"The seals, seal blood, son… All we have to do is drink the blood and we'll be cured!"

The old mariner ran like a boy to tell the captain the good news. The news about the seals spread quickly. The more experienced seamen knew exactly what had to be done. Captain Harrison sent fifty armed men to the seal colony. A short time later, he sent others to accompany them. Everybody was required to drink the blood. Those who couldn't walk by themselves were carried.

The armed men reached the seals before they could escape into the water. Gunshots rang out and only a few of the awkward creatures succeeded in escaping the shower of bullets. Several dozen lay dead on the ice. With raised knives, the men got down to the task at hand. Though difficult at first, many forced themselves successfully to drink the blood. Others drank the blood only to vomit it a short while later. Some turned back in disgust.

It was dark by the time they returned to the ship. Nobody touched his dinner. They went to bed with the fishy taste of the seal blood still in their mouths.

The days passed slowly. As they drifted further south, they discovered smaller colonies here and there. Those who drank the blood regularly showed steady signs of recovery. Those who, for one reason or another, refused to take the remedy lost their teeth and wasted away. There were one or two burials every day.

February arrived, and as the ice floe continued to drift south, all hopes of escape began to peter out. It was so cold that they had to rub themselves with seal blubber to stay warm. This, combined with the stench of their unwashed bodies, made the air on board nearly intolerable. For a while, the men made every effort to avoid each other, but eventually they became accustomed to the smell. Warm bath water was something they could only dream of now.

One morning, the men were out on their usual hunt when they spotted huge icebergs in the distance. These were bigger than any they had ever seen before. One was heading in the direction of the ice field. The men ran as quickly as they could in the direction of the ship. They were no more than a quarter of a mile from the vessel when a terrible shock suddenly rent the ice below their feet. The berg crashed thunderously into the sheet of ice. Other collisions followed. With a shrieking grind, they smashed further into the edge of the ice sheet. In the blink of an eye, the sheet broke into a million hairline cracks and opened beneath them. One of the hunters fell through and vanished from sight. All that the men heard were his screams. By the time they realized what was happening, it was too late: The man had been crushed to his death beneath the receding ice. Their own situation, meanwhile, was changing rapidly. They ran frantically toward the ship. Their lungs nearly burst from the cold, hard air. There were cracks everywhere now, so they had to make every effort not to fall.

The men on board the three-master knew that something wasn't right. They raced to the deck to witness something that was dreadful and wonderful all at once. The ice field lay broken all around them. The boat was free! Hearing faraway cries, they looked up. Their nine companions stood not 200 yards ahead, shouting desperately from the single remaining block of ice. It was drifting further and further away from the boat.

Captain Harrison immediately called for volunteers to get the large canoes and go after the men.

Half an hour later, the crew celebrated the successful rescue on board. The sails were untied from the masts, and the ship's sturdy bow slowly but surely pushed its way through the remaining chunks of ice. It was February 8, 1797, when they were finally released from their cruel prison and continued on their way to Chile.

According to Captain Harrison's calculations, the Storm had drifted 80 degrees west by 70 degrees south during the period of their captivity, and they were now very close to a group of islands. Despite the fact there were a thousand miles of sea still ahead of them -- and the obstacles that came with that -- their providential escape could be regarded as nothing less than an overwhelming victory.

The weeks passed and the Storm, with expert maneuvering, managed successfully to avoid the icy snares and shoals that littered its path. Another two months of suspense, and the long-awaited moment arrived. It was April 12, 1797 when the horizon finally spread itself before them. The free Pacific was theirs once again! They greeted it with loud cheers.

They were all in terrible physical shape. Some of them had wasted considerably, others had lost teeth or other extremities due to scurvy, or noses, ears, or toes in the punishing climate. They were thoroughly exhausted. Only the hardiest of them could help run the ship.

The difficulties encountered in the Antarctic had taken their toll: 30% of the passengers had perished. Terrible as this was, things could have been even worse. The ship itself was sorely in need of a dry dock. Its sails, decorations, bright work, and carvings had been stripped to the bone, and the hull itself was now worth less than a pile of junk lumber. Captain Harrison gave orders to go aground at the first green land or island sighted.

It was April 19, 1797. The ship dropped anchor on the southwest coast of Chile. The entire crew wept tears of joy, especially at the sight of vegetation and feeling the warm sun caress their skin again.

The sick were laid on makeshift beds in the shade. The other men then separated into small groups, one to hunt, the other to help unload the supplies needed to make camp. It was a wonderful feeling to be on land again, and they worked with great gusto.

The hunters returned with a large supply of meat. Some tried their luck at stealing turtle and bird eggs. They lit several huge fires and roasted all kinds of meat. When dinner was ready they were given rations they hadn't received in a long time, and they ate with great appetite, filling their empty stomachs to bursting.

The region was not completely uninhabited. They had spotted a few Indian tribes in the distance, but the tribes, seeing their great number, took care to avoid the men. That night they assigned watchmen around the camp to avoid any unpleasant surprises.

The next morning, they were up and about early. They performed some minor repairs to the hull and disinfected the hold. The ablest among them tended the sick. The carpenters also had plenty of work ahead of them. They had to build a new superstructure at the aft of the ship, and the mast had to be repaired and the yard replaced. Fortunately, they had all the carpentry tools they needed. They also had plenty of sealant, nails and stays.

Their sojourn on the coast lasted less than a month. They recovered most of their strength during this time. They weighed anchor, tautened the sails and cheerfully set sail.

Howell Harrison gave the order: "Direction, Valparaiso harbor!"

They had better luck this time. The Pacific Ocean remained true to its name: not a single storm occurred during the three-week journey.

On June 6, 1797, they put into port at Valparaiso. The patched and bootstrapped ship aroused no small attention from the port crowd. A crowd of curious onlookers surrounded them. The men could hardly wait to come ashore and be among people again. The harbor town was hot, a fact which was welcomed enthusiastically by these Antarctic-voyaging sailors.

Captain Harrison wished to have a few words with his men before allowing them to go ashore.

"Officers, soldiers and sailors, I feel it is my duty to reward you for remaining true to me when I was most in need of you. It was my fault that the ship became caught in the ice. This cost me and my employer alike…and you men! I would like to recompense you. Before you go ashore, you shall have the pay due to you - your wages - and I will also divide among you the money of those who could not be here today to receive their share."

"Hurrah! Long live the captain! Long live Valparaiso!" came the delighted shouts of the men.

"One more thing," the captain said, indicating the men to calm down. "I want four men to go ashore and purchase, at my expense, two barrels of rum from the first pub they find. We'll drink it before you go ashore, in celebration of the success of our trip and for the salvation of the souls of the deceased."

The cheering that followed shook the boards of the old Storm. When the men had calmed down somewhat, the captain brought his desk on deck and had the men line up to collect their money. During that time, the rum arrived and the men drank thirstily. That night, only a few watchmen and the captain remained on board. The other officers, soldiers, and sailors blended with the night crowd, and made up for lost time.

Wine, women, song, gambling – everything was available to them in the crowded taverns. That night the "starving" crew, their wallets thick, were given every opportunity to indulge themselves.

Captain Harrison brought his armchair on deck. He sat down, lit an aromatic cigar, and dreamily watched the busy life of the harbor town. He puffed at his cigar with pleasure, sighing largely and enjoying the fresh salt air. He was relieved that a difficult part of their journey had ended successfully. But now came the most important part. The hunt for gold – whoever heard of such a crazy thing?! There was no answer as yet to this question. He had involved himself in a seemingly impossible venture because of his friend. Would it be worthwhile? He had no way of knowing yet. The maps of Colombia still lay at the bottom of the sea chest, though if he closed his eyes the often-studied parchment drawings appeared before him. Soon they would approach the equator on their voyage to the Colombian coast and the mountain country. One thing was certain: If the trip succeeded, and even if it didn't, he would return to England and retire from the sea.

The Treasue

Thousands of stars sparkled like diamonds in the velvety sky. From its highest point, the waning moon cast a pale light over the jungle. Even so, one could feel the night coming to a close. Bird's songs began to take over the chirping of the crickets and cicadas.

In the east, the sky suddenly lightened. A pink flush appeared and the sun's first rays burst out like giant pillars of fire. The night's children, the moon and stars, faded into the blue sky. The burning orb of the sun ascended slowly above the jungle. Then it came to a sudden halt.

Storm clouds began to gather in the west. The sky grumbled ominously in the distance. Swift-moving clouds covered the sky and dimmed the sun. Lightning flashed over the ocean, and thunder began to boom angrily. The rising wind lashed the tops of the palm trees. Lightning struck an ancient oak. Fire, smoke, and the noise of falling branches filled the air. Then the thunder grew even louder and the rain poured down.

Susannah shivered beneath her warm blanket. She reached for William, but the boy appeared to be fast asleep. She pushed him over and snuggled close for safety. The boy didn't move, though he'd been awake since before the storm began. He watched the girl out of the corner of his eye, knowing she would do everything she could to disturb his sleep. She liked to be close to him during storms and needed him to tell her, "Don't worry, everything will be fine."

Susannah nudged William again. Groaning, he rolled over and pretended to go back to sleep. She shook him desperately this time, then sighed loudly and pulled the blanket over her head. William turned to her, grinning.

"Were you scared?" he asked, teasingly.

"No. Why?"

"You wouldn't let me sleep," he laughed.

When Susannah realized that William had been fooling her all along, she seized the llama skin and began to beat him with it. He took hold of it and pulled. She lost her balance and fell on him. He put his arms around her waist. When she resisted, he kissed her neck, and with his left hand gave her a sharp slap on the behind. Susannah shrieked, and they began to wrestle. Finally, exhausted, they fell on the bed and smiled at each other.

A year had passed. Since the death of Donald Hawke, they had enjoyed a life of undisturbed calm. Nothing could spoil their happiness now. The rainy season had returned, with its long, idle days. Often sheer boredom, rather than hunger, drove the Tongans into the wet jungle for fresh meat.

After finishing a hearty breakfast, William began to feel restless again. Adventurous soul that he was, he quickly tired of the indoor life. Things were very different for Susannah. She had to do all the cooking and cleaning. Even the worst weather was an excuse to have the boy at her side.

William gazed at his wife as she busied herself around the hearth. Susannah Gredford Anderson was so beautiful that her smile would have tempted a saint -- and no wonder. It was November of 1797, and she had just turned seventeen. She was beginning to blossom into womanhood. Aware that she was being watched from the bed, she turned around.

"What are you thinking about?" she asked.

"Oh, nothing," he hesitated.

"Oh, tell me. Or is it something I'm not supposed to know?"

"I was thinking about you."

"Me?" she asked, surprised.

"Yes. I just realized something," he continued, pretending to be serious.

"What?"

"It just occurred to me that we're married." There was a spark of mischief in the boy's eyes. She now had an idea where the conversation was going. She sat on the edge of the bed, but at a distance from the boy.

"And?"

"Married couples…" William paused for dramatic effect, not taking his eyes off the girl. "Married couples have certain obligations to each other."

Susannah's eyes widened with astonishment. She was even more surprised when William pulled her down beside him and started to undo her dress.

"Willy!" she cried. "What do you think you're doing?" But William quickly covered the girl's mouth with his own mouth to avoid listening to her objections. She tried desperately to escape from her position, but William's arms tightened. Her struggle for freedom soon ended in defeat. Secretly, she liked the game. The boy kissed her energetically, removing half of her clothing. William would have continued gladly, but the smell of burning food made him lift his head. Susannah sat up.

"Oh, no, my roast!" she screamed, pulling herself free. She ran to the hearth to find the meat burned to a crisp.

"It's all your fault," she muttered to her husband, who had thrown himself on the bed in a convulsion of laughter. Beside herself with rage, she picked up a clay pitcher filled with water and threw its contents on William. This did nothing to help the situation.

"Go ahead and laugh," she sniffed. "We'll see just how cheerful you are on an empty stomach."

"We'll have fruit!" suggested William, recovering enough to speak. He got off the bed and wiped himself dry with a blanket.

"Now I'm soaking wet, and it's all because of you!"

"Serves you right."

"Now what? Are you going to cook something else, or should we continue where we left off?"

"Oh, no!" Susannah protested. Suddenly realizing that her breasts were still bare from their scuffle, she blushed and quickly adjusted her clothing.

"I liked the way you looked before, too."

"Good!" she snapped, adjusting her dress even tighter.

"You know, that probably wasn't a very good idea. It makes undressing you that much harder." William ducked just in time to avoid a slap. He drew the girl toward him and kissed her.

"You're beautiful, my love," he whispered. "I'll go get some water. I'll be right back." He took the pitcher and winked at her. Susannah smiled and turned back to the fire. Unfamiliar thoughts began to occupy her mind; a strange excitement ran through her body.

William frowned when he realized that he was walking into the pouring rain, but his heart sang with joy. The Tongans were almost never outside in this weather. He quickened his pace to reach his destination as soon as possible. The cold air from the ocean struck him as he emerged from the canopy of trees. He shivered. He'd become so used to his warm home that such a minor thing as warm clothes hadn't even entered his mind.

He ran across the strip. A short while later, he arrived at the stream. He filled the pitcher with crystal-clear water and headed back home. On his way, he took a long look at the "great water". But nothing was out there, not a sail on the horizon, only the dull rain. Suddenly, it occurred to him that a reservoir could be built to make the transport of water much easier for the village. It seemed like a good plan, but his mind was elsewhere. He was thinking of Susannah. He knew that she was aware what was expected of her.

When he arrived home, Susannah looked up from her work. Lunch was almost ready. A fresh roast had a pleasing aroma. William set the pitcher down and seated himself at the table. The same thoughts he'd had on the shore began to repeat themselves.

A heavy silence fell upon the room. They couldn't think of anything to say to each other, but both were glad to put off the "scuffle" for a while. William made the first attempt at conversation.

"It's still raining," he announced. Susannah continued preparing the meal.

"The roast is ready!" she announced a short while later. The boy rose from the bed and sat beside her. They ate in silence. After the meal, they drank the fresh water William had brought. But they still couldn't find the missing thread of their conversation.

"You must be tired, Susie."

"Yes, a little."

After the meal, they lay on the bed but neither one could sleep. The same thought kept going through their minds. The minutes passed in silence and Susannah began to regret that the "scuffle" had been interrupted by the burnt roast. "Hmm… so he doesn't have the nerve to dare me to another game," she thought. "Well, now it's my turn to show a little courage!"

"Willy," she said aloud.

"Yes?"

"I've been thinking. Don't you think it's a little lonely here, with just the two of us?"

"What do you mean?" William asked, sitting up and looking closely at Susannah.

"Well…"

"Well?"

"What would you say if we had a baby?" she said finally. William gave her the same look that she had given him when he had mentioned their "marital obligations".

"Do you really mean that?"

"Yes! Mother always used to tell me about the day I would go from being a girl to a woman. But I never really understood what that meant until now. Do you remember Milla?"

"Of course."

"Remember what a scandal there was when Sagat discovered that she was pregnant? And how they let them marry even though Pang was still a "monk"? Well, I want us to have a baby too, Willy!"

Susannah buried her face in his shoulder. The boy could feel her trembling from head to toe. He felt a weight of responsibility he'd never known before. He held her close. Their eager bodies came together and something extraordinary fused them together. Their lips met, and the whole world stopped.

The rainy season brought the two closer together than they had ever been. This was the finest hour of their love – a day that had started in playful innocence and ended by being the most memorable of their lives. The long, wet days ceased to be dreary for William now that he had attained his greatest goal: The happiness and selfless love of his Susannah!

One morning, their meat supplies very low, the warriors set out hunting. It was the first clear day in months. William kissed Susannah goodbye. Taking their weapons, the men quickly disappeared into the thick of the jungle. By early afternoon, there was an abundance of meat, and William divided the men into two groups. One group would continue hunting while the other returned to the village to skin the animals. At first, William thought of continuing with the hunting party, but he reconsidered. He handed over the responsibility to Goko, his favorite hunter, and returned to the village with the other men.

Susannah greeted her husband joyfully. William skinned his game. Then he and Susannah went to the shore for a swim before lunch. After the meal, the boy returned to the stream for a fresh supply of water. After filling the pitcher, he rested on a flat rock and watched the stream flow eagerly towards the ocean. He could hear the distant laughter of the children, quick to take advantage of the pleasant weather, playing in the waves. William smiled. The villagers were happy on the island, and William knew that this was greatly due to him. The Tongans had chosen him as their leader, and it was a position he filled with great pride. He stood, stretched, and picked up the pitcher. Suddenly, he heard a loud cry. He turned and listened. "Am I imagining things?" he said, but the voice soon repeated itself.

"Help!"

"Somebody's in danger," he realized, setting out in the direction of the voice. He beat his way through the branches and underbrush. Seconds later, he was beside an injured man, who mumbled something feverishly and then lost consciousness. William lifted him carefully and carried him into the clearing.

He couldn't imagine how the man had managed to get so far into the thorn-laden bush. He had the look of one who had been chased or shipwrecked. These could be the only explanations for the ugly bruises and scratches on his arms and face and the nasty gash on his neck. The latter was probably caused by a knife. He also had what appeared to be an arrow wound in his left ankle. All things considered, it was clear that the man had not had an easy time of it. William wondered where his companions were.

Twice he had to stop and rest, sitting breathlessly beside the injured man. As he approached the island, he laid his heavy burden down again. The children flocked curiously around the white stranger.

"Susannah!" William called to his wife. Seconds later, she appeared in the doorway. On seeing the injured man, she turned white.

"Oh, Lord!" she cried, running over to them.

"I found him in the bush," William explained. "Come on, Susie, help me bring him inside." They carried the unconscious man into the house and laid him on the bed. Susannah immediately took care of the stranger's wounds, supported his head, and gave him water. They applied a poultice to his forehead to bring down the fever. Afterwards, they took a closer look at the man. He was approximately forty years old, broad-shouldered, tall, with brown hair and sharp features. His torn, blood-stained shirt revealed a hairy, deeply scarred chest. They removed the shirt and bandaged his wounds. They observed with horror the way gashes covered the stranger's body from head to toe. Then something else caught William's eye. On the left shoulder, there was a tattoo of a huge anchor. This meant that the man was a seaman of some kind.

The wounded man slept deeply. Susannah changed the poultice often. The fever gradually broke.

William sent one of the warriors to bring back the pitcher he'd left at the stream, and another to inform the elders of the newcomer's arrival. Soon, a large crowd gathered around William's house to catch a glimpse of the man. Before sundown, he was brought to the guest house where an old woman was assigned to care for him.

The patient regained his senses the following night. Though the sight of the Indian woman undoubtedly startled him at first, her friendly manner soon assured him of her good intentions. She brought him a jug of water and he drank thirstily. When he finished, he looked up to discover that the elderly lady was no longer there. She was on her way to William's house to inform him that the patient had regained consciousness. Susannah and William immediately followed the woman back to the house.

The man, Martin Cart, was surprised when he saw the white couple. Susannah's presence impressed him even more than William's. He thought he had seen the girl somewhere before, not long ago.

"Who are you?" he stammered.

"You'll know soon enough," replied the striking young man beside the beautiful girl. "Please understand," he added. "I think we should be the ones to ask the questions."

"Of course, of course. Forgive me. I'm a sailor on the Storm, a 3-master frigate. My name is Martin Cart. We sailed from England, around Cape Horn to the coast of Colombia."

"I'm sorry," interrupted William. "Our knowledge of geography is not what it should be."

"I understand perfectly," Cart said, slightly surprised. "I will be careful not to use any more technical terms. If I were to say the Andes, would you know what I mean, sir?"

"Yes. Please continue."

"As I was saying, we were heading north, to the north Andes. Our mission was to discover gold."

Martin Cart observed how the faces of the youths grew sullen on hearing these words, but continued.

"The crew was informed of this only halfway through the journey. And from that moment on, everything took a turn for the worse. We ran aground and wandered deep into the jungle. Just as the mountains came into sight, we were attacked by Indians. They assaulted us on all sides with arrows, spears, and knives. We were taken completely by surprise. Many of our men were killed immediately. To this day, we have no way of knowing what provoked the attack. Those who could do so, separated into groups and ran. We knew this was our only chance to survive. Once in the hands of angry Indians, there was no escape. Our captain, Mr. Harrison, told us where our ship would wait for us. It will head back to England come the new moon. Three companions and I managed to escape a few weeks ago. The Indians hunted us like animals. None of my companions survived. I received an arrow wound in one leg. I had to fight two Indians at once. I still don't know how I managed it; maybe the pain gave me strength I wouldn't have had otherwise. I wandered in agony for days until I reached the shore. I can't say when that was. But you can imagine how frightened I was just now to find myself among dark-skinned people!"

"You're safe here. I found you yesterday morning in the jungle. You called for help in English. I brought you home and my wife dressed your wounds. Your condition seems to have improved greatly."

"Yes! I can't thank you enough for your kindness. Thank you, young lady," he said, addressing Susannah separately. "If it had not been for your help, I wouldn't be here now. But if you don't mind, I wouldn't mind knowing something about you. How on earth did you come to live among the Indians?"

"If you truly want to know, Mr. Cart, I'll tell you. The story is rather long. My wife will help me to remember any details I may have forgotten, won't you, dear?" he asked, turning to Susannah. The girl nodded in agreement. William continued with the story.

Martin Cart could hardly believe his ears. When it was over, he could barely speak."I don't know what to say. After so many hardships, you the Tongan chief? An English sailor's boy, an Englishwoman's daughter? My lady," he said, turning to Susannah.

"Sir?"

"Could you tell me something about your mother, and about her life back in England?"

"I know next to nothing. My parents always kept their past a great secret."

"You mean, you don't even know how your parents came to live at New Holland?"

"That's right."

"Interesting! You mean to say you don't even know of the other places they left behind? A series of misfortunes must have forced them to wander from place to place. Just how many were they, exactly?"

"Fourteen."

"Fourteen, and they all took their secrets to the grave!"

"That's right, sir. That's exactly what happened. We don't know any more than you do," William replied, sadly.

"I have a feeling... I may be wrong, though…"

"What?"

"My lady, what was your mother's maiden name?"

"Raymond. Elizabeth Raymond."

"My God! That means…"

"What?" stammered William.

"Now I know everything," Cart shouted.

"Tell me, I beg you!" Susanna cried. "You have no idea how important this is to William and me."

"You, young lady," he said, turning to Susannah, "are the daughter of Countess Elizabeth Raymond!"

"Countess? What's that?"

"It's a position of great privilege in England. I will tell you the story. The year was 1770."

"That long ago?"

"Yes. I was a child myself at the time, but I remember as if it were yesterday. It all started with Captain James Cook's expedition…"

Martin Cart's words took them through their parents' history. They were told things they had thought would remain a mystery to them forever.

"That's why Mrs. Anderson's face seemed so familiar to me when you two entered the room! There's a chest in Captain Harrison's cabin. He has a medallion in the chest that he guards with his life. A short time ago, he showed it to me. It bears the image of your mother, Countess Raymond, at the age of seventeen. That portrait is the exact likeness of you, my dear lady!"

Susannah's eyes overflowed with tears. She threw her arms around the man who had returned what life had taken from her.

"Well, there's nothing else to do. I believe the place for both of you is back in England!"

The young people could hardly believe their ears. Martin Cart assured them that he would see them safely aboard the Storm. Once on board the ship, Captain Harrison would take over.

The world began to spin around the young couple. Here, at last, was their chance to travel to the land of their dreams, England, to begin a new life in civilization!

By the next night, however, it seemed that all their newfound hopes would be shattered. Martin Cart said that he had something urgent to tell them.

"What is it, Mr. Cart?"

"The ship," he groaned, resignedly.

"What about the ship?"

"It's sailing!" he cried, lifting a trembling hand. Through the small opening in the wall, he could see the sky and the new moon!

"How far is it to your meeting place with Captain Harrison?"

"Very far south of here. I don't think we can make it in time. I can hardly walk."

"Don't worry. My men will carry you on a litter all the way to the ship."

"Good, then there's no problem! I know Captain Harrison will leave a day or two later than scheduled," said the sailor, cheering up.

"Oh, but there is a problem," William said suddenly. "What will happen to the Tongans? What will become of my tribe? I'm their leader. I can't abandon them."

"Willy!" Susannah said. "You can't change your mind now. This could be our one and only chance to go home."

"Home," the boy echoed, bitterly. "What are you saying, Susie? I thought we were home." Saying this, he went outside.

"William, come back!" Susannah shouted.

Outside, William took a long look at the sleeping village. The rain clouds had scattered and the first stars were shining. Everything here was so perfect! Who knew what awaited them on the other side of the world? Once they left, they would never be able to come back.

What had happened to him suddenly? Not long ago he would have done anything to have this opportunity, and now that it had presented itself, he was afraid to go take it.

He walked to the center of the town, where the watch fires blazed, sat on a tree stump and continued to think things over. A few minutes later, he heard someone approach. It was the young warrior, Goko.

"You look very sad, chief. Why?"

"Why aren't you asleep, Goko?" William said, avoiding the question.

"I dreamed of a fire. Important things are soon to happen."

"That's right, Goko. There's a great deal on my mind. I'm not sure what to do."

"Every problem has a solution. You taught us that."

"This problem has no solution."

"But that's impossible. You have worked so many wonders – in this, you are not telling the truth."

"But I am," William said, sadly. Seeing that the warrior didn't want to trouble him with more questions, he continued.

"Goko, what would you say if I told you I was leaving?"

"By yourself? What about Flower of the Forest?"

"She would come with me."

"Would you be gone a long time?"

"Forever," William replied, heavily.

"Don't say such a thing. You would leave your tribe?"

"Yes."

"Why, did someone cause you harm? Tell me who, and we'll have him judged by the elders. We'll punish him!"

"No, nobody has harmed me. Everybody here is very good to us."

"I'm afraid I don't understand."

"Then listen to this." And William told him of the opportunity that had arisen. The young warrior listened with amazement.

"Now do you understand?"

"Yes. You must do what you think is right. Only promise that you will make a speech before you go." Goko's words fell heavily on William's ears. His heart sank.

"I promise, Goko." Suddenly, he reached over and embraced his great friend, the brave young warrior. The young man's face bore all the tenderness of his tribe. "You're a good man, a brave fighter, Goko," said William, feeling his eyes begin to well with tears. Goko nodded. Though he was glad of the praise, something was different suddenly. William and Flower of the Forest had lived among them; they were children of the jungle. He knew how sorely his tribe would miss the fine young people.

"Chief."

"Yes, Goko?"

"If you don't like it there, will you come back to us?"

"Yes," replied William, unconvinced of his own words.

"When will you and Flower of the Forest leave?"

"Tonight."

"Then let's go!" Goko exclaimed, and ran to call the Tongans together.

William didn't go with him. He went home. He knew Susannah needed him there with her, before leaving their youth and this wild land behind them forever. It was here that they had learned what it truly meant to be human beings – in so short a time, only two years! But they had had a good teacher, harsh but fair, life itself.

Susannah was waiting for him. As William entered the house, their eyes met in the firelight. The flames created a golden halo around her head. William was captivated by her beautiful eyes. They demanded nothing of him; they only pleaded, gazing upon him with sorrow. The decision was William's to make. If he said, "We're staying," she would not argue with him. She watched him anxiously. William could feel the incredible weight of the moment. Everything rested on his decision. Susannah spoke to him softly.

"What have you decided?"

"If it seems right to you, we'll go to England!"

The girl cried out joyfully and threw her arms around his neck, embracing and kissing him.

"I knew it, William!"

William smiled awkwardly.

"Let's hope it's the right decision," he whispered. "But before we start packing, come with me!"

There was the sound of drums outside.

"What is it?" Susannah asked, confused.

"A farewell. It's only right that we bid them farewell together."

The whole tribe was now assembled in the center of the town. They were anxious to know what the commotion was about and why this meeting couldn't wait until tomorrow.

The crowd parted for William and Susannah. Torches blazed everywhere now, their reddish light adding to the excitement. Hand in hand, William and Susannah mounted the stage. The Tongans didn't know that this was going to be their beloved chief's last speech to them.

William looked at his people. Tears rolled down Susannah's face, but she held her head high. The chief finally spoke.

"Good people," he began. "You have stood by me through good and bad. You have left your home of so many years. You did this because you had faith in me. You took us in when we were most in need. Together, we built this village so that we might dwell here in peace. And now we find ourselves in great difficulty. The hand of destiny has guided a man to our village, a seaman, who is one of our race. He is now giving us the opportunity to return to that land."

Murmurs of disbelief filled the crowd.

"Don't go! Don't leave us!" the people cried.

"We must leave tonight. We have come to bid you farewell."

"But you are our leader, our chief! What will become of us without you?" they pleaded.

"I know. I have chosen one to replace me."

"Who?"

"A brave young warrior. He has proven himself time and time again. Come here, Goko!" he called. Goko slowly realized what a great honor he was being given. He ran to William and threw himself at the boy's feet.

"Stand up, Goko," William commanded. The young Indian rose to his feet and gazed at his chief. William smiled at him reassuringly, and turned again to the people whom the rapid turn of events had reduced to silence.

"Do you accept Goko as your new leader?"

"We accept!" they roared.

"Then everything will be fine. Don't despise us for leaving you. You have shown us nothing but kindness. You are in our hearts forever, and no distance will ever be able to separate us."

Deeply moved, the people cheered. They lifted Susannah and William onto their shoulders and carried them to their house.

The couple was packed and ready to go in no time. Martin Cart was put on a large litter and four warriors carried him. Martin told them the way. All they had to do was head south along the shore. Ignoring the rain and the mud, nearly the entire village followed. They bore no anger toward the departing heroes, but there was a deep sorrow and an empty feeling in their hearts, and they wanted to spend every second with them.

The rising sun was greeted with joy. The light of their torches had been growing steadily weaker. Martin Cart looked on with baited breath. He pictured the sailors weighing anchor and sailing without them. But his fears were vanquished by a new discovery. Some three miles away, he could see the masthead. At the end of the mast waved the flag of England. He shouted to William.

"It's still here! It waited for us! Hurrah!" Martin shouted. But his joyful cries seemed to have no effect on the others. William and Susannah suddenly realized how hard this was going to be for them; another foreign land, abandoning their new home after so many years of exile and want.

The slightest misfortune would have been enough to make them turn back.

The three-master frigate was now in plain view. The Indians stared in awe at the man-made wonder.

They had just arrived at the sandy shore when cannon firing rang out – a signal to all on board that danger was near. Shortly afterwards, they heard the mad pealing of the tocsin. Armed men suddenly appeared on deck, and William and Susannah's group suddenly found the cannons aimed at them.

It didn't take long for Martin to understand the danger they were in. His frantic shouts were swallowed by the waves. Once the Tongan men lowered him to the ground, he rose and ran as fast as his wounded body would allow in the direction of the Storm. William followed him.

Martin began swimming toward the ship, shouting at the top of his lungs. But his strength soon gave out and he began to sink.

Several of the Storm's crew members recognized him, though they couldn't make any sense of his words. Seeing that their companion was on the verge of drowning, ten of the sailors dived in to rescue him.

Captain Harrison stood on the quarter-deck observing the Indians on shore through his powerful telescope. If they had plans to attack the ship, he could take care of them with a single blast from the cannon. But it was the young man who caught his attention now.

Ignoring the rescuing sailors, the boy raced to the unconscious man and pulled him toward the ship.

A quarter of an hour later, the boy was presented to Captain Harrison. The captain had yet to discover the identity of his guest.

William described Cart's arrival at the Indian village. He asked Captain Harrison to cease all hostilities, assuring him that the Tongans were peaceful in nature, and had only accompanied him. Captain Harrison immediately granted this request, and invited William to his cabin.

The ship's doctor had already examined Martin Cart. Apart from the unneeded exertion and some aspirated salt water, the sailor would be fine.

The doctor had Martin brought down to the crew's quarters, where a cabin boy was assigned to take care of him.

And now the time had come for William to state his case.

"Captain, sir! I would like to tell you my reasons for coming aboard."

"I'm all ears, Master Anderson."

"Back at the village, Mr. Cart agreed to present my case to you. I would like to ask you to bring me back to England with you, to our homeland. My wife is on the shore now, waiting for your decision."

"I understand perfectly, young man. However, before continuing this conversation, I recommend that we have a boat sent for the lady."

"Thank you, captain, sir."

Howell Harrison reached for the bell, and the first mate appeared almost immediately. He stood at attention.

"You rang, sir?"

"Yes. Have a boat sent immediately for my guest's wife, Mrs. Anderson."

"Yes, sir."

Clicking his heels together, the first mate left the cabin. Captain Harrison and William returned to the deck. The boat was lowered and four sailors rowed quickly toward the shore. And now the moment had arrived for Captain Harrison to welcome Susannah on board personally. Upon seeing the beautiful girl, the big man turned white.

"My lady, forgive me. You bear a very strong resemblance to someone I…"

"I know, sir," the girl replied tenderly.

"How?" the captain asked.

"I told her!" The captain turned around to see Martin Cart with a weak smile on his face. Cart's attendant was standing beside him, though it was obvious that he had reluctantly allowed the man to leave his sickbed.

Howell Harrison became more astonished by the second. He invited the couple to join him in the salon. With trembling hands, he poured drinks and asked William to tell him their story.

The story, as usual, took much time in telling. Finally, Captain Harrison took the young people's hands and expressed his deepest sympathy for all the hardships they had endured. His eyes misted with tears as he told them about the great love of his life, Countess Raymond.

"I knew, I knew that I would have her again. The only thing that mattered to me! They said I was mad to hope, but I was right after all. I've always longed for a family, and here you are! From this moment onward, I have my very own children."

All those present were deeply moved. That night, the ship's company and the Tongan tribe were invited to a feast. Susannah, William, and Captain Harrison joined hands. Seated, the young couple bombarded the captain with questions. When Harrison told them about the failed search for gold, William asked:

"Is the gold really that important to you?"

"Yes, son. But there's nothing to be done about that now."

"I wouldn't be so sure about that."

"What do you mean, William?"

"You'll have your gold -- maybe not as much as you imagined, but at least enough to keep you. And our future will be secure as well."

"Son, what in blazes are you talking about?"

"Susannah will tell you."

"You mean, Donald's treasure?"

"Yes. I'll be back by tomorrow night."

Saying this, William jumped up and set out to find Goko among the celebrants. He selected ten warriors to accompany him back to the village. They reached Goko's house before daybreak and rested there a while. At noon, they started into the jungle. The village was quiet. Only the children, their attendants, and the ailing remained behind.

The men arrived at the shore a little while later. They set out for the southern part of the island, for this was the fastest way to the wreckage of the Struggle. The Tongans, being excellent swimmers, would have no trouble retrieving the treasure from the sunken ship. They gathered stones to serve as weights and hung them around their waists. William was the first to enter the water. He swam quickly toward the wreck. The Tongans followed obediently. The cool water refreshed them, tired from the long, sleepless journey the previous night. A hundred yards from the shore was a place where the waves broke and the water churned. Any experienced seaman would have known right away that this was a shoal, and steered as far from it as possible. But William knew better. Here lay the sunken ship.

"I'll go down first," William told his men. "I want to have a look around." Without waiting for a reply, he descended.

Minutes passed. The Tongans began to grow restless. None of them could have remained under the water so long. In this, too, their "white chief" was exceptional. A burst of bubbles rose to the surface, and moments later William emerged, red-faced.

"Did you find it, chief?" asked Goko.

"Yes. I need three men."

All the warriors would have like to have joined William, but only Goko, Zamin, and Kodan were chosen.

"Stay close to me and be careful not to become caught in the rigging."

William wound a length of rope around his waist and dived again. The men descended into the crystal-clear water simultaneously. The weights they carried around their waists proved to be very effective. They took care to avoid the mesh of algae and sea anemones. William reached the gangway of the deck first and forced open the door. The men watched as the door to one of the guest cabins shut in front of them. This was where the chests were located, scattered helter-skelter from the sinking of the ship. They took the two smallest chests and swam to the surface with them. For the time being, the rope was left behind. The Tongans were nearly blue from lack of oxygen. They arrived at the surface coughing and gasping, and their companions took their expensive burdens from them.

Goko couldn't help but remark, "Chief William is like a lungfish!"

The chief smiled. When they had recovered somewhat, William sent four men to carry the treasure ashore. Then he turned to the others.

"Four of us are required for the remaining chests. The rest of you, stand by and pull the rope. We'll help you from down there."

"As you say, chief."

The men proceeded as ordered, only to discover that the four remaining chests were considerably heavier than the first two.

William and his crew descended again. They tied the remaining chests and brought the end of the rope with them to the surface. When it came time to bring up the load, however, the four men lacked air. The immense weight became too much for them to bear and the chests lay suspended in the water. All at once, the men let go and swam quickly toward the surface. Meanwhile, the other four men, knowing nothing of what had just happened, continued to pull. Then, to their great surprise, they were thrown off balance and flung into the sea.

A few seconds later, the divers explained everything to the unhappy men and they all laughed. They all went back to work cheerfully. The problem now was how to retrieve the chests from the bottom. It was a good thing they were locked, otherwise the treasure they contained would have been lost forever. Goko swam down for the end of the rope. The other group returned from the shore and helped haul the chests to the surface.

An hour later, they were sitting on the shore, drying themselves in the hot sun. Two of the warriors returned to the village for food.

The chests lay in the sand, filled with the gold that had cost so many innocent lives. Here it all was, in the right hands at last!

After the meal, the men hastened to take the six chests to the Storm before dark. They didn't stop to rest. When they finally emerged from the trees, the Tongan nation cheered and triumphantly marched them toward the arriving boats. In a hurry to return to his wife and the captain, William went back with the rowers.

Howell Harrison's eyes shone with joy when he saw the chests. They were to be opened only in the complete privacy of his cabin. Harrison was dazzled by the enormous quantity of jewelry and coins for which the convicts had exchanged a part of their gold. There was no shortage of gold, either! Three of the chests were filled with it.

"This is for you, Captain Harrison, to use as you see fit," William informed him.

"My boy, I really don't know what to say. There are enough riches here to last us a lifetime!"

"Wealth isn't the most important thing," William said calmly, putting an arm around Susannah. They left the cabin, turning their backs on the vast fortune. That it had a strange effect on the good captain's mind is perfectly understandable. Fortunately, however, it didn't take more than an hour for the man to return to his wise, thoughtful self.

The large boat was rowed to shore and it was now time for William and Susannah to say goodbye to the Tongan nation. This proved to be one of the hardest tasks they had ever had to face. But the Tongans were grateful for these last moments together, and waited eagerly for one last embrace or even the slightest touch. But everything, including this story, must come to an end.

The young couple boarded the boat. The oars guided them swiftly over the waves.

Susannah and William didn't take their eyes off the loving crowd for a second. The farther they traveled from shore, the smaller the tribe became.

Their faces grew blurry and indistinct, and by the time they reached the ship, they resembled tiny dolls – these, the kindest, most loyal people the world had ever known!

The long-awaited command was given.

"Sails, hoist!"

"Hurrah!" the crew shouted. And the Storm, spreading its wings wide and racing over the ocean, left the bitter tears and the sunny happiness of South America in its wake.

Epilogue

William, with Susannah beside him, continued to watch the horizon. As the hours went by, thick smoke appeared on the small island. William thought for a moment that maybe this was the Tongans' way of saying goodbye. Or perhaps the children had caused some mischief back at the village. But, no - it was their own house on fire!

This was a special Tongan custom: To burn the houses of those who had departed from them, whether it was physically or spiritually. This way, the spirit of the house could leave too, and they would have a happy home wherever they went.

THE END

www.ingramcontent.com/pod-product-compliance
Lightning Source LLC
Chambersburg PA
CBHW030342310726
48979CB00001B/148

9781425184117